Praise for *The Best Life Book Club*

"Don't we all want to become the heroine of our own story?...
When Karissa, Alice, Margot and Josie discover the power of books
and story to change their lives, they must decide whether to take
the chance for something new: cue laughter, tears and love. With her
trademark wit and warmth, Sheila Roberts delivers a story nestled
inside a story, a novel of pure delight!"
—Patti Callahan Henry, *New York Times* bestselling author
of *The Secret Book of Flora Lea*

Praise for the novels of Sheila Roberts

"Sheila Roberts makes me laugh...and come away inspired, hopeful
and happy."
—Debbie Macomber, #1 *New York Times* bestselling author

"Roberts deftly chronicles, with just the right mix of love and laughter,
the search for happiness, artistic and romantic, by three generations
of endearing women."
—*Booklist* on *Mermaid Beach*

"A masterful blend of comedic timing with characters you believe in
and want good things for... A wonderful summer read for anyone who
wants to enjoy a well-told story."
—*Midwest Book Review* on *Sand Dollar Lane*

"Roberts does an excellent job of creating sympathetic and relatable
characters with real-life problems... [Roberts] will win over readers
looking for a comforting escape."
—*Library Journal* on *Welcome to Moonlight Harbor*

The
Best
Life
Book
Club

SHEILA ROBERTS

mira

ISBN-13: 978-0-7783-0548-4

The Best Life Book Club

Mira
22 Adelaide St. West, 41st Floor
Toronto, Ontario M5H 4E3, Canada
BookClubbish.com

Printed in U.S.A.

Recycling programs for this product may not exist in your area.

For the 400 Book Club.

1

LANDING BUTT FIRST IN MUD. HOW SYMBOLIC OF Karissa Newcomb's life. The old life. Not the new one, please, God.

She shouldn't have crossed that corner of the lawn where the grass was sparse and slick in the pouring Northwest rain. Now here she was, wet and caked in mud. Like the cardboard box she'd dropped. At least the towels were still safely inside it. Something to be thankful for.

"See? There's always a bright side somewhere," her mother would say.

What was the bright side to Karissa's marriage ending? There had to be one. It would be nice if she could find it before she turned thirty-five. It felt like a landmark birthday of sorts, but that was only a few months away though, so she wasn't holding her breath.

Gig Harbor, Washington, a small maritime city, was a good

place to start—close enough to Seattle for the obligatory bi-weekly child hand-off with the ex-husband, but far enough away that she wasn't constantly having to look at the scene of the crime. Out of sight, out of mind. Someday, hopefully. Meanwhile, she needed to get up and get focused.

Brush the mud off your rear and get it in gear. That should be a bumper sticker.

She picked up her soggy box of towels and followed her brother Ethan and his friend Ike, who were making their way up her driveway, carrying her couch. Her eight-year-old daughter, Macy, was sitting on it, giggling.

The excitement of the new house had temporarily distracted Macy from the fact that she'd left behind her best friend. Who happened to be the daughter of Karissa's former best friend. Like Karissa, Macy was going to have to find a new bestie.

Moving in the middle of February, in the middle of the school year, swimming through a deluge of icy rain wasn't ideal, but that was how events had played out. The house in Seattle on which Karissa had lavished so much care had finally sold and now she had this house—a blue, two-story, Victorian-inspired one with three small bedrooms and a front porch. And a need for paint. The price had been right. Motivated sellers, the real estate agent had said. Karissa knew what that meant. She'd been a motivated seller, herself. Divorce had a way of motivating you. The house didn't come with a water view like she'd originally dreamed of—water views were far outside her price point—but the neighborhood was pretty, and the street seemed quiet. She could hole up in her almost Victorian home and rebuild her life, the new start people expected you to make after your world collapsed.

"This is adorable," her mother had gushed when she and Dad had made the trip to check out the house with Karissa and her Realtor.

Her parents were as enamored of Gig Harbor and its waterfront downtown as Karissa was. "I think Gig Harbor will be a perfect place to write the next chapter of your life," Mom had told her.

"I hope I do a better job of writing this time around," Karissa had muttered.

"It wasn't you who messed up," her dad had growled.

But maybe it was.

She jerked her mind away from that thought. She had a new house and a new job waiting for her. Between that and the spousal and child support her ex was paying she'd be okay financially. Certainly not rich, but okay. And she had free moving help. Look at all the good things she could focus on.

Inside the house, she followed one of the butcher-paper paths she'd made and set the box on the guest bathroom counter. Then she went back for the one with her clothes, brought that into the primary bedroom, which would be hers, and dug out a fresh pair of pants and panties. *Think of this as peeling off all the bad parts from your past*, she told herself as she ducked into the bathroom and stepped out of her pants.

It was hard peeling off the bad though. It stuck to you like dog poop on a shoe. There was always some little stinky bit that hung on. Like the memory of Mark walking out the door for the last time.

Dog poop, mud. She needed a new image to focus on. *Rain*. Rain washing away past sadness, bringing a rainbow and a promise of something better. Yes, that was a good image.

Her butt hurt.

Her cell phone rang, and she fished it out of her jacket pocket. "Hi, Mom," she said, trying to sound the way a hopeful woman making a new start should sound.

"How's it going?" Mom wanted to know.

"The guys are moving the furniture in now."

"What's the weather like there? It's partly sunny up here."

"It's raining like crazy. I should have rented an ark instead of a moving van. I spent a fortune on plastic covering."

"At least it's not snow," Mom said. "And the rain is what keeps everything so green."

The Pacific Northwest was famous for its perpetual state of green and Seattle had been dubbed the Emerald City. Like Dorothy, Karissa had loved living in the Emerald City.

Until the witch showed up.

She heard a thump, followed by her brother's favorite swear word, along with wails from Macy. "Mom, I gotta go. I think something just got dropped. I'll call you later," Karissa said and ended the call.

She got as far as the kitchen and saw a tipped love seat and three boxes, including one containing her collection of signed books, lying sideways on the floor. Ike was making a hasty retreat and her brother was hugging Macy and saying, "It's okay."

"What happened?" she asked.

"Uncle Ethan dropped me," Macy exclaimed with a sob.

"Sorry, sis. She jumped on the love seat and I lost my grip."

"At least it wasn't my dishes," said Karissa.

"I just wanted another ride," Macy said in her own defense.

"Yeah, but warning somebody first would be good," said Ethan. Ethan needed to work out more.

Okay, not really. Unlike Ike, who had arms the size of pipe cleaners, Ethan was buff and tough. He was also the world's best older brother.

Karissa took her crying daughter's hand and moved her away from him as he put the box of books on the counter. "Let's have Uncle Ethan bring in your dresser next and we'll get your clothes out of the car so you can unpack them. How does that sound?" Karissa suggested. It sounded like something she should have thought to do from the beginning.

Macy sniffed up a sob and nodded, and Karissa helped her out of her rain boots and raincoat.

"Go decide if you want your dresser by the window or on the wall by the door, okay?" said Karissa and Macy bounded off, already recovered from her mishap.

"What the hell?!" Ike exclaimed.

Karissa turned to see him halfway into the living room with her favorite wingback chair, doing some interesting dance steps with a muddy-pawed dog who kept jumping on him, trying to get ahold of his leg for a doggy close encounter. The dog was some kind of mix, with the fur of a golden retriever paired with a curly tail of who knew what breed. He wore a collar and a leash with no human on the other end.

Unlike her moving crew, he hadn't bothered with the paper path. Now the cream-colored carpet had been broken in. *Ugh*.

The way her day was going, Karissa would have liked nothing better than to pull her hair and let out a screech. She settled for muttering a word her mother would have washed her mouth out with soap for saying. It was equally satisfying. Ah, the power of words.

A moment later a woman appeared in the doorway. She looked to be somewhere in her late fifties, short and a little chunky, with a pretty, round face framed by chin-length red hair fading to...carrot? She wore wet tennis shoes and a raincoat over jeans. It was obvious she and the dog had been out walking.

"Lucky! Come here this instant," the woman said, clapping her hands.

"Get off me," growled Ike, shaking his leg.

Lucky gave a bark and made another attempt to make contact.

Ethan the dog whisperer intervened, distracting the animal, catching his leash and leading him back to the woman, who got a firm grip on it and wound it around her hand.

"I'm so sorry," she said to Karissa as the dog barked and wagged his tail and strained to reunite with Ike's leg. "He saw the open door and got all excited."

"No, he saw Ike and got all excited," cracked Ethan.

"Funny," shot back Ike. "Where do you want this, Karissa?"

"In that corner is fine," she said, pointing. "And can you guys move the couch so it's facing the fireplace?" While the men worked, she walked to the front door, where the woman stood with Lucky.

"I'm so sorry. I'll pay to have your carpet cleaned," said the woman.

"No worries," Karissa assured her. "I have something that will work." Somewhere.

"I'm Alice Strong. I live next door, and this is my granddog. I'm watching him for my son and his wife while they have a weekend getaway."

Thank heaven Lucky wasn't a permanent resident. "That's awfully nice of you," Karissa said.

"Ah, well. How can you say no when your kids ask? Anyway, no grandchildren yet, so I have to be content with this little guy."

Little?

"He's only a puppy. They've been taking him to obedience school."

Where he was probably flunking out.

"Anyway, this is a terrible way to meet a new neighbor."

"It's okay, really." Compared to everything she'd gone through before moving it was nothing. And, she had to admit, the dog was cute. "I'm Karissa Newcomb." Macy had tired of waiting for furniture to show in her room and resurfaced. "This is my daughter, Macy," she said as her girl came running over, brown curls bouncing.

"I'm happy to meet you," said Alice.

Lucky was happy to meet Macy, too, and jumped on her, nearly knocking her down, which made her laugh. Lucky proceeded to give her doggy kisses, which made her laugh even more.

"Lucky, stop. Sit," Alice commanded, pulling the dog back

and pushing on his rump, forcing him to sit. "Be good and we'll have a dog treat when we get home. We'd better go and let you get settled," she said to Karissa. "Welcome to the neighborhood."

She left and the men fetched Macy's dresser while Karissa hurried back to the car to get one of the boxes of her daughter's clothes. *Never mind the buckets of rain dumping on you. They're washing away the past.* She allowed herself to envision a better future in this new house on this quiet street, lined with ornamental cherry trees. When they bloomed it would make a charming scene.

Her old street on Seattle's Queen Anne Hill had presented an equally charming scene with brick Tudors and small front lawns, a few bicycles lying on those lawns. Picture-perfect. Alas, the sad thing about pictures was that they never showed you what lay beneath the surface.

She couldn't know what lay beneath the surface here, either, but Alice Strong appeared to be considerate and kindhearted. It was a nice change from what Karissa had left behind. Not that she was going to get involved with her neighbors.

The men brought in the last of the furniture and Karissa sent out for pizza and pulled the pop from one of the boxes of groceries along with napkins and paper plates while they got to work setting up beds. Later that night she and her daughter would be sleeping in a new house.

Someone new would be sleeping in the house she'd shared with Mark while he slept right next door. In Allegra Gray's bed.

Don't think about it!

She didn't, not while they ate pizza, not while the guys got the TV hooked up, not while she helped Macy put her room to rights and finished setting up the bathroom across the hall. But she did think about it later when she was making up her bed.

She called her mom. She could hear the TV playing in the background.

"You guys are busy," she said. Her mother had a life. Karissa had to stop calling her ten times a day.

"No, not really. Your father's streaming an action flick and the bodies are piling up. I'm ready for a break." The TV sounds got softer, indicating that Mom had vacated the room. "There. Now I can hear. How are you doing now?"

"I got Macy's room organized and mine sort of put together." Karissa plopped down on her bed. "I'm about to crash. I didn't sleep very well last night. How did I ever sleep on a hard floor in a sleeping bag when I was a kid?"

"The power of slumber parties, but you girls never did much sleeping at those," Mom said.

She remembered those times with the two friends she'd finally found in fifth grade, little nerds like her, who also enviously read about the adventures of Nancy Drew and the students at Sweet Valley High. Those girls had been so important to her, and they'd stuck together all the way through high school. They'd both eventually moved away and married and the bond had loosened to occasional posts on Facebook, but they'd been there for each other when they were growing up. Every little girl needed a bestie she could depend on.

And she'd moved Macy away from hers. "I hope Macy's going to be okay."

"She will be."

It was all Karissa could do not to add, *And I hope I'll be okay.* Instead, she said, "It feels weird, being here by ourselves."

"I wish you'd moved in with us," Mom said.

More than once, Karissa had considered moving in with her parents, tucking herself away and living safely and happily ever after in the Northwest Washington island town of Anacortes. But that had felt too weak, and even though she was, in a sense, running away, she had enough pride not to run home.

"It wouldn't have been practical with shared custody."

"Some sharing," Mom scoffed. "You're doing most of the work."

"That's fine with me," Karissa said. She didn't want to share any more than she had to. It would be hard enough parting with her daughter every other weekend. And she didn't even want to think about Macy being gone over spring break. "I just...wish I wasn't sleeping in this big bed alone. I know it sounds silly, but—"

"It doesn't sound silly. It sounds human," Mom said.

"It's hard not to keep asking myself how I got here? Why didn't I see what was happening right under my nose?"

"Because you trusted the people closest to you."

She had. She'd thought she and Allegra were best friends. They'd done so much together—Costco runs, helping each other with their kids' birthday parties, watching romcoms at Christmas. She and Mark had gotten Allegra through her own divorce, for crying out loud. Mark had gone over to her house and done everything from cleaning her gutters to fixing a leaky bathroom sink pipe.

Allegra had needed more fixed than leaky pipes, obviously, and he'd been happy to oblige.

"You should have been able to trust them," Mom added.

Yes, she should have. "And to think I felt so sorry for her," Karissa said bitterly, and not for the first time. "All that crying at our kitchen table. All that 'Can I come over? I hate being alone' crap. Well, I don't like being alone, either."

Although now that she was alone, she could at least understand how Allegra had felt after her husband moved out. Loneliness and sorrow had a way of filling every corner.

But that didn't excuse Allegra. Or Mark. "It's not right, Mom."

"No, it's not."

"I don't understand. We were happy. How could he have done this to me? How could they?"

How many more times was she going to say that?

"It was selfish on both their parts."

"I love her," Mark had said. "She needs me."

"So do I!" Karissa had cried when he broke the news to her. "Please, Mark. Don't do this. We have a life together. We have a daughter."

Their life together hadn't been enough. It was true what people said, the grass was always greener on the other side of the fence. Shame on Mark for looking over there and wanting it.

"I hope you can forgive me," Allegra had said when she came to help Mark get his things.

"Maybe I can someday," Karissa had replied. When Mark is dead and I'm senile and in a nursing home.

"I keep blaming Mark and Allegra," she confessed, "but what if it's me? What if I wasn't enough?" She certainly hadn't been able to compete with Allegra when it came to looks. She'd always admired her friend's long, dark hair, the time she put into her appearance, the way she could turn her face into a work of art with makeup. Apparently, Mark had, too.

"You were more than enough," her mother said sternly. "You still are and you're going to be fine."

"Thanks, Mom. I guess I need to keep hearing that. And you're right, I am going to be fine," Karissa said.

Had she moved far enough away?

Sunday morning Macy woke up with a case of the wistfuls. "I miss Daddy," she said.

Poor Macy. First, Daddy had been in the same house with them and then he'd moved out. But at least he'd been right next door. Now he was almost fifty miles away. Not close enough for Macy. Not far enough for Karissa.

"I know, sweetie. I miss him, too," she said.

She did. Not the selfish Mark who had left her. She missed the man she'd once been happy with, the Mark who told her that her glasses were sexy. The Mark who didn't care that she seemed to be allergic to every brand of mascara ever invented. The Mark who had talked about them taking Macy to Disney-land and promised he'd go on all the rides with her.

Mark was enjoying a different ride now.

But how much would he enjoy that ride once the novelty wore off? Allegra wasn't perfect. She and her ex had always been fighting about one thing or other. Allegra liked to fight. She had a temper and had used it often enough on her husband.

Karissa hadn't lost her temper when Mark dropped his emotional bombshell. All she could do was cry. And beg. Maybe she should have thrown a fit, thrown some dishes, maybe that would have been sexy and exciting.

But that wasn't her. She always tried to be kind. And reasonable. And sweet. Like her mother. Nice girls finished last.

"Eat your cereal," she said to Macy, "and we'll get dressed and…" Not go to church. Going in alone to a new church and meeting a crowd of new people? She couldn't do it. She wasn't ready to explain why she was a single mom. "Go someplace special," she finished.

They had church at Dairy Queen.

Macy was perfectly happy to thank God for her strawberry sundae and Karissa was happy that they'd gotten past the Daddy moment. Macy would still be seeing Daddy, every other weekend.

Along with Allegra.

Karissa stabbed her ice cream and pretended it was Allegra's heart. So much for church at DQ.

Be grateful you've found an affordable place to live and that you've got some money in the bank and a job, she told herself. It was a job she was excited about starting, working at Heron Publishing.

"It's a niche market," the publisher and owner, Shirley Houghton-Smith, had explained during Karissa's second interview, "but an important one. We publish a small number of nonfiction and fiction books featuring all things Northwest written by Northwest writers. We have a great team here."

Karissa had already met one of the other members of the team, Edward Elliot, editorial director, who'd interviewed her with Shirley on her first interview. He was handsome—tall with dark hair and dark eyes—and a bit aloof, which had been a little intimidating, but she'd made the effort to put herself out there and tell him and Shirley both how eager she was for such a great opportunity, and it had put her in the final running for the position.

She'd been thrilled when she'd gotten it and rather liked the idea that there would be a small crew in the office due to most of their people working remote.

She hoped that maybe, someday as the company grew, she'd be allowed to move up to the position of assistant editor. No one had said that, but a woman could hope.

No matter what, this was going to be a great job. She'd been a Lit major in college and the idea of working at a publishing house, especially a small one, felt like a dream come true. Here she would be involved with something near and dear to her heart. Books. Meeting and greeting didn't come easily when you were shy, but she'd mostly overcome that as an adult, and surely meeting and greeting authors would be…okay, a little intimidating, but she could do it. Finding this job had been like finding a unicorn, and if her new boss Edward Elliot wasn't a big smiler, she could live with that. She got it. She'd lost her smile on the way to divorce court.

"You'll get your smile back," her mom kept predicting.

Her mom had also predicted it wouldn't rain on moving day.

"Oh, stop," Karissa muttered. It hadn't snowed. Things could always be worse.

On that semi-happy note, she drove to Safeway to pick up a few things. *You are on a great path*, she told herself.

Once in the store she forgot that she knew the value of a dollar, and forty minutes later she and Macy were leaving with bags filled with everything from cookies to Fritos. Yogurt and frozen berries and apples and lots of good sandwich makings, too, to balance the junk food binging. As for the four magazines she'd bought...someone had to help keep those companies in business.

To listen to her daughter, one would think she was a stingy meanie. "I wanted a candy bar," Macy whined.

"We got cookies instead and those will last a lot longer," said Karissa.

"Candy bars last a long time, too."

Karissa decided it would be best to ignore this argument. She pretended not to see the pouting face staring at her in the rearview mirror.

Somehow, she was so busy trying to ignore the pouting face she also missed the SUV as she was backing up.

They hit with a crunch and a bounce. Oh, great. There went her insurance rates.

"Mommy, we hit somebody," Macy informed her.

Yes, they had. And as he got out of his car, unfolding himself like the tall, elegant man he was, she realized they hadn't just hit any somebody. *Oh, no. Really?*

"Are you okay, honey bunny?" Karissa asked Macy. She studied Macy's face for any sign of pain or panic.

There was none. "That was fun," Macy chirped. "Just like bumper cars!"

Only a million times more expensive.

"Stay here. I need to talk to the man in the other car," Karissa said, and scrambled out to see how much damage she'd done.

Enough to make her stomach give a sick flop.

Edward Elliot, her new boss, was casually dressed in jeans and a sweater.

His car wasn't so casual, and she could almost hear it saying, *"I may not be a Ferrari, but I cost more than you'll ever be able to afford, and you shouldn't have hit me."*

No, she shouldn't have. Her recently-paid-off Toyota Corolla was crunched in back, but that didn't look as obscene as his dented door. Dents and luxury cars did not go well together.

"Mr. Elliot, I didn't expect to run into you here," she said, hurrying up to him. *Oh, good Lord in heaven, had she just said that?* "I mean, I didn't expect to see you. Like this."

He raised an eyebrow. "Yes, what a surprise." A sarcastic comeback coupled with…no smile. Yep, she could tell she'd made an impression on her future employer.

"I'm so sorry. Let me get my insurance information out of my glove compartment. Oh, and my license. And if I can get yours…"

He sighed. Deeply. Nodded.

They exchanged the necessary information. He was all business, and she was all mortification.

"I'm terribly sorry," she said. "I somehow didn't see you." *Looming large as life behind my car.* There went the eyebrow again.

She wanted to say more, anything. But she decided any more babbling on her part would only make things worse.

"I'll see you tomorrow," he said when they'd finished, which was preferable to him saying, "Now that I think of it, you might be happier working somewhere else, and I'd be happier if you did."

"I'm looking forward to it," she said.

He didn't echo the sentiment. Instead, he nodded and got back in his car.

She stood beside hers, watching as he slowly moved away down the parking lot. *It could have been worse*, she told herself. No one was hurt. No one got fired.

Her boss thought she was an airhead.

Well, she'd just have to prove him wrong.

"Can we go home now?" Macy asked. "I want a cookie."

"Yes, we can, and so do I." In her present frame of mind, she could eat the entire box single-handedly.

2

*"Everyone's in our life for a reason,
even the ones that we wish weren't."*
—from *Where There's a Will There's a Way*, by Annie Wills

"THANKS FOR KEEPING LUCKY, MOM," ALICE'S SON, CAL-
lum, said as he greeted his dog with a head rub. "How was he?"

"He was a good boy," she said. She waved to Callum's wife,
Kara, who was calling hello and waving from the car. "Don't
you two want to come in and have something to eat?"

"No, we need to get home. Kara has a bunch of prep to do
for a meeting tomorrow. But I'm supposed to pick you up after
work for dinner tomorrow night. She has a new curry dish she
wants to try out on you."

Curry did not do Alice's stomach any favors, but she couldn't
bring herself to tell her daughter-in-law that. Kara and Callum
had only been married a year and it seemed rude to start giving Kara a list of diet restrictions.

"You gonna wait till your stomach erodes to tell her?" her
older sister, Josie, had demanded. "Good grief, Alice, that's not
being rude, it's just stating a fact of life."

"I'll tell her eventually," Alice had said. Eventually hadn't come yet. She'd take a pill.

"That sounds great," she said to Callum.

"Okay, see you around five thirty."

"Five thirty," she repeated. "Bye, Lucky, see you tomorrow," she said, giving Lucky a final pat. Which inspired him to jump on her.

"No, you don't, buddy," Callum said, pulling him down. "We don't jump on people. Remember?"

Especially when they were trying to get moved in, Alice thought, and felt a fresh rush of embarrassment remembering Lucky's naughty behavior. She decided she needed to do something nice to welcome her new neighbor to the hood. Cookies. Who didn't like cookies?

She'd just save a few for herself.

"Just a few," she told herself. She indulged her sweet tooth entirely too much.

If only her husband was around to help her eat those cookies. It had been three years since she'd lost Charlie to prostate cancer. It should have been caught sooner. It should have been curable. He'd only been fifty-nine and she'd been fifty-four. She'd thought they had decades ahead of them. Sometimes his passing felt like forever ago. Others it felt like yesterday. And during those times it felt awful.

"You have to get on with your life," her sister often advised. "That's what I did after Joe died."

But not everyone was a Josie who charged on with an armored heart and a tongue like a broadsword. That had always been Josie, strong, bossy, determined. A human bulldozer, pushing her way through life.

"I am getting on with my life," Alice would insist.

And she was. She was dog-sitting for the kids so they could get away for romantic weekends and work on getting pregnant, baking for the neighbors, hanging out with her sister, reading and puttering in her garden. She supposed it was a small life but losing Charlie had shrunk its borders and after the incident with the car she'd lost the will to try and enlarge them.

In the kitchen, she pulled a few chocolate chips out of the bag for a quick chocolate hit—milk chocolate, not dark. She didn't care if dark was better for you. Some things weren't worth compromising on, and chocolate was one of them. She also sampled a bit of the dough as she stirred everything together. You weren't supposed to do that, but she'd been sampling cookie dough since she was a child, and she wasn't about to stop now that she was fifty-seven. Within minutes the first batch was in the oven and the aroma of baking cookies filled the kitchen and brought back the happy memory of coming home from school as a child to smell cookies baking in the oven. Cookies said love.

She sampled one after she'd gotten them onto the cooling rack. Was there anything better than a warm cookie? A warm cookie and milk. She poured herself a glass and grabbed another treat.

After the fourth one, she reminded herself that she was making them for her neighbor. She'd take some to Margot, too, get them out of the house before she consumed the entire batch.

Once she was finished, she put them in two disposable plastic containers, then she grabbed the first one, threw on her coat and went outside. The clouds from the day before had returned, promising to rain any minute. If Charlie was still alive, they'd have been taking a vacation in Arizona, soaking up the sun, out playing golf every day. She hadn't picked up a golf club in three years. She'd never been that good, anyway.

Her new neighbor's car was parked outside, a sign that she was home. Not in the garage, but that was probably full of moving boxes. Alice didn't envy the woman her job of unpacking. Moving wasn't for the faint of heart.

The car was crunched in the back. Interesting. Alice hadn't noticed that the day before. But then, she didn't have the best powers of observation. Anyway, she wasn't one to spy on her neighbors and make note of everything happening in their lives. She may have been alone, but she wasn't desperate. She had a TV. She had books.

She rang the doorbell, and it was answered almost immediately, the same little girl she'd met the day before, smiling up at her. The child had such a cherubic face—that cute little nose and rosebud mouth. And those adorable curls!

"Hello, Macy. Remember me?" Alice said.

"Yes," the girl said cheerfully. "Where's your dog?"

"He was only visiting." The child looked disappointed, so Alice added, "But he'll be back. He's my granddog."

"Granddog?" Macy repeated and giggled.

Her mother came up behind her and greeted Alice with a weary smile. "Alice, right?"

"Yes." Alice held out the container of cookies. "I thought you might enjoy having something to snack on while you unpack. I just baked these. They're chocolate chip. Do you like chocolate chip?" she asked Macy.

Macy nodded eagerly. "We bought some at the store today."

So much for her welcome gift.

"But store-bought can't compare to home baked," said Karissa. Very sweet. Her parents had raised her right. Alice smiled at her.

"Thank you so much," Karissa continued. "It was kind of you to think of us." She looked over her shoulder where several boxes sat unopened on the living room floor. Probably hoping Alice would scram so she could get back to work. "Would you like to come in?"

"Oh, no. I can see you're busy. I just wanted to welcome you properly to the neighborhood."

"I do feel welcomed. These were just what I needed."

"Good. I'll look forward to getting to know you," Alice said.

Karissa didn't respond with an "I'll look forward to getting to know you, too," but she did say, "Thanks again for thinking of us." She was probably shy. She did have good manners though and seemed nice. No sign of a man around the house, so she was probably single.

A nice, single mother with a cute child. What was her story? Alice would find out soon enough. Not that she was nosy, of course.

"No, Mom, I haven't found a job yet," Margot Burns said. She set her cell phone on the kitchen counter and got busy making herself an afternoon latte. Coffee inserted in the espresso machine, milk out of the fridge, caramel syrup ready. Good to go. She loved her lattes, and she saved a fortune making them at home. A good thing, since being jobless meant she didn't have a fortune to spend on lattes anymore. She didn't have a fortune to spend on cigarettes, either, but she'd bought a pack anyway, picking up her old bad habit like reconnecting with a dear friend.

She took out the pack she'd gotten and grabbed one.

"It's been over three weeks. You should have found something by now," said her mother.

Ugh. Smoke into the lungs or a meltdown? Margot lit up and inhaled and felt instantly calmer.

But still irritated. "I guess I could work at Burger King, Mom. Might be a little hard to make the house payment."

"There's no need to get smart," her mother said stiffly. "I'm only checking to see how you're doing."

And tell her what to do. And to think she'd stopped scrolling through TikTok for this.

"I'm doing as well as can be expected," she said, still irritated.

"You must have accomplished something."

Since Friday. Margot scowled at her espresso machine and urged it to hurry and heat up, then took another drag on her cigarette.

"I don't understand why you haven't found a job yet."

"There's not exactly a huge demand for people in middle management right now. Companies are scaling back right and left."

"Someone must want you."

Ouch. There was something about that phrase that touched a nerve. Margot started the espresso dripping and pushed the button on her frother. Took one more draw on the cigarette. *Okay, that's enough. Put it out.*

"It takes time to find the right fit, Mom. I'm in the process of updating my résumé," she said.

"How long does it take to update a résumé? Honestly, Margot, you can't just sit around."

One more puff for the road.

"You have to do something."

Yes, I have to make my latte.

The doorbell rang. *Saved by the bell!* Funny expression. Margot thought it had something to do with boxing. If that was true, it sure fit the moment.

"Mom, I've gotta go. Someone's here."

"All right. Call me later. We can brainstorm."

Oh, yes, brainstorming with her mother who'd never had to look for a job. That would be helpful. "Thanks, Mom, but I'm on it."

"Okay," her mother said dubiously. "Love you."

"Love you, too," said Margot and ended the call. "But you make me nuts."

She stubbed out the cigarette on a saucer, then went to open the door.

Her neighbor Alice Strong stood on the doorstep, holding a plastic container. With her round face and sweet smile, Alice would have been perfectly cast in a sitcom as the neighbor who always had something good to say to the main character.

"I baked cookies," she said.

"Perfect timing. Come in and have a latte."

"That's an offer I can't turn down," Alice said, stepping in. "Were you busy?"

"Talking to my mom. Or more like her talking at me."

"Checking in on your job-hunting progress again?"

"She's making me crazy. According to her I should have already had a dozen interviews and almost as many job offers."

"She worries," Alice said.

"No, she nags. You know that. She needs a life," Margot said as she led the way to the kitchen.

Not that her mother didn't have a life. She played bridge once a week, volunteered at Children's Hospital twice a month, and had been taking art lessons for the last five years. Margot had one of her paintings…hidden in the guest room. It was a location her mother was not happy about.

"We all mother in different ways," pointed out Alice.

"Elisa can thank God I didn't mother her like mine does me. I swear, every time Mom and I talk, she finds something to get on me about. You'd think I was sixteen instead of forty."

"Your children are always your children," Alice said.

"Not all children are created equal. She doesn't get on my brothers like this," said Margot.

"Mother-daughter relationships are complicated," Alice said.

"Ours wouldn't be if she'd just stop nagging me. I swear, if she ever managed a thumbs-up over anything I did I'd die of shock."

"She's trying to help."

"Some help," Margo muttered.

"We all make mistakes."

"Yes, I guess we do. I think I let Elisa get away with a lot when she was growing up. But she turned out okay." And with her daughter in college, Margot was allowing her to live her life without interference. Her mother should have been doing the same for her.

"You turned out okay, too," Alice said. She set the container of cookies on the counter and settled on a barstool.

Margot held up the bottle with her homemade caramel syrup. "The usual?"

"Yes. I love your caramel lattes."

And she loved Alice. They'd been neighbors for years. Alice had been there for Margot when she and her husband split, and she'd been there for Alice when her husband died. They had the neighbor thing down. Speaking of...

"Have you met our new neighbor?" she asked.

"I did. She seems very nice. Poor thing. Lucky got loose and muddied up her living room carpet."

"Lucky on the loose, huh?" Margot teased. "How did she take it?"

"She was very understanding."

"That's a good sign. Any friend of Lucky's is a friend of mine," Margot joked.

And really, the idea of making a new friend appealed to her. She'd had a couple at work but keeping in touch felt awkward with them still at the company and her gone. One of her brothers was married, but he and his wife were busy with their kids, and, like her youngest brother, the man child, they lived in another state. Ever since her job had gotten pulled out from under her she'd felt a little lost, and, even though she had Alice, a little isolated.

"I'll be interested to know more about her," Alice said, bringing Margot's attention back to the new neighbor. "I'm pretty sure she's single."

"Well, then, we'll have to induct her into our swinging singles club," Margot said. "Let's hope she likes chick flicks and sex on the beach."

Alice giggled. "What a name for a drink."

"Maybe someday it will be more than a drink. At least I can hope," Margot said and sighed.

Although, honestly, she didn't see that in her future. Jobless, manless, good grief, her life sucked. Her mother was right. She had to do something. Hopefully, she'd figure out what that something was sooner rather than later.

3

"Embrace the new!"
—from *Where There's a Will There's a Way* by Annie Wills

"ONE OF OUR NEIGHBORS BROUGHT US COOKIES today," Karissa told her mother later as she made herself a cup of tea.

"Sounds like you've got a good neighbor."

"She's sure an improvement over the home-wrecker."

"Tell me about her," said Mom, refusing to go down the thorny road of Karissa's recent past.

"She's maybe around your age, somewhere in her fifties, I'd guess."

"In her prime," Mom quipped.

"In her prime," Karissa agreed.

Her mother certainly was. She and Karissa's dad were always the last to leave the Elks club on a Saturday night, and to further prove she was at the top of her game, Mom had run her first marathon the summer before.

"She has a granddog," Karissa continued.

"Macy will love that."

Maybe it would stop her from asking for one. Karissa believed that every child needed a pet, but taking on an animal when she was adjusting to so many changes was more than she wanted to think about.

"I'm glad you've landed somewhere nice. And tomorrow you start your new job, right? Are you excited?"

"I was this morning, but now I'm dreading it," said Karissa, and told her mother about her grocery-store fender bender.

"Accidents happen," Mom said. "I'm sure he knows that."

"They don't happen when people pay attention to where they're going. I don't know what I was thinking, backing out so quickly. Honestly, Mom, I came across as a complete fool. I'm sure he's wondering what kind of woman they hired."

"You're not a fool, and they're lucky to get you."

"He may not be feeling that way right now."

"If he doesn't yet, he soon will," her mother predicted.

"I sure hope you're right," Karissa said.

Monday was a big day for both Karissa and Macy. Karissa woke up with butterflies dancing in her stomach. Macy didn't have butterflies. She had dinosaurs.

"I don't feel good, Mommy," she said when Karissa came to wake her.

"Oh, no." Karissa sat on the side of Macy's bed and put a hand to her daughter's forehead. No fever. "Where does it hurt?"

"My tummy."

Thoughts chased each other around Karissa's mind. What could she do with her daughter if she couldn't go to school? It probably wasn't bring-your-child-to-work day at Heron Publishing. She'd signed Macy up for an after-school program but hadn't thought ahead to a Plan B for emergencies. Why hadn't she done that?! She could hardly send her daughter to school sick.

"I don't want to go to school," Macy whimpered, revealing the cause of the tummy trouble.

"Do you think your tummy will feel better later today, after you've made some new friends?" Karissa suggested.

Macy's lower lip began to wobble.

"I bet there's a little girl in Mrs. Kimble's class who's been waiting all year for a new friend, wishing on a star every night."

Tears made Macy's hazel eyes shimmer, and it tore a fresh hole in Karissa's heart. Her little girl was smart and creative. She loved to read and make jewelry from kits. And she used to love school. Not for the first time, Karissa questioned if she'd been right to uproot her.

"Remember how nice Mrs. Kimble was when we went to meet her Friday afternoon?"

Macy nodded.

"And how she said she was looking forward to having you in her class?"

Again, another nod.

"Let's have a little breakfast and see how your tummy feels after that. What do you think?"

Macy wiped at her eyes. "I think my tummy will still hurt."

"How about an apple donut?"

That perked her girl up a little bit.

"And some hot chocolate. I bet your tummy would like that. And you can wear the new outfit we bought you."

Macy bit her lip. The promise of an apple donut and wearing a new outfit wasn't as magical a combination as Karissa had hoped.

She ran a hand over her daughter's tangled curls. "I'm a little nervous, too. I have to start someplace new today, just like you. But I'm going to have a good day. You know why?"

Macy shook her head, suspicious of where the conversation was going, but willing to listen.

"Because I'm going to make it good. I'm going to smile when I walk through the door. And smiles always make things better, don't they?"

Macy nodded. Slowly.

"If you walk into your classroom with a smile, you know what will happen?"

"What?"

"Your teacher will smile right back at you and think, what a nice girl Macy is. I'm so lucky to have her in my classroom."

"Will I find a friend?" Macy asked in a small voice.

"You will."

"How?"

"Look for another little girl who knows how to smile, too." *Please, God, let there be some kid in that class who knows how to do that.* "Come on. Get dressed and we'll have our apple donuts and get ready to carpe diem."

"Carpy demem?"

"Car-pay dee-em," Karissa repeated. "It means seize the day. Go for it," she added for clarification. "Every day has something good in it. You just have to keep your eyes open." *So do I.* She gave her daughter's shoulder a pat. "Let's get moving and start carpe diem-ing."

The pep talk worked, and Macy got out of bed and bounded for her dresser to pull out her new outfit, a pink sweater decorated with red strawberries and mint-colored jersey leggings, while Karissa made her way to the kitchen to make breakfast.

Apple donuts were just apples cut in half widthwise, frosted with cream cheese, and decorated with a few candy sprinkles. But sprinkles made everything better. Karissa made herself one, too, along with a very large coffee to fortify herself for whatever lay ahead.

Forty minutes later they were in the car and on their way.

Macy was fidgeting with the hem of her coat. So much for carpe diem.

"You are going to have a great day," Karissa told her.

Macy bit her lip and nodded.

They pulled up in the loading zone in front of the school. "Remember, smile and carpe diem," Karissa said after she'd leaned over and given Macy a kiss.

Macy nodded, took a deep breath, and got out of the car.

"I love you," Karissa called after her, and Macy looked over her shoulder and smiled.

There was something about that determined little smile that broke Karissa's heart. She remembered what it was like when her parents had moved, and she'd had to start at a new school. She'd been skinny and wore glasses, and even the new clothes her mother had bought for her couldn't make her as cute as she knew all the other girls would be. She'd been about Macy's age, preferring to hide behind a book rather than get out on the playground and tackle the jungle gym. She'd lurked around the corner of the building and watched while the other children played, wishing she could be with them, but not brave enough to join in. What an awful feeling that had been! She so hoped that wouldn't be her daughter on this cold February day.

Let her find her tribe quickly. It had taken Karissa a long time to find hers, but she had eventually. Macy would, too, and, hopefully, soon.

Not for the first time, Karissa steamed over the selfishness that had driven her away from her home, sent her searching for a new beginning in a safe place. Mark and Allegra were happily living together, and Allegra's daughter was still at the same school, the one where Macy had been perfectly happy. Maybe they should have stayed put…or moved somewhere in the same school district.

Except she hadn't been able to afford their house in Seattle on her own and she'd needed to escape that toxic environment and find a new place to begin. So, this was how it was, and this was where they were. *Carpe diem!*

She pulled up in one of the parking spaces behind the home of Heron Publishing and surveyed the scene of her new beginning. It was a white two-story building with gray trim that sprawled across the lot. After she'd accepted the position Edward Elliot had given her a polite but stiff tour. She knew that the lower level housed Shirley and Edward's offices as well as a small break room. Upstairs was a conference room, an office used by their sales rep, and the office of their cover art genius and marketing expert, André Babin, who she'd also met, along with a large room that was used to house office supplies and extra copies of Heron Publishing books. Beyond the conference room lay a rooftop deck complete with a patio table and some chairs. *Office parties on that deck in the summer?* she thought hopefully. Small and intimate gatherings, not the kind where you were packed in like sardines, trying to find a way to stand out in the can, er, crowd. It was a short walk from their offices to the downtown that ran along the harbor, and she could already envision herself visiting Devoted Kiss Café for a latte or maybe even the occasional lunch.

While the outside of the building said modern, the inside harkened to another era when publishers gave unlimited time to their authors and those authors were celebrities. The reception area held a heavy, old mahogany desk which served as the receptionist's station, a grandfather clock slowly ticking in a corner, and a tall barrister bookcase displaying the many books published by the company. The art on the walls, however, refused to cooperate with the theme and instead paid homage to the company's name. A four-piece painting of a heron fishing took up one wall and another of a bird standing at the water's edge hung on the wall behind that mahogany desk. A traditional wingback button-tufted oxblood chair sat beside a small, carved table with a marble top, ready for a visiting author to relax with a cup of tea or coffee while waiting to see either Shirley or Edward.

"Our authors like that personal touch, and we like them to feel appreciated," Edward had explained.

Karissa could handle that. Although the idea of meeting successful authors did make her nervous. Not something she'd chosen to share with her future employer.

The room was welcoming, but if you asked her (not that anyone had), the huge oriental rug covering a beat-up hardwood floor needed replacing. It was bloodred and spattered with flowers and looked threadbare in a couple of places. If you asked her (again, who had?) it took away from the elegance of the furnishings and décor. A gray hardwood laminate would look so much better. If she was in charge (which she was not) that was what she'd put in. It was still a lovely work environment, though, and she was excited to start.

She hung up her coat on the coat tree by the door, adjusted her glasses, and settled in at her desk. Now, what should she do? She couldn't get into the laptop on her desk yet as she didn't have the password. No author was waiting in the chair to be greeted. Maybe she should find her way to the kitchen off in the side wing and make coffee. Or boil water for tea in case someone in the office wanted some.

She was still seated, captive to inertia, when Edward's office door opened and he stepped out, tall, dark, and elegant in black slacks and a crisp, white shirt. Edward Elliot looked like he belonged in a picture on a department store wall, modeling clothes. He was the kind of man women stared at on Instagram. But not the kind of man who gave women like her a second look. Anyway, he was her boss and also part of a species not to be trusted.

"Ms. Newcomb, I see you made it in with no problem," he greeted her.

As in, with not hitting any cars en route? She wasn't sure how to reply to that, so merely nodded.

"Your car is running all right?"

"Yes, thank you," she managed to reply. She hadn't seen his parked behind the building and wondered if that black model was a loaner.

He cleared his throat. "Good." He held out a Post-it with a combination of letters and numbers written on it. "Here's the password for the laptop. You can begin by sorting the emails that come to the general inbox. Requested material you will send to either Shirley or myself, depending on which one of us it's addressed to. Any submissions that don't say requested material in the subject line, the standard reply is, 'We're sorry. We are not accepting any submissions at this time.' Sincerely, etc. Save your fingers and cut and paste."

"Aren't you worried you'll miss out on something great?" Karissa ventured.

"Not really. At the moment we don't have the time or staff. We recently lost an editor. And frankly, most of the queries we get aren't worth reading. We've found our best writers at local writers' conferences, or they've come recommended from the authors we already have. Shirley's email is her full name followed by at Heron Publishing dot com," he continued. "Mine is my full name, also at Heron Publishing dot com. This should be a fairly quiet day for you. We're not expecting anyone in as we reserve Mondays for meetings and catching up on paperwork. Tomorrow I have a lunch date with one of our authors. Lystra"—the former keeper of the gate, who Karissa was replacing—"kept our calendars on the laptop as well as in a physical planner, which she kept in this drawer," he continued, pointing to the top right drawer. "She liked to have a backup. Shirley attends chamber of commerce meetings the first Thursday of every month and takes no appointments after ten. I'll want you to always keep my calendar clear on Fridays from three o'clock on, and, as I said, on Mondays. None of us will take calls on Monday mornings, either. Other than that, you may put people through to us, and fill in appointments anywhere between 9:00 a.m. and 4:00 p.m."

"Yes, Mr. Elliot," Karissa said, all humble efficiency.

"We usually go on a first-name basis around here. I assume that's all right with you?" Kind words. They would have felt more welcoming matched with a smile.

"Yes, Mr., er…"

"Edward."

"Edward," she repeated, feeling awkward.

He nodded. "All right then, Karissa. I'll leave you to get settled. I'm sure you remember where our break room is. Feel free to help yourself to coffee before you get started." He hesitated a moment, then added, "Just please be careful not to spill it on the laptop."

As if she would. It wasn't good employee behavior to frown at your boss, but she couldn't help herself. Still, she supposed she couldn't blame him. After their encounter the day before maybe he thought she was a modern-day Lucy Ricardo, bringing chaos and disaster wherever she went.

He cleared his throat, said, "I'll, uh, let you get to it," and then ducked back inside his office.

She went to the break room, which housed a kitchenette and a small drop-leaf table with four chairs, popped a pod in the Keurig, and made herself a mug of coffee. Someone had baked oatmeal cookies. She helped herself to one of those as well, hoping it was all right. They were, after all, on a paper plate, sitting right there on the table, which had to mean they were meant for everyone.

She was just biting into it when a female voice behind her said, "I see you found the cookies."

She choked on a crumb and turned to see Shirley Houghton-Smith smiling at her.

Shirley had an Audrey Hepburn figure and wore her gray

hair spiked and made glasses a fashion statement with her hot-pink frames. She dressed like Audrey Hepburn would and wore the confident smile of a woman who knew her worth. Karissa wished she could evolve into a Shirley someday.

This morning Shirley was wearing black slacks and a form-fitting black turtleneck sweater accented with a black-and-white scarf bearing a print of the Eiffel Tower.

"Sorry, I didn't mean to frighten the whiskers off you," she said, giving Karissa's back a pat.

"I assumed it was okay to have one," Karissa said in between coughs.

"Absolutely. I have a sweet tooth and so does André, so there's often a plate of temptation sitting around. Anyway, it's nice to have something for those afternoon slump times or for when an author happens to drop in, which they like to do."

Karissa cleared her throat and took a swallow of coffee. "These are really good."

"We have a couple of great bakeries around here. And André gets inspired to bake once in a while. Those oatmeal cookies he makes are his specialty, and he also makes an amazing Millionaire's Shortbread."

That sounded decadent. And fattening. How much had Lystra weighed by the time she left?

"I'm glad to see you're settling in. Did Edward make you feel welcome?"

Was that a trick question?

Karissa was spared from answering by the appearance of André. He didn't dress the way Karissa always thought an artist should dress. There was no ascot, no flamboyant shirt or jewelry, or high-top Converse sneakers—just pleated khakis, conservative shoes, and a white shirt as crisp as Edward's. Only a little more stylish and rolled up at the sleeves. Maybe he saved his artist look for his social life.

He was tall and skinny and had a longish face with a long,

thin nose to match, and his hairline was receding like a low tide in progress. To make up for it, he'd grown a beard, which made him look…no better. But he had the kind of smile you could warm your heart against. And, anyway, looks didn't matter.

It was what she kept telling herself, but every time she thought of Allegra the words lost their power.

"Reinforcements have arrived," he greeted her. "It's good to have you here."

"I'm glad to be here," she said.

"Not half as glad as we are to have you," Shirley told her. "Thank God we finally have a new friendly face for Heron Publishing. With that desk sitting empty it's looked like we were about to go on the auction block."

"Don't even say things like that," André told her with a mock shudder. "I'd have to get a real job."

Shirley smiled tolerantly and helped herself to coffee. "Midmorning fuel-up," she said to Karissa.

Midmorning? It was only a little after eight.

"She gets here before the birds," André explained. "The downside of being captain of the ship."

"Here's to smooth sailing," Shirley said, raising her mug to him. Then she disappeared.

"The woman is amazing," said André. "But then, so is Edward. Amazing runs in their family."

"Family?"

"Edward's her nephew. He was a big shot in New York before he came here. Really helped her get this business off the ground."

Interesting. Why would Edward have abandoned being a big shot in New York to come work at a small publisher? None of her business.

"It's a good place to work." André grabbed a cookie. "Sugar's my drug of choice," he explained to Karissa.

"Mine, too," Karissa said, and wished she had André's fast metabolism.

"Kindred souls," he said, and turned to the coffeemaker.

"I guess I'd better get out to my desk," she said.

"Good luck. Enjoy your first day."

"I plan to," she said, and went back to reception.

The first call she took was a woman wanting to talk to Shirley.

"Who may I say is calling?" asked Karissa.

"Just tell her it's her favorite author," said the woman.

Hopefully, Shirley would know who her favorite author was. What if she didn't?

"I'm new here, and I'd love to know the name of Shirley's favorite author," Karissa said.

The woman gave a quick laugh. "This is Avery Black. I wrote *A Death on Hartstone Island*. Maybe you've read it."

Probably not. Karissa had never heard of Heron Publishing until she submitted an application to them. She vowed to get her hands on a copy of Avery's novel as soon as possible. Since she was going to be greeting Heron Publishing's authors, she wanted to be familiar with their work.

"No, but it certainly sounds intriguing," she said, and hoped it wouldn't be too gory. She always tried to skip over the gory parts when she read a mystery and much preferred cozies, where the author kept the bloody graphics to a minimum.

"I have some extra author copies. I'll bring you one next time I stop by."

"Thank you," said Karissa. *Free books, a great job perk*, she thought as she buzzed Shirley. "You have a call from Avery Black," she said.

"Ah, my favorite author."

"Really? That's what she said."

"That's what she thinks. That's what they all think," Shirley said, and Karissa could hear the smile in her voice. Shirley obviously knew how to make her authors feel special.

Karissa put through the call and turned her attention to emails. The Heron Publishing inbox was filled to overflowing with queries and unrequested submissions. How did Edward and Shirley keep from drowning in them? Oh, yeah, they drained the pool.

It seemed a shame that so many hopeful writers contacting them would never get past the gate and onto the grounds of the Heron Publishing estate. She opened one with a heading that read *Your Next NYT #1 seller*, and out of curiosity, read the author's pitch.

This is what you've been waiting for. I have written the untold story of the ghost of the Tacoma Narrows bridge.

The bridge had a ghost?

It wasn't gale force winds or poor construction that made the first Tacoma Narrows bridge, which became known as Galloping Gertie, collapse. It was an unseen force, the ghost of a woman bent on revenge.

Okay. Maybe that wasn't the next Pulitzer Prize winner. She sent the form reply, then deleted it and tried another.

This is the enchanting love story of our Poodle Derriere and our Siamese cat Twinkle…

Uh, no.

She read one more. *The Vampires of Freemont is an edge-of-your-seat story about a group of vampire cats that live beneath the Freemont Bridge in Seattle.*

After that she pasted in the response to the rest without reading the pitches.

Still, she felt guilty doing it. All those hopeful writers out there—how depressing it had to be getting rejected, how hard to have someone take one look at your created baby and say, "Not interested."

Shirley stopped by her desk on her way out to meet her "favorite author" for lunch. "How's it going?"

"Great," said Karissa, but then couldn't help adding, "I have to admit though, I feel sorry for all those authors I had to turn down who contacted us with a book idea."

"I know. It's hard," Shirley said. "People have hopes and dreams and you hate to be the one to crush them. But the people with true talent, who don't give up, eventually find their way. Remember, there are other publishers out there besides us, most of them bigger."

But maybe not anyone who wanted to hear the story of Derriere and Twinkle. Maybe sometimes rejecting someone was doing everyone else a favor.

Edward and André were the next ones out of the office. "We close from noon to one," Edward said, handing her a key to the front door. "If you want to try one of the local restaurants, be sure to lock up."

She took it, tried a smile on him.

It didn't fit well. He managed half of one in return paired with a nod, and then followed André out the door, a whisper of cold air sneaking in to make her shiver as they left.

The rain was back, mixed with snow. She was glad she'd packed a lunch.

The rest of the day passed without incident. She talked to two other authors on the phone who offered her a free book. André gave her a cheery goodbye. Edward came out, told her to feel free to leave and that Shirley would be another hour and would lock up. Then he offered a stiff goodbye and left. Edward Elliot was what a nineteenth-century author would describe as brooding. What did a handsome man who was a big part of a successful business have to brood about, anyway? The man was a puzzle.

Which she wasn't going to solve on her first day at work.

She went to pick up her daughter from her after-school care program.

On seeing Macy, it was evident that Edward Elliot wasn't the only person who was brooding. Oh, dear.

4

OTHER CHILDREN WERE RACING TOWARD THEIR PARents' cars, laughing, shouting, smiling. Two little girls were running toward an SUV, holding hands. Macy was dragging her feet and her backpack, her head down.

Taking in her daughter's crestfallen expression, it was all Karissa could do not to cry. "What's wrong, honey bunny?" she asked as Macy buckled up and slumped into the back seat.

"I hate it here," Macy said, and burst into tears.

There were still children milling about. Karissa knew better than to climb in back for a counseling session with so many witnesses around. It wouldn't look good for Macy. In the world of childhood insecurities, showing weakness was inviting ridicule.

"Let's go home and you can tell me all about it," she said.

Macy was in no mood to wait. "I don't want to be here," she wailed and what had started as a trickle of tears became a river.

Karissa set her jaw, forced herself not to speed in the school zone although she wanted desperately to race home and console her daughter. This couldn't wait another ten minutes. She drove a couple of blocks, turned a corner, and then joined Macy in the back seat.

Macy threw herself against Karissa and sobbed, while Karissa rubbed her back and kissed the top of her head. "I'm so sorry, honey bunny." *Sorry your father turned our world upside down, sorry I couldn't stay in that world.*

"Nobody likes me," Macy declared between sobs.

Karissa felt a new fissure open in her already broken heart.

"Nobody knows you yet. When they do, they'll like you."

What was not to like about her little girl? She had her less than perfect moments and had thrown a tantrum or two during the divorce process as well as when she learned Karissa was selling the house and they were moving. But she was a naturally sweet, sunny child. This was an extra helping of unhappiness that she didn't deserve.

"I wanted to play with Marisol, but Amory said she wouldn't be Marisol's friend if she played with me," Macy said, and took a great, shuddering breath.

Ah, yes, playground politics. "Maybe Marisol isn't meant to be your best friend," Karissa said. "Or your friend at all." Amory wouldn't be getting any invites to birthday or slumber parties in the future. Neither would the cowardly Marisol.

"But I want them to be," Macy protested. "Nobody likes me," she repeated.

Karissa remembered that feeling all too well from her own childhood. Sadly, rejection felt as awful when you were an adult as it did when you were a child, and this probably wouldn't be the first rejection Macy would experience. If only Karissa could wrap her daughter in a protective bubble and keep her there for her entire life.

"I bet you're going to find somebody who does like you," she said, giving Macy another kiss.

Macy shook her head vehemently.

"Oh, yes you will. And you know why?"

Macy wiped at her damp cheeks and looked up at Karissa, somber but with hope in her eyes. "Why?"

"Because you are fun and nice. What's not to like about that?"

Macy bit her lip, thinking.

"You know why Amory did what she did, don't you?"

Macy shook her head again. "I wasn't mean to her."

"Of course, you weren't. But she's jealous of you. Marisol likes you and now Amory's worried Marisol will like you better than her. She's afraid of losing her friend, so she's making sure you and Marisol don't become friends."

Macy scowled. "That's mean."

"Yes, it is," Karissa agreed.

"I don't want to go to school tomorrow," Macy announced.

Karissa didn't blame her. "If you don't, you won't find that girl who's looking for a new best friend. You might miss out on the best friend of your life."

"I miss Charlotte."

Allegra's daughter. Once again, hurt and anger wrapped around Karissa, a vine she still had to keep cutting back.

"I know you do, honey bunny, but you'll get to see her when you stay with Daddy this weekend." Ugh. "Meanwhile, let's think about how you can make tomorrow a better day."

"I can't," Macy insisted.

"Are you sure?"

Macy nodded.

"How do you know?"

"Because Amory will be there."

"Well, nothing says you have to hang out with Amory. Do you sit by her in class?"

"No," Macy admitted.

"Do you have to be around her at recess?"

Macy shrugged.

"You don't. So instead of worrying about Amory, here's what I want you to do tomorrow. I want you to walk into class with a great big smile and say hello to someone. Is your smiler still working?"

Macy gave her lips a half-hearted lift.

"That's not your smile. Your smile is much bigger," Karissa coaxed.

Macy tried again. It was a little better.

"Okay, now, I want you to think of Amory walking into class wearing clown shoes and a big, red clown nose. How does she look?"

Macy giggled. "Silly."

"Ah, there's the Macy smile I know so well."

Macy sobered. "What if nobody smiles back at me?"

"Smiles are contagious. You can catch them, just like a cold. Someone is bound to catch yours. And you know what else you can do to make someone smile?"

"What?" Macy asked.

"Find something you like about that girl and compliment her."

"Like what?"

"Maybe her hair. Maybe her top or her shoes. We all like to hear good things about ourselves, don't we?"

"What if I can't think of anything?"

"Then just keep smiling. You'll find the person you're supposed to be friends with. Now, what do you say we go home and have some of the cookies that nice Alice next door gave us?"

Macy nodded, not as enthusiastically as she normally would, but it was a beginning.

That night Karissa had a counseling session with her mother. "I feel so bad for her."

"I do, too," said Mom.

"I'm sure she'll find a friend," Karissa said, as much to herself as her mother.

"It will take some time is all."

"Yes, but what eight-year-old understands that concept?" She sighed. "I feel like such a failure."

"Darling, you are not a failure."

Her marriage was over, her daughter was miserable. "I'm doing a pretty good imitation."

"This, too, shall pass."

Karissa sighed. Her mother was right. Life wasn't static. "Thanks, Mom. I need to remember that. I guess I'm no different than Macy. She wants her issues resolved overnight and so do I. But I am making progress," she said. "I had a great first day at work."

"Wonderful. Tell me about it."

Karissa did, and by the time she was done she was feeling much better about herself, even a little less worried about Macy. This new life she was building was going to work. She'd make it work.

The next morning Macy's concerns were back. "What if nobody likes me?" she fretted as she sat at the breakfast bar and pushed her scrambled eggs around her plate.

"You'll find someone." Karissa leaned her elbows on the counter so they were face-to-face. "Let's see your smile."

Macy managed a small one.

"Bigger," urged Karissa.

The lips went a little higher.

"Now this big," Karissa said, straightening and stretching her arms wide.

It worked and Macy obliged.

But by the time they'd pulled into the school's loading zone, it was faltering.

"Don't be afraid. Somewhere in this school your new best friend is waiting for you to find her," Karissa said, and prayed she was right. "And be patient," she added. "You might not find her right away, but she's there."

Macy bit her lip, nodded, and pushed open the car door.

"I love you," Karissa said.

"I love you, too," said Macy and walked toward the school entrance the child equivalent of French aristocracy headed for the guillotine.

"She'll be okay," Karissa told herself.

They both would.

Karissa's day started off well.

"You're looking good this morning," Shirley told her when she emerged from her office in search of coffee. She took in Karissa's turquoise blouse that she'd paired with black pants and nodded approvingly. "Turquoise is a great color for you. It shows off that lovely skin of yours."

Lovely skin. How high did that rate on the hot scale? Probably not very. Still, Karissa appreciated the compliment.

"Thank you. That was nice of you."

"I'm only speaking what's true," Shirley said with a smile.

"It's quite a compliment coming from you," Karissa said.

"Now who's being nice?" Shirley joked.

"You always look so put together."

This morning Shirley was in a royal blue sheath dress and heels so high it made Karissa's arches hurt just to look at them. She'd switched out her hot-pink glasses for ones with sparkly blue frames and she looked ready for a shoot for *Vogue*. Everything about Shirley said, "I am amazing, and proud of it."

"I do love clothes and makeup," she said.

"I wish I could wear makeup," Karissa said wistfully. She'd never progressed beyond lip gloss. She envied all those women on TikTok who looked so glamorous, but drama simply wasn't her and the few times she'd tried lipstick she'd felt like a fake. Eye makeup was a lost cause. "I'm allergic to mascara," she explained. "And eyeliner."

"You already have nice eyelashes," said Shirley.

But they were pathetic compared to Allegra's eyelash extensions.

Oh, no. What was she doing bringing Allegra to work with her? *Stay in Seattle where you belong.*

Edward came in, a stylish wool overcoat covering charcoal slacks. The morning drizzle had dampened his dark hair and made it shine like a raven's wing.

"Good morning, ladies," he said.

Shirley pointed to his laptop bag. "How's BJ's manuscript looking?"

"Polished as usual," he said.

She nodded. "Good news."

Edward turned to Karissa. "Do I have any appointments today other than lunch?"

"Let me check." She brought up his calendar. "You have two conference calls, one at ten and one at eleven thirty. Then it's your lunch with Emerald Austen at noon."

"Good. I can get some work done before then. Thank you, Karissa," he added politely, and slipped into his office.

Short and to the point. There would be no chatting with Edward Elliot. Did he chat with anyone? Was chatting in his wheelhouse? If not, she understood. It wasn't really in hers, either.

"I know I don't have anything on the docket, which is good," Shirley said. "Don't put any calls through to me. Just take messages. I have a pile of paperwork to wade through and edits to finish."

Editing a manuscript. Being part of turning someone's inspiration into a book that countless people would enjoy—what a thrilling job!

André was next in, carrying a Starbucks to-go cup and huddling under a trench coat that made him look like something out of an old spy movie.

She wished she was like these three, busy making book magic. She reminded herself that she was part of the team, too, keeping the magic machine well oiled by keeping the office running. It wasn't exactly on a par with writing a bestselling novel or bringing someone else's novel to life, but her job still mattered. Someone had to keep an eye on the magic machine.

"It's really starting to come down out there," André observed, inspiring Karissa to look out the window where a sloppy snow was failing to stick. "I think we need to hide inside and send out for pizza today. You up for ordering one in for us later? Or I can. You probably have enough to do."

"I'm happy to take care of that," she said.

She made note of André's preferences then shot off a quick text to Shirley.

Keep the anchovies on André's side, Shirley texted. Who wants to eat salty slug on their pizza? Shirley had a way with words.

The pizza had just arrived, and Karissa was calling André to let him know, pizza box in one hand, phone in the other, when the door opened and along with a strong gust of icy wind, in blew Emerald Austen.

Karissa blinked. Emerald Austen was somewhere in her forties—the ghost of Allegra future. Like Allegra, she had a perfect figure, slender in all the right places and curved where it counted. Her pouty lips were coated with bloodred lipstick, and she had long, thick, wavy hair like Allegra's. Only where Allegra's had been dark, this woman's was the color of polished copper. Her eyes were green, like Scarlett O'Hara's in *Gone with the Wind*, and dramatically framed by dark brown winged eyeliner and probably an entire tube of mascara. Karissa had never liked Scarlett O'Hara and she hadn't liked the book, either. Under her raincoat, Emerald wore black leggings tucked into stylish black boots. Her gloves were black leather with a faux fur trim. Was this an author or a lost movie star?

The woman brushed the snow off her raincoat, shook out her hair, and then inspected Karissa with a raised eyebrow. So this was what authors were describing when they talked about a withering look. Karissa felt herself shrinking.

Before she could manage to greet the newcomer, Emerald gave her a condescending smile and said, "You must be the new girl."

Girl? Seriously?

"Or else pizza delivery?" Emerald suggested with a smirk.

Oh, that was funny.

But maybe it was meant to be some sort of goodhearted teasing. Karissa smiled, giving her the benefit of the doubt.

"Not much better looking than the last one," Emerald muttered just loud enough for Karissa to hear.

Okay, so much for giving the woman the benefit of the doubt. For a moment Karissa envisioned herself walking up to this faux movie star and shoving the pizza in her face.

Instead, she set down the box and dismissed her Walter Mitty-style fantasy moment. She was much too professional for such shenanigans.

"I'm Karissa," she said with forced brightness. "I'm the new office administrator. And you are...?" She knew. But if they were going to play games...

"I'm Emerald Austen and I'm here to go to lunch with Edward. Shouldn't you know that?"

Ouch. Game, set and match to Emerald.

"Of course. I'm happy to meet you," Karissa lied.

Emerald didn't return the courtesy. "I assume he's still in his office, chained to his computer."

"Yes, but—"

"Good," said Emerald and marched to Edward's door.

"I'm afraid he can't talk right now. He's finishing up a call," Karissa said, hurrying after her.

Emerald didn't even slow down. What to do? Should she throw herself in front of the door and block Emerald's path? Follow her and pathetically whine, "I tried to stop her, sir"?

"No need to be a little guard dog," Emerald said. "Edward

and I don't stand on ceremony. Anyway, he needs to be done with his call. It's time for lunch." She threw open the door. "Edward, you workaholic," she said, her voice a purr. "It's time for you to take me to lunch."

The door shut in Karissa's face, and she marched back to her desk, fuming. Had the woman majored in rudeness in college? Oh, no, Emerald Austen probably had an advanced degree by the time she reached middle school.

A couple of minutes later, Edward emerged with her, an almost-smile on his face. "I should be back in an hour," he said to Karissa as he took his overcoat from the coat tree.

"Don't count on it," Emerald said with a grin that made Karissa think of a cat with a mouse between its paws. No, not a cat. A cougar.

Karissa watched out the window as they walked to where a black Mercedes was parked. Was Emerald making that much money as a writer?

André descended from his upstairs art lair. "Was that Emerald I heard just now?"

Karissa nodded. "She came to go to lunch with Edward."

"More like she came to eat Edward for lunch," cracked André. "Are they…"

"I don't think so," André said. "But she'd like to be. She's here often enough, that's for sure. She's our biggest selling author so when she wants Edward to go to lunch or out for a drink, he goes."

Karissa watched the Mercedes drive off. "She must be selling really well."

"She already had money before she came to us," André said. "Writing's more a hobby than an occupation for her. Good thing for us she enjoys her hobby. And she's good at it."

Writing may have been the woman's hobby, but Karissa was sure that chasing Edward was her occupation.

André pointed to the box. "I'll take that to the break room."

She handed it to him, then knocked on Shirley's door. "Pizza's here."

"Be out in a minute," Shirley called. "Save me a piece."

"Ha! The race is to the swift," said André. "Pizza is the food of the gods."

Yes, it was. What were Edward and Emerald having for lunch? Karissa wondered. Edward and Emerald—those two names went together so perfectly.

So did the people, if you looked on the surface. Edward Elliot was handsome, and she was beautiful. But that was where the perfect pairing stopped. In spite of his reserved manner, he seemed like a nice man. Emerald didn't seem to know the meaning of the word *nice*.

A few minutes after Karissa and André had sat down Shirley surfaced from her office to join them. André was on his second slice. Karissa was simply sitting, watching him.

"Aren't you going to have some pizza?" Shirley asked.

Karissa had lost her appetite. "I'm not very hungry. Anyway, I should get back to my desk."

"We break for lunch around here. Come on," Shirley urged. "Relax and have some."

"Yes. It will give us a chance to get to know you better," put in André. "Well, me, anyway."

"There's not much to know," Karissa said. "As I mentioned in the interview, I'm a single mom. I have a daughter named Macy."

"New to the area?" guessed André, who hadn't been in on her interview, and she nodded.

"It's hard being a single parent, although I did it and lived to tell the tale," said Shirley.

"I guess I will, too," Karissa said, and managed a smile more genuine than the one she'd given Emerald.

"How are you liking Gig Harbor?" André asked.

"It's great. I like my house, and I'm enjoying working here."

"I think you're set for success," Shirley said, smiling at her.

"I hope so." If Karissa couldn't have love, she'd take success.

"Life is what we make it," Shirley said.

"Or what gets dumped on us," André put in.

Oh, no. No more dumping. Karissa had had enough of being a dumping ground.

"Can you tell me a little more about our authors?" she asked. Especially the one who had just whisked in and insulted her before dragging Edward off.

"We've published quite a few since I started the company in 2014," Shirley said. "Edward's been instrumental in helping me expand. Some of our authors have moved on, either to bigger publishers or other adventures, but we have a talented core who publish regularly with us. Gerald McCrae is our top writer when it comes to nonfiction and memoir and writes about hiking and adventure in the Pacific Northwest. His new book will be out in June. Then there's Agatha Brown, who writes about Northwest history. Her latest one on Indigenous people has done very well."

"Morris Anderson," put in André. "He's our resident humorist. He's got a hero who's a ferryboat captain who is always dealing with crazy passengers. He's a retired ferryboat captain himself, used to work the Vashon-Seattle run. Love working with him."

"Truly Mason is another historical writer," said Shirley. "And you've met Avery Black."

"Yes, she seems really nice," Karissa said.

"Emmet Jones," added André.

Okay, this pump needed priming. "And what about Emerald?" Karissa asked. "Has she been with Heron Publishing for long?"

"Seven years and counting," said Shirley.

"We've seen that woman through divorce and widowhood. You'll find her in Wikipedia under Man Eater," André said.

"André," Shirley chided.

Unrepentant, he shrugged. "She's set for money now, so she's stopped digging for gold. Now she's looking for fun."

Edward Elliot didn't seem like a fun-loving type of man.

Shirley frowned at André. "She loved her last husband dearly and was devastated when he died."

"Yeah, so devastated that she used his death as inspiration for last year's novel."

"We all work through our grief in different ways," Shirley said, refusing to diss an author.

"So, she writes mysteries?" Karissa guessed.

"Yep. Dark, gory ones," André confirmed.

"They're all Northwest set and they all do well," Shirley said. "I keep waiting for the day she leaves us and moves on to someplace like Simon & Schuster."

That day couldn't come soon enough for Karissa. She'd only just met the woman, but she was rude and clearly entitled and seemed likely to make Karissa's new job a lot more challenging.

"Meanwhile, expect to see a lot of her. Edward is her editor, and she drops in frequently to see him," Shirley said.

"High maintenance," said André. "She always needs something. And when it comes to cover art, she's the pickiest of all our authors."

"It's good for you," said Shirley, putting another slice of pizza on her plate. "Keeps you at the top of your game."

"I don't need a prima donna author to do that," he retorted with a frown.

Karissa didn't need Emerald Austen there, either. Emerald, with her arrogance, was going to be the snake in Karissa's Garden of Eden. It was plain to Karissa that Emerald, like Scarlett O'Hara, was the kind of woman who took men's hearts for trophies and scorned other women. She'd like nothing better than to see Emerald gone with the wind.

You don't have to like her, Karissa told herself, *and you don't have to buy any of her books.*

But she did buy Emerald's latest mystery on her way to pick up Macy from her after-school program.

When you were a Mellie, you couldn't help yourself. You just had to know what made Scarlett tick.

5

"Some people were doers, and some were only wishers.
She knew which one she was."
—from *Shark Infested* by Emerald Austen

SEEING HER DAUGHTER'S HAPPY FACE WHEN SHE PICKED
her up made Karissa's day much better. Here was an improvement over the one before.

Macy bounded into the back seat of the car. "Hi, Mommy!"

"Hello to you," said Karissa. "It looks like you had a good day today."

Macy nodded eagerly. "I smiled at Lilith and told her I liked her unicorn backpack. We played fairies at recess."

The Fairy Feathers series was Macy's newest reading treat and she'd recently finished the latest installment. It appeared that this new friend Lilith enjoyed the same books. Relief trickled over Karissa like a hot shower, washing away the earlier unpleasantness of her day. Macy was finding her way on this new road stretching before them. That made Karissa's glass more than half-full of goodness.

Reading Emerald's novel later drained some of it. Karissa

stayed up half the night reading. It was well written and intriguing. Emerald deserved to be published.

But she didn't deserve to be liked.

"Be honest," Karissa told herself as she closed the book, "you're jealous."

Pathetic, but there it was. She couldn't help wishing she was...more. Prettier, bolder, better. Like Allegra only with a heart. Like Emerald only without the arrogance.

She could be more. After all, she was starting over.

She didn't have to keep dragging around her past hurt and she didn't have to let a certain rude bag of conceit get to her. What she had to do was keep moving forward. If she did, maybe at some point she would become...more.

With that in mind she went to work, did her job, and gave a properly enthusiastic yet professional response when Edward asked her if she was settling in okay. She was settling in, everyone had been welcoming, and it was kind of him to ask. Edward Elliot seemed to be a decent man, thoughtful and considerate. Certainly not arrogant. He could do better than Emerald Austen, for sure.

But Edward Elliot's life was none of her business. She had her hands full managing her own life. And she was going to manage just fine, thank you.

"I'm so glad things are looking up for Macy," said Karissa's mother, when she checked in with her later that evening. "I knew she'd find her way."

"I'm glad *you* knew," Karissa said.

"And how about you? Are you finding your way? How's the job going?"

"It's going great," Karissa said, opting not to tell about her Emerald-inspired moment of discouragement the day before. That was the past. It was a new day and she had moved on.

"I'm glad. I know this next year is going to bring good things into your life," Mom said.

"I'm ready for that," said Karissa.

"I hope so. Have you met anyone besides... What was her name? Alice?"

"No. Between work and Macy I haven't had time."

"You're still settling in. I hope you can find some new friends," Mom said.

"I'm sure I will," Karissa lied.

She was in no hurry to go looking. Those wounds in her back from where Mark and Allegra had stabbed her were still healing, and it was a slow process. Alice looked safe, but Karissa didn't know if she wanted to go beyond her.

The neighborhood seemed like a friendly one. On their way home she and Macy had driven past a tall, older man with white hair like a lawn in need of mowing. He'd been out walking his dog and he'd given them a friendly wave, and Karissa had waved back. Alice had brought over more cookies and they'd chatted for a few minutes. That was enough neighboring.

But the first Friday in March brought another neighbor standing on Karissa's front porch, holding a shamrock plant. She looked close to Karissa's age, maybe a little older, and, while she wasn't as intimidatingly hot as Allegra the Evil, she was a close second, in jeans and a cashmere wrap, her straight, highlighted hair tucked behind her ears to show off some very artsy glass earrings. She was tall and slender, with high cheek-bones and a perfect, oval face. A writer would probably describe her as striking. How long had it taken her to get her makeup so perfect?

Karissa took in the woman's smile and the plant—*I come in peace*—and commanded herself to smile back. No need to feel threatened.

"Hi, I'm Margot Burns. I live next door," the woman said, pointing to the red brick Tudor with the perfectly manicured lawn. "I'm a little late in welcoming you to the neighborhood. But better late than never, right?"

Did she want to come in? Macy was stuffing clothes in her backpack for her weekend with Daddy and they would be leaving in a few minutes to meet Mark for the kid hand-off. There was no time to entertain, which was a relief. The woman seemed nice enough, but then you never knew.

Still, Karissa had to be polite. "I'm Karissa Newcomb," she said. "I'm afraid I'm just getting ready to leave."

"No worries. I'm glad I caught you before you did though. I just wanted to make you feel welcome," the woman said.

Karissa had made the same gesture when Allegra had moved in next door. "I appreciate that. Thank you."

"If you need anything, let me know," said Margot.

"I will," Karissa said, but she didn't plan on needing anything.

"I don't think I should rush into any friendships," she told her mother later when they were talking.

"It's a good idea to go slowly," Mom agreed. "But you can't hide from people, either."

"Who said I'm hiding?"

"Are you?"

"No, I'm just going slowly, like you said."

"I said slowly, not stalled. Not every woman is an Allegra, darling. In fact, most women aren't."

"*Your* friends are great."

Karissa would have loved to clone them all. They'd invited Mom into their book club, The Bookies, shortly after the family moved to Anacortes. Those women had been there for her mom when she had breast cancer, taking her to treatments when Dad had to work, bringing over meals, sending flowers, watching over Karissa and Ethan. They'd all bought Campfire mints from Karissa when she was a Campfire Girl, sparing her from having to stand outside the grocery store and suffer the agony of approaching strangers. They'd sent condolence cards when Petunia, Mom's adored calico cat, died. True and loyal friends.

Karissa had been sure Allegra would be that kind of friend. But then she'd thought Mark would be the same kind of loyal husband her dad had been to her mom. Wrong on both counts.

"These women sound nice," said Mom. "You don't have to swing the door wide, but you could afford to open it a little. Give them a chance. Life's so much better when it's shared."

"I have you for that."

"You won't always."

Karissa frowned. "There's a cheerful thought."

"It's true. Put together your posse now. That way someone will always have your back when the hard times hit. Or when the Allegras ride into town."

It was easy for her mother to say. There wasn't a stinker on her block.

Maybe there weren't any on Karissa's, either. There was only one way to find out. She'd have to open the door, at least a little.

To help herself get there she decided to invite her two next-door neighbors over for coffee. She had to have met her rotten neighbor quota with Allegra.

Maybe she had. Both Alice and Margot were happy to accept her invitation and showed up with treats—coffee cake from Alice and a bottle of homemade caramel syrup from Margot. "It's great in coffee," she said.

"Or Margot's lattes," Alice added.

Karissa not only appreciated the kind gestures, but also how easy she found the women to talk to. Not that she shared a lot. Other than where she was working, which impressed them both, and that she was divorced.

That had come out when Alice asked about Macy and Karissa had replied, "She's with her father for the weekend."

"Been there, done that," Margot said, her voice filled with sympathy. "Thank God I had Alice here to help me."

"Like you helped me when I lost Charlie. My husband died three years ago," Alice explained to Karissa.

"We're our own support group," Margot quipped.

"What are neighbors for if not to help each other?" Alice added.

That was what Karissa had always thought. Until she realized neighbors didn't always help.

"Coping with shared custody is hard," Margot continued, "but you eventually adjust and take advantage of the time for yourself."

"I guess," said Karissa, although she wasn't sure she'd ever adjust. "What can you tell me about the neighborhood?"

"It's a friendly one, but pretty quiet," Margot said. "A couple of houses with teenagers. They're good kids."

"And we have a sweet pair of newlyweds down the street," put in Alice.

"Andrea Morgan across the street is great, but she isn't into doing much with anyone. She's got a stressful job and it pretty much sucks her dry," Margot said. "Kind of like what I had," she added, her smile disappearing.

"You'll find something," Alice assured her.

"You lost your job? I'm sorry," Karissa said.

"Maybe I was due for another cosmic punch in the nose," Margot said with a shrug.

Margot Burns wasn't so perfect after all. The discovery was a shock. And a bit of a comfort, which Karissa realized didn't say much for her own character.

"Maybe it's turning forty that did it," Margot continued. "Divorced at thirty. Laid off at forty. Is there a pattern here?"

"Something bad once every decade doesn't seem too awful," Karissa ventured, then regretted her words. Who knew how long it took to recover from a divorce? She had yet to find out. "I'm sorry, I shouldn't have said that."

"No, you're right. It doesn't seem like much," Margot said.

"It's more than enough," Alice told Margot.

"Yeah, I guess, if you toss in a couple of failed relationships in between. Love is not my specialty," Margot said with a shrug.

At least Karissa only had one love fail to recover from. "But now, getting laid off, that's tough," she said.

"I'm trying not to take it personally," Margot said. "When companies start trimming fat, middle management is often the first place they look, and these days everyone is trimming. So I'm moving on, working on figuring out what's next."

"A chance for a new start," said Alice.

"There you go," Margot said. "That's why I like this woman. She always looks on the bright side. But that's enough about me and my misery. Tell us more about working at Heron Publishing."

"Do they give out free books?" Alice asked.

"Alice is a bookaholic," Margot explained. "Don't ever take her to the library or a bookstore unless your trunk is empty."

"She exaggerates," Alice said, "but I do like to read, especially historical novels."

"Same here," said Margot. "I also like mysteries, and nonfiction, too."

"I like romance novels," Karissa said. "And historical fiction." She sighed. "But I'm thinking it would be good to read something that will help me sort out my life now that I'm starting over in a new city."

"I just downloaded one you might like," Margot said. She pulled out her cell phone and brought up her Kindle app, then turned the phone so Karissa could see it.

"Where There's a Will There's a Way," she read.

"I stumbled on it when I was looking around for some inspiration. I guess she's a big influencer."

Karissa turned to the About the Author page. "And she has a podcast."

"And a lot of followers," said Margot. "I figure the book's worth a try."

"It might be," said Karissa.

They enjoyed a little more coffee cake and a little more conversation and then her guests left. Karissa offered to send the last couple of pieces back home with Alice, but she said, "No, you keep it. I'm sure you'll want some for breakfast."

Karissa closed the door and grinned, feeling lighter than she had in months. Two nice neighbors, who seemed to understand the importance of supporting each other rather than stabbing each other in the back. It looked like she'd landed in the perfect neighborhood.

She sure hoped looks weren't deceiving.

"I'm glad you reached out," her mother said when they chatted later. "It looks like you've got some nice neighbors."

"I hope so," Karissa said. "I'd sure love to have what you have with your book club."

"You could," Mom said. "Why don't you start a book club of your own?"

"We don't know each other very well yet."

"I didn't know The Bookies very well when I first joined the book club," Mom said, "but I'm glad I did. I found my best friends there. You may never get beyond talking about books, but, on the other hand, you may end up with some solid friendships."

She could. Karissa liked both Alice and Margot, and they seemed safe. Still, committing to something like a book club with women she barely knew felt like taking a big step into quicksand.

"I'll think about it," she said.

The more she thought it over the more she warmed to the idea. Margot and Alice were always up for a chat if they happened to see her coming or going, and Alice invited Karissa and Macy over for dinner one evening when she was entertaining Lucky. Macy loved playing with the dog and Karissa enjoyed having someone nonthreatening to visit with. She and Alice exchanged phone numbers, and she wasn't sure who'd come away happier, Macy or her.

On Saint Patrick's Day weekend, Margot invited Karissa to come over on Saturday night for corned beef and cabbage and some Baileys. Alice had been invited, too, and was bringing Irish soda bread. Macy was with her father for the weekend, and Karissa had been feeling mopey, so she was happy to accept, and promised to bring some ice cream they could pour their Irish cream over.

"If there's any left by the time we get to dessert," Margot had joked.

Margot's house was a little bigger than Karissa's and decorated as stylishly as Margot liked to dress.

"This looks like something from a home improvement show," Karissa said, looking around. "The after, not the before," she quickly added, making Margot laugh.

The cream-colored sofa had eye-catching orange accent pillows; the coffee table sported a vase with fresh flowers. A stained-glass hand-painted clock depicting the four seasons hung on one wall. The wall in her dining area showed a colorful modern art piece of Murano glass shaped like a woman's face.

"I got that a couple years ago when I took my daughter to Italy," she said after Karissa had admired it. "Back when I could afford to travel. I still want to get to Ireland someday. For now, this will have to do." She held up the bottle of Irish cream. "My big, exciting life."

"Kind of like mine right now," said Karissa. "But at least I have a nice house and I've wound up in a great neighborhood."

"I can see you're a positive thinker," Margot said, as she poured them each a drink.

"I'm trying to be a glass half-full kind of woman," Karissa said.

"Half-full is better than nothing." Margot took a sip of her drink. "Although I'm ready to get my glass a little closer to the top. Maybe I'll win the lottery. Or maybe one of those hot heroes I like to read about will hop off the page and give me what I want."

"Sometimes fiction heroes are the best," said Karissa.

"You can say that again." Margot raised her glass. "Here's to those heroes and the books they live in."

"To books," Karissa echoed.

She could almost feel her mother at her elbow, urging, *Go for it. Start that book club.*

She should. What was she waiting for?

To be sure, of course, to have some kind of guarantee that all would be well. That these new friendships wouldn't end as disastrously as her last.

As if life gave out those kinds of guarantees. *Do it!*

She took another sip of her drink and then tossed the words out there before she could wimp out. "Speaking of books, I was thinking it might be fun to start a book club. Would you be interested?"

Margot cocked her head and considered. "You know, that might be fun. I've actually never had time to be in one. I've sure got time now. What would we read?"

"I don't know. Whatever we want," said Karissa, and then held her breath, waiting for a positive response.

"A little of everything maybe?" suggested Margot.

"And maybe things we might not normally read. Like that book you downloaded."

"I wouldn't mind having someone to talk about it with," Margot said. She gave a decisive nod and said, "Let's do it," and Karissa felt a warmth blooming in her chest that had nothing to do with the Irish cream she was consuming. "And let's invite Alice. She'll love this. She doesn't get out much."

"Really? She seems so sociable."

"She is, but she doesn't drive."

"Not at all?" Karissa asked, surprised.

"Not since her husband died. She gets panic attacks."

"Which explains the trips together to the library?" guessed Karissa.

Margot nodded. "Alice loves to read. And she'll love to make goodies for our meetings. A win-win, right?"

"Absolutely," Karissa said happily.

"So, what do you think?" Margot asked Alice after she'd arrived, been given a drink and been filled in on the plans for a book club.

"I think it sounds like fun," Alice said. "I manage fine without driving, but my horizons could use some expanding. It's been a rough three years since I lost Charlie." She blinked but couldn't hide the tears rising in her eyes.

"I'm so sorry," Karissa said. Which was worse, losing your husband to death or losing him to another woman? There was no worse. Both were awful.

"He was only fifty-nine. I was fifty-four. He was going to retire early, and we were going to get a camper and see the country." Alice bit her lip, stared at her tumbler and then downed the last of her drink.

"Maybe you'll still get to see the country," Karissa said.

Alice wiped at the corner of one eye. "Through books, anyway. So count me in."

"All right," Margot said. "We're going to start out with that book I just downloaded, *Where There's a Will There's a Way* by Annie Wills. I'll pick up a copy for you tomorrow."

"Great. Thanks," said Alice. "Say, you know who else might like to join us? My sister. I think it would be good for Josie. She's going through some challenges right now," Alice added, and looked hopefully from Margot to Karissa.

Karissa hesitated. A woman she didn't know joining them?

"Sure, why not?" said Margot. "It's about time I got to know your sister."

"Okay," said Karissa. Another Alice would probably make a good addition.

"Great," said Alice, beaming.

"Well, then, we're good to go," Margot said. "Meet in April to discuss?"

"Meet in April to discuss," Karissa agreed.

"Your place or mine?"

"Mine is fine," Karissa said. "Any day you prefer?"

"Gee, let me check my busy schedule," Margot joked.

"How about Wednesday nights then? Midweek break?" Karissa suggested.

"Sure. Middle of the month?"

"That works for me," said Alice.

And that was that. New friends and a book club. Things were looking up.

6

"Your attitude feeds your outlook on life.
How's your attitude?"
—from *Where There's a Will There's a Way* by Annie Wills

"I THINK YOU'D ENJOY IT," ALICE SAID TO HER SISTER,
Josie, as Josie helped unpack the treasures Alice had scored on
their latest thrift store hunting expedition.

Alice had brought up the subject of the book club on their way
home and had been surprised at her sister's lack of enthusiasm.

Josie removed the newspaper wrapping from a chintz teapot
and handed it to Alice to wash. "They'll probably want to read
nothing but depressing World War II books or some literary
gobbledygook with deep hidden meaning nobody cares about.
Remember the book club we were in years ago with Georgia
and Karen and Beth? The only books that were any good were
the ones you and I picked, and eventually the whole thing turned
into nothing but a bunch of booze and bitch sessions."

"It won't be like that with these two," Alice assured her.
Granted, the girls both had challenges in their lives, but that
didn't mean they'd do nothing but complain about them. "Any-

way, if they do need to vent once in a while or need advice, so what? We have a lot of wisdom to share."

"As if the young ever listen," Josie scoffed.

"Sometimes the old can learn from the young," Alice pointed out, which inspired a snort from her sister.

"Have they picked a book for their first meeting?" Josie wanted to know.

"They have," Alice said.

Here was where it got tricky. The girls' first pick wasn't one Alice would have chosen, and it was one Josie was definitely going to scorn. But it was good to read outside your comfort zone, good to be exposed to different ideas and points of view.

At least that was what she'd told herself. In reality, she'd gone along with the selection because she'd wanted to be included. Joining a book club was hardly the equivalent of signing up for a world cruise, but it had felt like a big step to Alice.

She dried her hands and fetched the book from her nightstand, brought it back and laid it on the counter. "Margot picked it up for me yesterday."

Josie looked at it as if Alice had just set down a piece of raw liver and said, "Here, take a bite." She raised both eyebrows at Alice. "You've got to be kidding."

"It's not bad," Alice said.

Josie picked up the book, turned to the back and studied the author's picture. "She looks younger than our kids. And she's an expert on living, huh?"

"She's an influencer."

"Who's she influencing?" Josie sneered. "Not me. What does someone like that know of love and loss and dealing with adult kids and bursitis and…leg dandruff? Her skin is tight and moist, and she has no idea what it's like to look in the mirror and see your neck looking like a turkey's or to get up in the morning and run for the Advil. What are we supposed to learn from someone like that?"

"You won't know until you read the book," Alice said with a frown. Honestly, Josie could be so stubborn.

"I don't care what anyone says. You *can* judge a book by its cover," Josie argued, giving the cover of the book a thwack.

"You never know who might have something to teach you, and you're never too old to learn. Maybe you're afraid you might learn something," Alice taunted.

"Very funny," Josie snapped.

"Well, you do tend to know it all."

"I do not."

"Then come to book club with me."

"Not if this is the kind of thing they're going to read."

"You know how it works in book clubs. Everyone gets to take a turn choosing what to read. We'll have variety. And it's not like you don't have the time," Alice said. A bit of a jab but it was true.

"That doesn't mean I want to waste it," Josie said.

"All right. I thought it would have been fun for us to do together, but if you're not interested…"

That was all it took. Josie was never one to let her sister down. Over the years she'd been there for Alice, helping her through everything from a difficult pregnancy to the house remodel from hell, and then widowhood. Of course, Alice had been there for her, too. It was what sisters did.

Josie heaved a long-suffering sigh. "I'll get the book."

"Good. This will be fun."

At least it would be for Alice. She liked Margot and she was already becoming fond of their new neighbor. The book club would provide a pleasant way to get out more. Plus, she only had to walk next door to do it. No driving involved. She could handle that just fine.

Hopefully, Josie would handle it just fine also. Would Margot and Karissa be able to handle her? Josie could be…blunt. Alice hoped the other two would see past her sister's rather forthright method of communicating to her good heart. Josie would never admit it, but she needed an emotional boost.

Actually, she needed more than that. She needed someone to drive home a few painful truths to her, but Alice wouldn't be the one to do it. Who ever took advice from a younger sibling? Josie probably wouldn't take advice from two younger women, either. But you never knew. At some point maybe they would read a book that would be exactly what her sister needed. There was a perfect book match for everyone, and a book club was the perfect place to find that match.

A book club. How had Josie allowed her sister to talk her into this?

The answer to that was simple enough. Alice wanted to do it and Josie wanted to see her happy. She'd had a rough three years, and Josie would go along with anything if it would get her sister out of the house more and back to living life.

Life after death, it wasn't easy. Not when the one who died was your soul mate, and Alice's husband Charlie had been exactly that. They'd been so entwined that when he left, he'd taken huge strands of her with him. Even now, when Alice went out to lunch with Josie or they made their thrift store rounds or checked out garage sales, Josie often felt like she was hanging out with the shadow of her sister rather than Alice, herself.

"I miss Charlie so much," Alice would simply say.

"Well, of course, you do," Josie would agree. "I miss Joe, too."

But she knew it wasn't the same kind of missing, and sometimes she felt almost wistful that it wasn't. Of course, Josie had mourned Joe's death, but, unlike her sister, she'd been in training for the loss for years, losing pieces of him long before he finally left her, and by the time he did she was more angry than sad about it. It had been hardly noticeable at first, then slowly, as middle age marched on, the gap between them widened. She'd wanted to become more active and had looked forward to a retirement of travel and outdoor adventure. He'd become enamored of his easy chair, his snacks, and his TV programs. As he became more sedentary she became more frustrated, and the more she tried to motivate him to get out of the rut he was digging himself into, the more he resisted. She'd tried to whip the man into shape, but that only brought out his passive-aggressive side.

"You're going to eat yourself to death," she'd tell him.

"You're going to nag me to death," he'd retort and go out and buy a bag of chips.

In the end, she'd been right. Sometimes she hated being right.

Of course, she'd loved Joe, but she'd also been disappointed in him, and angry at him, and after he died, she'd been determined not to be disappointed in herself by throwing away the rest of her life. Since becoming a widow she'd taken up pickleball, made a train trip across Canada and enjoyed a senior travel tour to England, where she'd visited Haworth, the home of the Brontës.

She'd tried to convince Alice to go with her on a European river cruise to Christmas markets in Germany the Christmas before but hadn't been able to pry her out of the house. Instead, Alice had opted for misery, walling herself up with her memories and playing with that doofy granddog. And then there was the whole driving thing. Something had to be done.

Maybe this book club was a step in the right direction. Perhaps, it would help break down a wall or two. If so, then Josie was all for it, and if Alice wanted her to join as well, she would. Although she knew it was going to be a complete waste of time.

"Can Lilith come over and play on Saturday?" Macy asked as Karissa drove her to school.

Inviting a friend over to play. This was social progress, indeed.

"I think so," said Karissa. "Have Lilith give you her mommy's phone number so I can talk to her. Maybe they can both come over for a while."

Which would give Karissa a chance to get acquainted with both Macy's new friend and check out the friend's mother. She hadn't done the best job of keeping toxic people out of their lives in the past. She wasn't going to make that mistake again.

Except Allegra hadn't seemed toxic at first. She'd only turned out that way.

Karissa could still remember Allegra complimenting her eye for color when they went to a paint and sip party. (She'd always been good at flattery.) The party had been Karissa's idea. Allegra's husband had moved out and she'd wanted to cheer Allegra up.

"I hope we'll always be friends," a slightly tipsy Allegra had said when Karissa drove them home.

"Of course, we will," Karissa had assured her.

And then, only a year later, everything had fallen apart. Allegra and Mark had gotten together and Karissa had lost both her husband and her best friend.

"Lilith doesn't have a mommy," said Macy, pulling Karissa back into the present.

"No mommy?" How sad.

"She has a daddy. And a grandma."

"Well, then get her daddy's phone number and I'll call and talk to him and see what we can set up for Saturday."

"Yay!" whooped Macy.

It looked like they were both making progress in their social lives.

Macy displayed her friend's phone number, written on her palm in ink, when she got back in the car that afternoon. "Can we call right now?"

"As soon as we get home," said Karissa.

"We're going to start a book club, too," Macy announced.

"An excellent idea," Karissa approved. She loved the fact

that, like her, Macy was a reader. "What's your first pick going to be?"

"We're going to read Lilith's story, *The Fairy Godmother.*"

"So, Lilith's a writer."

Macy nodded. "She's going to be famous someday." Macy considered a moment. "Mommy, do you think I'll ever be famous?"

"I don't know, honey bunny. But one thing I do know. You'll grow up to be someone I'm very proud of. Just like you are now."

She checked her daughter's reflection in the rearview mirror. Macy was beaming. Every little girl needed to know she was special.

Every big girl, too. Karissa sighed inwardly. Special wasn't easy to achieve.

But happy was and seeing her daughter smiling dished up a heaping serving of it.

Once home, they transferred the phone number from Macy's hand to a piece of paper. Later, Karissa would put Lilith's father's number in her contacts, under some name other than Daddy.

She punched in the number on her phone and after a couple of rings a deep voice answered with a cautious hello. It sounded familiar.

"Hi. I'm Karissa Newcomb, Macy's mom. She and your daughter Lilith have become friends at school."

"Karissa?" the voice repeated in surprise.

"Yes, and I was calling to see if you could bring Lilith over for a playdate on Saturday. I'd love to meet you." Did that sound a little weird? "I mean, it's always nice to meet the parents of your children's friends."

"We've already met," said the voice.

That voice—it couldn't be, could it? Did that voice go with a tall, elegant man with dark hair and deep-set eyes? "Edward?" she squeaked.

"Yes."

"Oh. It's me, Karissa."

"So you said."

"Of course. I guess I'm a little thrown. I didn't realize you had a daughter."

"It is quite a coincidence, isn't it? I'd be happy to bring Lilith over," he said. "Macy is all she talks about."

"And Lilith is all Macy talks about. I'm glad she's found such a sweet friend."

"Me, too," said Edward. "What time should I bring her over on Saturday?"

"How does one work for you?"

"That will be fine. And I'll see you tomorrow."

"Tomorrow," she repeated. At work, and again on Thursday and Friday. And then on Saturday, at her house. A much less formal environment.

She found it hard to picture Edward Elliot outside the bounds of the office, sitting and chatting with her. And was it weird to have a single father over for a playdate? Her boss, no less? What would that look like?

It wouldn't look like anything. Their daughters were friends, not them, and that was how it would be. She and Edward hardly moved in the same social circle.

For a moment she tried to imagine what it would look like if they did, seeing a hazy image of them standing side by side at some business party, chatting with a small group of writers, him elegant in a suit and her in the black dress she'd recently purchased when doing some retail therapy in the little boutique downtown. The image dissolved into nothing.

Which was exactly where it should be. She ran the office, not the company.

"I'm doing great just as I am," she told herself the next morning as she pulled into her parking spot behind the building.

André took in her New York-style little black dress and pumps and told her she was looking trés sophisticated.

She felt trés sophisticated. She hadn't worn heels in ages, but the dress absolutely required them.

Edward was the next one in. "Shirley's going to be out today, so cancel all her appointments. And what time is Gerald coming in?"

"Ten thirty," she reported.

"Thanks. Hold all my calls, will you?"

"Or course," she said.

"By the way, that's a very nice dress," he said as he disappeared into his office.

"Thank you," she called after him. It was only a passing compliment, but she appreciated it. She went back to sorting through emails with a smile. It was going to be a good day.

But then it wasn't. The not so good moment arrived when Gerald McCrae, their popular outdoorsman and writer of such hot sellers as *Looking for Big Foot on the Olympic Peninsula* and *Meeting Mount Rainier*, came in. He was short but he seemed to fill the room.

He eyeballed Karissa. "You're the new Lystra, huh?"

It could have been a cute greeting, but Gerald's blunt delivery managed to rob it of its cuteness. He may as well have said, "You're the new copy machine."

"I'm Karissa," she said, determined not to take offense and pairing her correction with a smile. "And you must be the famous Gerald McCrae who's climbed Mount Rainier." She'd heard he'd be coming by to see Edward and she'd done her homework. "I see you've added a beard since your author photo was taken." It was a scraggly thing, certainly no improvement over his clean-shaven look in the picture.

"I've been camping on Hurricane Ridge," he said, fingering it. "Decided to let it grow."

"It's very…" What was a good adjective to use here? "Rugged."

"A lot less hassle than shaving. That's nothing more than a custom meant to tame men."

Or make them look civilized.

Gerald wasn't going for the civilized look though. He wore a North Face sweatshirt over khakis and hiking boots on his feet. Because hiking from the parking lot into the office was a dangerous trek?

"Mr. Elliot is on a call but should be off soon," she said. "May I offer you some coffee while you wait?"

He nodded. "Black."

Of course. Gerald McRae probably felt that using sugar or cream was for sissies. He probably took his coffee so strong he could bite it instead of drink it. She went to the break room, did her best to make sure what she brought him would be extra strong and filled one of their large mugs with coffee. She made her way back out to the reception area, the picture of elegance and charm, delivering a drink to their visiting author.

And she was doing a very good job of being elegant, until she caught the heel of her shoe on a spot where the carpet had sneakily gone from threadbare to pothole. It was just enough to make her foot wobble, and one wobbling foot was just enough to throw her off balance. Suddenly she was doing...the Dance of the Flowers? The Mexican Hat Dance? Maybe a little of both, combined with a drunken sailor jig as she tried to regain her balance, staggering this way and that in an effort to get her feet firmly planted. Sadly, she didn't succeed. Instead, she picked up speed, turning into a runner racing to break the tape at the finish line. Her momentum carried her forward with a panicked, "Ooooh," when she realized a collision was imminent. She attempted a sudden stop, even as she tried desperately to keep the coffee in its mug and the mug in her hand. She didn't lose the mug, but the coffee went flying, right onto Gerald McCrae's manly chest...right before she landed with her face between his knees.

He let out a screech like a scalded cat and jumped back against his chair, swearing and knocking her backward onto the floor.

The commotion ended Edward's phone conversation and he burst from his office with a "What on earth? Karissa, are you okay?" he asked.

If you didn't factor in humiliation. "Yes."

"Never mind her. She tried to scald me. What kind of incompetent have you hired?" Gerald roared, pulling his coffee-heated sweatshirt away from his chest and glaring at Edward. This was followed by a fresh string of angry profanity. He turned on Karissa. "What's the matter with you, woman? Are you trying to boil me alive?"

"I'm so sorry," Karissa said to him. Then, to Edward, "I caught my heel on a torn part of the carpet and tripped. Let me get something to clean your sweatshirt, Mr. McCrae." She tried to scramble up from the floor. Instead, she scrambled out of one of her shoes and went down on one knee. She did lose the coffee mug at that point, and it bounced off Gerald's boot.

"Don't get me anything! She's dangerous," Gerald snarled, still pulling at his coffee-stained sweatshirt.

"It was an accident," Karissa protested and looked to Edward.

His lips were clamped shut and he looked like he was in pain. Like Gerald.

Gerald sidestepped her and marched toward Edward's office, muttering about incompetent help.

Edward didn't follow him immediately. He still appeared to be stoically suffering, but he took Karissa's elbow and helped her up, kept her steady while she got her shoe back on. "Are you alright? Did you twist your ankle?"

"I'm fine," she said. As long as you didn't count feeling mortified.

He nodded. "We'll talk later."

She watched as he followed Gerald into his office.

André appeared from his upstairs office. "What's going on down here? Who's being assaulted?"

Karissa held up the mug. "I tripped on the carpet and spilled coffee on Mr. McRae. I feel terrible. He was so mad."

"He'll be fine," André assured her. "He likes to get mad. It suits his persona."

His persona sure didn't suit Karissa. She hated to think how their future encounters would go. She suspected there would have to be much groveling on her part.

But she didn't want to grovel, and she shouldn't have to. If Gerald McCrae had been any kind of decent human being, he'd have tried to catch her before she fell or at least said something kind, like "No harm done." Clearly Gerald McCrae's idea of masculinity didn't extend to gallantry.

Half an hour later he was on his way out.

"I really am sorry," Karissa said as he marched past her. He held up a silencing hand and kept going.

Yep, she and Gerald were going to become good friends. If he ever got a lobotomy.

A moment later, Edward appeared in his doorway. "Karissa, would you come into my office please?"

Here was where she got fired. She'd bought a house, moved her daughter into a new school district and now she was going to get fired. Where would she find another job, especially one like this—one that was so much a part of the business of books and allowed her to work so close to authors?

Maybe a little too close to some authors.

But Edward had asked her if she was okay, she remembered, as she smoothed her dress and walked toward the doorway. Would he have done that if he was going to fire her?

She bit down on her lip, took a deep breath and entered his office. And remembered *Where There's a Will There's a Way*, the book she'd started reading for her first book club meeting.

She was only a couple of chapters in, but she'd read something the night before that pinged in her brain now.

Have the right attitude for the right time, Annie advised. *You can get through anything with the right attitude.* What was the right attitude in this situation?

Edward sat down at his desk, and she shut the door, her heart beating anxiously. Her brother always said that a good offense was a good defense, so she went on the offensive. Righteous indignation was the right attitude for this situation.

"That was not my fault," she said. "There really is a bad spot in the carpet." And there had been no need for Gerald to yell at her. Or for Edward to let him. Now the righteous indignation was easy to tap into. "And you stood by and let that man insult me. And bully me."

Edward's response was to raise those dark eyebrows of his. Not simply one, but both. Had she taken the righteous indignation thing too far? No, she told herself. Gerald had been awful to her.

"Aren't you going to say anything?" she asked.

"I'm going to say you're right. I shouldn't have let him insult you. I'm sorry I did. Nobody blames you for what happened. I just wanted to reassure you of that."

"Gerald McCrae blames me for what happened."

"But it was an accident. I mean, you weren't out to get him, were you?" Edward did something surprising. He offered her a smile.

She smiled back. "No."

"That's good to hear, but remind me never to ask you to bring me coffee," he said.

Was he joking? She wasn't sure.

"I would never spill coffee on you," she assured him. "Well, not on purpose."

"I would hope not. I really am sorry about the carpet. It's

seen better days, but I didn't realize it was that bad. I'm glad you're not hurt."

"Only my pride." A new thought occurred. "Is he going to sue me? The coffee wasn't that hot."

"Over tripping? Come, now."

"He wasn't very happy when he left."

"Happy isn't how Gerald rolls. No harm done."

"There could be more harm to someone if that carpet doesn't get fixed," Karissa said. "Do you want me to show you where the tear is?"

"No, that's okay. It will be taken care of. I've been after Shirley to get rid of that thing for the last year. I don't care if it did belong to her grandfather. Also, I'm thinking that maybe we'll want to set up a coffee bar in the reception area. That way our visitors can help themselves. It's not the sixties and you shouldn't have to be serving people."

"I think that's a good idea," she concurred.

"Umm, would you mind setting it up?"

"Even though it's not the sixties?" she teased.

"Even though it's not the sixties," he said, and smiled. He had such a handsome smile when he chose to use it.

"I'm happy to do that," she said.

He nodded. "And let's try to always have some kind of treat there."

"You want me to bake?" Baking wasn't in her job description, and it wasn't her forte. She had all of two recipes in her repertoire, snickerdoodles and chocolate chip cookies.

He must have seen the panic on her face. "Donut holes from the store are fine. I'll make sure you have a company credit card."

Trusting her with a company credit card? Karissa suddenly felt like her job was much more secure.

Margot was on chapter three of *Where There's a Will There's a Way: Make a Plan*. Okay, here was the plan. First, she'd do her required three job search activities each week so she could collect unemployment.

Labor research was activity number one. She'd researched and found...nothing.

Activity number two: apply for jobs. Yes, apply for that invisible job that was hiding out there who knew where. She'd already contacted two employment agencies and neither had anything for her. She was overqualified.

Overqualified. Who knew that could be a handicap? Working hard, taking enrichment classes, moving up the ladder of success—how had that wound up working against her?

Then there was the third thing on her to-do list, which she'd gleaned from her online research: prepare an elevator pitch for job searching and interviews. Sum herself up in one paragraph.

It was hard not to be cynical. *Hello there, Future Employer. How lucky you are to be getting this moment with me. I'm exactly what you need—hardworking, diligent, bitter.* Uh, no. Scratch bitter. *Efficient. I'm efficient. You wouldn't believe how efficient I've been since I got laid off.*

She'd prepared and frozen enough meals to take her into the next millennium, made enough coffee syrups to stock a Starbucks, and already pulled every weed in her flower beds. Oh, yes, and efficiently rewatched every episode of *The Crown*. Now she was on to *Bridgerton*.

She was still staring at her laptop screen when her mother texted. **Have you found anything yet?**

Anything. There was a telling word. Anything would do, anything that paid the bills. She glared at her phone. Of course, she wanted to work. She wanted to make friends with a steady paycheck again. And she was frustrated that, after almost two months, she still hadn't found anything that fit.

Working on it, she texted back, and hoped her vague answer wouldn't inspire a call.

It did. She let it go to voice mail. Then she shut down her

laptop and went in search of a cigarette. She'd only bought one pack. That was all she was going to buy.

That was what she'd said when she bought the last pack.

"I don't care. I need this," she muttered.

You should never have started.

Good grief. Her mom nagged her even when they weren't talking. Of course, she should never have started, but she had, back when she'd been young and foolish, and felt invincible. She'd quit when she got pregnant. But she'd picked the habit up again when her dad died, and then again after her divorce. She'd started and quit two more times since.

She fisted her hands, growled, and turned from the drawer where she kept the pack of camel breath sticks. She needed a distraction.

There was always more shopping therapy, but she'd already done that, finding a gorgeous royal blue poet sleeve blouse online. It would bring out the blue in her eyes. Jackson had always said blue was her color.

Jackson. She should have tried harder to work things out. What she'd had with him had been better than anything she'd had since.

Too late now. And what was it Annie Wills had said in her book? *Don't look back. You'll only get a crick in your neck.* Annie was right. At some point further in the book she'd probably have something to say about picking bad habits back up, too.

"So, throw out the cigarettes," Margot said to herself.

No. Not yet. She wasn't ready. Those were her security blanket. Even if she didn't smoke one she still needed to know they were there.

Good grief. She should take up yoga or deep breathing or... something. Distraction, distraction. She needed a distraction.

Just in time, the package arrived on her doorstep. The blouse she'd ordered. Yes! She'd have a new blouse and a new elevator pitch to go with her updated résumé—she'd be fine.

She took her treasure to her bedroom and pulled it over her head. The thing hugged her boobs and middle like a hungry lover.

"You look like a blue mushroom," she told her reflection. Darn it all. She'd checked her measurements twice against the description, but something was definitely off. She wished, not for the first time, that there was a way to see what clothes would look like on you before ordering them. It would save so much grief.

First nothing on LinkedIn or Monster.com and now this. The cigarettes were calling.

She plugged her ears and went next door to visit Alice.

"Uh-oh," Alice said, opening the door wide. "Have you been talking to your mom?"

"That, too," Margot said sourly.

"Come on in and have some banana bread."

That was all she didn't need. "No banana bread, but I'll take some tea."

"What's going on?" Alice asked as Margot followed her into her kitchen.

"I bought a top online, that's what's going on," Margot said, opting for the tip of the irritation iceberg. She plopped down at the kitchen table and started drumming her fingers, wishing she had a cigarette between them.

Alice's table was vintage, with a yellow Formica top. She always kept a little vase of miniature silk daisies on it. Vintage decorative plates with fruit painted on them that had belonged to her grandmother hung on one of the pale-yellow walls, and a clock shaped like a teapot hung on another. There was nothing new or sophisticated about Alice's kitchen. It was charming.

"Not a success?" Alice guessed, starting her electric teapot.

"Total fail." Margot sighed. "I shouldn't be doing shopping therapy, but I figured it beat smoking."

"Back to that again? I thought I smelled a faint whiff of smoke on you the other day," Alice said.

"I haven't even gone through a pack."

"Well, that's good."

"I should throw them out."

"Yes, you should."

"I have to stop stressing."

"That would be good."

Margot half laughed. "That was succinct."

Alice held up her tea canister. "Lady Grey or Constant Comment?"

"Lady Grey."

Alice nodded and pulled down a mug from her cupboard. "You've gotten through worse than a layoff. Losing your dad, divorce, breakups. What's having to find a new place to work compared to having to find a way to move on without the people you care about?"

"You're right, of course," Margot said with a sigh. She accepted the mug of tea and played puppeteer with the tea bag. "Still, I do have to pay the bills. Unemployment and savings won't last forever."

Alice sat down opposite her, said nothing. Very diplomatic considering the fact she could have said, "Then why are you spending money?"

Why indeed? "I thought a new blouse would give me a lift. Silly, huh?"

Alice took a sip from her mug. "Not necessarily. Sometimes a little treat does make us feel better."

"But not for long. Especially not after I tried the thing on. Somebody should invent an app that shows you how you're going to look before you buy. I'd buy that in a heartbeat."

"That's a great idea," Alice said. "Why don't you make one?"

"Me?" scoffed Margot. "I don't know anything about creating apps."

"Aren't there people you can hire for that?"

"Yeah, when you're sitting on a mountain of money. I'm sitting on a molehill."

"How are you liking our book?" Alice asked, jerking them into a different conversational lane.

Margot blinked. "I guess that's the end of the therapy session."

"Don't be looking to me for therapy. Your best therapist is yourself."

"Yeah? Well, I'm ready to fire me."

"This Annie makes some good points in her book," Alice said.

Margot nodded. "You're right, she does. I am trying to plan and set goals. It's just, I don't know. I feel like I'm wandering around in a desert with no cell reception and no water."

"I think you'll find your GPS. Maybe you have to ask yourself what you really want out of life, like she says in chapter one."

"I know what I want. I want a job." Actually, she wanted more. What "more" looked like she wasn't sure.

"Is that all?"

Margot frowned. "A whole new me?"

"I don't think you need a whole new you. The you that you are is pretty special."

"Right," Margot said with a snort.

"Don't give up. Things will work out," Alice said. "You're creating a new life for yourself and that takes time."

"Creation is a slow process," Margot grumbled, quoting Annie Wills. Annie Wills was full of…advice.

"Yes, it is," Alice agreed. "You'll get there."

"I hope I get there before I go broke," said Margot.

"Have some banana bread," Alice urged.

Two slices of banana bread later, Margot was back home, on the couch and staring at the book on her phone. "I just had to download you, didn't I?"

7

*"Don't wait for what you want to come to you.
Go for it."*
—from *Where There's a Will There's a Way* by Annie Wills

A FLOWER DELIVERY ARRIVED THE NEXT MORNING AT Heron Publishing—pink, yellow, and white tulips, and they were for Karissa. Who on earth would be sending her flowers?

Sorry for what happened yesterday. Floor getting refinished next Monday. You can work remote.—Shirley & Edward

Karissa hurried to Shirley's office to thank her.

"It was Edward's idea," said Shirley. "Although it should have been mine considering it was my carpet that caused the problem. I would have felt terrible if you'd gotten hurt."

"The only one who got hurt was Mr. McCrae."

"Gerald's fine. I already checked," Shirley said. "Just tell me you're not planning on resigning after this."

"No. I love working here," said Karissa.

"Good. We're happy to have you with us."

It was nice to be appreciated.

"Oh, and by the way, Edward and André will be taking up the carpet of death this afternoon. Meanwhile, tread carefully."

Next, Karissa knocked on Edward's office door and stuck her head in. "Thank you for the flowers."

His cheeks flushed like a light sunburn, and he waved away her thanks. "They were from Shirley and me. And again, I'm sorry I didn't stand up for you yesterday. I should have."

What a wonderful quality in a man, to be able to admit when he was wrong.

Definitely not a quality all men shared. Mark sure hadn't admitted to any wrongdoing when he took up with Allegra. "It just happened," he'd said about their affair.

Just happened. What did that mean anyway? As if he was walking down the street, minding his own business and Allegra had popped out from behind a bush and grabbed him and hauled him off to her bedroom?

"It didn't just happen. You made it happen," she'd protested, wiping at the endless spring of tears.

"The heart wants what the heart wants," he'd said. Another cliché in his ever-growing repertoire.

Only a small and selfish heart could want something that would hurt someone else so badly. It had done no good to beg. She'd crumpled like a used tissue.

Karissa realized she was standing there, thinking about her past with her head leaning into her boss's office. He was looking at her expectantly.

"Anyway, they're lovely. So, thank you."

"You're welcome," he said. Then he cleared his throat, scratched the back of his head.

They were heading into an awkward moment. Actually, they had arrived.

"I'll let you get back to work," she said, and he nodded.

She sat back down at her desk and smiled. Flowers were always a treat, even if they didn't symbolize passion or undying love. Flowers at least meant she was appreciated and that made her happy.

The good feeling they had inspired took her through the day on a high note and she was feeling downright cheerful when she went to pick up Macy.

Until she saw her daughter's face.

Oh, no. What had happened?

"Lilith played with Marisol at recess," Macy reported. "I wanted to play Flower Fairy and she wouldn't."

"Marisol?"

"No, Lilith." Macy's tone of voice said, *Sheesh, Mom, keep up.*

"Why wouldn't Lilith play Flower Fairy?"

Karissa's question was met with a long silence.

"Macy?" she prompted.

"I just wanted to be Queen Lily," Macy muttered.

"And so did Lilith?" Karissa guessed.

"She said she should be queen because her name was almost the same as Lily. But it's not."

Not for the first time Karissa wished she and Mark had had a second child. It would have helped Macy master the skills of compromise and negotiation.

"I don't want to be her friend anymore."

It looked like Karissa would be canceling the girls' upcoming playdate. That would be awkward, but that wasn't her big concern. The sad thing was that Macy would be back to having no friends.

"You can take turns being queen, you know," Karissa suggested.

"But I said first," Macy protested.

"Sometimes, when you're being a good friend, it doesn't matter who says first. If you want to keep your friend, you might need to let her be Queen Lily once in a while. Sometimes we need to let our friends have their way."

But some friends didn't deserve to get their way.

Get your brain out of the past, Karissa scolded herself. *Listen to Annie Wills*. Looking back would only give her a crick in the neck.

"I said it first," Macy grumbled, still not willing to let go of her grudge.

"Well, you think about what I said. You'll have to decide if Lilith is a friend worth keeping."

Keep the keepers and lose the losers—it was another quote from *Where There's a Will There's a Way*. Annie Wills was a very smart woman.

Later that night as Karissa was listening to Macy say her prayers, she had to smile when, after asking God to bless everyone from Grandma to Daddy and "Aunt Allegra" (ick!) Macy added, "and help me be nice to Lilith tomorrow."

Karissa kissed her girl good-night. "I'm sure God will help you do that."

And Karissa needed to ask God to help her get over being furious with Allegra. Macy was adjusting to their new normal and Karissa needed to also. Allegra could keep her thick, long dark hair and her eyelashes, even the extensions. And she could keep Mark. Who wanted to be with a man who didn't want you, anyway?

She thought of all the times, in the month before the house sold, when she'd watch from the living room window as the two of them drove off together somewhere. Allegra was always dressed like a Kardashian, which would inspire Karissa to go online and search for that perfect outfit that would transform her into someone amazing. She never put anything in her cart.

She was done with that and she needed to live like it.

Ethan checked in later that night by text. How's the new job going?

Great. She still had a job. There was something for which to be thankful. And... I got flowers from my boss.

Is he hitting on you?

Yes, because she was such a man magnet.

No. Just thanking me for pointing out a potential problem. No need to threaten him with bodily harm.

Like he'd done with Mark. He'd almost gone through with that threat, too, until Karissa informed him that she didn't have money to spare for bailing him out of jail.

It couldn't hurt.

She sent back a laughing emoji and told him she was fine and all was well. Still, she appreciated his concern. Ethan was only two years older than her, but he'd taken his older brother status seriously, always watching out for her.

Ironic that, when she and Mark had first gotten together, Ethan had given him a thumbs-up. "He's a nerd like you. He'll be perfect for you."

And Mark had been. Until he wasn't.

But not looking back anymore!

It's about time some good stuff happened for you, Ethan texted.

Yes, it was. Now, if Macy's bumpy beginning would sort itself out life would be…not perfect but good, and good wasn't so bad.

The next day Macy's friendship drama settled down. She decided to crown her friend fairy queen at recess and the fickle friend who kept changing allegiances even joined them, so Macy's teacup of happiness was overflowing when Karissa picked her up after work. The playdate for Saturday was on again.

Edward over at her house. Again, she wondered what that

was going to look like. What on earth were they going to talk about? Work, she supposed. *Read any good books lately? Haha.*

Lilith and Macy raced off to Macy's room the minute she and her father came over on Saturday, which left the adults alone in the living room.

After "Please, sit down," and "Would you like some coffee?" their conversation hit a dead end. She was looking for someplace to go when he saved her by asking how she was settling into her new neighborhood.

"I have good neighbors," she said, and found herself, once again, looking for something more to say.

This was ridiculous. They worked together every day. They should have plenty to talk about. Why was she at a loss? Her palms were getting damp.

Her mind reached for something, anything. "We're starting a book club."

"That sounds like an excellent idea. If you ever want to use a book by one of our authors, I'd be happy to provide copies."

"That would be great. Right now, we're reading one on personal growth."

He nodded politely, didn't say anything.

"I guess books like that don't interest you," she ventured.

He shrugged. "I'm sure they help a lot of people."

She was unsure how to respond to that remark, so decided she should move into new conversational territory. But where to find it? Maybe she should have been reading a book on how to master the art of chitchat when you didn't have a chitchat kind of relationship.

Then she remembered the cookies. She picked up the plate from the coffee table. "Would you like a cookie?"

He took one. "Thanks. I always liked snickerdoodles. My…" He faltered. "I haven't had one in years," he said and took a bite.

His what? His whom? She was sure he was about to mention someone baking snickerdoodles for him.

"Did your mom make them a lot for you when you were a kid?"

"Not really. These are excellent."

There would be no more personal sharing on this topic, obviously, so she didn't press him.

Still, Edward Elliot fascinated her. His reserved manner and typically somber expression draped an air of mystery around him and drew her the same way a muffled sound coming from a locked room in an old English mansion drew a Gothic heroine.

For a moment she envisioned herself as one of those heroines, making her way down a dark hallway, wearing a long, white nightgown and carrying a lit candle. Her hair, golden and gently waving, hung down her back and she moved with catlike grace...no tripping.

And no door opening, either. She backed away and returned her attention to the conversation. "I'll be happy to send some cookies home with you," she offered.

The elusive smile almost appeared. "Thanks."

At that moment Macy burst into the living room. "We have a fashion show for you," she announced.

"I do like fashion shows," said Karissa, relieved for the interruption. Little girl fashion shows put her back on familiar ground.

"Uh, okay," said Edward, obviously not on familiar ground.

"Mommy, will you put music on your phone?"

"Of course," Karissa said, and obliged.

A moment later, out strutted Lilith, her school clothes dressed up by a red, sequin-spangled shawl Karissa's mother had contributed to Macy's dress-up collection. She'd paired it with several strings of Mardi Gras beads and a veritable sleeve of bracelets. Next came Macy, wearing an old, tie-dyed shirt Karissa's mom had made for a seventies party along with an old top hat (a thrift store find). Both girls were showing off their best catwalk moves, and Karissa applauded. Edward caught on quickly and also clapped. The girls scampered away and returned a moment later, this time in glittery evening tops that hung on them like dresses.

"This is what everyone will be wearing to the Fairy Ball this spring," Lilith announced.

"I must get one," Karissa said, playing along.

"Will you get one, too, Daddy?" Lilith asked Edward.

He nodded. "Of course."

Two more clothing changes were modeled—Western shirts and a cowboy hat and two princess skirts in colorful layers of tulle. "This is what we'll be wearing to the coronation of the Fairy Queen," said Macy. "We're both going to be queen," she added.

"An excellent compromise," Karissa murmured, as the girls bowed. She held out the plate of cookies. "You'll probably want to take these for the coronation party."

"Yes!" cried Macy. She grabbed the plate and she and Lilith scampered off to her bedroom to work on getting a sugar buzz.

"I have more," Karissa said to Edward, and fetched a fresh plate. "It looks like the girls are having fun."

He took another. "I think so. It's been nice for Lilith. She's a little shy."

"It's been great for Macy, too," said Karissa. "It's not easy being the new kid in school, especially when the school year is half over. We moved when I was in grade school, and it about killed me. I was shy, myself, as a child," she confessed, then felt her cheeks warming. *Oversharing, Karissa.*

"You seem to have gotten over that," he said.

Had she? Some people burst into a room like a firecracker. That had never been her. She'd always preferred to ease into a room. And, after what she'd left behind, into friendship.

She helped herself to a cookie, took a nibble. "It's always a challenge starting over." *Especially when your self-confidence is shot.* No way was she sharing that bit of information.

"We're glad you're starting over at Heron Publishing," he said. "We try to be supportive of both our authors and our employees, so don't hesitate to say if you need something."

"Thank you. That's really kind."

"That's the advantage of being a small company. Shirley and I are both determined to keep that same close-knit atmosphere even as we grow."

"André was telling me you've been with Shirley almost from the beginning."

"Pretty much. Lilith was just a toddler when I came on board."

"You were in New York before that?"

She felt more than saw him stiffen. "Another lifetime ago." He cleared his throat. "We should probably get going."

His abruptness was startling. "Oh," Karissa managed. What on earth? Had she come across as nosy? She'd only been making conversation.

"We don't want to overstay our welcome," he added.

Overstay? They'd only been there an hour.

"It's no problem," she said. "We don't have any plans."

"We really need to get going. I will take some of those cookies if the offer is still good."

"Of course. I'll tell the girls," she said, then moved off down the hall, wishing all the way she could have thought of something brilliant to say or do that would have made him want to stay longer. In spite of the awkward moments, sitting and talking with this man had felt good, hinted that she was getting back to a normal life—a better normal than what her life had been after what happened with Mark. The abrupt end to the afternoon had her feeling confused and a little hurt.

Annie Wills advised her readers to go for what they wanted.

Karissa wanted her guests to stay longer, maybe for an early dinner. Lilith would certainly love to, she was sure.

She was halfway down the hall. She turned, ready to go back and invite him to stay. She bit her lip, stood there for a moment, imagining him accepting her invitation and offering to help her in the kitchen. They'd stand side by side at the kitchen counter, chopping vegetables and drinking wine. He'd smile at her. She'd smile back at him the way good friends did.

Too late. He was putting on his jacket.

She sighed and continued down the hall.

The girls were seated on Macy's bed, eating cookies and giggling. It was a sweet picture.

"Your daddy's ready to go," she said to Lilith, making the little girl's happy expression vanish.

"Already?" Macy protested.

"I'm sure you'll have more chances to play in the future," Karissa said.

"I wish you didn't have to go home already," Macy said to Lilith.

Karissa knew exactly how she felt. She wanted to say the same thing to Lilith's daddy.

"I'll get those cookies bagged up for you," she said to him when she returned.

"Thanks," he said, and shoved his hands in his jacket pocket. Even in jeans and an old, beat-up bomber jacket he looked elegant.

And uncomfortable. Maybe it was just as well she hadn't asked him to stay for dinner.

8

"Don't be afraid to try new things with new people."
—from *Where There's a Will There's a Way* by Annie Wills

THE NIGHT THE BOOK CLUB MET ALICE ARRIVED WITH
her sister, Josie, who was a head taller and several pounds thin-
ner. She had gray hair and a steely glint in her eyes. Alice wore
yoga pants and a sweatshirt. Josie wore jeans, and she had on a
sweatshirt as well, hers proclaiming that she drank wine, read
books and knew stuff. That should have been a good sign. But
the lines between her brows and beside her mouth looked like
the Grand Canyon, testifying to a strong tendency to frown.

Not a good sign, no matter what her sweatshirt says, thought
Margot.

"I swear, the traffic just keeps getting worse and worse," she
said after Alice had introduced her and apologized for them
being late. "People need to stop moving here," she added as
Karissa took their coats.

"Except for nice ones like Karissa," Alice quickly put in.

"Alice has told me about you. Sounds like you're going to be a great neighbor," Josie said to Karissa.

Okay, maybe she'd be all right after all.

"Between Karissa and Margot, I think I've hit the good neighbor jackpot," Alice said, smiling at them.

"Hard to find good neighbors these days," Josie said. "I have a couple of real stinkeroos in my neighborhood."

What to say to that?

Margot didn't have to say anything. Luckily, Karissa was already answering. "I understand. I had a stinkeroo in my old neighborhood, too."

Interesting. This was the first Margot was hearing about it. Had the neighbors taken sides when Karissa and her husband split? You never wanted it to happen, but in the marriage wars people always took sides. Fortunately for Margot, she and Jackson had both walked away with the friends they'd brought into the marriage so there'd been no hard feelings.

Josie turned her attention to Margot. "I can't believe I never met you all these years with you living just two doors down from Alice."

"Strange, isn't it?" Margot said. Maybe Alice had been afraid to turn her loose.

"Well, you were working long hours," said Alice.

"True." Those days were gone. So was the handsome salary.

"Sit down, please," Karissa said to the sisters. "I have wine and coffee and tea and crackers and shrimp dip."

"Don't let Alice have any of that dip. Shrimp will make her lips swell up like a blowfish and she'll choke on her tongue," said Josie, and Alice's face turned as pink as a cooked shrimp.

"Oh, my gosh, no." Karissa looked horrified. "I should have asked if anyone had allergies."

"It's okay. I'm fine with tea," Alice assured her.

"And I'll eat her share," said Josie. She pulled a box of chocolates out of the bag she'd been carrying. "I figure everybody likes chocolate, right?"

"Right," said Karissa.

"Oh, yes," agreed Margot. Okay, score a point for Josie.

Karissa's daughter came out to greet the women. She was already in pajamas printed with Disney princesses, her hair still damp from her bath. She showed off the book she was taking to bed to read.

"My son loved those Redwall books," Alice said. "Who knows, Macy? Maybe someday you'll have a book club, too."

Macy nodded eagerly. "I'm going to start one with my friend Lilith."

"An excellent idea," Alice approved.

"Speaking of reading, if you want to get some reading time in, we'd better get you into bed, honey bunny," Karissa said to her daughter.

That was enough to send Macy racing down the hallway.

"I'll just get her tucked in and be right back," Karissa said.

"Cute kid," Josie observed, and her frown lines took a break. "I remember when my girl was that age."

"Does she live around here?" Margot asked, trying to make conversation.

The frown lines dug back into Josie's face, and she gave a one-shouldered shrug. "Yes, but I don't see much of her these days."

"That's too bad," Margot said, hoping it was the right thing to say.

"Her choice," Josie said and even though it was April it suddenly felt February-frosty in Karissa's living room.

Karissa returned and invited everyone to the table to help themselves to refreshments. In addition to her deadly shrimp dip, she'd also set out a plate of fancy store-bought cookies.

"I love these," Josie chortled as she helped herself to one. "I never have 'em in the house. I'd eat the whole package."

"As if you'd ever buy store-bought cookies," Alice teased. "Josie could have her own cooking show," she said to the others.

"I do like to cook, but Alice is the baker in the family," said Josie.

They settled in the living room, and Josie sampled Karissa's shrimp dip. "This is worth taking a Benadryl for," she said to Alice. "Is this your own recipe?" she asked Karissa. "It's fabulous."

Okay, she's not so bad, Margot thought, watching her new friend smile in response.

"I found it online," Karissa said. "I'm really not that good in the kitchen."

"If you can make something like this, you're good," Josie said to her.

They continued to visit, or rather Josie continued to interrogate Margot and Karissa. "So, both divorced," she said with a frown. "Seems like nobody stays married these days."

Subtract one of those points Josie had scored earlier.

Karissa's brows dipped and her lower lip did a wobble. Margot was ready to bean Josie with her book. How was it these two were sisters?

"It wasn't my choice," Karissa said in a soft voice, blinking back tears.

"I'm so sorry," Alice said.

"The bastard," Josie growled. She looked questioningly at Margot.

As if Margot was going to tell this woman her life story? "Mine's not a bastard," she said, and left it at that.

Josie nodded. "Good. If you're going to split, it's nice if you can at least stay friends."

"What about you?" Margot asked, deciding it was time to do some prying into their interrogator's life.

Josie frowned. "Joe died on me."

Margot could feel her eyes popping wide.

"The man refused to take care of himself. He had high blood pressure and diabetes. Never stuck to any diet I put him on. And if that wasn't bad enough, he kept sneaking those nasty cigars. One day he keeled over at the dinner table, did a face plant right in his spaghetti squash, and that was that. I was so mad, if he hadn't already been dead, I'd have killed him."

Margot had no idea what to say to that. She shot a look at Karissa, who was also staring at Josie.

"I'm sorry," Karissa managed.

"This is life. You have to pick up and carry on," Josie said. She shot a look her sister's direction that made it plain for whom that observation was meant.

"I think I'll have a little more tea," Alice said and bolted for the refreshment table.

"It is hard to start over, but I hope I can," Karissa said.

"You already are," Alice told her as she poured fresh tea into her mug. "And starting a book club is a wonderful way to do that."

"Well, should we get started?" Karissa suggested.

"Sure," said Margot as Alice seated herself back on the sofa.

"What did everyone think of the book?" Karissa asked. "Did we all finish it?"

"I'm halfway through it," Margot said. "I have to say, I think it's a little simplistic in places, but I've found some helpful suggestions."

"Me, too," said Karissa. "I think her suggestion to get a goal buddy is a good one."

"Pigeon poop," Josie scoffed.

Margot blinked. *Don't hold back. Tell us what you really think.*

"It's not a bad idea," Alice said.

"It's pigeon poop," Josie insisted. "A goal buddy," she scoffed. "As if a woman can't set her own goals."

"Anyone can set goals," Margot argued. "Making a plan and sticking to it can be another thing. Sometimes it's nice to have someone to be accountable to. It can help keep you on track. That's why we had team meetings at the office."

"And managers," put in Alice, smiling encouragingly at her.

"Goal buddies don't work if people don't listen to them," Josie said, and slid a convicting look toward her sister.

"People are all at different places in their life," Alice said, and Margot was sure this statement was meant for Josie rather than the entire group. There was obviously more than one conversation going on in the room.

"And who is this woman, anyway?" Josie continued.

"She's an influencer," Margot said.

Josie gave a snort. "At her young age? Who does she influence?"

Margot frowned. Ageism in reverse. "She has a hundred thousand followers. I'd say that's not too shabby."

"Lemmings," Josie muttered.

Karissa spoke up. "I think there's a lot to be said for books like this. We can always learn from each other, no matter what our age."

"That's what I think," Alice said with a nod.

"A waste of money if you ask me," said Josie. "I'm glad I got the book from the library."

"Well, that's the beauty of a book club. Different opinions make for a good discussion," Alice said.

"They never change anybody's mind," said Josie.

At least not hers, which appeared to be stuck in dried cement.

"Josie has strong opinions," Alice said when her sister went to use the powder room.

"We noticed," said Margot.

"But she's got a good heart."

Where?

"So, what's next?" Josie asked after she returned to them.

"I found a book I thought might be interesting," Alice said, and pulled a hardcover book out of the canvas book bag she'd brought with her. She handed it to Karissa. *Close Calls*, the title read. "Remember when I got this at the library?" she said to Margot.

Margot nodded. "Yeah. It looked interesting."

"I've already started it and it is. It's all about people who wound up making last-minute decisions or had things happen that prevented them from ending up in situations where they would have lost their lives. Like Waylon Jennings, winding up taking the bus instead of getting on the plane with Buddy Holly before it crashed."

"That sounds...unnerving," said Karissa.

"But interesting," added Margot.

"Wait a minute. Is this the book you were telling me about this morning?" Josie asked her sister. "About fate and listening to that little voice? Being grateful you missed the bus."

"Yes," Alice said, her tone defensive.

Josie rolled her eyes. "More pigeon poop."

Another point lost. "I'm fine with it," Margot said, and hoped the newcomer got the message.

"If we all take turns suggesting a different book, we'll get all kinds of interesting perspectives," said Karissa.

"Fine," Josie said with a frown. "I want to pick the next book then."

By all means, take over, thought Margot.

"I don't know about her," Margot said to Karissa after the sisters had left.

"Well, like Alice said, she does have strong opinions."

"And they're always the right ones," Margot observed.

"I believe Alice. Josie probably does have a good heart. She brought chocolate, after all."

"It was a bribe to make us like her." Margot shook her head. "I can't believe she and Alice are related. Alice is so sweet."

"Just because people are related doesn't mean they're the

same," Karissa pointed out. "My brother and I are totally different. He's a slob and a party animal and has gobs of friends."

"My grandma always said if you have one good friend in this life who will stand beside you, you've got it made," Margot said.

Karissa looked suddenly sad.

"What?" Margot prompted.

Karissa got busy scraping the last of her shrimp dip off her plate with a cracker. "I thought I had a friend like that. I was wrong. She stabbed me in the back."

Margot frowned. "Women like her give friendship a bad name." She hesitated before continuing. She and Karissa were new friends. Would any assurances from her sound false? Maybe. Or maybe assurance was what Karissa needed. "I'm not like that," she said. "I believe in loyalty. And if you need a reference, I'm sure Alice will give a good one," she finished with a smile.

Karissa reflected it back to her. "I'm sure she will. I can't let my past influence my present. Sometimes it's hard though. It's hard to trust."

"Anyone who's been through a divorce can identify with that. Not that I had trust issues with my husband," Margot hurried to add. "We were just two workaholics who grew apart. But I have sure come to the point where I don't always trust my own judgment."

"I don't either," Karissa said with a sigh. "But you know what, I don't think we've made a mistake by letting Alice include Josie in our group. At least I hope not."

"I guess we can give her a chance. Everyone deserves a chance." Even the Josies of the world.

"At some point you need to get back behind the wheel," Josie said to Alice as she drove them to El Pueblito for lunch later in the week.

"I do just fine without a car," Alice insisted.

"Yeah, thanks to me and your neighbor and everybody else taxiing you around."

"I always pay for the gas, and I'm paying for lunch today," Alice reminded her, "So it's not like I'm imposing."

"That's not the point. You're too young to stop driving. You give up your independence when you give up your car."

"There comes a point when we all have to give up our independence," Alice said.

Josie shot a scowl in her sister's direction. "Not at your age." Honestly, Alice had to get past this.

"I'm fine. Stop worrying," Alice said.

Stop worrying? As if it was a faucet Josie could turn off? She'd always worried about her younger sister, especially after Alice lost her husband. She'd lost her way and then she'd lost her nerve.

"I never get tired of the view from here," Alice said as they settled at one of the restaurant's colorfully painted window booths that offered a view of the marina. "I think I'm going to have the chimichanga and a Chi Chi."

Obviously, she thought their discussion in the car was finished. It wasn't. They gave their orders to the server and Josie started in again.

"You have to get back on the horse," she said. "Callum's being a good son and keeping your car battery charged and you're still insured. Isn't not quitting the kind of thing that pigeon poop book we read said we shouldn't do?"

Alice stared at her water glass. "I can't do it, Josie. Don't you think I've tried?" She looked up and the pain in her eyes hit Josie in the heart. "Just opening the car door makes it hard for me to breathe and I start sweating like a pig."

Josie reached across the table for her sister's hand. "Go back to therapy."

Alice shook her head. "It didn't help."

"You didn't give it enough time."

Alice bit her lip.

"It wasn't your fault," Josie insisted. "That kid came shooting out of nowhere on his bike."

Alice didn't meet her gaze. Instead, she stared out the window.

"He wasn't even hurt that badly. Nothing more than a broken arm."

Alice turned back to her. "I could have killed him, Jos. I wasn't paying attention."

"You were distraught. We'd just buried Charlie."

"I could have killed him," Alice repeated. Their server arrived with tortilla chips, and Alice gave them an angry shove toward Josie. "Have a chip."

Josie frowned and grabbed one, took it and crushed it between her teeth. "There might come a time when you need to drive."

"No there won't. I can always call an Uber. And anything I need I can buy online. I go to the library with Margot, Callum takes me out to eat, and I order my groceries and they get delivered right to my door."

Josie took another chip and pointed it at Alice. "Do you really like somebody picking your produce for you? And you have to pay a delivery fee and tip the driver."

"So? I can afford it."

"I don't know why you bothered to read that book. You obviously didn't get anything out of it," Josie said in disgust.

"Did you?" Alice shot back. "How are things going with Coral?"

Josie stiffened. "She's still being a brat."

"You made her mad."

"Me? All I did was point out some things she needed to change in her marriage. It was for her own good. Errol needs to grow up and man up."

Alice said nothing.

That made Josie more uncomfortable than when she'd spoken. "Don't be turning the tables on me. We're talking about you."

"I'm not the only one who's got problems, and if you ask me, mine aren't half as bad as yours."

"I don't remember asking you," Josie said, irritated.

"And I don't remember asking you, either. People who live in glass houses, Jos."

Their drinks arrived and Alice took a big slug of hers. Josie had ordered a Chi Chi, also, but without the vodka since she was driving.

Alice the nondriver could drink away. Josie frowned and took a big sip. "This isn't half as good without the booze," she grumbled. "I hope you're enjoying yours."

Alice smiled, her sister's guilt arrow bouncing right off her. "I am. Oh, good. Here comes our food."

And that was the end of the sisterly shrink session.

"So, you never said. What do you think of Margot and Karissa?" Alice asked once they'd both smoothed their ruffled feathers.

"They seem nice. They have terrible taste in books. Not that your choice is much better," Josie couldn't help adding.

"You don't have to join us if you don't want to," Alice said stiffly. "I thought it would be fun for you and me to do together. I guess I was wrong."

"I love doing things with you. You know that."

Alice smiled. "Garage sale season is almost here."

Josie smiled back. "Yes, it is."

And she'd be the designated driver for those outings as well. Honestly, Alice really did need to take some of the advice in that book to heart. Most of Annie Wills's advice was just a bunch of rah-rah psychobabble, but the chapter on facing down your fears hit the target. Yes, Alice needed the tips in that book. Not Josie.

"So, you're going to keep coming with me?" Alice pressed, returning to the topic of the book club.

"I will," Josie said. "I hope I like the one you've chosen better than advice from Dear Blabby." Although she wasn't holding her breath. She was sure it would be full of metaphysical nonsense.

"You will," Alice predicted. "I think there's always something we can take away from a book."

"Except for the ones you don't finish," Josie said, determined to have the last word. Alice couldn't have finished their first book. If she had, she'd be making Josie her goal buddy and getting more therapy, getting on with her life.

"I thought Annie Wills made a good point about doing something nice for someone every day. That was excellent advice," Alice said, feigning obtuseness. "And she's right. You do feel good after you've done something good."

"As if we don't already know that," Josie scoffed. "And don't you feel good about picking up the tab for lunch?" she teased.

"Actually, I do," Alice said. "You leave the tip and you can feel good, too."

"I will. Twenty percent," Josie said.

But it didn't make her feel all that happy. Pigeon poop.

"Don't bring a lunch tomorrow," Shirley said to Karissa. "We're all taking you out for Administrative Professionals Day."

"Really?" Karissa had been an administrative professional before, but her bosses had never bothered to take her to lunch. This was most likely prompted by a sense of duty, but she appreciated the gesture, especially since she was still new on the job. "That's very kind of you."

"Edward thought you might enjoy Anthony's at Gig Harbor. It offers a lovely view of both the harbor and Mount Rainier. Is that okay with you?"

Only the day before Edward had casually asked if she'd had a chance to try any of the city's restaurants. When she told him no, he'd said, "Well, we'll have to change that situation," and she'd wondered if he was making up for his truncated visit with his daughter. Or...who knew what because a call had come through for him and he'd gone into his office to take it and never brought up the subject again.

"Yes. I love seafood," she said. "Thank you."

"Thank Edward. He's the one who reminded me."

She'd been so thrown by his sudden cold snap the day of Lilith's playdate that she worried her prying had destroyed any chance they had at a friendly relationship. Hearing that Edward had been the one behind taking her to lunch warmed Karissa's heart.

Don't let it get too warm, she told herself. *He's only doing what bosses are expected to do.* They weren't living out a remake of *Jerry Maguire.*

But the next day, he sent her one of his rare smiles from across the table at Anthony's, and she thought she felt herself beginning to fall for him.

Shirley raised her glass of the wine she'd ordered for everyone and said, "Here's to Heron Publishing's newest treasure."

"We appreciate how hard you're working to make our office a pleasant place to work and keeping everything running smoothly," Edward added.

"Loving the coffee bar," André put in, "and the daily dose of Lindt chocolates you're providing."

She murmured her thanks, sipped on her wine, and felt happy bubbles dancing in her heart.

Edward appeared relaxed, and seeing his rare smile appear had been better than dessert. It never quite erased the sadness deep in his eyes though, which left her with an instinctive longing to help him dig it out.

"I hate to admit it, but I'm becoming fixated on him," she confessed to Margot as they chatted over a late evening chocolate binge in Karissa's living room.

She turned her phone so Margot could see the group picture

the server had taken of all of them at the restaurant. Shirley had been on one side of Karissa with André at Shirley's elbow. Edward sat on Karissa's other side, with a hand on the back of her seat. His white shirt showed off his dark hair and deep brown eyes and molded lovingly to his pecs. How could a woman not fall just a little for such a perfect specimen? He'd smiled for the camera, not broadly but it still counted. She'd smiled, too, although hers had been self-conscious.

Being made the center of attention and feted simply because she was doing her job had felt awkward, even if she had been thrilled to be invited out.

"He is gorgeous," said Margot. "And a single parent, right?"

"He is."

"Well, then?"

"He's my boss."

"That boss-employee thing does happen."

"Not to me."

"How do you know? What's he like outside the office? How was it when he came over with his daughter?"

"Polite. Reserved. He didn't share a lot about his life. He ate a couple of snickerdoodles and then bolted."

"If snickerdoodles don't make him fall for you, he's not human," Margot joked.

"I'm not glamorous enough to be with someone like him, even if he weren't my boss." Karissa sighed and proceeded to tell her friend about Emerald who had cornered the market on glamour and probably on Edward's heart. "That's not even her real name," she finished in disgust. "I found a copy of her contract in the files. Her real name is Mary Morgan."

"Emerald Austen definitely makes a statement," Margot said. "But hey, what's in a name?"

"She's more than a name. She's gorgeous. She reminds me of the woman who stole my husband." Karissa hadn't meant to mention her past but there it was. Her cheeks flamed.

Margot picked up the bag of chocolates she'd brought over and held it out to her. "Your past doesn't have to become your present."

"Was that in the book and I missed it?" Karissa asked and selected a salted caramel.

"No. That's from me. I've told it to myself often enough that I'm almost starting to believe it."

Karissa smiled. "Thanks for listening. And for the advice."

"Hey, just being a good neighbor."

"More than I can say for Allegra."

"The woman who stole your husband?"

Karissa nodded.

"She was your neighbor?"

Karissa nodded again.

"Good thing you moved," Margot said. "And don't worry. You're safe here. Alice is the wrong age and I'm not a man poacher."

"Good to know," Karissa said. "That's enough about me. How's it going with you?"

"Let's see. I did apply for a job, but they hired someone else. My mom is now giving me advice on how to interview even though she's never held down a job. I've started smoking again."

"Oh, no," Karissa said, horrified.

"So far today I only had two though. One after I learned I didn't get the job. The other after I talked to Mom." She popped a chocolate in her mouth. "I have to learn to deal with stress better."

"Chocolate?" Karissa guessed.

"Yeah, that's doing wonders for my thighs. Lately I keep dreaming about creating this app. Ever since I mentioned it to Alice the idea's been growing on me. The job hunt is getting discouraging and starting my own business is looking better and better."

"What's the app?" Karissa asked.

"It shows you what clothes from online retailers would look like on you. Kind of a virtual try-on."

"I'd put that on my phone."

"I don't have anywhere near the money I'd need to invest, and I can't be raiding my 401(k). The penalties would kill me. I did read an article online the other day that said some banks will loan you money if you don't have a job, as long as you have collateral. I've got a lot of equity in my house and I've been toying with going to the bank and seeing if I could get a loan."

"You should," Karissa said. "What have you got to lose?"

"What have you got to lose?" Margot asked herself as she pulled into the Harbor Anchor Bank parking lot. *Confidence. Hope.*

Those were renewable resources. She could do this. Anyway, she had to start somewhere.

She'd done her research. She had impressive statistics and a solid business proposal. So, into the bank she marched, wearing a V-neck dress with a black top and houndstooth skirt. She'd matched it with black pumps and her black-and-red Dooney & Bourke purse. She'd tucked her hair behind her ears to show off discreet, small gold hoops which she hoped would hint at success and impress Oliver Blackwood, the loan officer with whom she had an appointment.

He appeared to be impressed, but more with what was under her business smart attire than the clothes themselves. Oliver Blackwood looked to be fresh out of business school, a junior banker who had no authority to make decisions and who was merely posing as a loan officer.

He shook his head sadly after she made her pitch. "Without a job…"

"As I said, I have considerable equity in my house."

"But no job."

"I'm launching a new career," she said, resisting the urge to grind her teeth.

"I can appreciate that, and your idea is a good one, but I'm afraid we simply can't help you. Once you find employment, I'd be happy to revisit this."

At the rate her job hunt was going they wouldn't be revisiting this until menopause. She pasted on her most professional smile and held out her hand to shake. "Well, thank you for seeing me."

He took it, took another glance at her boobs. "If you'd like to get together and brainstorm."

She was obviously stirring up a storm somewhere other than Oliver's brain. Maybe Oliver would like to come to her rescue and become an investor in the C.I.G.—Cougar Investment Group. She wasn't old enough to be a cougar yet, was she? At what age did a woman turn into a cougar?

Never mind that. At what age did a woman lose her scruples? Good grief. Still, maybe it couldn't hurt to offer him the opportunity of a lifetime. Not being with her, but...

"If you had some money you'd like to invest," she said.

The color fled from his plump baby cheeks. "I'm afraid I don't."

"Then I guess I'll have to find someone else to brainstorm with," she said, and slid her hand free.

She held her head high and walked out of the bank like the successful woman she wanted to be. Then she got in her car, started the engine and turned the air a lovely shade of blue as she drove away. She could hardly wait to get home and get a cigarette. Maybe somewhere in the cloud of smoke she'd find inspiration.

9

IT WAS TIME TO HAND MACY OFF TO HER FATHER. MARK was waiting in the parking lot of Chuck E. Cheese, where he was taking Macy and her best friend Charlotte for dinner. Thank God he'd kept his promise not to bring Allegra along. It was hard enough for Karissa to give up Macy for the weekend. Having to watch her skip off with Allegra would have been agony on top of the misery she was already feeling.

He'd seen them coming and got out of Allegra's Mustang—the Mustang she'd gotten in her divorce settlement. He looked good—slimmer, more fit. Not that he'd ever been overweight, but he had carried a little extra around the middle. Karissa hadn't minded. It looked like Allegra did. She must have dragged him to the gym. His hair was getting a little longer. It was—sigh—sexy. Everything about him looked sexy, from the new hair to the jeans and open shirt and fancy loafers. An Allegra makeover success.

Karissa wondered why Allegra had never offered to make her over. Afraid of the competition? Not likely.

She checked out her reflection in her rearview mirror. There was nothing remarkable about her face or her chin-length dull brown hair. Maybe there was nothing remarkable about her at all. No wonder Mark had been lured away. Why stay with someone unremarkable when fascination personified lived next door? She may have moved to a new neighborhood, but she was still the same her.

Allegra's daughter Charlotte hopped out of the car and ran to hug Macy. Okay, there was the one good thing about this weekend. Macy would get to hang out with her friend.

Mark followed at a slower pace. He gave Macy a hug and then sent the girls on inside ahead of him. He gave Karissa a nod. "You look good, Rissa."

Good, but not good enough. She felt a salty sting in her eyes and bit down hard on her lip. Nodded back. "I'm glad we could meet halfway."

Such a polite thing to say. She felt like she was talking to a stranger. In a way she was. She didn't know this man anymore. Maybe she had never really known him.

"A little more than halfway for me," he said.

If he was expecting her to compliment him on his gallantry, he was going to be disappointed. She made no response.

He cleared his throat. "How's it going?"

As if he cared. "How's what going?"

"Everything. The new house, the job." It was the same thing he'd asked the last time they'd met and it was just as empty.

"Fine. My boss is still great and I still love the house. My neighbors are all really nice."

At the mention of neighbors, guilt put some extra color in Mark's cheeks. He nodded. "Good. That's good. Well, I'd better get inside. Meet back here on Sunday?"

"Let's meet at the Tacoma Mall. In front of The Cheese-cake Factory."

It wasn't pizza and arcade games, but it was in the mall, and she and Macy could go shopping after they'd eaten. She had no problem asking him to drive the extra distance. In the fancy Mustang. Let him learn to go the extra mile. It was the least he could do.

She got back in her car and told herself she was fine, that co-parenting was working out fine. And her weekend without her daughter would be fine. It was only two days, for heaven's sake. So everything was fine, fine, fine.

She went home via Krispy Kreme.

Margot's lights were on when Karissa pulled into her drive-way. Karissa took a chance on her being home and went over with her box of donuts.

"Hi, come on in," Margot said, swinging the door wide.

"Were you busy?"

"Just talking to my daughter, but she had to go. Unlike her mom these days, she has a social life. Come on in." She motioned for Karissa to sit down. "Is that temptation in a box I'm seeing?"

Karissa set the box on the coffee table and opened it.

Margot joined her. "You got here just in time to save me. I was about to raid the cigarettes again." She frowned and shook her head. "I have to start running more, doing yoga. Something. I need to find better ways to manage my stress."

Yes, you do, thought Karissa, but she kept her mouth shut. Everyone looked for stress relief in a different way, and her friendship with Margot was too new for her to be offering advice. Not that she was an advice-offering kind of woman, anyway.

"I guess the bank loan didn't go well," she guessed.

Margot scowled. "No, and because it didn't, I'm perversely more determined to find a way to develop that app. I even thought of a name for it—My Dressing Room. What do you think?"

"I like it."

"I just need to find an investor somewhere."

"I wish I had money to spare. I'd invest in a heartbeat," said Karissa.

She was no business genius, but she suspected the kind of app Margot was talking about would be a hit and make whoever was involved with it a nice bundle of money. For a moment she imagined herself as a millionaire, riding around in a car ten times as impressive as Allegra's. A Lexus. A BMW. A Tesla.

"There's someone out there, some way to make it happen. I need to open my eyes wider and look around more," Margot said, and helped herself to a donut. "Maybe sugar will inspire me."

"Maybe," Karissa said and helped herself to a donut, too, although she wasn't looking for inspiration. Only consolation.

She delivered the rest of the donuts to Alice the next day and took her along as flower guide to the local nursery to pick up some plants for the flower bed and some grass seed for the lawn. The expert at the nursery was able to advise her on grass seed and Alice suggested pansies to brighten up her flower beds and convinced her to buy two large pots to set on her porch and fill with geraniums.

"For a pop of color," she said. "It will look lovely, and surrounding yourself with beauty is good for the soul."

"Anything that's good for the soul works for me," Karissa said, "especially this weekend, with my daughter gone."

"She'll be home before you know it," Alice assured her.

"After spending the weekend with my husband and his girlfriend," Karissa muttered.

"That is unfortunate but try to think of this as some time for yourself."

There was the bright side. The glass was half-full.

If only Karissa could get it closer to the top.

"Let's get back and I'll help you plant your flowers," Alice said.

Prettying up the house did help. Alice invited Josie over and the three of them had lunch at Alice's house.

"Flowers are always a good idea," Josie approved. "They're something you can always count on to make you feel good."

An interesting statement. What was going on in Josie's life? She'd been quick enough to share about losing her husband, but she seemed to have moved on from that. Karissa had the distinct impression something wasn't right. She also had the distinct impression Josie wasn't going to talk about it.

Margot didn't like Josie, but Karissa felt a little sorry for her. She wasn't a happy woman.

She was a walking warning sign. *If you're not careful, you could end up like me, negative and bristly.* Karissa could not let herself go down that road. *Glass half-full, glass half-full.* And half-full was a lot better than empty. Allegra had stolen Karissa's husband, she was probably, at that very moment, trying to steal Macy's affection, but Karissa was not going to let the woman drain her glass. For each selfish sip Allegra took Karissa would find something to bring the level of good back up. She was in a battle for her self-esteem and her happiness. She was not going to lose it no matter what.

To prove it to herself, she found a church the next morning, walked in all by herself, managed to smile at people, and even say good morning to an older woman who invited her to have a cup of coffee before the service began. She politely declined and hurried into the sanctuary. She got out a little ahead of the crowd after the service ended so she wouldn't have to talk to anyone, but so what? She'd showed up.

She was feeling triumphant and proud of herself when she picked up Macy later that day. Until Macy started chattering about all the fun she'd had at Aunt Allegra's. Aunt Allegra and the girls had gotten mani-pedis. "Even Daddy got a pedi," Macy said with a giggle.

Karissa had smiled around gritted teeth as Macy showed off her fancy multicolored nails. Very nice. Aunt Allegra was so much fun. Ugh.

"When is Daddy going to quit staying at her house?" Macy wanted to know. "Why doesn't Daddy want to live with us?"

Because he's a selfish man.

Karissa bit back the words and said for what felt like the millionth time, "Honey, you know Daddy and I aren't going to live together anymore. We decided that was best."

Macy's mouth drew down at the corners. "I wish you and Daddy would change your minds. It's not fair. Charlotte gets to see him every day."

Karissa hoped Macy wasn't getting replaced just like she had been. But no, she assured herself. Mark adored his daughter. That would never change.

"Not every day. Charlotte goes to spend time with her daddy, just like you do," she pointed out.

"I'm glad she was with us this weekend," Macy said, and then went on to continue describing all the fun she'd had at her father's new house.

Fun? Karissa could do fun, too. After cheesecake she took her daughter shopping at The Gap. They went home and streamed movies until they were on Disney overload. *Ha! Take that, Allegra. I guess I showed you who's the best mommy of them all.*

Later, as she heard Macy's prayers, she clenched her jaws while Macy prayed, "And God bless Aunt Allegra."

With a horrible bowel disease.

Sorry, God.

"I wanted to follow up on our meeting last Thursday," Margot said over the phone to the woman who had interviewed her at T-Mobile's sleek Bellevue office. "I'm excited about the prospect of getting to work with you."

The woman cleared her throat. "I was about to email you. You were a great candidate, but I'm afraid we went with someone else."

Margot's heart took a downhill tumble. She'd been so sure she'd get that position. She had experience, was actually overqualified. The interview had gone well. She'd thought she was a shoo-in.

"Of course, you have to go with the person who's right for you." *Which should have been me.* "I would love to know if there was, perhaps, something in my résumé that gave you pause." It was a difficult question to ask, but necessary.

A moment of silence ensued, followed by, "You were overqualified for this job, Margot. But then I'm not telling you anything you don't already know. I'm sure there's something better out there for you."

"Thank you. I'm sure you're right," Margot lied.

She set down the phone and drummed her fingers on the counter. Why, oh, why had she thrown out her cigarettes? She'd have gone outside and dug them out of the trash can if the garbage collectors hadn't already come. She needed something. She was going to climb out of her skin.

Her eyes strayed to the pantry where she still had a half-full package of mint Oreos. That probably wasn't a good idea either.

It's all about choices, Annie Wills had written in her book. *The wrong ones will take you backward, but the right ones will help you get what you need. Every small need you meet is a stepping stone to fulfilling bigger needs.*

What Margot needed was to burn off steam, do something good for herself that would put her in a better frame of mind. The sun was shining, and April was going out on a warm note. She put on her shorts and running shoes, stretched, and then set off down the street at a jog. She slowly picked up the pace, found her rhythm and found a smile. Okay, that job wasn't meant for her. She'd find something that worked. She would get her life sorted out!

"How does Anthony's sound for lunch for Mother's Day, Mom?" Callum asked when he called to check on Alice. "You and us and Kara's mom. And then Kara wants you both to come to the house afterward for dessert. She has some fancy thing she's making."

"That sounds like fun," Alice said. More fun than her sister was going to have. "Say, what about including your aunt Josie?"

Her son's answer came swiftly and firmly. "No."

"I think it would mean a lot to her."

"She has a kid," Callum said.

"Yes, but," Alice began.

He cut her off. "She and Coral are gonna have to work out their issues."

"I hate to think of her all alone."

"She doesn't have to be, Mom. She's brought this on herself."

Josie had made some mistakes with her daughter, but still... "She'll be alone on Mother's Day."

"Yeah well, like I said, she's got a kid. She doesn't get to stomp all over your day with your kid and his family."

Alice wanted to argue that his aunt Josie had been a good aunt to him, baking him treats, giving him his first job, helping with inventory years ago when she had her kitchen shop, that if he ever needed anything she'd be right there. Yes, her sister could be bossy and opinionated and, okay, a little negative sometimes, but she was hardly Cruella de Vil.

"We'll pick you up at 12:30 p.m., okay?" End of discussion.

"Okay," Alice said. She set aside her phone and tried not to feel guilty that she was going to have a great day with her son and her sister was going to be alone and miserable.

"So, I guess you're going out with the kids this Sunday," Josie said when she called that evening.

"Yes, I am," Alice said.

"I hope Callum's taking you someplace expensive."

"Anthony's."

"Not bad," said Josie. "I always loved that restaurant."

Josie was hoping for an invite to join the party. Alice's stomach clenched and she scrambled around in her mind, looking for something to say—anything but, "Why don't you join us?" Callum would not be happy, and one sister with a child not speaking to her was enough in their family.

"How about you and I go there tomorrow night. We can split a Sunset Dinner."

"No, that's okay."

"I'll pay."

"I don't need a sympathy meal, if that's what you're thinking," Josie said irritably.

"I wasn't thinking anything," Alice lied.

"Good. Because I'll be busy tomorrow. And Sunday," she added. "I'm going to get Georgie over to help me try out my new pasta maker."

Josie should have been making pasta with her daughter, not her neighbor. She and Coral had done a lot of things like that when Coral was younger.

"Looks like it's almost time for *Jeopardy*," Josie said. "Got your TV on?" The two of them always watched *Jeopardy* together, trying to see who could get the most answers right.

Alice knew the subject of Mother's Day and any possible suggestions she could make regarding her sister and her niece repairing their relationship was officially closed. She gave up. Callum was right. Josie and Coral were going to have to sort out their problems on their own.

"Turning on the TV right now," she said, grabbing for her remote.

★ ★ ★

Mother's Day was just a day like any other, really. Telling herself that didn't make Josie feel any better. She hung around her house all day Saturday in case a surprise flower delivery showed up. Even if she and Coral weren't speaking, it wouldn't surprise her if Coral sent flowers simply out of guilt. They'd had their little run-ins in the past, especially when Coral was a teenager, but they'd always made up.

No flowers came.

On The Day Josie kept her phone nearby all morning but it remained silent. She drank her coffee and cried.

Then she wiped away her tears, got in her car and drove to the nursery, where she bought herself a hanging basket for her back deck. She'd be able to look out her kitchen sliding glass door and see it hanging there every morning when she drank her coffee. She would look at it and remind herself that she'd been a good mother, always there when Coral needed something. She'd always been there for her nephew, too, the little shit. Nice of him to take Alice out and snub her.

She wished her own mother was still alive. It would have been good to be able to talk to someone who understood how she felt, who would agree, who would say, "Not speaking since February? Coral should be ashamed of herself."

Sadly, Josie and Alice had lost their mother long before she died. Dementia. It had been a horrible thing to go see the woman who had always been there for her look at her, brows pulled together in concentration as she tried to figure out who Josie was.

I'm the one who watched over Alice when you were getting chemo and were so sick you couldn't get out of bed. I'm the one who cooked the meals and went with you to the doctor's when Daddy had to work and Alice was in school. I'm the one who kept us all going when you eventually forgot who we were and slipped away someplace where we couldn't follow.

Josie had been a good daughter. And a good sister and a good mother. But now, here she was, alone on Mother's Day.

Coral should have called.

Karissa and Macy went to Anacortes to spend Mother's Day weekend with Karissa's mom. They brought gifts—Godiva chocolates from Karissa along with a mug that showed cartoon versions of her and her mother sitting side by side, captioned *Best Friends Forever*, and a special story Macy had written for her grandma featuring a grandmother who made pink birthday cakes topped with special candles where every wish a little girl made came true. Of course, in the book, the girl's daddy moved back home and he and Mommy and the girl lived happily ever after. It was a cute story, and both Karissa and Grandma praised Macy. Neither ruined the moment by mentioning the fact that life did not always imitate art.

There were many games of *Sorry!* played with Uncle Ethan and a special mother-daughter walk on the beach. There were hugs and encouraging words and predictions of great things waiting for Karissa in the future. Even a gift of lavender from her brother ("Mom said you'd like it.") for Karissa to plant in her flower bed—a gesture which had touched her deeply. She returned home with her glass three-quarters full.

"I think mine might be emptied," Margot said, when the book club met to discuss Alice's pick, *Close Calls,* and the subject of Mother's Day came up. "My daughter took my mom and me to a movie. The movie was great because she couldn't give me job hunting advice. But she still managed to on the way home."

"Maybe you need it," Josie suggested.

"No. I don't," Margot snapped. "I should have been born a boy. She never got on my brothers about anything. Still doesn't. She saves it all for me."

"Mothers and daughters, they don't always communicate well," Alice said, and Josie scowled at her.

"What does she think about your idea for the app?" Karissa asked.

"I haven't told her. I'm sure she'd shoot it down. Anyway, it's out of reach. It would cost more than I can afford to develop."

"What app?" Josie wanted to know.

Margot elaborated but didn't look happy about it, and Karissa wished she hadn't brought up the subject.

"Never shop online," Josie said after Margot had finished. "When it comes to buying clothes, you need a mirror. Even buying something off the rack they never get those sizes right."

"Or you're stuck two sizes in the past," Alice teased.

Josie rolled her eyes. "Okay, so I'm not a size twelve anymore, but I'm still fit enough to hold my own on the pickleball court."

Karissa could imagine. Josie would be a formidable opponent on any sport court.

"Anyway, Mom just wants me to get a job and be done with it. As if I'm not trying," Margot added, and grabbed a chocolate from the See's box on Karissa's table.

"So much for that pigeon poop book," Josie sneered.

Karissa decided she needed to defend Margot's book choice. "It wasn't all pigeon poop. I took Annie's advice about having the right attitude at work and it paid off." She proceeded to share about the coffee fiasco at work.

"What a jerk," muttered Josie. "The writer, not your boss," she clarified. "Although he sounds like a wimp to me."

"He's not. He's really nice," Karissa said. Which made Josie raise a speculative eyebrow. "Anyway, the book helped," she finished.

"I have to admit, it hasn't necessarily moved me closer to my dreams, but reading that book has helped me move away from penalizing myself with stupid choices," Margot said. "I tossed the cigarettes, and I've started running again."

"Good for you," Alice said.

"You could have done that without the book," Josie said.

"I could have, but it was the push I needed," Margot insisted.

"I did like the idea of planning for things you want to do," Karissa added. "I know I need to do that. I do want to exercise more. I think I need a goal buddy for that one," she added, bringing out a disdainful snort from Josie.

"Yeah? I could be your goal buddy," Margot offered. "How about taking up running with me?"

"At this point in life I'd never run unless a bear was chasing me," cracked Josie.

"Run?" Karissa echoed weakly. "Umm."

"Okay, walking? We could meet on Saturday mornings for starters."

Everyone was looking at Karissa expectantly. "Okay," she said, half wishing she'd kept her mouth shut.

Still, why not give it a try? She'd never been athletic, and the idea of working out at a gym had sounded like torture. But walking with a friend? That was something she could handle. And it wasn't an activity Allegra had poisoned. They'd never walked together. Allegra had preferred the gym. Now Mark did, too. Maybe he'd drop a forty-pound weight on his foot.

"Well, there you go," Alice said cheerfully. "Now you both have a plan."

"But what's your plan for making money?" Josie asked, pointing a finger at Margot.

"I don't know," Margot confessed with a frown. "I'm not getting anywhere putting out résumés so far. I've had a few interviews, but they've gone nowhere. I'm either overqualified or underqualified for everything out there."

"So do something else," Josie said. "You won't get anywhere whining."

"I'm not whining," Margot snapped, and her frown turned into a glare.

Josie shrugged and dug a chocolate out of the box.

"What about our book for this month?" Alice asked, and Margot sent her a grateful look.

"I don't know what to make of it," Josie said. "Like the part about the people who should have been on the *Titanic* and for some reason or other weren't."

"Like Milton Hershey," said Karissa.

"The chocolate king. I'm glad he didn't go down with the ship," said Margot, who had recovered her composure.

"But then you think of all the people who died," Josie said.

"It wasn't their time yet," said Alice. "None of us knows when that is."

It was a sobering thought. The women fell silent for a moment.

"Has anyone here had a close call?" Karissa asked.

"I did," said Alice.

"When?" her sister demanded.

"Don't you remember Axel Broom?"

Josie frowned and nodded. "Oh, yeah, him."

"He was the most handsome boy in the whole school," Alice said.

"He was," Josie agreed. "But he was a shit."

"Definitely a bad boy," Alice said. "He was a senior and I was only a sophomore. I was smitten, and I thought I'd won the love lottery when he asked me out."

"To a kegger," Josie supplied. "If I'd known that I'd have locked you in your room."

"I didn't know," Alice said. "I just thought it was going to be a party. Anyway, I got a bad case of cramps that night and couldn't go. He took another girl instead. Got completely wasted and, driving home, he crashed into tree. The girl was crippled for life, and he was an emotional mess afterward. That girl could have been me."

"Wow," said Karissa. "That was a close call."

"You and I had one, too," Alice reminded her sister. "Remember that big pileup on I-5? We only missed it by minutes. I guess we're still supposed to be here."

"Wish I knew why," Josie muttered.

"Anyway, there's another reason not to drive. It's dangerous," said Alice.

"You need to drive," Josie told her sternly.

"No, I don't," Alice insisted. Her cheeks began to turn pink. "I don't like to drive," she said to Karissa.

"She's afraid to," Josie elaborated.

"For good reason," Alice said, frowning at her sister. "I almost killed a child."

"You hit a reckless boy on a bike who wasn't watching where he was going and rode right out in front of you," Josie corrected.

"How awful," Karissa said.

"How badly was he hurt?" Margot asked.

"Broken arm," Josie answered for her sister.

"How badly he was hurt is not the point. I hit him and we're all better off if I don't get back behind the wheel." Alice sent a warning look to her sister, then changed the subject. "What about you girls?"

Margot took a deep, thoughtful breath. "I'm thinking about my post-divorce love fails, especially the last one. He was like your hot guy, Alice, but I quickly realized he had big-time substance abuse issues. And a temper. I think if I'd wound up with him, he'd have been abusing more than substances."

"Yikes," Karissa said.

"Things have a way of working out for the best," Alice said. "Have you had any close calls, Karissa?"

Karissa shook her head. "My life's been uneventful. Well, except for my divorce."

"Maybe by splitting with him you've escaped more unhappiness in the future."

"I don't know how much worse it could have gotten than cheating," Karissa said, and hoped Josie wouldn't accuse her of whining. She wasn't whining. She was…sad.

"He's some other woman's problem now," Margot told her.

"Allegra's a problem all by herself," Karissa said bitterly.

"Then I guess your husband is getting what he deserves," said Josie. "Sounds like they both deserve each other."

But I didn't deserve to be betrayed. Karissa kept the thought to herself. It was all in the past and that was where she needed to leave her hurt. The present was good. She had a satisfying job, great neighbors, and her daughter was off enjoying McDonald's goodies with her new best friend. She had no love life, but she had people who loved her. It was enough.

"Okay, so much for that book," Josie said. "Is it my turn to pick the next read?"

"Go for it," Margot said. It almost sounded like a dare.

"I say we read a classic. How about *Jane Eyre*?"

"Oh, I have the movie on DVD. The one with Ciaran Hinds, remember?" Alice said to her sister.

"I've never read that book," Margot confessed.

"You haven't read *Jane Eyre*?" Alice sounded shocked. "Well, then, you're in for a treat. Everyone should have to read at least one Brontë book."

"I read *Wuthering Heights* when I was in middle school," Karissa supplied. "It tore me up."

"This book ends better," Josie assured her.

"Let's read it," Karissa said, and so it was decided.

As the women freshened their drinks, conversation returned to Margot's job hunt. "I'm okay," she said. "I've still got unemployment and money in savings. But I'd rather be working and so far everything I apply for bombs."

"Sounds like you're only interested in superstar positions," Josie said.

"I'm interested in management positions because that's what I'm good at," Margot shot back at her, "and because they pay well. But I'm not too proud to take something else if it comes along."

"What about working odd jobs for a while or launching a new business?" Josie suggested. "Besides that app one."

"Any suggestions?" Margot challenged.

"How about something that would take advantage of your skills at organizing?" Alice suggested. "She helped me clear out my garage when I lost Charlie," she explained to Karissa.

"That's right. I remember you telling me," Josie said to her sister. "You wouldn't be able to collect as much unemployment, but it could lead to something." She turned a thoughtful gaze onto Margot and Karissa was sure she saw Margot stiffen. "You know, I could use some help getting organized."

Oh, no. No, no, no. The last person in the world Margot wanted to work with was Josie. She'd find a job somewhere. Sanitation. Digging ditches. Waiting tables. She'd done that in college.

"I don't think that's a good idea," she said.

"Weren't you saying earlier you'd like to get some money coming in?" Josie challenged.

"I'm not sure we'd work well together," Margot said, opting for polite honesty.

"You never know. We might."

Margot was about to say, "I doubt it," when Josie mentioned an hourly rate that made dollar signs jump in front of her eyes.

"I couldn't charge you that much," she protested. Josie was a widow, probably on a limited income.

"I can afford it. Joe left me well provided for."

"This could turn into a business," Alice added.

Or a nightmare.

Still, it was hard to turn down Alice's offer. And Margot did like organizing things. All those labeled containers stacked so neatly in her freezer testified to that. She liked managing people.

Although she couldn't imagine managing Josie.

Hmm.

10

"Look beneath the surface.
People are always more than they appear to be."
—from *Close Calls* by Gisella Strom

WORKING FOR JOSIE TURNED OUT TO BE AS FRUSTRATING as Margot had suspected it would be.

"Josie, you have three different sizes in this closet," she pointed out after looking through Josie's clothes.

"I need three different sizes," Josie insisted. "One for my size now, one for if I outgrow this size and one for when I shrink down a size."

"How long have you been working at shrinking down?" Margot asked.

"Never mind. Just know I'm working on it."

"Some of these clothes are long out of style," pointed out Margot.

"Who cares? I like them. And I need all of them. Anyway, I'm not an influencer," Josie finished on a sneer.

"You do remember that you're paying me to help you, don't you?" Margot said.

"Of course, I remember, and you are." Josie pointed to two pairs of shoes she'd decided to part with. "I need to be able to find stuff more easily."

"All right. Let's put everything in sections. That will make it easier."

"They were once upon a time," Josie said, "but I get busy."

She was retired. What was she busy doing? Margot decided not to ask. They finished with her bedroom closet, organizing everything by occasion and color, and moved to the next thing on Josie's list, the basement, where she admitted she had a few things she could part with.

A few? Two walls of shelving held everything from an old espresso machine ("I need a backup for when mine breaks.") to an ancient toaster still in its original box ("I might need a wedding present down the road and that's never been opened.")

Margot pointed out that giving someone a ten-year-old toaster might not look like a very thoughtful present.

"Okay, fine. It can go to Goodwill," Josie snapped. "You are sure bossy."

"I'm supposed to be helping you. How can I help you if you don't listen to me?"

"You're supposed to help me organize, not get rid of everything I own," Josie said with a scowl. "Now, come on, help me organize this stuff."

"All right, all right," said Margot, and got to work. It could have been overwhelming to a lesser woman. Toilet paper and paper towels were jammed in every which way between cleaning supplies, old cans of paint, duplicate bags of potting soil and old clay flowerpots. Several cardboard cartons containing who knew what weren't labeled. And the woman had enough old plastic bags to stock a store.

"I don't like paying for bags," Josie explained.

"A little hard to access them down here, isn't it?" Margot said.

"These are spares. I have some in the pantry."

Margot could well imagine. "All you need are a couple of reusable bags."

"No, I don't. I have all of these. And I'm keeping them."

Margot gave up. "Okay, okay."

As they worked Josie complained about how her lower back hurt and how clueless her doctor was. Next, she dissed the neighbor two doors down who never cleaned up after her dog and complained about another whose teen son shattered the peace and quiet of the neighborhood roaring up and down the street in his beater in need of a muffler. Once those subjects were exhausted, she poked her nose into Margot's non-love life and advised her to get out there and find someone before it was too late.

By the time they were finished Margot was done with Josie.

"I guess that income stream has dried up," Karissa said when the two friends took their Saturday morning walk.

Margot sighed, shook her head. "No, she asked me to come back."

"You're going?" Here was a surprise. "You don't even like her."

"What can I say? She begged. Well, as much as Josie is capable of begging. It was more like, 'Don't be a quitter and I'll pay you an extra five dollars an hour.'"

"Interesting," Karissa said.

"That was very diplomatic," Margot teased. "I know, only an extra five and I'm going back for more irritation. I'm easy to buy. But truthfully, I kind of feel sorry for her. I know she's got Alice. And she's got a daughter, but something's not right there. She seems…broken. I know it sounds funny considering how unbroken she's acted at our meetings so far, but people break in different ways, and they show it in different ways. And what the heck, I still haven't found a job, so I may as well do this."

"Well, you're a braver woman than I am," said Karissa. "I kind of like Josie, but I'd be terrified to work for her. Speaking of brave, Gerald McCrae came in the office again yesterday and I was ready to run out the back door."

Margot chuckled. "I take it you didn't."

"No, but I thought my heart was going to bang a hole in my chest," Karissa confided. "I was pure professional though. I greeted him with a smile and pointed him to our coffee bar. I even asked him how he liked the refinished floor."

"What did he say?"

"He grunted and said that now I wouldn't have an excuse if I tried to take him out."

"We should match him up with Josie and see who'd come out of that encounter the winner," Margot cracked.

Now, there was an idea. "Do you think she'd like to get married again?"

"It would give her someone to boss around. Her husband probably died just to get away from her."

Josie was, indeed, a force of nature. Maybe it would be good for her to have someone equally forceful in her life. "I don't see her succeeding in bossing around Gerald," Karissa said.

"I'd love to see her roll up against another boulder," Margot mused. "My grandma always said iron sharpens iron."

"I wonder," Karissa said thoughtfully. Maybe when it was her turn to pick their next read, she'd pick one of Gerald's books and ask him to come join them.

Margot was at Josie's again for more frustration. This time they were in Josie's well-stocked but disorganized pantry. Her house was so clean it would pass any white glove test, but it seemed once you opened a cupboard or closet door chaos reigned supreme and it was like a whole different person was living in the house. Maybe Josie had multiple personalities.

More than one version of Josie, that was a little scary.

"I don't know how you find anything in here," Margot said, looking at the mismatched food items. Cake flour sat next to rice (to make rice cupcakes?) and regular sugar and flour were nowhere near the brown sugar or the extra boxes of baking soda. Three of them. Margot picked one up and read the expiration date. "Josie, this is two years past its expiration date."

"I can still use it," Josie said, snatching it out of her hand. "I'll put it in the fridge to soak up odors."

"Okay, fine," Margot said. She looked at the expiration date on the other two. "But these are going out. Get your trash can."

"Hey, you can use baking soda and vinegar to clean a clogged sink," Josie protested, reaching for one.

Margot held it away. "You can use the one you're going to stick in your fridge. Where, I'm willing to bet, we'll find another one."

Josie pretended not to see Margot's cocked eyebrow. "Okay, fine. Toss 'em."

Margot looked at the shelf piled high with pots and pans. "What's with all these?"

"I used to have a kitchen shop."

"And these are the only pots and pans you have left from that?"

"Of course not. I have more in my cupboard."

"You're not old enough to have come through the Depression. Or World War II. What's with this hanging onto everything?" Margot asked.

"Because you never know," Josie snapped. "You should probably be more mindful about what you throw out, Miss I-Don't-Have-a-Job."

Margot was ready to dump one of the boxes of baking soda over the woman's head. "I have a job right now, and you're making it hard for me to do. Get the trash can already."

"All right, all right."

Josie fetched the trash can from under her kitchen sink and brought it over. It was almost empty. Margot was willing to bet they'd have it full to overflowing by the time they were done.

"Okay, we're going to put all your baking goods together. It looks like most of your breakfast items are already in the same neighborhood, so that's good."

"Do I get a gold star?" Josie sniped.

"Do you want me to leave?" Margot snapped.

Josie took a deep breath. "Sorry. I guess I don't take orders very well."

"I guess not," said Margot.

Josie picked up a jar of coconut oil and studied it. "It's hard to do when you're used to being in charge. I had my shop, and then I was a supervisor at Macy's for years. Then I retired and just supervised my husband."

This was said with a smile, so Margot smiled back, acknowledging Josie's attempt at humor.

"My parents were older. We had some hard times financially when Alice and I were teenagers. My mom was sick. We had bills. We had to be pretty darn careful with money." Josie shook her head. "It's hard to buy into this throwaway society, even though I grew up in it."

That explained a lot. "I get it," Margot said. "So, you're the older sister?" she guessed. It wasn't difficult to tell, watching how the two sisters interacted.

"Yep."

"I have two younger brothers. I get that whole thing of being in charge."

"Bossy older sister?"

"Oh, yeah. I'm two years older than James, four years older than Tyler."

"Old enough to know more than both of them."

"Oh, yeah. Of course, I don't tell them that anymore."

"You should. I tell Alice all the time. I might know more than you, even."

"Except about organizing."

"Oh, I know about that," Josie said, waving away the jab. "I just don't like to do it. You're a smart woman. Hard to imagine a company giving you the heave-ho."

"All kinds of people get the heave-ho when companies start worrying about their bottom line," Margot said, and shifted a can of peaches onto a different shelf. "I have to admit, I didn't see it coming."

"Thought your job was secure, huh?"

"I did."

"There's really no such thing," Josie said. "The one thing we can always count on in life is change, and that's not always for the best. But you got to keep truckin'."

Margot handed her a package of instant cocoa mix. "How about putting that with the breakfast items."

Josie complied. "Even if you have your own business, it's no guarantee, but at least nobody can lay you off."

"I don't know if I want to do this as a business," Margot said.

"Look how good you are at it," Josie said. "Anyway, you have to do something. You can't sit around like a princess and wait for somebody to bring you a job on a satin pillow."

"I'm not sitting around," Margot said shortly.

"Hey, don't get so prickly. I never said you were."

"You could have fooled me."

"What about that app thing you were talking about? There must be a way you can make that happen."

"Right now I don't have the money to hire a developer."

"I've got some spare money kicking around."

Margot was touched by her offer. "It's probably not a good idea to borrow money from friends," she said. Did Josie qualify as a friend? Probably not.

"Why not? You'd borrow from the bank."

"That's different. I'm not in a book club with the bank loan officer."

Josie laughed, harder than Margot expected.

"Besides, do you know how much it could cost?"

"I don't know. A couple thousand bucks."

"Try more like between fifty and seventy thousand."

"What? That's ridiculous. Just to make something for people to put on their phone?"

"It's tech stuff and that doesn't come cheap."

Josie blew out a breath. "I've got money to spare but not that much."

"Nobody has that much," Margot said bitterly. "At least not sitting around. I sure don't."

"I bet you've got some kind of retirement plan."

Margot shook her head. "I looked into that, believe me. The penalties for withdrawing from my 401(k) are way too stiff."

"Well, you were in business. Don't you know some movers and shakers?"

"One."

"Then what's stopping you from cornering that person?"

"He's my ex."

"Ah. Still enemies?"

"No, we get along fine, but I don't think borrowing money from your ex is a good idea."

But when you were out of good ideas, maybe a bad one was the next best thing.

Karissa walked to her parking lot in the lot behind Heron Publishing, out into the sunshine after a lovely day, to discover her car had a flat tire. She'd stayed a little later than she'd intended but hadn't been concerned about picking up Macy on time. Until that very moment.

"Noooo," she wailed. She hadn't changed a flat tire since she was seventeen and her father had made her. They should have had a few pop quizzes in the years following.

"You can do this," she told herself, and went to fetch the jack from the trunk. If she needed help, that was what Google was for.

She had the jack in hand when Shirley happened to come out, on her way to meet an author. "Oh, no. What have we here?"

"We have something that's going to make me late picking up my daughter," Karissa said as she put the jack together. At least she remembered how to do that. "Serves me right. I ignored the low-pressure symbol on the dashboard. I figured I could put some more air in the tire after picking Macy up."

"You need more than air now," Shirley observed. "But you are not going to do that yourself, are you?" She looked at the jack in disgust. "That is dirty work, and that's what roadside service is for."

"Sometimes you have to do dirty work," Karissa said. "I don't have time to wait for help."

"Put that thing down," Shirley commanded and punched some numbers on her phone. A moment later she said, "Get out here. We have a car emergency."

"Oh, don't bother poor André," Karissa protested. "His clothes are way too nice to mess up."

"So is your dress. And I didn't call André," Shirley added as Edward emerged, rolling up his shirtsleeves.

His clothes were too nice to mess up, too.

"I can do this. Really," Karissa said to him.

"I know, but I want to help," he told her. "I'm behind on my good deed quota, and I'm sure Macy will be waiting for you. Lilith would never forgive me if I stranded her at school."

It was hard not to argue even though she felt the need to prove that she was totally self-sufficient. Whether that was to Edward or herself she wasn't sure. Maybe both. Still, her daughter would be waiting, and she suspected he'd be a lot faster than she would.

"This would definitely count as a good deed," she said, and handed over the jack.

"My job here is done. See you two tomorrow," Shirley said, then got in her own car and drove off.

Edward had the spare on the car and the flat stashed in the trunk in under ten minutes.

"Thank you," Karissa said to him. "I'm sorry I had to bother you."

"It was no bother," he said, and smiled down at her. A genuine smile that reached his eyes and its warmth hit her right in the heart. "I'm glad I could help. Don't worry about work when you're making an appointment to get the tire fixed. We can manage without you for a while."

"Just not permanently, I hope," she joked.

"Not permanently," he agreed. "We like having you around. See you tomorrow."

"See you tomorrow," she repeated and climbed behind the wheel.

Edward Elliot was a good boss. And a good man, the kind of man a woman's heart found hard to resist. *Don't fall for him*, she lectured herself. But it was too late.

Shirley asked Karissa about her tire situation the next morning.

"I have an appointment at Costco for noon to get the tire mended, so I can go on my lunch break."

"Good. Flat tires are such a pain. I'm glad you didn't get yours on the road somewhere. I once had one on I-5 at ten at night. Talk about terrifying. It happened right at an exit, so I was able to get off without killing myself, but still it was no fun."

"I felt bad that Edward had to change it," Karissa said.

"Don't. He likes doing good deeds. Sometimes I think that man was born in the wrong time. He should have been a nineteenth-century poet."

"He does seem to have a poetic soul," Karissa said. "He's certainly a kind father," she added.

"He's a great dad," Shirley agreed.

"It's got to be hard raising a child alone." Fishing, fishing. There had to be someone special in his life. Like Emerald?

Shirley didn't rise to the bait. "His mom's a big help. He and Lilith live with her." She checked her Fitbit. "I have that conference call in ten minutes, don't I? I'd better get my notes pulled together." With that she was off to her office.

Karissa frowned. How was a woman supposed to get vital information these days? She hadn't found anything useful on-line when she'd searched the night before. Not that she was an expert when it came to online sleuthing, but there should have been something about Edward Elliot, other than references to Heron Publishing and his address. (Kind of creepy that anyone could go online and learn where you lived!)

Asking him about his life would be tacky. And intrusive. He'd already shown he wasn't open to talking about his past. If he'd wanted her to know more about him, if he was even remotely interested, he would have shared. And if he wanted to get to know more about her, he would have asked.

She was probably only zeroing in on Edward because she was lonely and love-starved. When you were hungry, all you could do was fantasize about cookies, cupcakes and bread, things you weren't allowed. She needed distraction.

Maybe I should try online dating, she texted to Margot that night.

Just marry your boss, Margot texted back with a laughing emoticon.

There was an enticing fantasy. The more she saw of Edward the more she wished she could have him. She'd once read somewhere that there was something about beauty that made people want to possess it. How true! Edward was a treat for the eyes. But there was more to him than a handsome exterior. He was handsome on the inside, too, and that was even more attractive. If only the attraction was mutual.

I'll get right on that. Thanx.

Welcome.

Maybe I'm meant to be single forever. There was a charming thought.

Or not. What do I know? Check out some sites. You may have better luck than me.

I guess I'll think about it, Karissa texted, but she knew, when it came right down to it, she wouldn't be brave enough to jump into online dating. She'd used up most of her bravery reserves moving and starting a new job.

And her poor banged-up heart had already been through so much. So, no online dating and no more fantasizing about Edward.

Not listening, said her heart. *I want more of him.*

"We're not going to get more than we already have," she told her deluded heart with a sigh.

Hearts didn't listen very well.

11

"None of us are simply one thing.
We are multi-faceted. Like a diamond."
—from *It's Never Too Late* by Muriel Sterling

KARISSA RETURNED FROM STOCKING UP ON COFFEE
and treats to find the offices of Heron Publishing empty. She
knew Shirley had a lunch date. Edward and André had probably wandered off in search of something as well. The warm
May weather beckoned her to the rooftop deck to enjoy her
lunch break with *Jane Eyre*. She was finding the story fascinating. And a little unnerving.

She stepped out onto the deck to discover Edward there alone.
He wore his usual finely pressed slacks and crisp white shirt,
but his posture was relaxed. He was half slumped in his chair,
with his long legs stretched out in front of him, and he appeared
to be engrossed in a book. She'd have loved to ask what it was.

But she knew better than to interrupt someone's reading.
Rather than look like she was stalking him, she started to back
up, planning to slip back the way she'd come. She and Jane
could as easily find a spot at the little waterfront park.

He must have possessed a highly refined sixth sense, for he turned as she was backing away. "Karissa," he said in surprise.

"I'm sorry. I didn't realize you were up here," she said.

"It's a nice day. I thought I'd get some vitamin D. Join me. There's enough room for two."

His invitation surprised her, but she was happy to accept. "More than that," she said, taking another seat at the patio table. "Do you ever entertain authors up here?"

"We have occasionally," he said.

She thought of Emerald Austen up there, leaning into Edward and clinking champagne glasses, and forced herself not to frown.

"What were you reading?" she asked.

He held up a copy of John Grisham's latest novel.

"I love him," she said. "Well, his legal thrillers."

"You didn't like *Playing for Pizza*?"

Was he teasing her? She wasn't sure. He was smiling, so maybe. She gave a one-shouldered shrug. "I'm afraid I'm not into football."

"It's really quite entertaining," he said. "The book," he clarified.

"I assume you like football," she said.

"Not as much as basketball. I played some in high school."

It was the most personal sharing he'd volunteered, and she appreciated it.

"You don't have to know all that though," he added.

"It's nice to know something about the people you work with," she said. "It makes you feel like more than just a cog in the machine."

"I hope you don't think of yourself that way. You're a valued member of our team." He cleared his throat. "Anyway, you might enjoy this. It's one of my favorites. I pull it out every once in a while and reread it."

"I understand rereading books," she said. "I've read *Pride and Prejudice* half a dozen times."

He gave a bit of a snort. "Ah, yes, Mr. Darcy, the man every woman loves. I've never understood quite why."

"Because in the end he proves he's truly noble. He and Elizabeth merely misjudged each other."

"And thus began a favorite romance trope," he murmured. Not smiling. "What are you reading now?"

He'd already passed judgment on Jane Austen. She supposed poor Charlotte Brontë wouldn't fare any better.

Sure enough. She showed him the cover and he frowned.

"It is a classic," she argued.

He said nothing. He was no longer looking at her. Instead, he was staring out at the harbor, with its blue waters and boats at rest. "I assume this is another book you've read countless times."

"Actually, I never have," she said. "My book club is reading it and I'm finding it fascinating, although it makes me glad I'm not a woman living in the nineteenth century."

"Every century has its problems, Karissa," he said. He stood. "I'd better get back to work. I'll leave you to read in peace. Enjoy the sunshine."

And then he was gone, leaving her wondering what had just happened. One moment they were in comfortable conversational territory and the next they weren't. They'd taken a wrong turn and she wasn't sure how.

But he was right. Every century had its problems. What were his?

Karissa would be making the trip to Anacortes to visit her family for Memorial Day weekend alone. Mark and Allegra were taking the girls to Great Wolf Lodge, a resort that offered everything from indoor and outdoor water parks to family events and arcades. Karissa and Mark had talked about taking Macy there. Now he was finally following through, just not with her. She supposed Disneyland would be next.

Yet another thorn to pull out of her heart. Divorce, the gift that kept on giving.

"I'm sorry you won't have Macy this weekend," her mother said, "but it's a good trade-off as you'll have her for the Fourth of July."

"True, and I'm glad about that. But look where they're taking her. How am I supposed to compete?"

"You're not. But even if you were, you'll be bringing her to her favorite beach neighborhood to hang out with the friends she's made over the years. Amanda and Elsie and their parents will be visiting Grace and Martin, and the girls all love playing together. We'll have fireworks and homemade ice cream, and the zip line."

Yes, the zip line her dad and brother were going to finish up over the weekend would be a big attraction. Not that it was very long or very high up. Strung between two trees, the ride would last about ten seconds. But it would still be fun. Plus, Macy would have a real beach to play on, not a bunch of chlorinated water pushed through plastic tubes.

Kids loved those tubes.

Never mind. Her mother was right. She was getting the better end of the deal having Macy over the Fourth of July weekend. Maybe they'd invite Lilith. It would be perfect. For Macy, at least. Karissa wasn't sure she'd ever catch sight of perfect again. Unless Edward came, too.

That wasn't perfect, that was fantasy, and she wasn't doing fantasy. She'd been allowing Edward increasingly more space in her thoughts and it was time to stop. It was a waste of time. Better to focus on the good things she already had, the things that were certain.

The weather could be off on Memorial Day weekend, but this time it was nice enough to complete the zip line and share a late-afternoon bonfire on the beach with neighbors. Sunday night she and her brother and parents gathered around the kitchen table and played cards and enjoyed the pie Mom had baked from the last of the blackberries in the freezer, which had to be used up to make room for the upcoming summer harvest. Karissa had contributed snickerdoodles to the evening snack fare, because with two hungry men in the household that pie disappeared faster than you could say blackberry.

The only thing missing to make the weekend perfect was Macy, and Karissa struggled to keep a positive attitude.

"You'll be all right," her father told her as the family made their way to the military section of the cemetery on Monday to lay flowers on Grandpa's grave. "Divorce is hard, but there are worse things in life."

Yes, like war, she thought. Her own battle felt smaller as she took in the sea of grave markers where men who had lost their lives when they'd barely had a chance to live lay buried. She at least still had her life before her, had a chance to rebuild and live it. It was a humbling wake-up call.

"You can do this," she whispered to herself. "You *are* doing this."

So what if she wasn't an Allegra? *Be the best version of yourself*, Annie Wills had advised in her book. *That's all you've got and that's all you need.*

Even humble Jane Eyre had managed to find her HEA. Karissa could, too.

Margot and her mother flew to California to spend Memorial Day weekend with her brother and his family. "Let's not talk about my unemployment, okay?" Margot had said once they met at their gate.

"You should have told your brother," Mom chided. "You should have let me."

"He doesn't need to know. He's got enough to worry about just taking care of his own family. Anyway, I'm fine."

"Are you sure?" Her mother studied her, much the way she had when Margot was a child and Mom was sure Margot was lying about having gotten into her perfume. She had been, but that was another story.

"If you need money…"

Her father had left Mom in good financial shape, and she was carrying on fine without him. Their trip to sunny California wasn't so much about visiting Dad's grave in the veterans' cemetery as it was about dinners out and visiting James, one of Margot's brothers, Mom's pride and joy. James wasn't making a fortune as a teacher, but at least he was steadily employed and doing something applaudably noble, while Margot was…not.

Not that her mother didn't love Margot. Margot knew she did. But it was a love that always found something in need of improving. Margot supposed she'd earned some of that. Between the bad habits she'd picked up as a teen, ending her marriage and then stumbling around trying to replace the man she probably should have stayed with, she was sure she'd given her mother half the gray hairs she kept hidden under that artificially brown hair. James, on the other hand, could do no wrong.

Literally. He'd watched and learned when Margot got in trouble for breaking curfew, sneaking Dad's cigarettes, trying marijuana long before it was legal. And the worst. Getting a D in English Literature. Horrifying! Margot figured she'd read enough books since then to make up for it. She'd graduated cum laude from the University of Washington, landed a good job, gotten promoted, done well. Her father had bragged about her to all his friends. So had her mother. But then came the trials of adulthood and the nagging from the teen years returned.

It was the last thing Margot needed. She felt crappy enough about being ejected from a job she'd been good at. Enough of her identity had been wrapped up in her work that having it taken away had left her angry and frustrated, and yes, insecure. Especially when nothing seemed to be working out. Mom was not helping.

It would be nice if her mother could be a little more like

Margot's daughter, endlessly confident in Margot's abilities. "You've got this, Mom," Elisa said when she'd called to see how Margot was doing after getting laid off. Margot had been so grateful for her support that she'd put fifty dollars on her Starbucks card. Buying her daughter's loyalty was money well spent.

She wasn't spending freely these days. Thank God she'd had enough points with Alaska Airlines that she could score two free tickets. James had three kids, one about ready to graduate from high school. No way could he have flown his family up to Washington for a party weekend, and she would never have dreamed of asking him to fly her down. It hadn't occurred to her mother to offer to pay for the tickets. Mom had been a trophy wife. She was used to selecting goodies off life's platter, not putting them on it. She would be paying for dinner out on Friday night though. That had been settled before they left.

After the plane took off and Mom had settled in with the latest novel everyone was talking about, and Margot pulled up the copy of *Jane Eyre* that she'd loaded onto her phone. *Having a mother to nag you beats being an orphan*, she told herself.

On Monday, when they were picnicking at McKinley Park in Sacramento, the adults enjoying lemonade and chatting while the kids swam, Mom forgot her promise not to blab. "I'm glad at least *your* job is secure," she said to James.

"Unless I crack and quit," he joked. Then he got the underlying message. "Wait a minute. Margot, what's going on with you?"

"She got laid off," Mom answered, and Margot glared at her. "He asked," she said with a shrug.

"It's okay," Margot said to him. "I'll be fine. I'm picking up some side gigs consulting." Organizing people was a form of consulting.

"You didn't tell me." Her mother looked accusingly at her.

"They're only small jobs. I'm working on some other things, too," she added.

"Do you need money?"

As if James could spare any.

"No," Margot said firmly.

"What are you working on?" he asked.

Talk about my app idea in front of Mom, the equivalent of exposing my neck to a vampire, or run away from the subject?

She should run away. Mom, who wanted her to land safely at a big corporation and be done with it, would douse the whole idea with ice water. But part of Margot wanted to show her younger brother that she was still big sister, in control of everything. Especially her own life. Pride won out over sensibility.

"I'm working on an app," she said. That was stretching truth to the breaking point. She had an idea for an app and no funding.

"Yeah?" James, the technology early adopter, was all ears.

"It's for women," Margot said.

"Well, that's sexist," her brother teased.

Margot went on to talk about her idea of making online clothes shopping easier for women. She already knew she was onto something, but the way her sister-in-law, Rolanda, leaned forward confirmed it.

"I would love to have that app," Rolanda gushed. "When will it be in the App Store?"

Maybe never. "I don't know, but I'll keep you posted."

"You're still looking for a job though, aren't you?" Mom asked.

"Of course." But the more doors that closed the more Margot wanted to be her own boss. There had to be a way she could exchange having to be employed for becoming an entrepreneur.

Josie took her triple threat caramel chocolate cake to the annual Friends of the Library picnic. Alice was the better baker of the two of them and it was her recipe, but Josie was never above accepting compliments.

This was an event she never missed, as one of the library's friends had a mansion on the bay with a huge deck and sweeping lawns. And, of course, a dock and a boat and a boat house. It was like knowing Jay Gatsby.

Josie had been involved with the Friends of the Library for years. In the past, she'd come to this gathering with her family in tow. And then, when it was only the two of them, with Coral. She'd also brought Errol the loser, the year before. He hadn't bothered to talk to anyone, had gone back for seconds and thirds at the buffet, and then been ready to go as soon as he'd finished dessert.

"As long as Coral's happy," Portia Berg had said.

There was a difference between being happy and being deluded. Portia was a fool.

And now, here she came, ambling up to where the bottles of Perrier, high-end sodas, white wine, and microbrewery specials had been set out. "No Coral with you this year?" she asked.

"No, she had other plans," Josie said shortly.

Her tone of voice should have been enough to tell Portia to back off, but, of course, she didn't. "Oh? What's she up to?"

"Off raising money for the homeless," Josie lied. Okay, so she didn't want to admit she had no idea what her girl was up to with that loser she'd married. So, sue her.

"Well, that's our Coral. Tell her we missed her here today. I'd have loved to see her little girl, Blossom."

So would Josie.

It was time to change the subject. "How's your son doing these days?"

Last she'd heard Portia's son was in rehab. It was an underhanded tactic to turn the magnifying glass on Portia's life, but Josie knew for a fact that it was the only way she was going to get Portia to move along and find some other stewing pot to stick her long nose in.

Portia got suddenly busy selecting something to drink. "He's doing well, thank you."

"Glad to hear it," Josie said.

Portia was searching the crowd now. "Oh, there's Janice. I need to talk to her about the newsletter."

"Good idea," said Josie, and went to find someone who would chat about something other than kids.

She found her old pal Marigold settled in an Adirondack chair with a glass of white wine and sat on the empty one next to her.

"I do hope you have something to talk about besides your child," Marigold said. Marigold was in her late sixties. She'd never had children and found all discussions about others' offspring boring. In the last two years she'd taken two singles cruises to Hawaii and one in the Mediterranean. She was widowed and on the hunt for a rich husband. No luck yet but she kept on cruisin'.

"I always have something to talk about," Josie said, and Marigold chuckled.

"That you do," she said. "What's new?"

It was a relief for Josie to visit about other things and leave behind her family issues. She bragged about the new book club she'd joined. "It's Alice and I trying to whip two starry-eyed young things with awful taste in books into shape."

She went on to describe their first book club read and Marigold shuddered. "Sounds abysmally clichéd."

"I must admit, my sister's pick wasn't much better. I'm making them read a classic."

"Oh? Which one did you pick?"

"*Jane Eyre.*"

Marigold pulled down her sunglasses and regarded Josie over them. "Really? That melodramatic mess was the best you could do?"

"That book was groundbreaking for its time," Josie argued. "And women making money as writers! Those three accomplished a lot. Anyway, everyone should read at least one Brontë in her lifetime."

"Yes, I suppose you're right," Marigold said but didn't sound convinced.

Marigold was a snob, and Josie was willing to bet nobody had asked her to join a book club.

"I think book clubs are a little silly, anyway," Marigold continued. "Just an excuse for women with no lives to pretend they have a life by sitting around and drinking wine."

Was there a reason Josie had decided to join Marigold? She couldn't remember. The view of the bay was picturesque, but Josie had seen all she wanted to see. It was time to go home and read her melodramatic mess.

Margot and her mother flew home Tuesday. That night Margot went for it and called her ex, the one person she knew had enough money to invest in her idea. He was doing well, on track for partner at his law firm and he had made some smart investments—ones he'd been kind enough to suggest to her and she'd passed on. There was a life lesson in there somewhere.

"I think I have an investment for you that will pay off big," she said after they'd gotten past the we're-still-friends chitchat.

"Yeah?" He sounded suspicious. "Don't tell me you're investing money in something right now when you don't have a job."

"I'm working some side gigs," she said. A couple of jobs for Josie was stretching it, but business was all about facades. "Anyway, this isn't something I'm investing in. It's something I'm starting."

This was met with a very long silence.

"Jax? You still there?"

"I'm listening."

Warily. She plunged on. "You know how much money women spend on clothes."

"All the women in my life have given me a good education," he cracked.

But lightheartedly. She took it as a good sign and plunged on. "These days a lot of us get tempted by the things we see online."

"There's an understatement," he said, and she could envision the eye roll. Margot knew that Wife Number Two spent a lot of time on TikTok, and, like Margot, she loved cute clothes. Unlike Margot, she could still afford to shop.

"Well, I have an app that is going to be what every woman needs."

"What every woman needs, huh? Does it print money?"

"Spoken like a true jaded family man," Margot said. "But I'm serious here."

"Okay, sorry. You've got my attention," he said.

She moved into her pitch, sharing the same business plan she'd presented to Oliver Blackwood, cowardly loan officer. "I'd pay you back and give you ten percent of the business."

"Yeah? For old times' sake?" he teased.

"And because it's only right. You could stand to make a lot of money," she finished.

"Only if it works."

"It will," she assured him.

"That's a pretty generous offer, Margot."

"Fair is fair, and I can't do this without the extra cash."

"Knowing you, I'm sure you have pages of documents for me to wade through."

"Yes, I have a business plan. How'd you guess?"

"Email the documents to me and let me take a look."

Once he saw all her facts and figures he'd be on board. Jackson didn't like to miss out on an opportunity to make money. Plus he was enough of a visionary to see this as a good investment.

It was nine the next morning when he called. He had some questions and they ironed out a few more details, then he finally said, "Okay, I can loan you fifty K."

Yes! That plus what she had in savings should just about do it.

"Thanks, Jax. I owe you."

"Yes, you do," he said, and chuckled.

All right! She had money. She could hire a developer.

She'd started doing her research weeks earlier so she'd be ready if and when the time came and had already found one in nearby Tacoma. *We can make any app,* bragged App Apes on their website. *Here at App Apes, we offer both the skill and the imagination needed to help you succeed with your project,* it said in the About Us section. *Andrew Logan worked ten years providing cyber security before launching his business and his expertise gives him a clear understanding of what is needed to make a successful app.* A clear understanding, a tech expert—that was what she needed.

She called and got voice mail. "If we're not picking up it means we're helping a customer create a successful app. Please leave a message and someone will get back with you as soon as possible."

Well, okay. She left her message.

Twenty minutes later someone did, indeed, call her. It was Andrew Logan, himself. He had one of those voices people labeled as pleasant, a kind of friendly voice that said, *I am all about making you successful,* and Margot was hoping that voice could deliver.

"I have some time tomorrow at four o'clock. Would you like to come in then?" he asked.

"Let me check my schedule." She paused a moment, a busy creator, looking at her calendar. Haha. "That should work fine."

"All right, I'll see you tomorrow."

The address wasn't in the business district where she'd worked, but that didn't bother Margot. This was probably a small business, and so many people, especially techies, worked remote now. Maybe this Andrew Logan had set up shop in his basement. Who knew? Geeks and computer nerds did what they wanted.

The next day she pulled up in front of a small, gray house with a big view. This place was worth a few pennies. The office was in a separate building which probably at one time had been a detached garage.

There on the window of the entrance was the company logo, an ape wearing glasses and working over a laptop. She opened the door and walked in to see a desk holding a laptop with a couple of midcentury modern chairs in front of it. A bookcase housed a varied collection of books—some looked like textbooks and others she thought might be novels. Over it hung a painting with a cynical kid sitting on an upturned crate, painting a quote for Diogenes: "One Original Thought Is Worth a Thousand Mindless Quotings." Interesting.

And rising from the desk, talk about interesting. Andrew Logan was tall and lean with sandy hair and hazel eyes hiding behind designer framed glasses. He wore Levis and a long-sleeved brown cotton shirt that made her think of chocolate. He made her think of chocolate—yum! No wedding ring on the finger.

Here to do business, remember? Anyway, he looked younger than her.

Not that much. And she was not a cougar.

Yet.

"You must be Margot Burns," he said, coming around the desk to shake her hand.

He had nice hands, with long tapered fingers—not calloused, but firm. Did he have some kind of electric buzzer implanted in his palm? She hadn't felt a zing like that in a long time, bringing heat up her arm and nearly to her face.

"I am," she said. "I found you online. It looks like you've got what I need. For my business," she added, more as a reminder to herself than for him.

"I'm good at what I do," he said.

"I bet you are." Good. At what he did. "At what you do." Margot cleared her throat and shifted into business overdrive. "I did have one thing that concerned me. I didn't see a lot of testimonials from satisfied customers."

"That's because I haven't had a lot of customers yet," he said. "It takes time to develop an app." He held out his hands. "As you can see, it's only me. I'm a fairly new start-up, and there's only so much time. I've been pretty selective about who I work with. An idea has to excite me."

Margot raised an eyebrow and said lightly, "Who's interviewing whom here?" This felt like some kind of power play.

He laughed. "Don't get me wrong. I need business, same as anyone else, but, like I said, there's only one of me. If you need to find a bigger firm, I get that. They'll charge you more."

"Okay, let's talk money. How much will you charge me?"

"I can only give you a ballpark price. I'd need a couple of days to work up an accurate quote."

"So, take me out to the ball game," she said.

He smiled at that. "I like your sense of humor."

And she liked him, but the bottom line was, would she like his work? "Here's what I'm wanting to do," she said, and explained the app to him.

He nodded when she'd finished. "Rad. I think this could go big for you. If you've done your research, you'll know stuff like this doesn't come cheap though," he said.

"I have and I know. But, back to the ballpark."

"Here's my best guess off the top of my head, but don't hold me to it," he said, and gave her a number.

"I can work with that if you come close. I've got some money of my own and I have an investor."

"If we decide to go forward, I'll need a third of the money up front," he said.

"Not a problem."

"Well, then, let me do some calculating and I'll call you in a couple of days. I'm pretty good at reading people, and I think we could work well together."

Yes, they could. "Great," she said. "Meanwhile, I'll want to talk with your previous client."

"No problem."

She did talk to his satisfied customer, and that satisfied her. She made a run to the grocery store and got champagne, as well as crackers and some fancy dips. While waiting in the checkout line she called both Alice and Josie. "Come on over and help me celebrate. I've got funding for my app and I'm getting started."

Both sisters promised to be there, and Alice said she'd get busy baking.

Karissa was invited as well and promised to be over as soon as she'd dropped Macy off at the library for a special kid event that was going on. So excited for you, she texted.

I'm excited for me, too, Margot texted back. She was doing something she never had dreamed she'd be doing when she was let go. No, call that what it was—kicked to the curb. That was in the past now. She'd make her millions and thumb her nose at Groundwork Planning, Inc.

It was seven forty and the women had enjoyed Alice's lemon bars and were getting ready to toast Margot's success when she got the call. She'd texted Jackson earlier to let him know that she'd found the perfect company to help her develop her app, and he probably wanted details.

"Hey there," she chirped. "I guess you're wanting some more details."

"Umm, not exactly."

There was no excitement in his voice. She could feel the blood rushing around her body, scrambling to get away from the coming tidal wave and she braced herself.

"I'm afraid I've got some bad news."

12

"Looking back, he realized that missed opportunity
not only saved him from a disastrous investment,
but also turned him in a new direction and enabled him
to launch what is now a multi-million-dollar company."
—from *Close Calls* by Gisella Strom

THE OTHER WOMEN SAW MARGOT'S SMILE CRUMBLE
and their happy chatter stopped. The whole room turned
silent as the sky before the thunderstorm broke.

"What is it, Jackson?" she asked, even though she already
knew.

"I can't help you out after all."

Oh, no. "Do you need a bigger percentage of the company?
Want me to pay you interest on the loan? I will."

Sales pitches after someone's mind was made up never
worked. It was like hurling yourself against the Great Wall of
China and expecting it to topple. She was feeling light-headed
and set her glass of champagne on the coffee table.

"Look, it's not that I don't want to, but Clarice is not on
board with this."

"You'll make your money back and then some," Margot said,
still hurling herself against the Wall.

Josie was scowling, ready to put the hurt on whoever was messing with Margot. Margot should sic Josie on Clarice.

"You know the situation. I have one more year of tuition to pay for Elisa and the twins are graduating this year. They both picked out-of-state colleges and it's going to cost me a bundle. They're not exactly college scholarship material."

That was for sure. Someone had turned the dimmer switch way down on his stepsons' brains.

And someone had sure turned down the dimmer switch on Jackson's for him to let his wife talk him into backing out of a business agreement. Sure, no papers had been signed yet. The last papers they'd signed had been their divorce papers ten years earlier. But since then they'd both always been as good as their word. She'd never imagined he'd go back on his.

"And I promised Clarice I'd take them all to Spain this year."

"Did you tell her the money you're going to make with this deal could buy her a house in Spain?"

"I'm sorry, Margot, I really am. I shouldn't have made such a big financial decision without talking to her first."

Margot sighed. "Of course not. But damn it all, Jackson, you sure screwed me."

"If it's any consolation, I know I'm gonna regret this," he said.

If she wasn't so frustrated and disappointed and just plain mad, she'd have smiled. "Yeah, you are. Maybe I'll buy that house in Spain and rent it to you guys."

"Rub it in," he said. "And look, if it turns out you only need ten K, circle back. I can probably kick in that much."

"Thanks. I will," she said. But she knew she wouldn't because she didn't know anyone else with a huge pile of money to gamble. Ten thousand wouldn't add enough to her money pile to take her where she wanted to go. She was done. She ended the call and drank her entire glass of champagne without coming up for air.

"Okay, what happened?" Josie demanded.

"I lost my investor. I'm at a dead end. I thought my ex was going to come through for me, but his wife stopped the deal."

"We could invest," Alice said.

"Not the kind of money she needs. Our financial managers would lock us up," Josie said.

Margot shook her head. "I couldn't ask you to, anyway. I think it's a great idea, but it is still a gamble. My ex could afford it, but I wouldn't do that to you guys."

"Damn, this sucks," said Josie.

Yes, it did.

"Something's got to work out," said Alice. "Have a lemon bar."

If only it was a gold bar.

Her friends did their best to console her, then left her to mourn her loss with the remaining lemon bars. Forget the lemon bars. She got in her car and drove to the store to get cigarettes.

She got in the checkout line, looking like the human version of Oscar the Grouch. Fumed. Wished all manner of evil on Wife Number Two.

Then realized that she'd have done the same thing in Clarice's shoes. *Lend your ex fifty thousand of our money? Are you nuts?*

It was only an idea. The idea would still be there once she got a job. If she got a job.

She slapped away that negative thought. She'd get a job, of course. And then she'd go back to the bank and try again. Her dream wasn't dead. It was…sleeping. A change in circumstances would wake it up.

And what was she doing? Was a cigarette going to help her?

She left the line, left the store, and drove home, pawed through her nightstand drawer and pulled out a piece of nicotine gum. Then she got online to see what new job opportunities had surfaced since the week before. None.

Well, something would. She'd figure things out. Meanwhile, she had a phone call to make.

Her call to Andrew Logan at App Apes went to voice mail. "If we're not picking up it means we're helping a customer create a successful app..."

She sighed. That someone wouldn't be her.

At least not yet.

Alice's grocery delivery arrived. As always, she tipped the delivery person ten dollars. She didn't care what Josie said about the money she was wasting doing this. It was worth it to her, and what was ten dollars here and there?

She began to unpack the goodies. Bananas, yes, and still partly green as she'd requested. There was the cream of mushroom soup—store brand, so much cheaper than name brand. Look at all the money she saved doing that. There were the frozen raspberries and blueberries. But where was her pint of Ben and Jerry's chocolate chip mint ice cream? And what was this? Frozen sausage rolls? She hadn't ordered that. She wanted her ice cream, darn it all.

She went online to the store's site and started filling out the proper form, grumbling all the way. "I'm not paying for sausage rolls," she muttered. Since they were now in her freezer, well, maybe she'd try them, but they were a poor substitute for ice cream.

She was still typing and muttering when she received a call from her old friend Donna. "Guess where I am," Donna sang.

Who knew? Donna lived in Idaho, but she was always traveling somewhere.

"I give up. Where?" Alice asked.

"I'm in Seattle. Remember I said I was going to take an Alaska cruise? Well, I am. We don't ship out until later today and I thought maybe you could run on into the city and we could have lunch. It's been ages."

It had. In fact, she and Alice hadn't seen each other in years. Charlie had still been alive the last time they'd gotten together.

Charlie. The memory of sitting next to his hospital bed, holding his hand as he took his last breath brought the tears swimming to her eyes and, for a moment, made it hard for her to catch her own breath.

Then the thought of driving into Seattle—across the bridge, on the freeway!—had her almost hyperventilating. "I'm sorry, Donna, I can't. I've got too much going on." *Inside my head.*

"Oh, darn. Well, it's my fault. I should have given you more notice. I could have come in a day early and we could have stayed at the Edgewater."

"That would have been fun," Alice said wistfully.

"Well, hey, here's an idea. Maybe I'll change my flight and stay an extra day or two when I get back."

"Oh, no, don't do that for me," Alice said. "I really can't do anything now. I'm still sorting things out here."

"Still, after all this time?"

Donna was divorced, had been for years. She didn't understand the concept of loss. She would one day, though. Death eventually stole into everyone's life and took away someone special.

"I'm sorry," Alice said.

She was. Sorry to disappoint her friend, sorry to miss spending time with her, to miss out on the fun, sorry that parts of her life were shrinking. But sorry was all she had. Sorry was all she could do.

"Well, let's look ahead. Maybe later this year. Or next year. We could take a cruise together."

"I'd like that," said Alice. But really, would she? Without Charlie?

★ ★ ★

Margot was back at Josie's house, this time organizing the kitchen.

"How long have you had these cookie sheets?" she asked Josie as she held one up. The things looked like they'd been around since World War I.

Josie snatched it away. "They were wedding presents. And I still use them."

Margot sighed. "Okay, no throwing out crappy cookie sheets."

"Very funny."

"I don't know why you keep hiring me if you don't want to let me help you."

"You *are* helping me," Josie insisted. "And we've had this conversation before. I don't see the point in throwing things out simply because they're old. I'm old."

"You wouldn't fit in the garbage can," Margot teased, and was surprised she could find any humor in anything. Her last conversation with her ex still lay heavily on her, a disappointment hangover.

Her crack brought a smile from Josie and a slow shake of the head. "Anybody ever tell you you're a cheeky little brat?"

"You." Margot continued her search of the cupboards. "Okay, you do not need two colanders. Don't even try to tell me you do."

"Okay, fine. I'll keep the blue one. The other one can go to Goodwill."

"And you don't need two double boilers, so which one is going to go?"

Josie sighed and pointed. "That one, I guess."

"It will be a lot easier to organize your cupboards with the duplicates gone," Margot said.

"I suppose you're right."

Josie admitting someone else was right? Mark that on the calendar.

"You gonna stay for lunch?" she asked as they filled another box with donations. "I'm making chicken curry sandwiches on olive bread."

"Sounds great. I'm staying."

Josie knew how to put together a sandwich. "This is amazing," Margot said as she reached for a second helping. Josie had laid them out on a plate, cut in quarters and garnished them with parsley.

"Yeah, these are my daughter's favorites."

A mention of the invisible daughter. "Am I ever going to meet her?" asked Margot.

"Maybe. Have the parsley, too," Josie said, moving them away from the subject of her daughter. "It's good for your breath."

"It is? I never knew that."

"Handy to know. Eat a mouthful before you go on a date. It's better than breath mints."

"I'm not planning on going on any dates," Margot said.

"Why the heck not? Is your life that busy?"

"Dating is a waste of time. I've never been able to get relationships right."

"Who does? But you're still young. You shouldn't give up. Get out there and find a man. Go dancing, have sex. You know what they say, use it or lose it."

"You're a fine one to be giving advice," Margot said, pointing a sprig of parsley at Josie. "I don't see you looking for a man."

"I don't need one anymore. And besides, I had my time."

"You make it sound like you're ancient."

Josie's brows pulled together, and the frown line canyons made their appearance. "I didn't say that. I just said I had my time. Now it's over and that's that. Anyway, at this age, men just want to sit around in recliners and watch TV and get waited on."

"How did you get so cynical?" Margot scolded.

"Years of training," Josie cracked. "I'm serious here. You're still a young woman. There's more to life than looking for jobs and organizing cupboards. And apps," she added.

And apps. Margot sighed.

"If that app idea of yours is meant to be it will work out eventually. Meanwhile, you need to get out and have some fun."

"Book club is fun," Margot argued.

"Yeah, it is, but if we're all there is to your social life you've got trouble, girl." Margot made a face and Josie continued. "I mean it. We all need stories, we all love stories, but we also need to live our own stories. Books should encourage you to do that. They shouldn't be a substitute."

"I have a life." She walked with Karissa, took her runs around the neighborhood. Had lunch in Seattle with her daughter once a month. Josie's cocked eyebrow dared her to continue. "I can only focus on so many things at once."

Josie had a comeback for that. "We women are multi-taskers."

"That's a myth," Margot said flatly. Anyway, she didn't want to add looking for love to her list of tasks. That would be a bigger waste of time than looking for a job.

Andrew Logan strolled into her thoughts. There wouldn't be anything happening with him now, business or otherwise.

Margot shoved away her plate. "Let's get back to work."

"That's the trouble with the young. They never listen," Josie muttered and started clearing the table. "By the way, I told my neighbor Victoria about you."

"Didn't you once say your neighbors were stinkers?"

"Not all of them," Josie said stiffly. "Victoria's a sweetie."

Lucky Victoria, she'd won the Josie seal of approval.

"She wants to hire you to help her sort through her things."

"Thanks for the referral," Margot said.

"I want to see you get some money coming in."

Margot was touched. "I appreciate that," she said.

And she appreciated Josie's concern for her. The woman was the human equivalent of a porcupine—all quills on the outside, something softer underneath.

"You may not thank me after you see the house," Josie replied. "Just remember, it's money. And another reference for future clients. I told her I'd bring you over when we were done here."

When people said, "Just remember," it usually meant they were about to suck you into something you wanted to forget. What was the deal with Josie's neighbor?

An hour later they walked across the street to Victoria Adams's house. The first impression wasn't too bad, although the flower beds needed weeding and the lawn was a little scruffy.

"She needs a gardener?" Margot guessed.

"She's got a lawn service coming to mow the lawn. She needs some help with the inside of the house."

Some? thought Margot once they were inside. Where was Victoria's living room floor? Buried under boxes, furniture, and piles of scrapbooks and photo albums. The coffee table held columns of old magazines. A bookcase overflowed with books, and its surface was a clutter of crafted knickknacks. Skeins of yarn in various colors were trying to climb out of one box. A suitcase was propped up against an overstuffed chair holding a stack of quilts. A suitcase. Was Victoria planning on running away? If Margot had to live in this she'd be planning on it, for sure.

Victoria, herself, was a slender woman, with white hair and a face crisscrossed with lines. She was dressed neatly in a pair of gray slacks, a flowered blouse and comfy-looking pink sneakers. She didn't look like a hoarder. Although who knew what a hoarder looked like?

"I'm not a hoarder," she said as if reading Margot's mind.

"I've watched those shows." She looked around at the mess in front of them. "My grandson's been after me to get rid of some things and I've been trying but I'm not making much progress." She let out a breath. "I feel a little overwhelmed."

"I can understand that," said Margot. She felt a little overwhelmed herself.

"Josie thought you might be able to help me."

"She will," Josie said. As if Margot had already agreed to work with this woman.

Maybe it was a given that she would. How could she not? Still, this was… a lot, and now Josie had baked her into a guilt corner.

"I lost my daughter to cancer two years ago this coming week, and I must admit I haven't had much desire to bother with anything since," Victoria said.

"I'm sorry for your loss," Margot said. The words felt unsubstantial and useless, incapable of holding up in the light of the kind of loss Victoria had suffered.

"We all die. You just never expect to see your child die before you." Victoria shook her head. "I used to love to garden, you know. And quilt. My daughter was the knitter. The yarn was hers. She lived with me."

Which was why the yarn was still living with Victoria. "What's in the other boxes?" Margot asked.

"More yarn," Victoria answered with a sigh.

"I'm done with Margot for the day," Josie said to Victoria. "Why don't you use her for the afternoon?"

What was she, a garden tool to be shared? Margot frowned at Josie. Referrals were one thing. Running her life was a different matter.

"That would be wonderful. Could you help me?" Victoria asked.

"Of course, she could. She's an expert in organizing," said Josie, fitting flattery and bossiness into one sentence.

"I think I could use some expert advice," said Victoria.

She could use a dumpster.

"But I doubt I can afford you," Victoria said to Margot.

"It's all right. I already paid Margot for today, but we got done early. Right, Margot?" Then, before Margot could speak, Josie added, "So you may as well take advantage of her expertise for a couple of hours."

"Could I?" Victoria looked hopefully at Margot.

The woman needed help and it would have been callous to refuse. "Of course," Margot said.

"All right. That's that. I'm out of here," Josie said and started for the door.

"I'll walk you out," said Margot.

As soon as the front door was shut behind them, Josie and Margot both began to speak at once.

"You could have warned me," Margot said.

"I'll pay you double," Josie said.

Margot frowned at her. "You don't get to decide who I take on as a client."

"You wouldn't leave her in that mess, would you?" Josie argued.

"No, I can't, but I don't need you making my decisions for me. And you don't have to pay me."

"Are you trying to mess with my good deed?" Josie demanded.

"Maybe. Maybe I'm capable of doing a good deed occasionally myself."

"Don't be a drip. You need the money. And stop standing out here arguing with me. Victoria's waiting."

Yes, she was. "We'll talk about this later," Margot threatened.

Josie wasn't intimidated. She gave Margot a superior smile and walked back to her house.

Margot went back inside to deal with Victoria. She suspected that there would be more reminiscing than there would organizing.

Victoria did, indeed, need to reminisce. They looked through photo albums and Margot heard all about her life and, more important to Victoria, her daughter's life—her sports awards, her community service, her two children who, sadly, did not live in the state and weren't able to visit often.

"After she lost her husband, she moved in with me. She was determined to take care of me in my old age. We had such fun at first—trying new recipes, doing quilt projects together. She loved crafts of all kinds and was teaching me how to knit. I'm not very good at it though," Victoria confessed, "and I'm getting arthritis in my fingers, so it's a little painful."

"Maybe your daughter would say it's okay if you donated that yarn to a thrift store." There was enough in all those boxes to stock an entire yarn shop. "I'm sure some other knitter would consider it a real find." Hopefully. Margot knew nothing of knitting. "It would be one small way to honor her."

Victoria brightened. "You think so?"

"I do. I could put those boxes in my trunk and drop them off today."

Victoria bit down on her bottom lip, regarded the boxes. Parting with them probably felt like giving up a secret treasure stash.

"I really think your daughter would approve," Margot said softly.

Victoria was still biting her lip, but she nodded.

"And what about the suitcase?" Margot asked.

"I think I'll just put that back under the bed in the guest room."

"Are you sure?" She had hauled it out.

Victoria nodded again. "We were going to take a trip." She stopped and pressed her lips together so hard they turned white around the edges.

"I think under the bed in the guest room is probably fine," Margot said.

"It's down the hall on the right."

Margot stowed the suitcase under a bed that had seen a population explosion of dolls and stuffed animals. There was barely room underneath, between shoeboxes and tote bags and more carry-on suitcases. Even a violin case. Time and memory were both big collectors. Once the suitcase was stowed she parked her car in Victoria's driveway and loaded up the boxes of yarn before Victoria could change her mind.

She also convinced Victoria to let her take her photos to a company that would digitize them. "You're not getting rid of them. You're simply putting them in a form that's easier to store. Also, I can put them in a digital picture frame where you can play them to run any time you want. Better than watching TV, right?"

Victoria looked dubious. "You're not going to lose them," she fretted.

"I'm not. I promise."

"Are you bonded or insured?" Victoria demanded.

Crap. Margot hadn't thought of that. She should have.

"I am," she lied. She would be as of that afternoon. It was a business necessity.

And one thing she knew for sure, even if she only continued it as a side gig, she was going to keep growing this little business of hers. Seeing floor space open up in Victoria's living room, knowing she was offering both practical help and the comfort of a listening ear gave her a feeling of accomplishment she hadn't felt in a long time.

"I think I'm ready to quit for the day," Victoria said, looking at the quilts.

Margot could well imagine. Going through precious possessions and deciding what to keep and what to part with, remembering the emotional highs and lows of life—it was draining.

"You accomplished a lot today," she said. The room almost looked like a living room again.

"*We* accomplished a lot," Victoria corrected her. "And I must say, I feel somehow lighter. Could I hire you to come back again and help me a little more?"

Margot thought of the crowded guest room bed. There was a lot of little left. "I think that could be arranged."

But could Victoria afford her? She lived in a nice neighborhood and had a nice house which, hopefully, was paid for. But she was probably on a fixed income. Was Josie planning on subsidizing her? Margot couldn't let her do that.

"Do you take checks?"

"I do."

"And what do you charge?"

Margot felt guilty naming a price. "Price is negotiable," she said. "You tell me what you can afford to pay and that's what I'll charge you."

"Ten dollars an hour?" Victoria looked hopefully at her.

Less than minimum wage in Washington. "That will be fine." It would also be no way to run a business. If she did that for everyone she'd go broke. "But that's my special Victoria rate, so keep it top secret."

Victoria beamed. "Thank you."

"My pleasure." And it had been.

She dropped off the boxes at Goodwill and then went home, got on a site where she could create business cards and got busy designing. She decided against any cute graphics, instead putting her name in bold block letters. Under it went her new company name, Simply Organized, LLC. Doing the proper paperwork for that would come next, along with lining up insurance.

This was crazy. Her mother would say she was crazy. She needed a secure job and dependable income. But until that time came, she had to do something. This was something. And if more somethings showed up, she'd do them, too. Jump and the net will appear.

Who had come up with that, anyway? What a ridiculous saying.

Her mother called right after she'd finished talking with an insurance agent. "I was just thinking about you and thought I'd check in," Mom said.

Oh, boy. Margot braced herself.

"How's your job hunt going? Do you have any interviews lined up?"

"No, but I've got my side jobs, so you don't have to worry."

"But then what about your unemployment?"

"I've already dealt with all of that, and Washington State and I have it worked out."

That shut her mother up. But only for a moment. "I hope you're not wasting time on that silly app."

Margot was trying to formulate an answer that wouldn't start a fight when another call came in. She knew that number. "Sorry, Mom, I've got to take this call."

"Is it a job offer?"

"It's business," Margot said and ended their call.

"This is Andrew Logan from App Apes," said a male voice. "I got your message. Sorry to hear you lost your backer, but I think you might be onto something with this, and I have a proposition for you."

A proposition. Hope exploded in her chest and her heart began to beat as if she was running an Olympic track event. "What did you have in mind?" *Please let it be something good.*

13

"I'VE BEEN THINKING ABOUT THIS APP OF YOURS AND
I think we should meet and talk further," said Andrew.

Margot would have liked nothing better than to meet with
Andrew Logan, but talking business would be a waste of time.
"There's no point since I no longer have my financial backing."

"I got that. But I've got a business proposition for you."

"Okay," she said slowly. "I'm listening."

"Let's talk it out in person. Where do you want to meet?"

"Gig Harbor." Let him come to her.

He did. They met the next day at Fog and Fern Coffee
House, and she didn't need that Americano to give her a jolt.
Simply seeing Andrew Logan walk through the door with a
messenger bag slung over his shoulder, the sun at his back, did
that. He looked casual and classy in jeans and a blue, light-
weight sweater with the sleeves pushed up to show off beautifully sinewed forearms.

Business, she reminded herself. *You're here to talk business.*

So, of course, she had dressed like the professional she was, in gray slacks, a white blouse and a navy jacket, black heels on her feet, small gold ball earrings in her ears and a square opal wrap bracelet on her wrist. She'd thought she looked classy hot when she'd checked herself in the mirror before leaving. Seeing Mr. Casual, she felt overdressed, like she was trying too hard.

She stood up and extended her hand like a good little professional. He shook it and for a moment she found herself thinking some very unprofessional thoughts, picturing those long fingers roaming through her hair.

"I think, after this we can bag the handshake, don't you?" he suggested.

There was a lot to unpack in that sentence. After this? After what? And bag the handshake? What did that mean?

"That's more for strangers meeting for the first time. I don't want to be strangers."

Funny, neither did she. "What did you have in mind?"

"Looks like you already got your coffee," he said, pointing to her cup. "Mind if I get one?"

"Not at all."

"Can I get you anything to go with that?"

"No, I'm good."

"Be right back," he said, and she watched as he walked to the order counter. Lean and…lithe. Andrew Logan was the whole package—brains and bod and, so far, nice.

The world was one of facades though.

Coffee in hand, he returned and settled across from her at the table. "Let me just say this up-front. I know what I'm about to propose requires a major leap of faith on your part, but it could be a win for both of us."

"I'm listening," she said. She took a sip of her coffee and braced herself.

"I think this app really has potential and I'd like to work on it with you. But—"

Here came the but.

"I need to eat and pay the bills. You said you lost your funding and I'm wondering if you lost all of it."

"I had some money of my own," she said cautiously.

"Well, I'm thinking, if you can give me something up-front, say, ten thousand, then, instead of you having to foot the bill for the rest of the work, I'll develop this for you in exchange for twenty-five percent of the business once it's up and running. A sort of partnership."

She almost choked on her coffee. "Twenty-five percent?" She'd only offered Jackson ten percent, and they knew each other and had a history together. Plus bringing in a relative stranger felt risky.

"I know it sounds like a lot."

"It does."

"But when you consider how much time I'd be investing, I don't think it's unreasonable."

"I think it is. Twenty-five percent of my profits forever?"

"I'm developing the app and I'd be the one keeping it updated."

She studied him. "I hardly know you. You could really mess me over, copyright the code in your name."

"I'll walk you through the process and you can do the copyrighting. Get a contract written up that nails me to the wall if I try to mess you over."

She could do that. Jackson would, at least, put together a contract for her. Being a lawyer, he'd make sure she was legally protected.

"I get what you're saying though," Andrew continued. "You don't know me, I don't know you. We're both taking a chance. In a way, I'm taking the bigger chance because I'm pretty much doing this on spec. If it flops, I'm out a lot of time and have nothing much to show for it."

"Except for what I'm giving you up-front," she reminded him. "And I'll be out a chunk of change."

"That could happen even if you found the funding and hired someone else to develop this and it tanked. It's a gamble. A pretty smart one, though, I think. That's why I'd like to be part of it."

She sat for a moment, considering. She wanted to move forward with the app. He was offering her a way to do it. She'd been willing to pay out a large amount of money. She'd still end up paying, but with this option it was considerably less, and she wouldn't have to get a loan. Of the two of them, he was the one taking the bigger gamble in offering to forgo a large chunk of income.

"All right," she said. "But first, let's talk more about you and your company."

"The business version of speed dating?" he joked.

"Something like that."

"What do you want to know?"

"Everything about your business looks good on the surface."

"You're wanting to look beneath the surface."

"Just a little."

"Go for it. I've got no problem with that."

"I talked to your last client, and he spoke highly of you. I know you said you're a new startup, but how long have you been in business? Your website doesn't say."

"Two years."

This definitely qualified as a new start-up.

"Don't worry. I know what I'm doing," he added. "My qualifications are right there on the website. I do good work, and I work my hump off."

Margot could identify with that.

"How's your cash flow?" she asked.

He grinned. "Worried if I'll be able to keep the lights on?"

"Just wondering."

"I saved enough to live on when I first started the company, so it gave me a cushion. I'm in good shape."

Very smart, she thought.

"Makes it a lot easier to work when I'm not stressed about paying the bills. I don't have to worry about side gigs."

"It's good to be able to pay the bills," she said. She was going to have to get busy and pick up a lot more work, herself. But back to him. "I guess your cushion's gotten a little flat since you started?"

"I have expenses, like everyone else."

"Of course," she murmured.

"How am I doing here?"

"Okay," she said.

The big question was, how was she doing? She'd been working toward this moment, trying to pull this together. Now that the moment had arrived, she felt like a kid on a diving board, looking down at that water and deciding whether or not she really wanted to jump.

But of course, she wanted to. She could always find a way to make more money. She wouldn't always stumble on a great idea. It was now or never, and Andrew Logan had just offered her a way to make it now.

He drank some of his coffee, slung an arm over his chair and settled back. "Tell me more about you."

She'd been perfectly happy to dig around in his life. She supposed fair was fair. "I was in management and got let go when my company decided to cut costs. I still think they made a bad decision when they cut me loose," she added.

"I bet they did," he said. "Looking on the bright side, would you be trying something like this if you were still working?"

"Probably not. I wouldn't have had time."

"Well, there you go."

She frowned at her half-empty coffee mug. "Employment

has its advantages, especially when you're trying to get a business loan."

"That why your funding fell through? The bank wanted you to have a job?"

"Collateral and savings don't impress as much as a steady paycheck. I'm working up something on the side now, but it's way too new to count. That wasn't what fell through. I had something else lined up." No way was she telling him what. "Maybe it's for the best it didn't work out."

If, heaven forbid, this app didn't go like she anticipated, she'd have been years paying Jackson back. And if the bank had loaned her money on her house and it bombed…? Partnering up with Andrew Logan really was the safest bet.

"Maybe. Things have a way of working out the way they're supposed to," he said. "You know this is going to take time to develop."

She'd done her research. "I know."

"And it is a gamble."

"Are you trying to talk yourself out of this?" she teased.

"No, just making sure your expectations are realistic."

"I'm well aware of the risks, and since you're asking for a percentage of the profits, I assume you are also," she said.

"I am. I just want you to understand what you're getting into."

Wasn't that why she'd been asking questions, checking up on him? "I said I was aware of the risks."

"You get this testy this quickly?"

"Only when people insinuate that I'm incompetent."

"Never said that."

Now he had her feeling small. "Sorry," she said. She'd let her mother's constant nagging turn her into a prickly pear.

"It's okay. Better to be honest about what you're feeling than bury that stuff. In the end, it makes for an easier working relationship. So, what do you say? Are you up for doing this?"

"Yes, and I promise I won't be hard to work with."

He laughed. "That's what they all say."

"No, really. You're the expert. I have some ideas for how I want it to look though. We can discuss them once we have a signed contract."

"Bring it on," he said and smiled at her. He had the kind of smile that reached to his eyes and warmed his entire face, and that warmth spread out to touch her. "I'm looking forward to working on it with you."

The little kid in her wanted to clap her hands and cry, "Yippee!" She had to remain professional, but she did allow herself a big answering smile. "I'll have my lawyer draw up the contract."

"Shoot it to me when it's ready and I'll have mine look it over."

Contracts and lawyers, all very professional. Margot half wished they'd met under different circumstances. Andrew Logan was someone she'd have liked to do all kinds of things with besides business. Oh, well. You couldn't have everything.

Macy had been invited to Lilith's house for dinner. House? *More like a mansion,* thought Karissa as they pulled up in front of a mammoth home perched on a hill overlooking the harbor. It was white and pristine, with a large front yard encased in a trimmed laurel hedge. Karissa was very happy with her home, but she still felt a moment of house lust as she followed her daughter, who was skipping up the stone walkway to the double front door. Edward Elliot lived like a prince.

Lilith had been watching for her friend and swung the door wide. "We're having lasagna and French bread," she announced, pulling Macy inside, "and my grandma made cupcakes for dessert, and we get to decorate them. And Grandma wants to meet your mom."

As if on cue, an older woman with stylish gray hair, wearing a gray turtleneck top and jeans with pink flats appeared in the hallway. "Hello, I'm Honor Elliot. It's lovely to get to meet Macy's mother. And Edward has told me how valuable you are to his team."

He had? Karissa felt her face flush like a kid who had just been praised by her teacher for doing a good job on her homework.

"Thank you," she murmured.

"I hope you'll join us for dinner," said Honor.

Would that be professional? Would Edward mind? Had his mother consulted with him?

"Oh, I don't know," Karissa began. Except Edward had been to her house with his daughter and dropped her off to play several times since. They weren't simply boss and employee, they were parents whose children were friends. And work was over for the day.

"Please, do. Edward is off at the racquet club playing tennis and I'd enjoy the company."

No Edward. Karissa smiled to hide her confusing mix of disappointment and relief. "Thank you. I'd love to."

Karissa stepped inside and tried not to gawk, although the place looked like it should have been featured in *WestSound Magazine*. To her left she saw a door opening onto a library with shelves filled with books reaching from floor to ceiling. It housed two fat leather armchairs, an antique writing table and a window seat. Before her stretched a huge living room with an entire wall of windows offering a sweeping view of the harbor, the water glistening in the early evening sunlight. Thick area rugs spread over hardwood floors and the furniture was all in shades of tan and cream. A showroom.

The kitchen and the great room beyond it looked less for show and more for living. The quartz countertops were cluttered with canisters, a bowl of fruit, an open cookbook and some scattered homework papers. A rack of cupcakes sat on one end, along with a bowl of frosting. The promised cupcakes.

The family room area was an extension of the kitchen. Karissa imagined this was where the family put up the Christmas tree and opened presents. This was where friends came and hung out. It held a couple of worn easy chairs and a large couch. A silly painting of dogs. A large TV was mounted over a fireplace, and a painting of Mount Rushmore with a bright yellow rubber duck replacing Teddy Roosevelt hung on another wall.

Honor saw her looking. "My son's warped sense of humor. Don't ask me what he saw in that."

"I'm not sure I even want to ask *him*," said Karissa.

The painting felt at odds with the man she knew. Maybe this was an artifact from a happier, more carefree time.

They dined at a cozy booth built into a corner of the kitchen, on plates Honor said had been hers since she was a newlywed. She'd gifted them to Edward and his wife when they got married.

Karissa was surprised to learn they were still using them, but she kept that thought to herself. It was hardly the thing to say in front of the children. Or to Honor.

"Grandma's going to give them to me when I get married someday," Lilith announced.

"My grandma has dishes with daisies on them," said Macy, not to be outdone. "She lives at the beach."

And so the moment to learn more about what happened to Edward's wife was gone. Maybe that was just as well. Talking about lost loved ones could be depressing, and, much as she wanted to know more about Edward's past, she realized it would have been tacky to introduce a topic that could have been painful. Especially in front of Lilith. And really, was it any of her business? Of course, it wasn't.

As dinner progressed, the girls kept up a steady chatter, and much of it required the involvement of Grandma and Karissa. In between, Edward's mom kept the conversation focused on

Karissa, asking her how she was liking Gig Harbor and how she liked her job.

"I'm proud to be part of Heron Publishing, and I love helping to keep things running smoothly, and I'm really enjoying getting to know the authors," Karissa replied. "Avery Black stopped in recently and gave me a book and I'm excited to read it."

"I do like her books. Edward has some excellent authors writing for him," Honor said. "Although some of them are entirely too demanding, if you ask me."

Karissa thought of Emerald, who had been in earlier that day, insisting Edward take her to lunch, but she kept her lips locked and simply nodded.

"He's worked so hard to help Shirley build the business, and you know what a challenge publishing is these days. His father would have loved seeing how much the company has grown over these last years. He was so proud of Edward's success in New York. Did he tell you he owned a small publishing company there?"

Karissa shook her head. She wished he had. She would have loved to hear about that part of his life. No one would ever accuse Edward Elliot of oversharing.

"He sold that and returned home to help my sister build Heron Publishing. We were all glad he came back. Good for Lilith to be with her family. Right, Lilith? You like living with your grandma, don't you?"

Lilith nodded enthusiastically. "Can we decorate our cupcakes now?"

"Of course," said Honor. "Plates to the sink first."

The girls obeyed and Honor got them set up for cupcake decorating at the kitchen bar.

Karissa cleared the rest of the table and then helped Honor load the dishwasher. "It was really nice of you to include me for dinner."

"It's nice to have company. I love to entertain. I'd like to see Edward feel free to do some entertaining himself and have some fun."

Here was Karissa's opportunity to probe. She couldn't pass it up. "It can't be easy raising a child alone. But he has you," she hurried to add.

"Yes, he does. I'm glad I was around and able to help."

Edward entered the house, ending the conversation.

"Daddy!" whooped Lilith and ran to greet her father. Macy raced off right behind her.

"He's a wonderful father," Honor said. "He deserves to be happy."

The way Honor was smiling at her seemed to telegraph permission for Karissa to be part of that happiness. But was she imagining it?

And then the man who deserved to be happy was there in the huge kitchen with them, his daughter in his arms and Macy skipping along beside him.

He wore warm-up pants and a light jacket, and his hair was damp along his forehead, proof that he'd been exercising hard—the elusive Edward Elliot, at home in his natural surroundings.

He smiled at the sight of Karissa, but it seemed an uneasy one. Still, his greeting was warm. "Karissa, hello."

"Hello," she said. "Your mother invited me to stay for dinner," she added, feeling the need to explain her presence since the invitation had been for Macy.

"I've been enjoying getting to know Karissa," said his mother.

"Good," Edward said. "Uh, I'm glad."

He looked more flustered than glad. Honestly, was it that strange that his mother would invite her to stay for dinner, considering what good friends their daughters were? What was it about her that made him so uncomfortable?

"We're decorating cupcakes, Daddy," Lilith said, pointing to the bowls of colored frosting and the many jars of sprinkles.

"I see that. Are they fairy cupcakes?"

Karissa's heart gave a flutter. It was touching watching this man, determined to be part of his daughter's world.

Lilith nodded. "I'm going to do a special one for you."

"Thank you," he said, setting her back down.

"You ready for some lasagna?" Honor asked her son.

"Later, thanks. I'm going to get cleaned up. Nice to see you, Karissa," he said, although she doubted it. Then he was gone.

The girls finished their decorating then devoured their cupcakes and Karissa decided it was time to leave. Edward would want time with his family.

"Thanks again for having us," she said to Honor, as she and Macy stood by the door, saying their goodbyes.

"It's been a pleasure. We'll have to do it again," Honor said.

Karissa didn't see that happening.

Or did she? A pleasant vision of a future dinner visit sprang to mind. She'd be buttering up French bread to go with Honor's lasagna. Edward would come in from playing tennis, all sweat and smiles. He'd drop a kiss on her neck and she'd ask him how his game went. He'd brag a little, she'd flatter a little. He'd offer to teach her to play.

Reality slapped her out of it and jerked her back onto the front porch. *Don't get attached to this man, don't long for this life. Neither one is for you.*

The next day Karissa was reading a book, another gift from one of Heron Publishing's authors, Selma Rodriguez, though she had written it under a different name for a larger publisher. It was a charming romance with witty banter. Karissa had finished *Jane Eyre* and was enjoying a lighter read. She'd taken it up to the rooftop deck during her lunch break and was just coming back down with it when Edward entered the office, returning from a lunch meeting with their sales rep.

"I see you've been taking advantage of the sunshine again," he said. He seemed more at ease than he had the other night.

Maybe because she wasn't invading his home. She was back in her proper place, the office.

"I am," she said.

He came and stood next to her, looking over her shoulder.

His cologne hovered next to her nose, encouraging her to take a nice deep breath and enjoy. It was hard to resist. Her hormones went on red alert, sending the blood pumping to body parts that had been neglected for too long.

"What are you reading?" he asked. "Something new?"

She turned it so he could see the cover with the cartoon couple on it, sharing a beach umbrella.

He looked like he'd just been forced to drink cod liver oil.

"It's very cute," she said.

"And the world needs more cute?"

His sour tone of voice took her aback. "Maybe it does."

"Those books are ubiquitous," he said in disgust.

"People like to read them. *I* like to read them," Karissa added boldly. "They're fun and…hopeful."

His whole body stiffened. "And unrealistic," he said, and started for his office.

"They sell well."

He paused and turned. "They offer false hope and Heron Publishing will never be involved in peddling that." He continued his march into his office and shut the door. Rather forcefully.

It wasn't her place to tell him that Selma Rodriguez, one of his authors, wrote those ubiquitous romance novels when she wasn't producing tomes on Northwest history for him. Surely, he knew. Then again, maybe he didn't. If he didn't it was probably for the best. He'd haul Selma into his office and sternly reprimand her for having the nerve to write something so frivolous.

Whatever Edward Elliot had against romance novels, it had to be related to his own life experience. That had left him prejudiced, and blind to an opportunity to tap into a lucrative market.

It was too bad, really. But then people had been sneering at love stories ever since the days of *Jane Austen*. Maybe the sneering would never stop.

But hopeful readers would still want a good romance, no matter what. Maybe someday she'd find a way to convince Edward of that. Maybe someday, Heron Publishing would stumble on just the right manuscript to convince them to start a romance line. Her mother liked to say, "Books are like chocolate. It only takes one good one to get you hooked."

By the end of the workday Edward seemed to have recovered his equilibrium and was back to his normal, well-mannered self. Almost friendly again.

And then Emerald showed up, decked out in a purple pencil skirt, heels so high they could have doubled as stilts and a low-cut black blouse which she'd paired with a lavender cardigan. Her perfume skipped over and whispered, "Not only do I look better, I also smell better than you," to Karissa, who was wishing she'd worn a spring dress to work instead of her boring pants and efficient white blouse.

This time Karissa managed to get to Edward before Emerald could march past her and into his office unannounced. It gave her a perverse little thrill.

"I'll be out in just a minute," he said, and kept typing on his laptop.

"He'll be out in a minute," she reported.

"Aren't you quick on the draw today, Melissa," Emerald jabbed, deliberately getting her name wrong.

Karissa didn't bother to correct her. She merely smiled. *Yes, I am… Emma.*

"Edward, you're finishing just in time," Emerald said when Edward came out a moment later. "I need someone to go to dinner with me and make sure I don't cheat on my diet."

She gave her long mane a toss and smiled at him. Karissa wanted to kick her.

"I'm afraid I can't. I have to pick up Lilith from her after-school art class," he said.

"Your secretary can do that and take her to your mom's." How easily Emerald Austen managed other people's lives to suit herself.

Edward was getting a boy blush. "Oh, I don't think…"

"Melissa doesn't mind," Emerald said blithely.

Karissa tapped down her ire. "Actually," she began.

Emerald cut her off. "See? I told you."

Karissa gaped at the woman. Did she think she'd been a queen in another life? "I'm sorry, I can't help you," she said firmly, giving Emerald a look that dared her to keep pushing. Doormat was no longer her middle name.

"I'll see if my mother can pick her up," he said. He pulled out his cell phone and stepped back into his office.

"You don't go the extra mile for your boss, do you?" Emerald huffed.

"I have a child, too," Karissa said stiffly.

"And a cute little crush on Edward, just like his last secretary. I'm not saying this to be unkind, really, but don't get your hopes up. Men like him don't fall for women like you."

Maybe not for women like you, either, if they open their eyes and really see you, Karissa thought as Edward returned.

"My mom's going to help me out," he said.

"Good," said Emerald, and beamed at him.

"But I'm afraid it will have to be only appetizers," he added.

Emerald lost her smile. "Well, then, let's get going. Honestly, this is hardly worth the time."

"Would you like to reschedule for a later date?" Karissa asked sweetly. *Like around the Twelfth of Never?*

"No, I would not," snapped Emerald.

"We can go to Anthony's. You do like their clams," Edward said to her.

"Clams it is then." She took his arm and led him off, barely giving him time to grab his jacket.

"Honestly, Edward, your girl is not very accommodating," she said as they went out the door.

"I hope you get a bad clam," Karissa muttered as the door shut behind them.

André emerged from his upstairs kingdom as they exited. "I guess Heron Publishing is feeding Emerald again," he said with a shake of his head.

"It looks that way," Karissa said.

"She's never going to get him to see their relationship as anything beyond business. He hasn't dated in years."

"I wonder why," Karissa mused. How long had he been a widower?

"I don't know his story," said André.

Shirley had emerged from her office in time to catch the end of their conversation. "His story is his own business," she said firmly. She did have a near-sympathetic look to spare for Karissa. "Just because a man doesn't wear a wedding ring it doesn't mean he's free."

Karissa bit her lip and nodded, willing away the heat on her cheeks. "Of course."

There it was, laid out in the open. Edward Elliot was, for whatever reason, not available. There would be no romance novels published at Heron Publishing and there would be no romantic entanglements, either. The book on his story would never be opened and that was that.

And yet, in her own small way she was part of his story. They were developing...something like a friendship. Their children were pulling them closer, just as Jane's charge had pulled her closer to the mysterious Mr. Rochester.

Comparing herself to a heroine in a novel, now there was a

sensible thing to do. *Don't rest until you get what you want,* Annie Wills had advised in her book. If Karissa listened to that advice, she'd spend the rest of her life restless. *Be happy with where you are and what you have,* she told herself. It was much better advice.

Macy was holding a pink envelope containing an invitation to Lilith's birthday party when Karissa picked her up.

"It's gonna be at Lilith's Grandma and Grandpa Peretti's house and there's gonna be a bounce house, and her grandma's making fairy cakes and we all get to wear crowns," Macy squealed, hardly able to contain her excitement.

"It sounds wonderful," said Karissa.

She'd met Edward's mother. Now the other grandma was coming into the picture. Karissa wondered vaguely whether Edward would be there since his deceased wife's parents were hosting. Perhaps it would be an opportunity to sneak a peek at a few more pages of the Edward Elliot story.

How quickly she'd forgotten both Shirley's words and her own advice to herself. Shirley was right, of course. Edward's story was his own business. He didn't have to share it with his administrative assistant.

"Still, I don't think it's wrong to want to know about a person you're spending time with," she said later that night when the book club gathered to talk about *Jane Eyre* and toast Margot's good news with the champagne Josie had brought. "I mean, we work together, and our kids are friends."

"I'd want to know," said Margot. "And I'd especially want to know what Shirley meant by that cryptic remark of hers."

"I'd want to know, too," said Josie, "and I'd come right out and ask him."

Of course, she would, because she was Josie.

"I wish I was…bolder," Karissa said. "Even though I don't like Emerald, I wish I was more like her."

"Ugh," Margot said. "No, you don't."

"Who's Emerald?" Josie asked. "Have we talked about her and I missed it?"

"She's one of Heron Publishing's authors who likes to make Karissa feel inferior," said Margot.

"A bitch, huh?" said Josie.

"She is, but she gets what she wants," Karissa said. "I just sit around and wish. Like Jane Eyre."

"Jane got what she wanted in the end," Alice pointed out.

"Yeah, very convenient how she didn't have to work to get it," Margot sneered.

Josie pointed a finger at her. "That's not the point of the story. The point is that if a woman stands by her principles everything will work out in the end."

"For Jane. Not so much for Rochester's wife," Margot argued. "He locks her in a room and gives himself permission to become a bigamist."

"There is that," Josie admitted. "I sure thought the book was romantic when I first read it as a young girl."

"Romantic? It's a horror story," Margot protested.

"I felt sorry for Jane. She went through so much before she even got to Thornfield Hall," said Alice.

"Sometimes I feel like Jane, like I'm nothing but an observer," Karissa mused. And where did observing get you in the real world?

"You haven't exactly sat around. You found a job and started a new life," Alice said to her.

"I have," she conceded. It all looked impressive on the surface.

"You took control of your life and moved," Alice continued.

But Karissa had moved because she couldn't stand up for herself. She couldn't bear to stay in the same neighborhood or even the same city as Allegra and Mark. Yes, her neighborhood had become unaffordable, but she'd been glad to get away. Relieved.

"I ran away so I wouldn't have to see my ex-friend and my ex-husband together. As for the job, I had to live on something." She sighed. "I wish I was beautiful."

"What? Where on earth did that come from?" Josie demanded.

"There's nothing wrong with the way you look," Alice argued, offended on Karissa's behalf that she would fail to see her own worth.

"I'm not pretty like Emerald." Just saying the woman's name left a bad taste in her mouth. She'd left Allegra behind and here she was, stuck with Allegra's sister from another mister. Every time the woman came into the office it was a reminder of how little Karissa measured up as a woman. She reached for her champagne and took a sip. "That isn't even her real name," she muttered. "It's Mary."

"So, there you have it. She's a fake," Josie said. "Men see through that eventually. It's more important to have heart. In the end that trumps beauty. I should know. Charlie sure didn't pick me because I looked like Gia Carangi."

"Who?" asked Karissa.

"Never mind," Josie snapped. "I'm trying to make a point here. We all know better than to judge a book by its cover. There's a lot to you, Karissa Newcomb."

"Not enough to compete with women like Emerald," Karissa said miserably. *And Allegra.*

"Then don't try to compete. Just be yourself," said Josie.

"Sounds like something from a book we read," Margot taunted, referring to the Annie Wills book Josie had dissed, and Josie told her not to be a smart-mouth.

"We women waste a lot of time comparing ourselves to others," said Alice. "I always wanted to be tall like Jos."

"So people could say things like, 'How's the weather up there?'" Josie said, rolling her eyes. "I hated being tall."

"And I wanted to look like Loni Anderson," put in Alice. "Our mother wanted to look like Audrey Hepburn."

"I wanted bigger boobs," said Margot. "Alice talked me out of going down that road."

"The bigger they are the farther they fall," Alice said.

"Alice is right. We waste a lot of time wanting to look like somebody else. Don't you be doing that," Josie said to Karissa.

"And remember, Jane may have thought she was plain, but Rochester didn't," put in Alice. "You'll find your Rochester. Meanwhile, you've got a lot of living to do."

Their encouragement was touching. "Thanks, you guys, I appreciate the support."

"What are friends for?" said Margot.

Friends. How lucky she was to have met women who lived up to the word. "I sure moved to the right neighborhood."

"Yes, you did," Alice said, beaming at her.

"Now, back to Rochester and Jane," said Josie.

Forty minutes later the book had been thoroughly discussed, Karissa had managed to lock up her unhappiness and insecurity, for the night at least, and it was time to pick the next month's read.

"What do you want to read, Karissa?" Alice asked.

"No more Brontës," said Margot, and Josie frowned.

"One of our Heron Publishing authors has a new nonfiction book coming out. I thought it might be interesting to read it and then we could invite him to join us. He lives right here in Gig Harbor."

Josie narrowed her eyes. "He who?"

"Gerald McCrae," said Karissa.

"You're not talking about that uncivilized beast who yelled at you when you accidentally spilled the coffee on him, I hope," Josie said.

"I thought it might do him good to meet some strong women," said Karissa.

Half of Josie's mouth quirked upward. "Ha! You want to put him in his place."

"Maybe."

"I'm happy to help with that," Josie said, and Margot laughed.

"Poor man," Alice said. "I hope for his own good that he says no."

"Were you hoping to see fireworks before the Fourth?" Margot asked Karissa after the sisters had left.

"We did talk about maybe matching those two up. I think Gerald needs someone in his life who's not afraid to chisel off his rough edges."

"Josie is a walking chisel, that's for sure," said Margot.

"You never know. They might hit it off."

"Or kill each other, right in front of us."

There was that.

"But hey, why not?" Margot said. "And, speaking of why not...don't give up on Edward."

"I need to. Shirley as much as told me to, and she's right. He's so out of reach. And she says he's unavailable anyway. I only hope Emerald doesn't somehow manage to hoodwink him into something. It would be so wrong. That woman is a narcissist."

"You may not be able to stop her from snaring your boss, but don't let her snare your self-esteem. You're worth ten Emeralds."

"I don't even look like one Emerald."

"I get that she's beautiful, but there are all kinds of beauty. You really need to take what Alice and Josie said to heart."

It was easier said than done when you had emotional scars, and Karissa did. They were buried deep, but they came out of hiding and held up a filter for her to look through every time she stood in front of her mirror.

"I've never really felt good about myself. Maybe that was why when Mark came along, asked me out, wanted to be with me, I fell for him so hard. And then when he left me for my prettier friend…"

"You fell again, but not in a good way."

Karissa nodded. "I like to think I'm working on getting past it, but it's two steps forward and one step back. And some days it's one step forward and two steps back."

"Healing takes time. You'll get there," Margot assured her.

"I wish I had a fairy godmother with a magic wand."

"If you're wanting new clothes for the ball, I can help with that. Makeup, too."

"I'm allergic," Karissa said. She sighed. "I sound like a whiner. Come to think of it, I am."

"You're not whining. You're working through your issues."

"Slowly."

"Slowly is better than not at all," Margot said.

She supposed Margot was right.

When Karissa went to bed that night she was still thinking about all the things her friends had said. They were right. It was a waste of time to wish she looked like someone else. It was wrong to keep putting herself down. Even Jane Eyre had a sense of her own worth. Maybe that was part of what Mr. Rochester saw in her. Maybe that was why she got her happy ending in the end. She did things to deserve it.

Karissa's happy ending didn't have to look like Jane Eyre's. It didn't have to look like anyone else's. It was her own to write. She could continue to fill her life with good things. She wasn't running away anymore, she was running to, running to lasting friendships, special times with her girl, running toward growing into more responsibility in a meaningful job.

But it would be nice if that job didn't include having to deal with a certain man-eating narcissist.

14

*"Envy is a waste unless you turn it into fuel
to get out there and do something with your life."*
—from *Where There's a Will There's a Way* by Annie Wills

LILITH'S OTHER GRANDMA LIVED IN A HOUSING DE-
velopment outside of town. The house was modest with a well-
kept front lawn and a fence separating the backyard from the
front. The roof of the promised bounce house peeked up over
it and Karissa could hear childish squeals as she followed her
excited daughter up the front walk.

Macy was clutching a wrapped box like it was treasure. If
you were an eight-year-old girl and into fairies, it was. The box
contained the newest book in the series the girls were reading
and a feather fairy crown as well as a wishing stone—choose
the one with your favorite fairy on it (great merchandising).

Lilith's grandma, Sylvia Peretti, opened the door and introduced herself. She smiled at Macy and said, "The girls are
in the bounce house. I'll put your present with the others and
you can go join them." She motioned to a sliding glass door.

"Thank you," Macy said, and hurried to the door.

"Thank you for inviting Macy," Karissa said. "When should I come back for her?"

It was the polite thing to say since the invitation hadn't been for Macy and Mom. There were adults present though. She saw Edward standing by that sliding door, looking out at the rockin' bounce house and talking with an older man, Mr. Peretti most likely. A woman somewhere around Karissa's age sat on the couch while another woman, also similar in age, lounged in an easy chair, her feet on a footstool. Family members, perhaps? Both of them eyed Karissa like cats, the aloof Egyptian goddess kind.

Edward turned and waved at Karissa and smiled. It seemed that he smiled more lately, and this one reached his eyes.

The two women kept their hands around their drink glasses, and neither one called, "Come, join us."

"We'll be done by four," said Sylvia.

Karissa nodded, promised to return, and went back to her car, disappointed. There would be no nosy chats, no helping serve cake. And no discovering who the unwelcoming committee was. For all she knew, one of the women could have been there as Edward's guest. Although if that was the case, wouldn't he have been sitting with her?

Karissa drove to Invitation Bookstore to console herself. A good book was always a woman's truest friend.

At the bookstore she stocked up on novels by some of her favorite writers—the two Susans (Susan Wiggs and Susan Mallery), Marie Bostwick, and Rachel Linden. One of the Friends & Fiction ladies had a book on the shelves. She loved their podcasts! Oooh, and here was a new one by Brenda Novak. And...she needed to stop before she blew up her credit card. She rationalized her book binge by reminding herself that she was supporting authors, helping them pay their bills. Look what a good thing it had turned out to be that she hadn't been invited to the party. Look at all the imagination exercise tools she'd have missed out on.

She settled in her car, picked up a book and opened it to the first page.

She got four chapters read in Susan Mallery's latest and then it was time to go pick up Macy.

This time Sylvia invited her in, and she seemed a little more welcoming. Maybe because she knew Karissa wouldn't be staying long?

The girls were finishing up their cake and Karissa supposed Sylvia could hardly leave her standing on the porch. The two women Karissa had seen earlier were helping with cleanup as Karissa followed Sylvia into the kitchen.

"These are my daughters, Arletta and Meagan," she said, and the two women said a quick hello and then went back to stowing away leftover goodies.

The girls hadn't lacked for food. In addition to the fairy cakes, which had been given little cake wings, they'd enjoyed ice cream, chips, fruit, and tiny tea sandwiches. They all wore costume butterfly wings on their backs and glitter in their hair, and smiles on their faces.

"Let's get a picture before you all go home," Sylvia said to the girls. "Lilith, put your cousins on either side of you."

Which left Macy, the best friend, on the outside of the inner circle.

Cousins trump best friends, Karissa reminded herself.

Macy didn't care, she was beaming with ice cream on her chin, an arm around one of the cousins.

Edward and the older man came into the room at that moment. "Karissa," Edward greeted her. "I thought you'd stay."

Your mother-in-law didn't invite me. "I had some errands to run."

He nodded. "Of course."

"You didn't miss anything but chaos," said the older man. "Come on, girls, time to scram. Grandpa's pooped."

The little girls all giggled and Sylvia shook her head at him.

"Time to go, Macy," Karissa said to her daughter. "What do you say to Mrs. Peretti?"

"Thank you for having me," Macy said. "And thank you for the fairy wings!"

Fairy wings for all. Sylvia Peretti wasn't stingy, that was for sure.

"You're more than welcome," she said to Macy. "Nice to meet you, Karissa. I didn't realize you were Edward's secretary."

Ah, that explained the change in attitude.

"Administrative assistant," he corrected.

"Administrative assistant. All these changes in terminology," said Sylvia. "I remember when secretaries were secretaries and garbage men were garbage men."

Karissa wasn't sure what to say to that.

"Times change," Edward said. "I'll walk you and Macy to your car, Karissa."

He did, but he didn't say anything about his in-laws. Instead, he thanked Karissa for coming. "It meant a lot to Lilith to have Macy here."

"I can tell she had a wonderful time."

"I'm sorry you had errands to run. I thought you might have enjoyed staying."

Had he wanted her to? She wished she'd been invited.

"I'm sorry, too. It looks like it was a great party," she said.

"Magical," he said with a slight head shake.

Was that glitter she saw in his hair? "Is there...something in your hair?"

"They made me be fairy king. I'm going to take two Advil when I get home."

They had reached the car, and Macy bowed to Edward and said, "Thank you, King Thistlebottom. I was honored to be your loyal subject."

Karissa choked back a giggle. "King Thistlebottom?"

He frowned and shook his head. "Don't ask."

"I guess I shouldn't address you as such at work on Monday then?"

"I guess not," he said firmly, and she laughed.

"Very well, then. I can call you Your Majesty if you prefer."

He was already a handsome man, but that smile took handsome to a whole new level.

"Edward will be just fine," he said, opening the car door for Macy.

"Oh, that's right. You probably want to keep your magical kingdom and powers a secret," Karissa teased.

"I think that would be best. See you Monday."

Karissa wore sandals to work on Monday, which paired nicely with the pedicure Macy had given her as part of their mother-daughter Sunday fun. She had on a floral print dress and a cute denim jacket, which she also felt like she was rocking. She didn't look glam but she looked...summery. And she felt good about how she looked, and that was saying something.

"You look loverly," Shirley said when she emerged from her office for her morning coffee fix.

"I feel loverly," Karissa replied. Okay, slight fib. She was no transformed Eliza Doolittle, but she did feel happy with the outfit she'd put together and was sure Margot would have given it a thumbs-up. "My daughter gave me a pedicure."

She stuck her leg out to the side and gave her foot a little chorus line flick just as Edward walked in. His eyes widened at the sight.

The leg got instantly pulled back and banged on the corner of the desk in the process, and it was hard to stifle a yelp.

"Are you okay?" he asked.

"I'm fine," she said through gritted teeth and rubbed her shin. As usual, she'd managed to make herself ridiculous in front of him. "Macy gave me a pedicure and I was showing it to Shirley," she added. Her cheeks had to be as red as a lobster.

He nodded slowly. "It looks very nice. Well, don't let me interrupt," he said, and hurried into his office, and as he passed, Karissa noticed his face was a little pink.

"I do have a way of impressing my boss, don't I?" she muttered.

"You impressed this boss," Shirley said. She got her coffee along with one of the lemon bars André had brought in, then went back into her office.

Karissa opened her computer and got busy with emails. So what if she'd looked a little silly? There was nothing wrong with showing off her pedi. So there.

Come lunch hour, she and her sack lunch were on their way to the marina to soak in the scenery and leaving the same time as Edward and André. "Dining al fresco," she quipped to prove she wasn't even remotely embarrassed over doing the pedicure can-can, and held up her sack.

"And dining in style. Love the outfit," said André.

"And the pedicure," added Edward. "You look very nice today."

She watched them walk off in the direction of El Pueblito, then she, too, left the office, an extra swing in her step and a smile on her face.

The smile lasted through lunch and the rest of the afternoon. But it got lost when Emerald Austen waltzed in, a perfect sour note on which to end the workday.

Didn't the woman have anything else to do besides haunt Heron Publishing. And Edward? Maybe she'd like her own desk.

Right across from Karissa so Karissa could throw spitballs at her all day.

"I assume Edward is still in, trying not to have a life," she said to Karissa as she started past her desk. At a good clip this time.

"Actually, he's right in the middle of something," Karissa lied. "Let me tell him you're here," she said, and stood.

"Oh, stop with the little secretary guardian of the gate thing, Melissa," Emerald said. "It only makes you look insecure."

"It's my job," said Karissa, starting for the door. "And I can't afford to lose it."

Anyone with a heart would take a seat. Emerald didn't have a heart.

"If you behave, I'll make sure you don't get fired, little guard dog," Emerald said lightly.

She swept past Karissa and pushed open Edward's door. "Oh, look, it's a workaholic in his natural habitat," she joked and shut the door behind her.

"Oh, look, it's a cougar stalking her prey," muttered Karissa, sitting back down at her desk. "And now, she's dragging him off for the kill," she grumbled when, ten minutes later he was following her out the door.

"I know your little girl will love the place I have in mind for dinner," Emerald was saying.

So, she was already on to phase two of the hunt. Bring in the offspring.

"Not your business," she told herself as she drove to pick up Macy from her summer daycare program. Telling herself was one thing. Listening was another.

"Everything about her bugs me," Karissa confessed later when Margot, Josie, and Alice came over for an unofficial book club hang. She went on to tell the others about Emerald's high-handed manipulating of Edward's schedule and how blithely the woman always shifted his family responsibilities onto other people so she could have him to herself. "She just barges in whenever she likes as if she owns the company. And him."

"Which is probably what she wants," said Josie.

"I guess if I'm being honest, I have to say the main reason I don't like her is because I'm jealous," Karissa admitted. "Which is pretty small of me. I mean she can't help it if she's beautiful and talented."

"But she can help it if she's rude and selfish," Margot argued. "The woman is a bitch with a capital *B*."

"You're right. She is. She's so full of herself and condescending. And this whole nonsense of calling me Melissa... I know she knows my name."

"Of course, she does, but pretending she doesn't makes her feel like she's got power over you," said Margot.

Karissa frowned and dredged a carrot through the dip she'd set out. "I guess she does. I'm letting her bring out the worst in me. I'm starting to wish all kinds of awful things on her." She sighed. "If I was a writer I'd put her in a book and bump her off."

"Have you ever tried your hand at writing?" Alice wanted to know.

"Oh sure. I wrote stories as a child and dabbled in college. But I never tried to sit down and write a whole book. That felt too overwhelming."

"What about now?" Alice asked.

"I bet you could get inspired," put in Margot.

Karissa closed her eyes and envisioned Emerald, with her long copper hair, holding a plate of clams and walking along the boat dock. Catching her foot on a loose board, falling into the water, her clams flying every which way. Going down before bobbing up like a red-topped cork and sputtering, "Help! I can't swim." Her murderer, the woman whose man she'd stolen, would be sitting with her back turned, listening to music on her headphones.

"I could write a book about a conceited cougar," she said, her eyes still closed. "She writes...murder mysteries. But she's not that bright. She has a ghost writer."

"Ooh, I like that," said Margot.

"Yes, a ghost writer," Karissa decided.

"Is the ghost writer the one who kills her?" Alice asked, leaning in.

Karissa grinned. "Yes, I think so."

"And does she get away with it?" Josie asked.

"I think she should," Karissa said. "And the publisher, a handsome man who the cougar has been chasing, falls in love with the ghost writer."

"Of course," Margot murmured.

"And they wind up getting married and the ghost writer becomes the new star at the publishing house." Very satisfying, except… "I guess it couldn't be a murder mystery, because in those the murderer has to get caught, and I don't want my killer to get caught." Karissa wanted the satisfaction of getting away with murder…in fiction, of course.

"So, some kind of dark thriller," Margot guessed.

"Maybe. I could set it in the Pacific Northwest. Maybe on an island. I could push her off a bridge. Or a ferryboat." The possibilities were endless.

"Or beat her over the head with one of her books," Alice suggested, and Margot laughed.

"Alice, I never knew you had such a strong violent streak," she teased. She turned her attention back to Karissa. "Writing this could be therapy."

"I bet you could even sell it," Alice said.

"A first novel? Probably not," said Karissa, being realistic. "But I do like the idea of writing one as therapy. Maybe you guys can help me come up with ideas."

"I'm all over that," Josie said.

"I probably wouldn't be any help," said Alice.

"I don't know. Murdering my victim with a book sounded pretty good to me."

"What would you call it?" asked Margot.

"I have no idea," Karissa said. *"Sick?"* There was a fitting title. Imagining ways to bump off Emerald was more than a little sick. And very unkind. But if you did it in fiction, what did it matter? Then it was simply...writing. And maybe a good way to get her frustration out of her system.

"Interesting title," said Margot.

"Kind of reflects my current mental state," Karissa said.

"*Murder, She Wrote,*" said Alice. "Except that's been taken. Oh, how about this? *Murder She Wrote No More.*"

"That has a ring to it," Karissa said.

"And writing it sounds like fun," said Margot. "Can I help?"

"I'll take all the help I can get," said Karissa. "It can be a book club project." They were only doing it for fun, anyway. It would never be good enough to sell, so why not?

"I'm going to go home and try not to have nightmares about my murderous neighbors," Alice joked.

"Don't worry. If I ever put you in a book, I'll let you live," Karissa told her.

"Thanks, you guys," she said later, as she walked her friends to the door. "I feel better for having been able to vent."

"I hope you turn that venting into something positive," Alice said.

"Let's write it and sell it. You can dedicate it to all the women who've had to deal with women who are conceited and self-ish," Margot said.

That made Karissa smile. "Maybe I'll dedicate it to Allegra. And Mary," she added.

"Mary, aka Emerald?" guessed Margot.

Karissa grinned. "Yep."

"I have a better idea. Name the murder victim Mary."

"Mary Austen?" suggested Alice.

Mary Austen. The name had a nice ring to it. Maybe too close to the real-life villain. "Mary Black," Karissa said, trying out the word. "No, too on the nose." And Avery Black, Heron Publishing's mystery writer, probably wouldn't appreciate Karissa taking her last name for her murder victim. "Mary Blackworm," she said, and Margot gave a snort. "No, that's just silly," she decided. Then she had it. "Mary Goodall."

"Yes, that works," Margot approved.

It did. Karissa liked the irony of it. There was nothing good about her victim or the woman who had inspired her.

The next day, on her lunch break, Karissa made a run to the store and bought a large legal tablet. The June weather was turning nice. She could sit up on the rooftop patio and commit murder. And not have to worry about life in prison. Books were a wonderful thing.

15

"Keep looking forward, keep moving forward."
—from *Where There's a Will There's a Way* by Annie Wills

JACKSON DELIVERED THE REQUESTED BUSINESS CONtract to Margot, along with his regrets that he hadn't been able to help her after all. With everything working out she could easily say, "No hard feelings." Although she suspected there would be some hard feelings on his part if her app became successful. Well, he'd had his chance.

After several back-and-forth negotiations with Andrew over a few small points the contract was ready to sign. They could have done it electronically, but he suggested making it a historical moment in person.

"We can take some shots for Insta, maybe do a reel," he'd suggested.

That worked for her. It would make for good promotion when they rolled out the app.

They met at a Starbucks in Tacoma late in the afternoon and he was kind enough to buy her a frap. She'd taken care to make sure she looked as on trend as possible so she'd be camera ready. She was willing to bet when he was working at home he was in sweats and a T-shirt but today he was dressed business casual and definitely looked ready for a photo op.

They took pics of themselves signing the contract, one of them toasting each other with their fraps, and did a couple of reels talking about the app. She felt like a little kid right before Christmas vacation.

"Brewers Row has a great happy hour menu. Feel like toasting to our future with something more potent?" he suggested when they were done.

It was perfectly normal to go out to eat with someone you were in business with. This was not a date.

Still, it felt like one as they settled in at an outdoor café table and ordered margaritas. "I think this app is going to fly high fast," he said after the server had brought their drinks and taken their orders. "I told my sister about it and she's ready to download it as of yesterday."

"That's a good sign," Margot said. "It's all about finding something people want and then giving it to them."

"And I'm all about that," he agreed.

Sitting across from Andrew at that small table, she could think of things she wanted that had nothing to do with apps. She reminded herself they were simply business associates.

"I love your office. I assume that's your house I saw when I first went to meet with you?"

"It is now. It was my folks'. They downsized and I'm buying it from them."

"A smart investment," she said.

"I'm all about being smart with money. Not that I think that's all there is to life."

"Oh? What else is there to life?" she asked.

"You gotta have some fun. I'm semi-addicted to gaming. Like to read. Work out at the gym so I can eat Cheetos and drink beer. I've got two older brothers who were jocks and nicknamed me Elon. Fine by me. The guy's a zillionaire."

"Are you going to help him populate the moon if you make a zillion dollars?" Margot teased.

"Maybe," Andrew said with a wink. "But really I'd just want enough to buy a '57 Crown Vic. After that I'd donate a bundle to Habitat for Humanity and The Nature Conservancy. I like them both a lot."

"Are you like President Carter?"

"Nah. I'm a Libertarian."

"You know what I mean."

He chuckled. "Yeah, I've helped build a few houses."

Good grief, this man was too good to be true. How was it that he was still single?

"How come you're not married?" she blurted. So inappropriate. Her whole face felt like a fireball. "I mean, you're noble, you've got your own business." *You make my mouth water.*

"I blew through a couple of relationships. They didn't like my addiction." He showed off his gaming ability with his hands.

"Girls like to game, too."

"Not the ones I dated. Do you?"

She laughed. "Does *JoJo's Fashion Show* count?"

"*JoJo's Fashion Show*, huh?"

"Don't judge."

He smiled. "It does explain the app."

"No, getting frustrated with online shopping explains the app," she said with a frown.

"So, you saw a need and wanted to fill it."

"Something like that."

He pointed to her bare ring finger. "No man in your life?"

"I'm divorced. Been too busy since."

"With JoJo?" he teased.

"I took her off my phone a couple years back. I was getting way too sucked in."

"She probably misses you."

"Maybe someday we'll get back together," Margot said, and he chuckled.

"Or maybe I'll have to introduce you to one of my games," he said. "So, when you're not working, what do you do for fun?"

"I like to run."

"Yeah? Me, too."

"And I love to travel. Right now, that's on hold."

He nodded. "I wouldn't mind doing some traveling. I still haven't gotten to Hawaii."

"Everyone should see Hawaii at least once."

"Yeah? Where would you say I should start?"

"Oahu. It's got fun tourist shops and great night life, and there's Waikiki Beach and, of course, Pearl Harbor. You can hike to Diamond Head, and if you want to relax you can drive to the North Shore. I like Kauai too. It has great beaches and gorgeous waterfalls. Then there's Maui. Those fires were awful, but the people have rebuilt and it is well worth the visit."

"Sounds like you've done it all."

"Oh, yeah. I'd do it again in a heartbeat."

"Yeah?"

She liked the way he was looking at her, with that gleam of interest in his eyes, that easy smile. Maybe, at some point, if they got to know each other better, she'd offer her services as tour guide.

That would take a lot of getting to know each other. This man felt like someone she could spend a lot of time with, but she knew better than to trust her feelings.

They continued to visit, and she learned that in high school Andrew had been a nerd. No big surprise there.

"The problem with labeling people though, is there's usually room for more than one label, and people tend to forget that," he said.

"You didn't like being labeled."

"Who does? But you know the joke about nerds—my dad used to say it to me all the time."

"What's that?" she prompted.

"What do you call a nerd?"

She'd heard that one and couldn't help smiling. "Boss?"

"Yep," he said, and raised his glass in a toast to the nerds of the world.

"So, boss," she said, "now that we've got a contract and everything's official, let me share my vision for the app."

"Okay." His tone was neutral. He'd probably had some crazy ideas run past him before.

"I want it to look like you're stepping into a dressing room when you open the app. Can you do that?"

He nodded. "Rad, and yes I can."

"And I want to call it My Dressing Room."

He nodded approvingly. "I like it, let's make it happen."

Making something happen with him certainly appealed to her. By the time they'd finished their happy hour nachos they decided they needed to hang around and have dinner, and by the time they were done with dinner she'd fallen halfway down the love stairs. Her common sense grabbed her and said, "No, you don't."

No, she didn't.

But after he'd walked her to her car and they were standing there, closer than business associates should stand, she was about to fall down the stairs once more. She felt like she was in some old movie, with visible current running between them. She could tell he wanted to kiss her, and she wanted it, wanted to feel his arms slide around her.

He bit down on his lip and took a step back. "I guess we should keep this on a professional level."

That would be the common sense thing to do. Common sense was highly overrated.

She forced herself to nod. "Yes, we should." For the time being, at least. "Until the app is done," she said.

There went his lips in another smile, and she felt that zing she'd felt when they'd first shaken hands all over again. "Until the app is done."

If, by then, the sizzle had stopped they could live their separate lives and share the profits. Hopefully, there would be some profits.

I am miserable. What's the point of pretending otherwise? Death is the only solution. Not mine, though. Why should I be the one to die? I'm a good person. I work hard, do my job, try my best. No, I don't deserve to die. But there will be a death in the future. I know that.

Karissa reread the opening lines she'd written for her novel. She hadn't thought about the plot or any of the characters beyond her frustrated main character and, of course, the awful Mary, who would be killed in honor of Emerald. What Mary would do to deserve death she didn't yet know. She had simply plunged in and let her thoughts flow. And the flow felt good. Writing had felt like mental waltzing. Reading what she'd written felt cathartic. No wonder people became writers.

She took her notebook to work with her the next day, determined to write on her lunch break. Someplace far from the office where no one could see what she was doing.

It was a perfect Pacific Northwest day. A blue sky with a few puffs of cloud hung over water that was postcard cerulean blue, and Mount Rainier hovered in the background, its white top dusted faintly pink by the sun. It was a count your blessings kind of day, and she did. Her daughter had found a friend and she'd found some as well, the kind of friends a woman could trust. She had her house, her job and now, she had a new hobby to try out. A hobby that could very well turn into a passion. And passion on the page was better than no passion.

Here was where the counting stopped. She missed having a husband. She'd have loved to feel a man's hands on her again, love to feel lips sliding over hers and tasting her neck. She missed having a body up against her in bed, missed being able to roll over and lay her hands on a solid chest. No solid chest, no solid relationship. She should have realized sooner that hers and Mark's was going soft.

Looking back will only give you a crick in the neck. The words from their first book club read settled on her shoulder, giving it a gentle pat. Annie Wills said to keep moving forward. It was advice worth following.

So, back to murder. She opted for working at the waterfront park, settling in at a picnic table and writing in bold letters at the top of the page, *Ways to Kill*.

Was there any new way to murder a person? Not really. She tapped her chin with her pen. Stabbed with a pen? That would take a lot of force. Beaten with a book? That had been Alice's idea and Karissa had liked it. But it would take a lot of strength and energy to beat someone to death with a book. And who would stand around and let you do that? How about a laptop? One good swing to the back of the head would do it. But again, how to manage that? Karissa wasn't sure she had a killer instinct.

If the killer printed out pages for Mary to read the killer could hit her from behind with her laptop right on the head while she was reading, she scribbled. But that had no finesse. How else could you murder someone with a computer?

Inspiration struck and she had to call Margot. "I've figured out how to kill Mary!" A woman walking by with her purse puppy gawked at her, and she lowered her voice. "Poison."

"I've always read that poison is a woman's tool, but I don't know if that's true anymore. Although it could be. It's subtle and…elegant," Margot approved.

Karissa giggled. "And you should always be elegant when committing murder." The woman was passing closer, pulling out her phone, probably ready to call 911. "I'm a writer," Karissa said, and held up her notebook. *I'm a writer.* It felt good to say that.

The woman blushed, nodded, and hurried on past.

"Announcing it to the whole world now?"

"Only to a woman who looked ready to call the police on me," said Karissa.

"What's the clever way you've thought of to poison the bitch?" Margot asked.

"Something topical. My murderer will put it on the keys of Mary's laptop."

"Except the murderer's the ghost writer. Wouldn't she be the one using the laptop?"

There was that. "Yes, but Mary still has to write emails and guest blogs, right? I think I can make it work. If that doesn't work I can always make the killer her underpaid assistant."

"That works, too. Want me to research poisons?"

"That would be great. Thanks."

"It'll be fun. Of course, Alice will be disappointed you're not going to beat Mary to death with a book. I think she was ready to write that scene."

"I'll let her come up with a different scene," said Karissa. She checked her phone. "Looks like my lunch hour is over. I'd better get back to work."

"Me, too," Margot said. "I have to get my website for the new business set up. If you hear of anyone who needs organizing, send 'em my way. I'm expanding my business."

"I will," Karissa promised.

The opportunity to help her friend came sooner than expected when Avery Black dropped by with a book for Karissa. She was middle-aged and the opposite of Emerald—a modest, unassuming woman perfectly happy to wander around in jeans and a sweater and sneakers.

"I'm in town to meet my pals Marie Bostwick and Rachel Linden for lunch. Since I promised you a book, I thought I'd drop one off for you."

Getting a free book was like Christmas coming early. Karissa reached for it eagerly. *"Death in Deep Waters,"* she read. "I like that title."

"So did I, and I was happy when they let me keep it. Authors don't always get to keep their titles."

There was a sad thought. "Really?"

"It's all about marketing, you know, and what will sell well. And I'm all for sales. Although Heron Publishing isn't my main source of income," she confided.

"It's not?"

"I have another publisher."

"Another publisher?" Wasn't Avery happy at Heron Publishing?

"I write romance novels like Selma. In fact, we have the same publisher. Only my novels have lots more sex. You know what they say, sex sells," Avery added with a laugh.

Another romance writer working for someone else. Look at the money Heron Publishing was losing.

"I have to admit, though, juggling two publishers and keeping up with social media is enough to make me nutty. I'd love to find a virtual assistant."

Virtual assistant. Was that something Margot might like to tackle? "I have a friend who's starting her own business. She might be able to help you. Would you like her contact information?"

"Oh, yes," Avery said. "I'll call her today. I'm glad I stopped by. The universe was sure looking out for me today."

Karissa wasn't so sure the universe cared much about whether or not Avery found a virtual assistant, but she kept the thought to herself and thanked Avery for the book.

Inspiration and a free book—this was what a great day looked like. The rest of it passed happily, with fielding phone calls, setting up appointments and even consoling and then troubleshooting for a writer, whose author copies had gone astray.

At the end of the day, Karissa was at the office door, juggling her purse, her keys, her new book, the package of donut holes about to go stale that Shirley had insisted she take home and her notebook when the juggling failed. The donut holes had done it. She knew she should have tossed them. Now there they went, the box popping open and the little rolls of sugary dough bouncing all over the new floor like escaped ping-pong balls, shedding white powder as they went. The book landed with a thud and the notebook fell open.

Edward's door opened. "Is everything all right?"

"Yes. I just dropped some things," she said, bending to pick up the scattered donut holes. It looked like she'd be tossing them after all.

He hurried over. "Let me help you."

This wasn't as awful as backing into his car or as mortifying as spilling coffee on Gerald, but it was still embarrassing. "You don't need to, really."

"I don't mind," he said. "It looks like you were a little loaded down."

"Pilfering donut holes. Actually, Shirley gave them to me."

"Good. We wouldn't want them going to waste."

"Oh, they'd have gone to my waist all right," she said. A silly pun. Her cheeks started to burn.

"I don't think you have to worry about that," he said. He picked up her notebook. "It looks like you might be journaling."

"Oh, no, nothing like that." She snatched the notebook back.

"Are you working on a story, then? Not that it's any of my business, but I remember you saying you majored in literature in college."

"A book idea." She had just confessed that to her boss, a man who published experienced writers. A three-alarm fire burst out on her face. "It's just for fun."

"If it ever becomes something more than fun and you want someone to take a look, I'd be happy to," he said.

"Thank you," she murmured. She put it back on the desk,

then returned to picking up donut holes. "I'll have this cleaned in no time," she promised.

He nodded but continued to help her. André came down from his office. "What's this, a new game? Can anybody play?"

Karissa dropped the last donut hole into the box and got to her feet. "I'll get a broom."

"I miss all the fun," André cracked.

Fun. Was that what you called embarrassing yourself in front of your boss? At least he hadn't read what was in her notebook. Thank God he was too polite to insist.

Half of her almost wished he had. Would he have read it and commented on how raw and real her writing was? Or would he have said something polite, like, "You have to get the words down. That's what first drafts are for," which was polite speak for, "Don't quit your day job." Now she'd never know.

That was probably for the best.

Josie and Alice had been bargain-hunting in their favorite thrift stores. Josie's trunk already held a large vase shaped like a frog that Alice had fallen in love with and a good as new three-in-one turquoise breakfast maker that included a toaster, an egg cooker and a small griddle. She'd seen the same thing on-line for fifty-nine dollars (plus shipping!) and she'd gotten that baby for twenty. She'd also scored on some great jeans and a sweater. They were on their last store of the day and Josie was checking out a necklace in the jewelry section.

Alice came up behind her, a shopping basket filled with books over her arm. "That would look lovely on Coral."

The same thought had drifted into Josie's mind, but hearing her sister say it motivated her to put it back.

Alice scooped it up. "If you're not going to buy it, I will."

"For yourself?" She'd better be.

"For when you come to your senses and make up with your daughter," Alice snapped, and marched off to the checkout aisle.

Josie picked up her basket, with the kitchen towel she'd found, and followed her sister, her jaws clenched.

It was a silent ride back to Alice's place. "Come in and have lunch," Alice said.

"I can't. I have things to do."

"No, you don't," said Alice.

"Yes, I do. I have a scene to write for Karissa's book and I want to get it down while the idea is fresh in my mind."

"You got inspired by the thrift store?"

"I did," Josie lied. "I'll see you later."

"Okay, fine. Just remember, I have the necklace."

"Out!" Josie commanded, and her sister gave a judgmental head shake and climbed out with her bag of books.

Josie popped the trunk and Alice got her vase and slammed the trunk shut. Then Josie sped off down the street as if she was driving one of her nasty neighbor's muscle cars. Coral didn't deserve to be rewarded for the way she was behaving. And Errol deserved to die.

At least on paper.

Once home, Josie made herself a cup of tea and settled on her recliner couch with her feet up and got busy tapping on her laptop. She may have been typing about a woman, but with every word she pictured her useless lump of a son-in-law who was responsible for the rift between her and her daughter.

The woman was deceptive and evil and lazy and needed to have her head severed from her neck.

The image made Josie frown. Was that too violent? Of course not. They were murdering someone, after all.

A very gory image popped into Josie's mind, one of Errol's head, rolling down the sidewalk in front of her daughter's house. Good Lord! She needed to wash her brain. She didn't want to sever the loser's head from his neck, she just wanted to sever him from their lives. She wanted her daughter back. And she wanted to see her granddaughter.

Alice called later to check in on her. "How did the writing go?"

"It went fine," Josie said.

"Did you bump off Errol?"

"No, I bumped off that Emerald woman," Josie lied.

"I'm glad you didn't bump off your son-in-law, even if it was only in your head. Even though you'd like to."

"I don't want to kill him. I just want him gone," Josie said. "You don't understand," she continued. "You have a perfect daughter-in-law."

"I know. I lucked out. But Jos, it's too late to get rid of him. They have a child."

The very reminder of her granddaughter made tears rise in Josie's eyes.

"Look how hard life is for Karissa having to share her daughter back and forth. Do you want that for Coral?"

Over the years Josie had seen her share of unhappy kids, dealing with being shuttled from one home to another. It wasn't ideal. But then neither was marrying the wrong person.

"Coral could have done so much better," she grumbled.

"She loves the man, Jos."

"God alone knows why," Josie said in disgust. Coral pulled most of the load in their marriage. She was always exhausted. It wasn't right.

"So does Coral. You need to give him more of a chance, see what she sees in him."

"Nothing. Love is blind."

"Maybe you need to be a little less eagle-eyed."

Josie gave a grunt. "Maybe."

But when her birthday came and it was only her, Alice, and her two neighbors at her house eating cake and not even a birthday card from her daughter, all bets were off. How could Coral treat her like this?

16

KARISSA'S ENCOUNTERS WITH GERALD MCCRAE SINCE the great coffee incident had been, if not cordial, at least polite. Rather coldly polite on his part, which left her with a rapidly beating heart as she punched his number in her phone.

"This is Gerald," barked a male voice.

The grump. What had possessed her to think it would be a good idea to have him visit their book club? And why had she even picked his book when there were much nicer writers on the Heron Publishing roster? She was toadying, as any nineteenth-century writer would say. Sucking up. Although she certainly didn't need to suck up to Gerald. He wasn't her boss. Still, it bothered her that he disliked her. It was an undeserved dislike.

"This is Karissa from Heron Publishing," she said, keeping her voice pleasant.

"What do you need?" he demanded.

For you to be nice. "I'm calling about your new book."

"Is there a problem with it? Did some reviewer with the IQ of a walnut give it a bad review?"

"No, not at all. My book club is reading it and I was hoping you would meet with us and share some of your adventures."

"Oh?" The sharpness in his voice dulled somewhat. "I didn't know you had a book club."

"There are a lot of things you don't know about me, Mr. McCrae," Karissa said as politely as possible. "One of the things you don't know is that I like to read."

"Well, good for you."

"And I've actually read a couple of your books so far and found them interesting." That was no lie, they were.

"Really?" Suddenly he was sounding almost friendly.

"Yes, really."

"Well, uh, thank you."

"Would you be interested in a visit with our book club?"

"How many are in it?"

So, numbers mattered, which made Gerald a book club snob.

"Four," she said. "They're all very intelligent women."

"All women." He didn't sound pleased.

"All interested in reading your book. Isn't that how authors grow a readership, one reader at a time?"

"I don't need a lecture on how authors grow a readership," he snapped, and then was silent a moment.

"Obviously, you're not interested in meeting with us," Karissa said. "We'll switch to a different Heron Publishing author. I'm sorry I wasted your time."

The threat of her book club choosing a different author to read belted Gerald where it hurt, his pride. "I didn't say I wasn't interested in meeting with you," he said.

"That's the impression I got."

"Well, it's a wrong one. I never turn down an invitation to meet with readers."

Which was very wise of him. He was hardly a *New York Times* bestselling author and couldn't afford to be a snob.

"When are you meeting?"

Karissa gave him the date and time and he promised to put it on his calendar.

"Wonderful," said Karissa. "Thank you."

The charming response would have been, "No, thank *you*." Gerald was not a charmer. "You're welcome. Text me the address. I'll be there." And then, in case she might have forgotten how important he was, he added, "I can give you one hour."

"And we can give you refreshments," she said, proud of her clever response.

He grunted and said goodbye and that was that.

The next day Shirley and Karissa enjoyed a chat in the break room over the orange nut muffins Karissa had brought in. Alice's creations, of course.

"That was sweet of you to invite Gerald to your book club meeting," said Shirley.

"I think he's coming out of a sense of duty. He wasn't exactly enthusiastic when I invited him."

Shirley pulled off a piece of her muffin. "Trust me, he's thrilled."

"How do you know?" Karissa asked.

"I know because I had an email waiting for me this morning. He plans to bring a free book for everyone and wanted advice on which one he should pick."

"What did you tell him?"

"I told him anything but the Sasquatch one. It sells well, but really, it's rather a ridiculous book. Don't ever ask him if he believes there is such a thing. He'll never shut up about it. He's sure he spotted one once."

"That could make for interesting conversation," Karissa mused. And would Josie have fun with it. Gerald considered himself a toughie, but Josie's tongue would cut him to ribbons. "Anyway, I'm glad he's okay with coming."

"Oh, yes. Any time Gerald can pontificate he's a happy man." Shirley paused a moment, then continued. "I know you two didn't exactly get off on the right foot, but really, under that gruff exterior of his beats a kind heart. He sent me flowers for my birthday last year. And when we were all locked down during COVID and I was complaining during a Zoom meeting about not being able to find toilet paper, he was on my doorstep the next day with a package of four. He claimed it was the last one left on the pallet in Target and he outran two teenage boys to get it."

Karissa giggled. "The adventures of Gerald."

"Probably truer than some of the ones in his books," Shirley said. "Anyway, he's a good raconteur."

"At least that's what Shirley said," Karissa reported when she and Margot were doing their Saturday morning walk. Margot had picked up the pace from when they first began, and Karissa was pleased that she was keeping up.

"Gerald and Josie in the same room will definitely prove interesting," Margot said. "By the way, I've been researching poisons to use on our evil Mary."

"Did you find one?"

"I found several—arsenic, cyanide, even something awful called dimethylmercury. But none of those quite fit the bill. There is one called Ricin, that you can absorb through the skin. I read about it being used on an exiled Bulgarian dissident. But he didn't collapse immediately, so that's probably not very dramatic. You'd have to send her to the hospital."

"I do like the idea of her collapsing over her laptop," said Karissa, envisioning their villain with her head on the keyboard, her copper-colored hair—greasy because she hadn't washed it—spread out. "What are the symptoms?"

"Fever for one."

"Hmm. She could keep typing and ignore the fever."

"That could work if you've decided to change the ghost writer to her assistant. Mary could be right in the middle of an important scene and determined to finish it."

"Or the killer could sprinkle the poison on some pages she's proofreading. I do prefer the desk though. Death should be quick enough that she's stuck there. And painful."

"Very painful," Margot agreed.

"It will be great if you can find a poison that will do that."

"If not, we can invent a poison. It is fiction, after all."

"True," Karissa said. She thought a moment. "If we can't make the poison work quickly enough, maybe Mary doesn't die at her laptop. Maybe she dies in bed."

"With a lover?" Margot suggested.

"No, all by herself. I wouldn't wish dying alone on anyone in real life, but in fiction to make a selfish and heartless woman die without anyone with her who cares feels like the best kind of poetic justice."

"Fiction is often the only place you get it," said Margot.

"And the safest," Karissa said, and they both laughed. Then Karissa sobered. "It's kind of a petty way to get back at someone you don't like."

"Don't tell me you're feeling guilty about killing off a real-life bitch in a pretend story."

"Maybe a little."

"I bet authors do it all the time. And wouldn't it be great if Heron Publishing did decide to publish the story?"

"A first book, the odds aren't in our favor."

"You never know if you don't take the gamble."

"You all are having so much fun helping me with it. I hope none of you are disappointed if nothing comes of this," Karissa said.

"We won't be. It's fun playing around with it. Josie is turning out to have quite a way with words, and I know Alice is enjoying thinking up scenes for you. No matter what, we're all in."

The declaration of loyalty was water for a parched soul.

"I'm so glad I moved in next to you," Karissa said.

"And I'm glad you did," said Margot. "We're all glad you moved here."

Her friends, the book club, this project, her job—all had come as a result of something devastating. She thought of the Phoenix, the legendary bird that would rise reborn from the ashes of fire and destruction. She was the Phoenix. *I've got liftoff.*

It was a good feeling, and that good feeling stayed with her all the way to the Fourth of July. She had Macy for the long holiday weekend, and Lilith had come with them to Anacortes as well. It was as perfect a day as anyone could have asked for, with a cloudless sky and a breeze from the beach keeping the temperature pleasantly warm. Her parents' house was her favorite getaway, with its sweeping views and beach access. Her grandparents had built it when they were first married and waterfront was affordable for a hardworking couple. It wasn't so affordable anymore, and Karissa felt blessed to be able to have it as a retreat to run to.

"They're having a good time," said her mother as they sat on the deck, watching the girls race up and down the beach.

"They are. I'm glad Lilith could come with us."

She hadn't been sure how Edward would feel about parting with his daughter for three days, but he'd been both appreciative and complimentary. "Her grandparents are on a cruise, and I'm buried in work, and my mom actually had some plans, so this is great timing. It's nice of you to let her tag along. But then, I shouldn't be surprised. You've got a kind heart, Karissa."

It had only been a casual compliment, but Karissa's heart had taken it in and swelled anyway.

"We love having her with us," she'd said. It was true. Lilith and Macy had become like sisters.

"She's a sweet girl," said Mom. "I imagine her father is just as nice."

"He is."

"Do you know if he has anyone in his life?" Mom asked casually.

"Very subtle," Karissa teased.

"You never told me."

She hadn't. Too much sharing about Edward with her mother would have leaked her feelings and put ideas in Mom's head, and Karissa already had a hard enough time managing her own thoughts.

"There's no wife in the picture, but he spends a lot of time with one of our authors," she said. It was all she could do not to frown.

"Strictly business?"

"Who knows?" If Emerald had her way it wouldn't be, and it sure looked to Karissa like she was determined to get her way.

"I'd love to see you find someone nice."

"Maybe someday," Karissa said. "I'm not holding my breath."

"Timothy Bracken is up visiting for the weekend with his boys. I hear he's divorced."

Timothy Bracken. In grade school he'd chased Karissa and her best friend around the school playground with lizards or garter snakes or any other creepy thing he could find, threatening to put them down their tops. She'd squealed and carried on but had secretly loved the attention. When they were in middle school, he'd kissed Karissa as part of a kissing game some of the neighborhood kids were playing at a poorly supervised party. It had been the highlight of her young life, but not his. He teased her about being a bookworm when they started high school and then forgot about her.

"Not surprised he and his wife split," Ethan said later when they all walked down two houses to the neighborhood block party where the Browns had set up food tables under a tent. "I'm surprised the woman stayed with him long enough to have kids. He's a fungus."

"Mushrooms are fungi and look how many people like them," Karissa pointed out.

Ethan pointed a finger at her. "Don't even think about it."

Easier said than done. He was even better looking than he'd been in high school. He'd filled out in the thighs and chest, and the smooth face of youth had become more chiseled and manly.

"I wonder what happened to end his marriage?" Karissa mused.

"I heard he couldn't keep it in his pants," said Ethan.

"Don't be crude," chided their mother.

"Okay, he's a mushroom that can't control his stem."

Karissa giggled and Mom gave Ethan a motherly look that threatened punishment and never mind how old he was.

That was his cue to wander off.

"Honestly, what am I going to do with him?" Mom muttered.

"Keep adoring and spoiling him," said Karissa, and they exchanged smiles.

They watched as he sauntered over to another one of the old gang, a pretty woman named Jill, who was single again after a failed relationship.

"I always liked her," said Mom. Mom wanted two things out of life, for her children to be happy and to have more grandchildren.

The evening passed pleasantly, with all Karissa's mother's friends wanting to know about how Karissa's glamorous job was going.

"You are living the life now," said one of them.

Yes, she was. She had liftoff.

She was helping herself to a cupcake from the dessert table

when Timothy Bracken appeared at her side, smiling and smelling like beer. "Hey, Rissa, long time no see."

Only because he hadn't looked. She'd been around. She didn't know whether to feel insulted that he'd ignored her so long or flattered that he was finally seeing her. Flattered, she decided.

"Hi, Timothy," she said, opting to keep her response casual.

"I hear you're single these days. How's it goin'?"

Suddenly, after all these years, Timothy wanted to hear about her life? "Everything's going great," she replied cautiously.

"I hear you're a big shot at some publishing house."

"I'm not a big shot. I just run the office."

He took a swig from his bottle, nodded. "That's big, right? Do you meet a bunch of best-selling authors?"

"It's a small company."

"So, no hanging out with Lee Child? Man, I love that TV series."

"Have you read the books?"

"Nah. I'm a visual kind of guy." He winked and ran a hand up her arm.

Ethan was right. Timothy was a fungus.

"Hey, Timothy." Ethan had arrived and he slung an arm around Karissa's shoulder. "You're not thinking of messing with my sister, are you?"

"Of course not," said Timothy, although that sudden sunburn on his face said, "Yep, busted."

"Good. 'Cause she's not interested."

"What? Rissa can't speak for herself?" Timothy demanded, finding his bravado and puffing out his chest.

"I can, and I'm not interested. Sorry."

Timothy's shocked expression was enough to make her laugh. He didn't join in. "Just bein' friendly," he muttered.

"Go be friendly somewhere else," Ethan said to him. "Horny little drunk, he'll hit on anything," he said as red-faced Timothy walked away. The words were barely out of his mouth before his eyes popped wide. "Hey, I didn't mean that the way it sounded. You're not anything. I mean, you're fine the way you are, so don't be getting all desperate and encouraging tools like him. You deserve better. And Mark was an asshat for leaving you," he added.

Her brother's kind words and loyalty made her smile.

Smiling was something she seemed to be doing a lot more lately. It was progress.

Time heals all wounds, the saying went. *And time wounds all heels.* She liked that saying better. But at this point, it didn't matter what happened to Mark.

"Yes, he was," she agreed. "But he's in the past. I'd rather concentrate on the future."

Ethan gave her shoulder a one-armed hug. "Well said. You know, Dad's been bragging about you to everyone and Mom's already trying to figure out how she can score more free books for her book club. Did she ask you yet?"

"Not yet, but I'm sure I can get some for her."

"You're kind of a celebrity now."

"No," she scoffed.

"It's true. We're all proud of you, sis," he said.

"This sounds like sucking up to me. What do you want?"

He grinned. "That Gerald McCrae book about Big Foot."

"One of our top sellers."

"Can you get me a signed copy?"

"I can," she said.

"Yes! Okay, now I'm going to go back and talk to Jill some more. Think you can manage to keep the drunk horn toad away without my help?"

"Man magnet that I am, I'll try."

"You'll be a magnet for the right one, Rissa."

She thought of Edward. "Probably not," she murmured as her brother sauntered off.

★ ★ ★

Alice had rented a cabin on Hood Canal for the holiday weekend for her son and daughter-in-law and herself, and the granddog, of course, and had invited Josie to join them. They'd grilled oysters for dinner to go with the potato salad Josie had made and then enjoyed Alice's chocolate cake with buttercream frosting.

The table was cleared, the dishes were done, and Lucky had been given a doggie sedative so he would survive the night. Next on the agenda came a game of cards before darkness fell and everyone along the canal started setting off fireworks.

It had been a relaxing day, sitting on the beach and watching the kids kayak, throwing sticks into the water for Lucky to chase. But in spite of all that relaxation Josie had felt like extra baggage, hauled along but not necessary.

"This is for you and the kids," she'd protested when Alice invited her. "You don't need me."

"This is for family, and I do," Alice had insisted. "Anyway, I'm paying for the cabin, so I get to say who shares it with me. There's plenty of room."

Not for an extra who should have been with her own kid. Coral's absence was the proverbial elephant in the room that nobody wanted to talk about. Or maybe they did. Maybe Callum wanted to tell his aunt Josie to quit being a monster mom and fix things with Coral.

Everyone sided with Coral, Josie was sure of it.

Jealousy took a sharp bite out of her soul as she watched how easily Alice interacted with her daughter-in-law. Of course, who didn't love sweet, happy Alice who never had a bad word for anyone? Who always wanted everyone to love her. That was why she was so beloved. She was a people pleaser. If her son looked at a sunny sky and said, "It's going to rain," Alice would agree because her boy could do no wrong.

Although Josie could remember a few times when Callum

was a kid that Alice had yelled at him. And when he and Coral had gotten into it when they were tweens and he'd hit her, Alice had picked him up like he weighed no more than a one-pound bag of sugar, plopped him at the kitchen table and practically snarled, "You don't hit your cousin. For anything. Ever."

"She started it," Callum had whined.

"And now I'm finishing it. You will sit here all afternoon and think about how important family is. We never do mean things to each other. Ever!"

Josie had applauded her. Moms had a right to tell their kids things they needed to hear.

No matter what their age.

This weekend felt all wrong without Coral present.

"You in, Aunt Josie?" Callum asked.

Josie had looked at her poker hand but not seen it. "I fold."

Coral should have been with them.

17

"Only a fool doesn't answer when adventure calls."
—from *Meeting Mount Rainier* by Gerald McCrae

THE NIGHT WAS WARM, AND ALICE'S BACKYARD SMELLED
like the honeysuckle growing along the side of her house when
the book club gathered for their July meeting there. "Let me
host since you don't need to be home," she'd offered. "I'd love
to take a turn."

Macy was spending the night with Lilith, so Karissa had
agreed.

"I'm glad we're meeting out here," she said as she sat down
next to Margot at Alice's patio table and poured herself some
lemonade from the pitcher. "It's nicer than being inside."

"Patio furniture should be on sale soon," said Margot.

"Josie and I have been keeping our eyes peeled at garage
sales," Alice said, "but we haven't found anything for you yet."

"That's sweet of you," Karissa said to her, "but I think I'd
rather get something new."

"At fifty percent off," added Margot.

"At fifty percent off."

"Tell me how your Fourth of July weekends were," Alice said. "I have yet to hear."

"Not much to mine," said Karissa. "Unless you count an ego boost from a drunk."

"Were you in the bars up there in Anacortes, trying to pick up men?" Margot teased.

"Nope. Neighborhood block party."

"Do tell," said Margot, so Karissa related her encounter with Timothy the tool.

"Losers, you find 'em everywhere," said Margot.

"What about you, Margot?" Alice asked.

"Busy," she said. "Andrew and I worked until late on the third."

"Oh?" Alice prompted.

"Don't get all excited. There's nothing going on."

Alice's eager expression dissolved. "That's too bad. What did you end up doing on the Fourth then? Were you with Elisa?"

"No." Margot got suddenly busy with a cracker and Alice's artichoke dip.

"Then what?" Alice persisted.

"I hung out with Andrew's family. His grandparents have a place on Raft Island."

"Just hung out with his family, but there's nothing going on?" Alice sounded disbelieving.

"We're in business together," Margot said primly.

"You're blushing," Alice observed. "Don't be keeping secrets."

Josie came out through the kitchen slider. "Hey, everyone. Sorry I'm late. Who's keeping secrets?"

"Margot," said Alice. "She was with Mr. App Ape and his family on the Fourth."

Josie set down the seven-layer dip she was carrying. "Yeah? Did you set off some fireworks?"

"The kids did," said Margot.

"Not that kind," Josie said and frowned at her.

"What all did you do?" Alice asked.

"The usual. Grilled burgers, ate potato salad, did some water skiing, drank wine coolers. It gets a little fuzzy after that."

"Thanks to a few wine coolers," Karissa surmised.

"Only a few."

"And then you set off some fireworks," Josie crowed. "About time you got a love life."

"I don't have a love life," Margot insisted. "It's gestating."

"A gestating love life. Now, that's interesting," said Josie.

"We need to keep things professional," Margot said.

She hadn't been advising Karissa to keep things professional with Edward. Not that Karissa had a love life, not even a gestating one.

"Well, I hope it works out," Josie said. "If this guy's at all decent you should grab onto him. Good men are hard to find."

Karissa immediately thought of Edward. He was, indeed, a good man, one she would have loved making a new start with. She sensed that he needed a new start, too, needed to show off that smile more, needed to laugh. Emerald, for all her beauty, wasn't succeeding in growing his smile. Not for the first time Karissa wondered who could.

"How soon before you think your app will be done?" Alice was asking.

"Hopefully in another few weeks," said Margot. "I think it's going to be great. I just wish my mom would quit nagging me to get a real job," she added, using air quotes. "As if I'm working my tail off for nothing." She shook her head. "She makes me nuts with all her nagging."

"You should be glad she does," Josie said sharply, making Margot frown. "Your mother cares for you."

"My mother wants me to be perfect," Margot snapped.

Josie wasn't intimidated by Margot's irritation. "She only wants what's best for you. Mothers always want what's best for their kids, and kids should respect that. How would you feel if she wasn't around to nag you?"

"Relieved."

Karissa stared in shock as tears appeared in Josie's eyes. She blinked furiously. "I need to pee," she said, and rushed back into the house.

"What the hell?" asked Margot, looking to Alice.

"Josie and her daughter aren't speaking."

"I didn't know. Crap. I didn't mean to upset her," Margot said.

"It's not your fault," Alice said. "And she's got to work this out."

"Is it reparable?" Karissa asked. She couldn't imagine not being on speaking terms with her mother. They were best friends.

"It is. But Josie's going to have to be the one to repair it, and she's stubborn."

The three women sat in silence until Margot mused, "Why is mother-daughter stuff so hard?"

The slider opened. "I'm back so you can all stop talking about me," Josie growled as she stepped back onto the patio.

"Oh, please. We have better things to talk about than you," said Margot.

It was the perfect thing to say. Josie poured herself a lemonade and grabbed a plate. "Like our stick-up-his-ass author. You can tell by the way he writes he thinks he's something else. Probably sees himself as the next Hemingway."

"I suppose somebody needs to be the next Hemingway," Alice said.

"Not him."

"I don't know. I enjoyed the book," said Karissa.

"Did you really?" Josie challenged.

"Yes, I did," Karissa insisted.

"Well, you can suck up to him if you want, but I'm not going to," said Josie. "Where is he, anyway?"

As if on cue Alice's doorbell sounded. "I'll go let him in. Be nice," she said to Josie, who simply rolled her eyes.

"Let the games begin," said Margot.

Josie lowered her voice and said to Margot, "I'm sorry I snapped at you."

"I'm sorry I hit a nerve," Margot said. "And maybe you're right."

The slider opened and Alice stepped out, followed by Gerald who was wearing cargo pants, a T-shirt and his favorite hiking boots. Dressed for the occasion. He also carried a book bag with author copies of one of his older books for everyone.

"Here's our guest," Alice announced.

"We've got eyes," Josie said.

"Thanks for coming, Gerald," Karissa hurried to say. "I was just telling everyone how much I enjoyed your book."

"I did, too," said Alice.

"That's nice to hear," he said, smiling at her and demonstrating that he could be charming when he chose to be.

She beamed and blushed. "Would you care for some lemonade?"

"Don't mind if I do," he said, taking a seat.

"And we have artichoke dip and a seven-layer dip," Alice said.

"It's full of frijoles, like a lot of writers these days," put in Josie.

He raised an eyebrow. "Are you a critic?"

"I'm a reader," she said. "And I can recognize a sentence fragment when I see one. And I saw plenty in your book."

He lowered his eyebrows. "Writing styles have changed since the nineteenth century." Josie merely shrugged, which seemed to irritate him almost as much as her earlier remark. "You know, I'd love to see all those readers who like to get online and diss a writer's hard work sit down and write something."

"Maybe some of us are," Josie said.

He gave a snort. "Yeah, I guess you don't have to be a genius these days to puke something on the page and put it up and say, 'I are a writer.'"

Maybe this had not been such a good idea. The verbal sparring had started much too quickly, and it was making Karissa uncomfortable, but she found herself at a loss for how to stop it. She looked to Margot. Margot was watching Josie and Gerald over her lemonade glass, smiling like she was enjoying a good movie. She'd be no help.

"Authors all have their own unique styles," said Alice, and Josie rolled her eyes. "I'd like to hear about that encounter you had with a cougar," Alice continued.

"Yes, that was a good bit of fiction," said Josie.

"That was not fiction," Gerald snapped. He turned back to Alice. "The thing with cougars is, you don't want to run. That will trigger their predatory chase instincts. You have to stand your ground and face them. If a cougar looks like it's going to attack you try to make yourself look bigger than it."

"So, you should gain weight before hiking in the mountains," cracked Josie.

Gerald frowned but refused to look at her. "But if you just stand still, chances are it will keep moving on. Look at its feet. Don't look it in the eye. You don't want to appear aggressive."

"I've done my share of hiking and I've never encountered a cougar," said Josie.

"Lucky you," Gerald said, dismissively.

"I bet you haven't, either. Are you really as badass as you sound?"

"He sounds pretty badass to me," said Margot, a glint of humor in her eyes.

At least someone was enjoying this.

"I never said I was a badass," he said. "I'm just a writer."

"And an outdoorsman," put in Karissa. "Gerald has done some impressive hikes—the Oregon Badlands, the Wild Rogue River Trail."

"Forty miles of beauty," he said.

"My husband used to love to hike," said Alice.

"So did mine until he turned into a couch potato," muttered Josie.

"I'd love to try hiking again, but I'd want to go with someone who's experienced," Alice continued and smiled at Gerald.

"Since when do you want to hike?" Josie challenged her.

"Since reading Gerald's book," Alice said. "Gerald, would you take us on a hike?"

"Hiking requires a lot of stamina," he said.

"Are you insinuating we couldn't keep up?" Josie demanded. "What do we look like, a bunch of cream puffs?"

"I think I could manage," said Margot.

Yes, she could. In addition to their Saturday morning walks, Karissa knew that she got up early and ran every morning. Last Karissa had heard, Margot was up to five miles.

"Let's all go together," suggested Alice.

Hiking and getting exhausted and sweaty didn't sound like fun to Karissa. "I have Macy," she said, hoping for a way to wiggle out.

"We can pick a day when Mark has her," Margot said, easily wiping away Karissa's excuse.

"I'm sure Gerald doesn't have time," Karissa said.

"He probably doesn't want to actually prove he's as tough in real life as he is in his imagination," said Josie.

She'd said it under her breath, but he'd heard.

He frowned at her. "I can make time. Green Mountain in Kitsap County is an easy one and you get a nice view at the end."

"That sounds perfect," Alice said, beaming.

"It sounds like torture," Karissa complained after their meeting was over and she and Margot were walking back to their houses.

"It'll be good for you," Margot said. "And it should definitely prove entertaining."

"You are sick, you know that?"

Margot laughed. "You're the one who suggested his book and invited him to book club."

"I didn't know it was going to lead to a forced march."

"You might enjoy it."

"I doubt it," said Karissa.

Karissa's prediction regarding her enjoyment of their hike had proved true. Margot couldn't help but laugh at her friend's stoical expression as they made their way up Green Mountain's Gold Creek Trail.

"You really are a cream puff," she teased.

"There's nothing wrong with cream puffs," Karissa retorted.

"Just another mile," said Margot.

"Another mile? Ugh, I'm already sweating to death. People should hike in the fall when it's cool."

"No complaining," called back Josie, who was keeping pace with Gerald. "You're getting a chance to breathe clean air and enjoy nature. Look at those rhodies."

"I'm not sure I'm an enjoy nature kind of woman," Karissa said.

"I need to rest a minute," said Alice, who was straggling behind all of them.

"I'll rest with you," Karissa offered.

"You don't want to lag behind. We might encounter a cougar," Josie called back to her sister. "Of course, we have Gerald here to show us what to do."

"Did anyone ever tell you that you have a smart mouth?" Gerald snapped.

"I have a smart brain to go with it," she retorted, and Margot laughed.

"I can't believe I let you women sucker me into this," he grumbled.

"Oh, you're loving showing how masculine you are," Josie taunted.

"I think I need to turn back," Alice called.

Everyone stopped and looked at her. She was still sitting on a fallen tree, holding her half-full water bottle, Karissa next to her.

"Come on, sis, you can do this," Josie urged.

Alice shook her head. "I need to get in better shape before I get serious about hiking."

"Okay, I'll go back with you." Josie started down the trail toward her.

"We can all go back," Margot offered.

"Oh, brother," Gerald muttered.

"No, I don't want to ruin this for all of you," Alice protested.

"I'll go with her," Karissa offered. "We'll wait for you at the parking lot. I need to use the porta-potty anyway."

"I'd better go with you," Josie said.

"You keep going. We'll be fine. We've got pepper spray, and I know how to make myself look big." Karissa demonstrated by raising her hands high like a wizard about to zap someone.

"I'm not waiting," said Gerald.

Josie frowned at him. "Who says chivalry is dead."

"They'll be fine," Margot assured her. "Come on. We don't want to miss that view."

"Hey, if you need to quit," Gerald said to Josie.

"No, I don't," she said, and turned and began marching back up the trail.

"A tough thing, aren't you?" he said.

"You bet, and I can keep up with you just fine, Mr. Mountain Man."

Better than reality TV, thought Margot as she followed them. It reminded her of a few friends-to-lovers romances she'd read.

Josie and Gerald as lovers. There was an image that didn't need to hang out in her brain. She'd wind up scarred for life.

"So, tell me about all the hikes you've been on," he said to Josie. It was a dare.

"Did the Twin Falls trail, the Skyline Trail Loop."

"That's a hard one," Gerald said.

"Did it with my husband when we were young. Those glacier views were something else. I always wanted to go back but we never did."

"A shame," he said.

"Things don't always go according to plan," said Josie.

Margot remembered some of the comments she'd made about her husband and wondered if one of the things that hadn't gone according to plan had been her marriage.

They finally reached the top. The view from the outlook was worth the effort. Thanks to the clear sky they could see the city of Bremerton, and beyond that the Olympics to the west and Mount Rainier in the distance to the east.

"This was worth the sweat," said Josie as she opened her water bottle. "Nature is amazing."

Gerald smiled. "Yes, it is."

"I'm glad we did this," she said.

"Good," he said.

"Thanks, Gerald," said Margot.

"My pleasure."

It looked like chivalry wasn't dead after all.

They started back down. "Coming down is always harder than going up," said Josie. "My knees are already pissed at me."

"You gotta stay in shape if you're gonna hike," said Gerald.

Margot was in the lead, so she couldn't see either of her companions, but she didn't need to see Josie to know she was scowling.

And then she heard it, the scuffle of boots on gravel, followed by an oomph and a squeal.

18

"You can't be too careful when on the trail.
Nature doesn't suffer fools lightly."
—from *Meeting Mount Rainier* by Gerald McCrae

MARGOT TURNED TO SEE GERALD AND JOSIE LAID OUT
on the trail like two fallen logs, him flat on his back and her
on her side. Josie's water bottle had rolled away and Gerald's
wide-brimmed sunhat was tipped over his eyes.

"Are you okay?" Margot asked as Josie struggled to her feet.

"What the heck?" Josie demanded of Gerald. "You took me
down like a bowling pin."

"Damned loose gravel. I didn't see it," he said as he pushed
his hat back in place.

"That's what you get for looking at my legs," Josie told him
as she picked up her water bottle.

"I was not," Gerald snarled, but his sunburned cheeks suddenly turned redder.

"Can you get up?" Josie asked him.

"Of course, I can." He got to his feet with an "Oomph,"
took a step and swore.

"You twisted your ankle," said Josie.

"Great deduction, doc," he growled, then limped another step, jaw clenched.

"Here, let me help you," she said.

"I don't need any help," he informed her, pulling away. He limped another step.

"Oh, for crying out loud. Don't be such a macho fool. Margot, come get on his other side. He can lean on us."

"We can't fit three abreast on this trail," he protested.

"Sure we can," Margot said cheerfully. "We'll just have to get cozy."

"Don't argue or we'll leave you here for the cougars," Josie threatened. "Now, come on."

So off they went, the three musketeers, making their way down the trail as best they could. Conversation was at an end and all that could be heard was the occasional tweeting of a bird and a few choice words from Gerald.

"Oh, my gosh, what happened?" Alice cried, hurrying toward them when they finally got back to the parking area.

"Gerald fell," Josie reported.

"Loose gravel," Gerald explained.

"He wasn't watching where he was going," Josie added. "Guess I shouldn't have worn shorts."

Margot had to admit, Josie was in pretty good shape, and she did have nice legs.

"I'm so sorry," Karissa said, looking concerned.

"Ice and Advil," Margot said.

"I know that," Gerald replied, irritated.

"And bone broth," said Josie.

He nodded. "I'll get some at the store."

"That store-bought stuff's no good," she said. "I've got some in the freezer. Give me your address and I'll bring it to you. Unless you live in a yurt somewhere in the wilds."

This was better than Netflix.

Gerald turned meek as a lamb and gave up both his address and his phone number.

"I can send along some cookies," Alice said.

"Leave your door unlocked. That way you won't have to get up and answer," Josie instructed.

"Give me time to get a shower," he said, his brows pulled together. "Unless you think I need help with that."

"You need help, period," she retorted, unfazed. "Alice, help me get him to his car."

"I think something much more than loose gravel is about to take down Gerald," Margot said to Karissa as the trio moved away.

Josie and Alice were in Invitation Bookstore a few days later, picking up copies of *It's Never Too Late*, the book club's next read, and Josie was complaining about the choice.

"You know, your complaining about our book club choices is becoming irritating," Alice said.

"The choices are becoming irritating," Josie replied. "You're obviously the darling of the group because this is the second time you've gotten to pick something."

"You picked something the meeting before last. Anyway, I like Muriel Sterling's books. And Karissa wanted to read it, too."

"Of course, she did. You ply her with cookies all the time. You've got that girl trained like a puppy."

"Oh, stop. This will be good reading."

"A book by a spoiled woman who thinks she knows it all."

"I don't think I'd call her spoiled. She's gone through some hard things," Alice said. "Widowed, like us. Twice."

"And now remarried. I can't feel sorry for someone whose family owns a chocolate company."

"I can feel sorry for a woman who lost the love of her life," Alice said. It was a hurt that never completely left your heart.

Josie softened. "I'm sorry, sis. I know Charlie was yours."

"As you always say, life goes on," Alice said.

Of course, life went on, but it was never the same. There were achingly lonely moments, times when she felt adrift without anything substantive to anchor her heart to. Callum had his own life, so did her friends. Maybe that was why Gerald McCrae had appealed to her. He possibly held the antidote to the loneliness.

But he hadn't offered it to her, even though she'd sent out signals that she was interested.

"Want to share some leftover chicken salad for dinner?" she offered after they'd made their purchases and were leaving the store.

Josie suddenly looked uncomfortable. "I can't tonight."

"Oh? What have you got going on?"

"I'm having dinner with Gerald."

"Gerald! You don't even like each other."

"I never said that," Josie insisted.

"Oh, great. You meet someone you can enjoy a good argument with, and you fall head over heels." It was ridiculous but Alice felt somehow cheated. "I'm the one who was nice to him, and he asks you to dinner."

Her sister looked guilty. So she should. "It's just payback for me bringing him bone broth."

"I sent cookies." Cookies beat bone broth any day.

"Why don't you come with us?" Josie suggested.

"I certainly won't. I wasn't invited."

"It's nothing, really," Josie insisted.

"Don't say that. I'm not stupid."

They got into Josie's car and she heaved a sigh, turned to Alice. "Look, we just got to talking and he suggested dinner. It wasn't a big thing." Alice's silence filled the car. "I didn't know you were interested," Josie continued. "I can tell him to take a hike by himself. It's not that big a deal to me."

But it was or she wouldn't be doing it, and it was wrong of Alice not to allow her the freedom to explore a new relationship.

Alice was being a brat, she knew it. Loneliness did funny things to a woman. It made her insecure and envious.

It also made her think about pursuing someone she wasn't even interested in, which, if she was going to be honest, was what she'd be doing if she went out with Gerald McCrae. He was interesting, but he was also gruff, and that gruffness would wear on her. There was a reason he'd been attracted to Josie. She was similarly wired. Josie had loved her husband, but in the end their marriage hadn't been what it once was. She deserved a second chance at love.

"No, you go out and have fun. When it comes right down to it, he isn't my type."

Josie studied her. "You sure?"

"Yes, I'm sure."

"It's nothing romantic, really," Josie said.

"Not yet, but you never know. I hope you have a wonderful time."

"You mean it?"

"I do," Alice said.

Josie smiled. "Never turn down a free meal, right?"

"Right," Alice said. "Just don't…leave me behind."

Josie stared at her. "Why would you even think a thing like that?"

Alice shrugged. "People get caught up in a new relationship and other ones fall by the wayside."

Josie frowned. "Not sisters, for crying out loud. And, really, Alice, this isn't a big deal."

"I think it might be bigger than you realize."

Alice was wrong. Josie and Gerald were simply going to share a meal—his idea of paying her back for getting him down the trail and putting him back on the road to health. It had only been a sprain, no big deal. And dinner was no big deal.

She put on perfume anyway.

They met at Anthony's at Gig Harbor, on the bay. Gerald cleaned up well, she'd say that for him. He was wearing a collared shirt and slacks and a pair of loafers and looked...not bad.

"How's the ankle?" she greeted him when he walked in.

"It's fine. It was never that bad to begin with."

"Which is why you couldn't walk on it," Josie said, raising an eyebrow.

"I could have. There was no point in making a scene with you two fussing over me." He turned to the host. "I've got a reservation. McCrae."

"Of course," said the host, and started to seat them at a table.

"By the window," said Gerald, and their host immediately changed course.

"I see you get what you want," Josie said once they were seated.

"When I've specifically requested something, I'd better," he said. "One thing I learned years ago, I don't like being walked all over. Not that I don't appreciate a strong woman," he added.

"Yeah?" It was an affirmation of who she was and it pleased her.

"But there's a difference between strong and bossy," he added, and that didn't please her.

"What's that supposed to mean?" she demanded.

"It means that no man likes being treated like a little boy. I see women doing that to their men all the time."

"Some men act like little boys," Josie argued, "and are you insinuating I bossed you around out on the trail when you couldn't even walk?"

"No, but now that you mention it, I could walk. I didn't see you having to carry me down."

She pointed a finger at him. "You are an ingrate."

"I am not. I'm taking you to dinner, aren't I?"

"Nobody said you had to."

"Nobody said you had to accept."

"Well, I did, so you and your indestructible foot are stuck with me."

He surprised her by laughing. "By Jupiter, you do like to give as good as you get."

"It's more blessed to give than to receive," she said, and he laughed again.

She chuckled, and their waiter who had been hesitating to approach came up and took their drink orders.

"You were right about your bone broth," he said after their drinks had arrived. "It was better than what I normally buy at the store."

"I'm a good cook," she informed him.

"I'm pretty good in the kitchen, too," he said.

"Yeah? What's your specialty?"

"Bacon wrapped pesto pork tenderloin."

"That is impressive. I thought for sure you were going to say something like lasagna."

"Why is that?"

"It's easy to make but sounds impressive."

"As in any fool can make lasagna?"

"Something like that," she said.

"Let's hear your specialty."

"Mushroom soup."

"Mushroom soup, huh? From a can?"

"Oh, real funny," she said, frowning at him.

The waiter was coming back for their orders but hesitated. "You're scaring the waiter," Gerald said, as he motioned the man over.

"Oh, you are a comic, aren't you?" she said. To prove how unscary she was, she smiled warmly at their waiter before ordering.

"I'll have the salmon, too," Gerald said. "Good brain food," he added after the waiter left.

"Exactly," Josie agreed. "But back to my soup. It's excellent. I make it with chicken stock and cream and sauteed onions and fresh thyme. Years ago, I used chanterelles. We'd go hunting for them ourselves—better than Easter egg hunting."

"At the price of those suckers now it's like hunting for gold."

"You hunt mushrooms?" Josie asked.

"I've been known to. You ask nice and I might take you this fall."

"You ask nice and I might show you the best place to find them," she shot back.

He shook his head. "Is everything a competition with you?"

"Not everything."

"Be sure to let me know when you think of something that isn't," he said, and she laughed.

That was the end of the laughter. The rest of the meal was spent debating everything from who the best modern writers were to which foods were overrated, and that led them back to comparing their cooking skills.

"The best chefs in the world are men," he said as he signed the charge bill.

"According to men," she retorted.

"Okay, I'll put my pork loin up against your mushroom soup," he challenged.

"Deal. I'll spring for the 'shrooms. Bring your pork to my house and I'll supply the bread. I make an awesome sourdough."

"Okay, I'll bring a Riesling. That goes good with pork, and if I don't like your soup I can doctor it with the wine."

"If you don't like my soup, it will prove your taste in food is as bad as your taste in literature. Who ever heard of someone not liking *Wuthering Heights*?"

"Or Hemingway!"

"You are hopeless," she informed him, determined to get the last word as they walked out to the parking lot.

Although, really, the last word had to be thanks. "It was a good dinner."

"Ours will be better. I'll call you," he said, and sauntered off toward his car.

Maybe it would.

She called Alice on speaker to report in as she drove home. "You know, he's not so bad when you get to know him. I think that tough guy persona is an affectation."

"He is manly," Alice said.

"Which makes him a rare breed," said Josie.

"Jos, you *are* falling for this man," Alice said.

"I am not," Josie insisted. "I don't need another man in my life. They're a pain."

"Not all of them," Alice said softly, and Josie knew she was thinking of her Charlie.

Sadly, there weren't enough Charlies in the world. Most men were Joes.

But maybe she had found herself a Charlie. Time would tell.

Karissa had become adept at guarding Edward's time at work, as requested, taking messages when he didn't want to be disturbed, and organizing his schedule. All his authors respected that and were fine with setting up appointments. Except for Emerald. She continued to pop in so often, Karissa joked to André, that they should put her on staff.

On Friday she kidnapped him for lunch and kept him away all afternoon. By the time he returned, Karissa had a stack of messages for him, which made him groan.

"I should start working remote so I can't be whisked away," he said.

The thought of him not being around the office made her sad. It seemed they were chatting more and longer every day before starting work. He'd ask how her book was coming. It was coming together nicely, but she'd always answer with a vague, "Slowly." She'd tell him what progress she was making in the club's latest book pick. His smiles were becoming increasingly lighter, which lifted her heart.

The only bug in the bread was Emerald and her constant appearances.

"I can always tell her you're not in," Karissa offered.

"I wouldn't want you to lie for me," he said.

"I'm happy to." That hadn't come out right. "I mean, I do want to protect your time."

"I need to do that for myself, but I appreciate you taking your job so seriously. In fact, I appreciate everything you do here, Karissa. I don't know what I'd do, what we'd do," he corrected himself, "without you." He cleared his throat. "I guess I'd better start returning these calls," he said, and vanished into his office.

19

"I took the hard path. It was worth the effort."
—from *Meeting Mount Rainier* by Gerald McCrae

"I'VE GOT TO ADMIT, THIS IS AMAZING," JOSIE SAID
after tasting the first bite of Gerald's pork tenderloin.

He smiled, wiped at the corner of his mouth with his napkin. "Paired with that soup of yours and this bread, we could have our own restaurant. Just kidding," he added in case she was naïve enough to take him seriously.

"Restaurants are too much work. You never own a business. It owns you."

He pulled off another piece of bread and dipped it in the soup. "You had a restaurant?"

"Close enough. I had a kitchen shop. Sold all kinds of cute gadgets and cookware. But then people started shopping more online and I got tired of little twits coming in and taking pictures of my merchandise and then leaving. I figured out that they were off to order it online cheaper. I finally said heck with it."

"People always want a bargain."

"You're right," she said. "Alice and I love hitting the thrift stores. But that's different."

"So you've never bought books online."

"Okay, I'll admit I have. But we also support our local bookstore, and I prefer bookstores," she said. "Great atmosphere."

"I'm surprised a reading snob like you can find anything to read," he taunted.

"Your pride still a little sore from our book club discussion?" she shot back, making him frown.

"It's easy for people to criticize something they've never done."

"Who says I'm not doing it now?"

He leaned back in his chair. "Are you?"

"I am," she said. "Actually, it's a group project."

"Writing a book together—my idea of hell," he said.

"So far this is fun. At least my part is. I'm not sure I'd ever want to write a whole book." And then she had to be honest. "I think you're right. Not everyone can do it."

He put a finger in his ear and jiggled it. "Did I hear you correctly?"

"Yes, you did."

"Is that as close as I'm going to get to a compliment from you?"

"I already complimented you on your pork," she pointed out.

"That you did," he said, and poured more wine into her glass. It was the second refill. "Tell me more about this book of yours."

"The book club's writing it. It's about murder, but it's not a mystery. It's about revenge. The killer deserves to get away with murder, and I have to say it's kind of fun coming up with awful things to do in fiction. Helps you work out some of your anger."

"You seem to have your fair share of that," he observed.

She downed a good-sized swig of her wine. "What makes you say that?"

"Seriously? You've got a razor edge to you, woman."

"Oh, and you don't."

"Okay, I admit, I can get..."

"Cranky? Snippy? Mean?" she supplied. "I heard how you went off on Karissa when she was first working at Heron Publishing."

His bushy brows lowered. "The girl tried to scald me."

"She tripped," Josie said sternly.

"Okay, okay. Not one of my finer moments. Anyway, that's all water under the bridge, and we're talking about you here, not me. You appear to be in good health and you're not a bad-looking woman."

"Damning with faint praise," Josie murmured.

"You've got friends. Got a nice place. Looks to me like your life is pretty good."

It was, on the surface, but the feud with Coral was chewing down her heart. "My daughter and I aren't speaking." She hated saying it out loud. She downed another healthy swig.

He gave a thoughtful nod. "Hard when things aren't going right with your kids."

"Have you got any?"

"A son. We get along okay."

"Lucky you. It's different with daughters." Josie could feel the sting of tears. She blinked hard and took another gulp of her wine.

"I take it she's all you've got."

She nodded.

"What happened to your husband?"

"He died on me." She held up a hand before he could say something he'd regret, like, *these things happen.* "I know people die, I know wives usually outlive their husbands, but Joe cheated us out of a lot of years together. Not that the years we had after we hit middle age were all that good, but still."

"How'd he do that?"

"By choosing his bad habits over me. He cheated on every diet I ever tried to get him on, he refused to quit smoking."

"You do know how hard it is to quit smoking, right?" Gerald said.

"I know how hard it is to keep living," she retorted. "He didn't have to have a heart attack. He could have taken better care of himself."

"Did he have a bad ticker?"

"He had high cholesterol. That could have been fixed with diet and medication."

"Oh, so you're a doctor?"

"No, I'm a widow," she snapped. "His doctor was after him for years to make lifestyle changes, but he didn't. After a while he didn't even bother with checkups. Who does that? People said things to me like, 'It was his time to die,' but it didn't have to be. He chose the time by clogging his arteries and stressing his heart. He left me, pure and simple."

"I'm sorry," Gerald said.

"And then my daughter ran off and married that turkey." She realized she was ranting, the wine loosening her lips more than she'd intended, and she pressed them together.

"A turkey for a son-in-law, huh?"

"I told her he wasn't right for her, but she didn't listen. Now she's stuck with him, and...oh, never mind." Josie grabbed her wineglass and headed for the living room couch. "I don't want to talk about it."

He followed and sat down next to her. "But you are. You know it takes some men a while to grow up. Did you give the guy a chance?"

"Of course," Josie insisted. "I tried to be a sport, tried to accept him. But he's a loser."

"Don't tell me, let me guess. You pointed that out to your daughter."

On more than one occasion. She'd tried to warn Coral when she and Errol were first dating. The boy drove a souped-up old beater and dressed like he didn't have a penny to his name. If he did, he didn't spend much on Coral. A far as Josie could tell, his biggest ambition in life was to sit around and play video games with his friends and drink beer.

"He's fun, Mom," Coral had insisted after they'd gone to the Fremont Fair, a silly free-for-all in Seattle's Fremont District.

As if fun was all there was to life.

It seemed that Errol thought that way. After they were married and Josie commented on his Peter Pan tendencies, Coral had leapt to his defense.

"So what if he doesn't mow the lawn?"

"And sits inside gaming while you do," Josie had pointed out.

"He's got hay fever."

"He's allergic to work."

"He works."

"Thirty hours, sometimes less, compared to your forty plus," Josie had argued. *"Stocking shelves. How is that a career?"*

"He doesn't do drugs and he's not abusive. Okay, so he's not ambitious. I don't care. Nobody's perfect, Mom."

Errol was as far from perfect as a man could get. Thinking about what her daughter had settled for was enough to make her blood pressure spike.

"I tried to give him a chance," Josie insisted, although at the moment she couldn't come up with an example of how. Her face felt flushed. It was the wine. She set her glass on the coffee table. "They have a child now and he still hasn't grown up. He hardly helps at all with the baby and he's a loafer. It's not right. And instead of taking my advice and making him turn into a man, my daughter sides with him."

That was a mild way of putting it. After their last discussion

Coral had blown up and yelled at her, picked up her baby and stormed out of Josie's house. They hadn't spoken since.

Gerald was judging her. She could feel it. "I suppose your life is so together."

"I never said it was. There's a lot of stuff that happened I didn't like. But what are you going to do?"

"Something," Josie argued.

"Looks like you did something with your daughter. How'd that work out?"

Not well at all. All Josie had been trying to do was help. And now here was Gerald the Great sitting there all smug and psychoanalyzing her.

"Who are you, Doctor Phil?" she demanded.

"I've still got my hair," he said, running a hand through his silver mane.

"While we're on the subject of you..."

"Oh, boy, here it comes," he said, and he, too, set his glass on the coffee table.

"You've got a hard crust on you, mister, so you're hardly in a position to be pointing fingers, you know."

"I wasn't pointing fingers. Why do you women always have to start throwing around accusations?"

"Why do you men always bluster when we tell you the truth?"

He frowned, picked his glass back up and took a drink. Set it back down. Josie waited.

"I'll cop to being crusty," he said. "And yeah, I'm carrying some baggage. By this time in life, we all do."

"What's in your suitcase?" she asked.

"The usual," he said with a wave of his hand.

"Divorce?" she supplied. "Or did she die?"

"Divorce." He took a deep breath, looked out her window, seeing something other than her monkey tree. "I never saw it coming. I liked my job, liked my life. Did the family vacation thing every summer. I was a biology teacher, so I got a lot of the summer off. We spent one up at Denali. The kid was a good kid, hardly gave us any trouble growing up. I thought everything was fine."

"Until?" Josie prompted.

"Until she got together with a fitness trainer."

"Shallow," Josie said with a shake of the head. "Is that when you decided to get buff?"

He laughed a little and shrugged. "I needed to do something with my time. Our boy was out of the house by then. What was I going to do, sit around and watch TV?"

"That's what Joe did."

"Well, not me. I took up hiking. Never bothered to replace her. Life's been good ever since."

"And the writing? How did that happen?"

"I kept some journals. Showed my buddy the English teacher and he encouraged me to turn them into a book. I eventually sent it to Heron Publishing on a whim and they took it. Now I'm retired. I can write as much as I want, hike wherever and whenever I want, do what I want."

"All by yourself."

"I like my own company."

"You should have a hiking buddy. In case you break a leg or get attacked by a cougar."

"Yeah? If you were my hiking buddy, would you save me from a cougar?"

"No, I'd run away while it chomped on you and be forever grateful that you died saving me."

That produced a reluctant chuckle.

"You know what else you need?"

"You're going to tell me, aren't you?"

"I am. You need a first reader who can give you input on your books."

"Uh, no I don't."

Okay, fine. Not everybody could take criticism. She shrugged and took another sip of her wine.

"But I wouldn't mind a hiking buddy. Occasionally," he hurried to add.

"I could get into taking a hike occasionally," she said casually as she set her glass back down.

"You want to try another this summer?"

"Yeah. Why not?"

"I'll find an easy one for you."

"And I'll try to keep you from falling on your keister."

He frowned. "Do you always have to have the last word?"

She grinned. "Yep, and nothing stops me from getting it."

"You need someone who can stand up to you once in a while." Suddenly he was looking at her in a way that made her heart catch. Naw. She had to have imagined that.

But she hadn't. "Come here," he said softly, hooking her neck and drawing her close.

"Oh, come on now. We're too old for this stuff."

"You're kidding, right?"

He didn't wait for an answer. He kissed her and what a kiss it was. She felt like she'd just discovered fire. And he'd stayed single all these years? What a waste of talent.

He pulled away enough to study her face, a self-satisfied smirk on his. "That shut you up."

"Oh brother. If you aren't the most conceited thing God ever planted in a male body."

"Am I going to have to shut you up again?"

Well, why not? "Yes."

It's so easy to see in others only the things that bother us and forget to focus on what's good. Is there someone in your life that you should be seeing in a different light? Margot read in Muriel Sterling's book.

The words left Margot unsettled. She set the book on her

nightstand, unimpressed, and turned off the bedside lamp. That was enough reading for one night.

But later the next day, after she got home from helping Victoria go through her closets, she picked up the book again—not because she wanted to but because she'd made a commitment to the book club to read it—and got hit hard.

We tend to take the people in our lives for granted, assuming they'll always be there. But they won't. We let small irritations pry us apart and think I'll deal with that later. *Later can arrive too late. The most important word I can share with you in this chapter is the word* Now. *Now is the time to tear down walls and rebuild relationships. Now is the time to reach out to friends you haven't talked to in a while. Now is the time to tell those important people in your life that you love them. Now is all you have.*

The word *now* inspired an answering word in Margot's heart. Mom. Her mother had been driving her nuts lately, but as she thought about the last conversation they'd had, how she'd brushed her mom off, and hadn't even bothered to answer her last call, she felt a rush of shame. Who cared more than her mother whether she got a job? Who else called and checked on her as much as her mother? She did take her mother for granted.

She left the book on her couch, got back in her car and drove to the Hallmark store where she found a properly gushy card. She sat in the car, trying to think of what to write in that card. She chewed on her lip and considered her options. *I'm glad you care enough to nag.* Not that. Much as the motives behind the nagging were good, she didn't want to encourage it. *Please don't die for a long time. Don't leave fast and unexpectedly like Dad did.* That would be heartfelt but way too morbid. She settled for *I love you.* Then she addressed it, drove to the post office, purchased a stamp and mailed it. A card was a small thing, but she hoped it would show her mother she appreciated her.

Two days later her mother called to thank her. "I got your card. What a lovely surprise!"

Her enthusiasm felt way out of proportion to what she'd received. "It was just a card, Mom."

"Not to me. It meant a lot." Was Mom crying?

Suddenly Margot wanted to cry. Her mother was so starved for appreciation that a simple card felt like the keys to the kingdom.

"Mom, I know I was a pain to raise."

"No, you weren't," Mom insisted.

"Yes, I was. And I know sometimes I don't appreciate your advice." There was an understatement. "But I also know you care and I'm grateful that you do."

"I love you, darling. You, being a mother, know how that works. Your children may grow up, but they're always your children. And you always care. And you always want the best for them."

"You're right. Thank you for always caring, Mom."

"I always have, and I always will. I love you."

That said it all. Maybe mothers and daughters didn't always get it right, but they loved each other. And it was important to remember that and to say it. Margot was glad she had. Thank you, Muriel Sterling.

"Pigeon poop!" Josie muttered on reading Muriel Sterling's latest so-called pearls of wisdom.

What did that woman know of ungrateful daughters who never listened to their mother, who turned their back on a once-close relationship in favor of one that was doomed not to last? She was not going to finish this asinine book, and if the girls kept choosing ones like it, she was leaving the book club and that was that.

Rashness is the enemy of us all, wrote the oh-so-perfect Muriel Sterling.

Another Muriel Sterling proverb. She had so many vapid sayings she could start her own line of inspirational merchandise—Muriel Sterling mugs, Muriel Sterling T-shirts, Muriel Sterling greeting cards. Every woman who wanted her life solved in one easy sentence would buy one.

Her phone rang. It was Gerald. "What are you doing right now?"

"Nothing important," Josie said, and slammed the book shut.

"How about dinner at Harbor Lights? We never did get around to talking about hikes."

"We do need to do that," she said. And she needed to get away from Muriel.

But Muriel was not easy to escape. One of the first things Gerald asked after they'd given the server their drink orders was, "What's your book club reading now?"

"Another stupid self-improvement book. We haven't even been together a year and we're already on our second one. If this keeps up I'm quitting."

"That bad?"

"I hate it when people who think they're perfect tell you what to do."

Their drinks arrived and she guzzled down half of her tonic water.

"Hit a nerve, huh?"

"Oh, stop," she said irritably.

He chuckled. "Yep, hit a nerve."

"I have no nerves to hit," she said, which made him laugh outright. "Okay, maybe I do. I'm human, after all."

"If you prick me, will I not bleed?" he said.

"Oh, good grief, you quote Shakespeare, too? You are a man of many talents."

He responded to her flattery with a shake of his head. "Everybody knows that quote. I don't much care for Shakespeare. I'd rather read Hemingway."

"Of course, you would. Way to lose points."

"He was a brilliant writer," Gerald said, lifting his Scotch in salute to Papa Hemingway.

"He was a misogynist who killed animals for sport."

"I think you should only judge a writer on his writing, not on his life."

"Can you disconnect a writer from his life?"

Gerald took a thoughtful sip of his drink. "I don't know."

"Don't try to be like him. The man killed himself."

"I'll try not to do that. What about the woman who wrote this book you're bitching about? How does her life measure up to her writing?" he asked, returning them to the subject of the irritating Muriel Sterling.

"Practically perfect in every way. She's had two husbands die on her but she's syrupy sweet and positive and beloved and… okay, maybe I'm a little jealous. I'm not a Muriel Sterling or a Mary Poppins, and it's too late to try and turn myself into one."

"Who says you have to?"

Josie bit her lip. Muriel Sterling, that was who. Not in so many words, but the underlying message was there for her on every page.

"I'm not the Wicked Witch of the West, either," was all she could say. That wasn't saying much.

"I don't know about that. You seem to have cast a spell on me," he said.

She rolled her eyes, feigning disdain even as her heart gave a girlish flutter.

"Now, let's talk about hikes," he suggested.

Good idea. They discussed a couple of possible hikes to take, traded dares and double dog dares and enjoyed a stunning view and delicious meal. And for a while Josie forgot all about Muriel Sterling and her platitudes and simplistic advice.

For a while.

20

*"If you're still here there's still a chance
to make right what's wrong in your life."*
—from *It's Never Too Late* by Muriel Sterling

KARISSA AND MARGOT'S WALKS HAD TURNED INTO JOGS,
and Karissa was proud that she'd reached a point where she
could jog and talk at the same time. "Everything's set for
Macy's birthday party this weekend," she said. "Mark's bringing Charlotte."

"Is he going to drop her off and go away, I hope?"

"I'm not inviting him to stay, that's for sure," said Karissa.
"I'm getting used to this sharing routine, and each time I see
him the hurt feels less raw, so that's progress. But I still won't
want him hanging around the house like nothing bad ever happened between us."

"I don't blame you," said Margot.

"I don't know how you and your ex managed to stay on
such good terms."

"Nobody cheated, that's how. We grew apart, we fell out of

love. You can get past that, even circle around to being friends. What Mark did is another ball game."

"I guess it is. He's a walking reminder that I didn't measure up. No, wait," she corrected herself. "He's a walking reminder that he didn't measure up."

"We have a breakthrough here," Margot said, and Karissa grinned.

Yes, they did.

The book club was on hand Friday evening to help with Macy's birthday party. "A chance to check out your rotten ex? I wouldn't miss that for all the Ghirardelli in San Francisco," said Josie. "And if he acts up we'll stomp on him."

"I love a party," said Alice.

"Me, too," said Margot.

It was going to be a book-themed party, so Alice had made cupcakes topped with tiny fondant books. Josie contributed a bowl full of mini-popcorn balls which she'd labeled fairy bowling balls in honor of Macy's favorite book series, and Karissa made a slushy-style punch from a mixture of frozen fruit juices and soda pop. Margot's contribution was candy for the children and white wine for the grown-ups.

Each of the guests was to come as her favorite character from one of the Fairy Feathers books. So far one unicorn and a witch had arrived. Next on the doorstep was Lilith, dressed as a fairy, with her father in tow. Edward was invited to stay and accepted with a genuine smile. Mark arrived on his heels with Charlotte, who was also dressed as a fairy. Mark was not invited to stay.

"We'll be done in two hours," Karissa told him as Macy gave him a hug.

He handed over his present, and after an enthusiastic, "Thank you, Daddy!" she and Charlotte raced off to the kitchen to inspect the cupcakes.

He looked to where Edward was settling in on the couch next to one of the moms, Margot offering him a glass of wine.

"I don't mind staying," he said.

Karissa minded him staying. Someday she'd get past that, but she wasn't there yet, and the idea of Mark watching her every move, rating it, and then reporting back to Allegra was not a pleasant one.

"I'm sorry, Mark. I'm not ready to explain to everyone why my ex-husband is arriving with my ex-best friend's daughter to our daughter's birthday party. You can celebrate with her when you have her next weekend."

He didn't seem to have anything to say in response, but he looked around the living room behind her as though searching for backup, before frowning at Edward.

"Come back in two hours."

"Fine," he snapped. "I'll go sit in the car and read."

"An excellent idea," said Karissa. "We do have some great restaurants in town if you want to grab something to eat," she added.

He turned and marched back down the front walk, flipping her off as he went.

She shut the door and smiled at Margot, who gave her a thumbs-up.

With all the guests present it was time for the games to begin. Josie had dubbed herself the bad fairy and kept the girls entertained in the family room by trying to tap them on the head with the magic wand she'd ordered online. Karissa invited the adults to enjoy the appetizers she'd picked up from the store and made sure everyone had their drinks and had been introduced. Then she took over with the little guests, leading them outside for the treasure hunt she'd set up for them.

While they were searching for net bags filled with party favors, she and Alice set the treats out on the table along with the mini-books Karissa had created. Everything was going perfectly, and Karissa felt like a perfect hostess.

Margot led Edward to the table to show off the tiny bound books wrapped in pink ribbon. "Karissa made them up," she said, making Karissa blush.

"It's a silly little story," she said. "And the girls helped write it. I had them each give me a character's name, a special fairy trick and the name of a pet. Then I just mixed them all together."

"Just mixed them together. Into a book. No big deal," Margot scoffed.

"That's ingenious," said Edward.

"It was fun," Karissa said.

"How's your other writing coming?" he asked.

"Slowly," she replied. That was one book they didn't need to be talking about. Even though the murder victim's name had been changed she was sure he'd see through the thinly veiled description of Emerald and her dislike of the woman would show like a neon sign. She needed to do a better job of disguising her pettiness before letting her boss see it on display. She went to the slider and called the girls in.

The rest of the party passed in perfect chaos with more games, lots of squeals, two bumped heads and a moment of tears, followed by story time with bad fairy Josie and then the opening of presents. By the end of the festivities Karissa was ready to sit down with a glass of the wine Margot had brought.

"What a lovely party," said one mother as she and her daughter left.

It had been, and Karissa was pleased with herself and grateful to her friends.

"That Josie," the woman added. "You should clone her."

"One is enough," cracked Margot, who'd heard.

Mark was back at the door to fetch Charlotte. Frowning.

"Oh, my gosh, he's pouting," Margot whispered to Karissa.

It looked that way. It was small of her, she knew, but Karissa enjoyed the moment anyway.

"Look what I got, Daddy Mark," Charlotte said, holding up her specially made book.

Daddy Mark. Ugh.

"Yeah, whatever," he said dismissively. "We need to get going. Mommy's waiting at home." It would have been an innocuous little sentence coming from any other mouth, but she felt the intended barb. "Be sure and pack a bathing suit for Macy next weekend. We'll be taking her to Wild Waves for her birthday," he added and accompanied it with a mean smile for Karissa.

Those little digs for no reason, other than he was irritated that she didn't want him hanging around, making things awkward for her—it was mean-spirited.

She refused to let it get to her. "That will be fun. I'll be sure and pack it." She gave Charlotte a hug. "Goodbye, sweetie. Thanks for coming."

Charlotte nodded and then raced off to the car.

"Thanks for bringing her down," Karissa said to Mark, determined to be civilized.

"A long way to come for two hours of sitting in my car," he grumbled.

"You should have tried one of our restaurants," she said, refusing to pick up the guilt he was laying down.

He scowled, then turned and followed Charlotte down the front walk.

"There he goes, your lucky escape," Margot said to Karissa.

"I guess he's right," she said. "It was a long way to come, but I couldn't not invite one of Macy's best friends. Macy wanted to see her."

The last of the moms was at the door, ready to leave, and Edward was right behind her. Karissa was sure they'd both overheard the conversation.

"Exes, can't live with 'em, best to live without 'em," the woman joked.

"Ain't it the truth," said Margot, speaking for Karissa, who had no idea how to reply to that.

"It was a great party," Edward said. "Pretty hard to top."

She'd tried her best. "I'm afraid trips to amusement parks aren't in my birthday party budget," she said, thinking of Macy's upcoming celebration with Mark.

"You made one right here," he said, showing that smile that once had been so rare.

His kind words removed the sting lingering from Mark's unkind behavior. "Thank you."

"What time do you want me to pick up Lilith tomorrow?"

They set a time and he left. The two girls vanished into Macy's room to play with her gifts and the women settled in the living room for their own after party.

"I can see why you're so into Edward," Margot said. "He is the epitome of kindness. And what a contrast from the jerk."

"There was a time when Mark wasn't a jerk," Karissa said.

Margot shook her head. "It was latent. A little fertilizer and out popped the real him."

"It was different when we were first together. Maybe back then he thought I was the best he could do." Karissa realized what she'd said. No more of that. She had her own unique gifts and talents. She'd just proved it by throwing a great party for her daughter. Even more important, she had principles. She had heart. When she and Mark split it hadn't been her loss, it had been his. His behavior earlier had proved that.

She quickly corrected herself. "But he didn't know what he had. His loss."

Margot saluted Karissa with her wineglass. "Yay you. I'm glad you realize that."

"You're making progress, kiddo," said Josie.

Yes, she was.

★ ★ ★

Words from Muriel Sterling's book were like sticky notes Josie couldn't seem to shake from her brain. *It's never too late to build a bridge*, Muriel insisted. *You'll feel so much better once you have.*

How did Muriel Sterling know how she'd feel?

The book was sitting right there on her coffee table when she sat down with her morning coffee. Against her will, her hand picked it up. Some invisible force seemed to be moving her like a puppet, making her open it and begin reading.

Imagine the rest of your life without the people you love in it. How does it feel? The answer to that is easy. Not good. Do you really want to sell your future happiness to your present feelings?

Ouch! But darn it all, Josie wasn't the one who'd cut off all communication. It was Coral. And Coral needed to be the one to fix this. She shut the book and tossed it back on the coffee table. That wasn't far enough away. She grabbed it and tossed it in the recycle bin. That took care of Muriel Sterling.

Until Josie was in the supermarket late that afternoon. Then Muriel's words came back with a vengeance and bitch-slapped her.

A mother with her little girl, who looked to be about five, stood in front of her in the express checkout line, waiting to pay for some frozen lemonade. The girl was a chatty little thing.

"Grammy likes lemonade, doesn't she, Mommy?" she said to her mother.

"Yes, she does," said Mommy. "That's why we're getting some."

"Will Grammy like my new shoes?" The girl bounced a couple of times, making the LED colored lights around the soles go into action.

"Yes, she will," said Mommy.

The conveyor belt moved forward, and the checker grabbed the lemonade and scanned it.

"We're going to my grandma's house to bake cookies," the child told her.

"That sounds like fun," said the woman.

The little girl nodded eagerly, making her blond curls bounce. Blossom had blond curls. Josie could envision her standing where this little girl was standing one day, bragging about going to her grandma's house.

A sudden ache hit her heart, making her tear up. At the rate things were going with Coral that wasn't going to happen.

That was when the first slap hit. *What are you waiting for?*

A time machine. She'd blown her relationship with her daughter to smithereens with her big mouth. It was too late.

It's never too late to build a bridge, Muriel insisted, giving her another good slap. *How badly do you want to see your daughter again? How badly do you want to watch your granddaughter grow up and be part of her life?*

Josie left the checkout line, and speed-walked up and down a few more aisles, adding items to her cart. Then she was back, mentally urging the checker to hurry up.

She paid for her items, raced home, and got busy baking.

An hour later she was standing on Coral's doorstep, knocking on the door almost as fast as her heart was beating. *Please open up.*

21

ERROL THE LOSER OPENED THE DOOR. HE WORE RIPPED jeans, a T-shirt promoting someone named Machine Gun Kelly, a ponytail, and a shocked expression. This was awkward. She'd hoped Coral would be the one to open it. That would have been difficult, but somehow not as unsettling. There was nothing like coming face-to-face with the person who had to know all the things she'd said about him.

It didn't take more than a second for his expression to go from shocked to resentful. Josie held out the container of peanut butter cookies she'd baked. "These are for you."

He took them and looked at her suspiciously.

"Don't worry. They're not poisoned. I want us to hit restart and figured maybe they'd help."

"Maybe," he said.

"My daughter loves you." *There's got to be a reason. Don't say that!* She cleared her throat. "You're family and you need to be treated like family."

"Does this mean you're gonna nag me?" he asked in sullen tones, infecting Josie with a desire to kick him in the shin.

It would be deserved as far as she was concerned, but hardly an effective way to build a bridge. She opted for humor. "If you're lucky. And now, I need to talk to Coral."

He stepped aside, letting her enter. She could smell dinner cooking, something with garlic in it. Coral had to be out in the kitchen.

She walked through the living room where a video game had been paused on the big-screen TV. Soldiers shooting each other. Charming. *Never mind that,* she told herself.

Her daughter was in the kitchen, standing at the stove, stirring a pot of what was probably spaghetti sauce. Spaghetti was one of Coral's favorite dishes. She'd learned how to make the sauce from scratch from Josie. They'd spent a lot of time in the kitchen together when Coral was growing up. There'd been none of that after Coral married Errol.

Little Blossom was corralled in her playpen, close enough to see her mother and for Coral to keep an eye on her. She was happily occupied with some kind of noisy toy. But with that sixth sense babies have, she realized someone new had walked on stage and looked up.

At the sight of Josie, she cried out, "Nananana!"

That made Coral turn around.

She was a lovely young woman, much prettier than Josie had been in her youth, with hair the same light brown Josie's had been before the gray sneaked in and contaminated it. The same hazel eyes looked back at Josie in amazement and her daughter's perfect full mouth dropped.

Like her husband, the surprise was quickly replaced by a much stonier expression. "Mom. What are you doing here?"

"I came to apologize."

There was no softening of the features. Instant forgiveness would not be forthcoming. Coral turned off the burner, leaned against the stove and regarded her mother with her arms crossed.

"Nananana!" cried Blossom, jumping up and down.

Josie longed to rush over and pick her up. She resisted the temptation because she longed even more to hug her daughter, to hear Coral say, "All is forgiven."

"You've got a lot to apologize for," Coral said.

It was humbling to hear. Josie sat down at the kitchen bar and took a deep breath.

Coral didn't give her a chance to speak. "What you said last time I saw you was unforgiveable. Wishing my child's father had never been born? Really, Mom?"

"Only in the sense that I wish he'd never come into our lives."

"My life, Mom," Coral corrected her. "He came into my life."

"And turned ours upside down," Josie protested. "Good grief. We were still mourning your father. You rushed into this relationship."

"I didn't rush. You never liked Errol. You've never given him a chance," said Coral, her voice rising.

There was a reason she'd never liked Errol. He was a lazy lout and was all wrong for her daughter. And what Josie was seeing was proof. Coral was busy getting dinner ready and was he helping at all? Was he playing with the baby? No. Josie felt all her righteous indignation build right back up inside her till she was nearly ready to burst. What was wrong with her daughter that she didn't see this?

She opened her mouth to speak, but Coral cut her off. "If you're going to start in again about what a waste of space my husband is you can leave. Because this house is my space and I get to decide who stays in it. And he stays."

Ouch. Josie deflated. "Look. I don't want to fight."

"Yes, you do, and you'll keep fighting until you hear that you're right. That's what you want."

"Nananana," Blossom tried again, her little voice anxious.

New emotions began to rise like a high tide, sorrow, love, and fear all about to drown Josie. "I don't want to be right. I want my daughter back. I want to be part of your life."

"You won't be, not without Errol in it, too. We're a couple, Mom. We have a kid. We're a family."

Josie saw the same tears in her daughter's eyes that she was feeling in hers. She'd caused those tears. Shame on her.

"I know," she said softly. "I know."

"So what if Errol's not perfect?" Coral continued, eyes flashing.

There was an understatement. Perfect and Errol lived in two different galaxies.

"But neither was Dad and you loved him."

"Oh, that is not fair. Don't you dare compare Errol to your father," Josie said hotly.

"I'm not criticizing Daddy. Not like you did. And I'm not going to get on Errol's case for every little thing he does."

Or doesn't do. Josie bit back the words. They would only fan the flame.

"He's trying, Mom," Coral said, her voice earnest. "He's picking Blossom up from day care now and he's learning to cook."

"You could have told me that."

It was the wrong thing to say. Coral turned back to stone. "Why would I?"

Josie sighed, wiped at a corner of her eye, nodded.

"Dad would have given him a chance."

Coral was right. Joe would have. Joe had always had ostrich tendencies.

But they weren't talking about Joe. They were talking about Josie and her tendencies. Quick to judge, needing to be in control. In her daughter's case, desperate to protect. It was no easy thing to choose a perfect mate.

"I only wanted you to be happy," she protested.

"I'm a grown woman, Mom. I get to decide what makes me happy, and he makes me happy. Which is more than I can say for you."

Her daughter's words sliced through Josie's heart. "You're right. I've been hard-hearted and unforgiving. I'm sorry," Josie said, and began to cry.

So did little Blossom.

"Errol, come get the baby," Coral yelled.

Errol appeared a moment later, scooped up the child and left the kitchen, glaring at Josie as he passed.

"Nananana!" sobbed Blossom.

Josie was sobbing, too. "I'm sorry. I really am."

And with that, Coral was seated next to her, taking her hands. "I need you to say more than that, Mom. I need you to admit you were wrong."

Josie still wasn't convinced that she was. Still, she'd been wrong to treat her daughter like she was fifteen instead of thirty. Coral hadn't specified that she say she was wrong about Errol.

Josie used the loophole. "I was wrong." Time would tell whether or not she was wrong about him, but it was Coral's right to be with whomever she chose.

Coral, wiped at her own eyes, nodded. "Okay. It's a beginning." She didn't hug Josie, but she squeezed her hands. It was, indeed, a beginning.

Josie sniffed, nodded, then said, "Now, how about I take you all out for dinner. It will give me a chance to get to know Errol better."

"I'll ask him if he wants to," Coral said and left Josie to fish around in her pocket for a tissue and hope that her son-in-law would say yes.

She could hear their voices. They seemed to be having a long conversation. She was glad she couldn't hear what they were saying about her, though she could well imagine.

At last Coral returned. "Okay. Let me put away the sauce.

Errol's getting Blossom ready," she added, which Josie suspected was meant to point out that she wasn't as observant of Errol as she claimed. Maybe she wasn't.

She let them choose the restaurant and they chose a nearby Applebee's. Errol still regarded Josie suspiciously as they settled into a booth and waited for the server to bring a booster chair for Blossom, who was once again happy now that the adults in her life were happy.

"Errol, I'll get right to it," Josie said. "I haven't given you a fair chance." Actually, she thought she had but maybe she'd been wrong.

He concentrated on the silverware on the table, didn't say anything in reply.

Coral did. "You're right. You haven't."

"I want my daughter to be happy. I worry about her. You've got a daughter now. I bet you can understand that."

Still nothing. Great. She was trying to converse with the Sphinx.

It took a round of lemonade and a double order of buffalo wings before he finally found his voice. "Coral told me all the shit you said about me."

Josie was supposed to be building a bridge, but she had a memory lapse. "Did you deserve any of them?"

"Mom!" Coral said sharply and Josie shut up.

But she didn't take back what she'd said. Instead, she regarded the man her daughter had chosen. She was still convinced Coral could have done so much better, but Coral was right. She got to decide what made her happy.

"Hey, I know I'm not perfect," he said. "But I love Coral and she loves me." The look he gave Josie dared her to question their love.

"I'm not so perfect, either," she said. "And I love her, too, so let's move forward from here. Okay?"

He nodded, took a big gulp of his lemonade, and Coral smiled.

"Nananana," Blossom said happily.

Josie let out a breath and relaxed against the seat. She had her daughter back. Life was good.

She wasn't going to get a dream son-in-law, not with this man, but so far she hadn't been a dream mother-in-law. Maybe they both needed to grow a little.

And maybe Muriel Sterling knew a thing or two after all.

It was a typical catch-up Monday, and Karissa was sorting through emails, passing on unsolicited submissions and dumping the unwanted hopefuls when one subject line caught her attention. *The Secret Spring.* What was the secret spring? She had to know.

The query letter informed her that the book was a nonfiction telling of the history of the sacred site of Licton Springs on Seattle's Duwamish River, which had become Seattle's first Indigenous Landmark. She opened the attached sample chapters and began to read.

She was still reading, captivated, when Edward came out of his office and started for the break room for coffee.

"I think I've found something you're going to want to see," she told him.

He stopped, raised an eyebrow. "You haven't been wading around in the slush pile, have you?"

"I have, and I think this is something that could be an important book for Heron Publishing. The subject matter is timely, and it's well written."

"Really?" He came over and stood by her desk.

Her senses were immediately aware of his physical presence—the smell of his cologne, the nearness of his body, the timbre of his voice as he spoke. She focused on her computer screen as she summarized her discovery. And her heart squeezed when he smiled down at her and said, "I think you may be onto something. Forward it to me. I'll have a look."

"I will. Would you let me do more of this?" she asked. "I'd love to be able to take some submissions home and read them."

"That's going above and beyond," he said.

"I know. But I want to."

He nodded. "Sure, if you want to. I don't think you'll find much."

"I'm pretty sure I just did. I really think I'm capable of doing more than fielding calls and organizing files."

"Of course, you are. I admire your ambition. It was a lucky day for us when you applied to work here."

"I'm glad you hired me," she said.

"So am I," he said.

For a moment she thought she glimpsed something in his eyes, something more than simply a boss's appreciation. But he cleared his throat, mentioned the need for coffee and moved away before she could take a closer look.

Don't be imagining things, she scolded herself. She was settling into contentment with her life and who she was. That was a boat she didn't need to rock, and hoping for something to happen with Edward would only rock it and, eventually, tip it. As Alice had said, someday her Mr. Rochester would come. Meanwhile, she'd keep her imagination reined in and her mind busy. All it took was discipline.

To prove it to herself, she kept her eyes on her computer screen when he went back into his office. The boat stayed stable.

The next day Shirley called Karissa into her office. "Edward sent me the submission you discovered, and I just finished it. You're right. It is something we'd like to publish."

Karissa grinned, delighted to hear that her instincts had been spot-on.

"Edward tells me you'd like to take on a little more responsibility."

"I would," said Karissa.

"I think if you want to scout out more potential authors for us that would be fine. We still haven't found a replacement for our editor who left earlier so we won't be taking on many new authors for a while, but if you find another like this one, we're open. Meanwhile, how about a new title?"

Karissa leaned forward in her chair. "Really?"

"Editorial assistant," said Shirley.

"I like the sound of that."

"It sounds more glamorous than it is. You'll still be doing pretty much what you've been doing all along and the bump in pay will be miniscule."

"That's okay. I just want to be more involved in the business."

"Looks like you are," said Shirley, pointing to her computer screen. "Great find."

Karissa practically skipped back to her desk. A few months ago she'd felt like her life was over. "Look at it now," she told herself.

Her mother said the same thing when Karissa called to tell her the news. "I'm so proud of you," she added.

"I'm proud of me, too," Karissa said.

"I can hear the confidence in your voice," Mom said.

It was newly found, growing a little more every day, and Karissa intended to keep it growing.

"All those hard things you've gone through, they've been the fertilizer that's made you blossom," Mom said.

"In other words, crap is good for you?" Margot joked when Karissa related what her mother had said.

"I guess so," she said with a laugh. "But I think I'm fertilized enough now." So no more crap, God, please.

22

"It's never too late to change,
so don't give up on yourself."
—from *It's Never Too Late* by Muriel Sterling

"THIS BOOK WAS A GAME CHANGER," JOSIE SAID, PAT-ting Muriel Sterling's book when the book club held their August meeting at Karissa's house. "My daughter and I are speaking again."

"Awesome," said Margot, and saluted Josie with her wineglass. "How did you manage that?"

"I followed Muriel's advice and built a bridge. And let me tell you, it wasn't easy."

"I'm glad everything is patched up," Alice said, and she couldn't help but feel a little proud of herself. After all, it was she who had recommended the book. She'd hoped maybe the chapter on reconciliation would get through to her sister.

"I have to admit, it spoke to me, too," Margot said. "My mom is still, well, my mom, but my attitude toward her has changed."

"Are you keeping her up to date on the app?" asked Josie.

"Uh, no. I want to maintain my new and improved attitude."

"I thought there were a lot of good things in the book, too," Karissa said. "That whole chapter on changing your attitude about your life is really helping me keep mine in the proper perspective. She's right. It's never too late to make a new start."

"It sure isn't," said Josie, and Alice didn't like the look she was giving her.

"What about you, Alice? What did you think about the book?" asked Karissa.

"I thought she made some very good points," Alice said and hoped nobody asked her to explain what she meant by that.

"Like what?" asked Josie. "I mean, you're the one who recommended the book to us. There had to have been something specific in there that you thought we needed to hear."

Alice could feel an uncomfortable sizzle on her cheeks. "Well, I thought the part about bridges would be especially helpful."

"For me?" Josie challenged.

"We all need to build bridges at some point," Alice said.

"And we all need to make new starts," Josie said.

Alice knew exactly what she was talking about. She feigned ignorance. "Karissa, you are showing us such a good example of that."

"Karissa isn't the only one who needs to make a new start," Josie persisted.

"We're always starting new on something," Alice said, parrying her sister's move.

Karissa was opening the book. "I really loved this," she said, and read, "I often hear people referring to themselves as a glass half-full or a glass half-empty person. What so many people fail to understand is that we each play a large part in how empty or how full our glasses are. Why not make the effort to fill that glass to the top with joy, accomplishment, time with family and friends? Why settle halfway for anything?" She looked around at the others. "I am happy to report that my glass is filling up."

"The new job title?" Margot guessed.

Karissa nodded. "In addition to working on our book I'm taking on more responsibility at work," she explained to Alice and Josie, and shared the details.

"Good for you. That's inspiring," said Josie. "How about you, sis? Are you inspired?"

"Yes, I am," Alice said. "Karissa, I think you found a book you thought we might enjoy reading for September. What was it?" she asked, ignoring her sister's frustrated frown.

"It's a time travel romance." Karissa reached for the book. "I thought we could use a change."

"Change is important," Josie said. If she circled back around to the subject of their last read Alice was going to put the banana cream pie she'd brought over right in her face.

"I'm all for romance," said Margot.

"Is there anything brewing between you and your app guy?" Alice asked, determined to keep them away from any more discussion of Muriel Sterling's book.

"We're spending a lot of time together," Margot said. "But we're keeping it professional. No distraction before we roll this thing out."

"How much longer before that happens?" Josie asked.

"We're almost there," said Margot.

"And who knows what might happen after that," said Alice.

"I wouldn't object if something did," said Margot.

"Hot, huh?" teased Josie.

"More than that. He's kind and hardworking and easy to be with."

"He sounds wonderful," said Karissa.

She sounded wistful, and, not for the first time, Alice felt for her. If anyone deserved to find love with a good man, it was Karissa Newcomb.

"I hope she can find someone nice," she said to Josie the next day as Josie drove them on their weekly thrift store bargain hunt.

"We make our own happy endings," Josie said.

"I can't believe you're quoting from Muriel Sterling, after all that squawking about not wanting to read her book."

"I'm living proof that people can change. And make new starts. That applies to you, too, you know."

"I think I've done a pretty good job of making a new start," Alice said.

"I'm still driving us around," Josie said.

"I'm still paying for the gas," Alice retorted.

"You need to get back behind the wheel," Josie insisted. "You can't let what happened defeat you."

"I don't want to have this conversation," Alice snapped, and folded her arms in front of her chest.

"You're stuck with it because you're stuck in my car," Josie pointed out. "If you were in your own car, you could drive off."

"I mean it, Jos. I don't want to drive, I'm not going to change my mind and you need to stop telling me what to do."

Josie put on her turn signal and turned into the Goodwill parking lot. "There's going to come a time when you'll wish you tried."

"Well, it's not now," Alice informed her and marched off into the store.

She couldn't concentrate on anything once they were inside. Instead, she wandered up and down the aisles and fumed. Josie always thought she knew everything. So what if she was older? It didn't give her lifetime privileges for bossing Alice around. Was Alice going to have to stop talking to her like Coral had for her to come to her senses?

"I can't believe you didn't find anything," Josie said once they were back in her car.

"I wasn't in the mood."

"You're mad at me."

"Yes, I am. Honestly, Jos, you never know when to quit."

Her sister was silent for a long moment. Hopefully, thinking.

"I'm sorry," she said at last.

"You should be. Your nagging only upsets me and makes me feel guilty that I haven't Josied up and marched on. I'm not you."

"I didn't say you had to be me," Josie protested.

"You might as well have. You've hounded me about driving for the last two, no, two and a half years..."

"I've been trying to help you!"

"You're not helping! All you do is make me feel bad. I don't want to talk about this anymore and I don't want to go to therapy, and I don't want to drive, and I don't want you to say another word."

Josie nodded. "Okay. Got it." Her cheeks were red, and she was blinking back tears.

Good, thought Alice. Josie was good at lecturing others. It was about time someone gave her one.

"I'm not feeling too good," Josie said a few minutes later. "Are you okay if we skip lunch today?"

"That's fine," Alice said stiffly. After this conversation they both needed a break from each other.

Gerald was downright cheerful when he stopped by the office. This was a new Gerald, one taken over by aliens, perhaps. Or by love. Josie, too, seemed like a different person. She hadn't lost her Josie snark, but she seemed happier, more positive. The power of love, Karissa's mom would have said.

"Just dropping off something for Shirley's birthday," he told Karissa, handing over a box of See's candies.

"It's Shirley's birthday?"

"Yep. All day long. You still have time to get your shit together."

"Thanks for the heads-up," Karissa said.

"Is she in?"

"No. Her daughter took her to lunch."

"Tell her have a good one," Gerald said, and then left.

Karissa wished she'd known. She would have loved to do something for Shirley.

Gerald was right. It wasn't too late. She was out the door behind him a moment later. By the time Shirley returned it was to find a cake and a vase of flowers waiting for her in the break room. And a card Karissa had managed to get André and Edward to sign in addition to the chocolates Gerald had dropped off.

"Oh, you guys, you shouldn't have," Shirley said after they'd sung happy birthday.

"Sure, we should," said Karissa as she cut the cake. "Birthdays should always be celebrated."

"Not after a certain age," said Shirley and passed on the piece Karissa held out to her.

"Especially after a certain age," André corrected her, digging into his piece. "Ask my eighty-year-old grandma. She'll tell you."

"I just finished reading an excellent book by Muriel Sterling," Karissa told her. "She says if you're still here you're here for a reason. I think she's right, and we should celebrate the fact that you're still here."

"I agree," said Edward, "and we want you here for a long, long time, Shirley."

"Thank you," said Shirley. "And if part of the reason I'm here is to be keeping us going at Heron Publishing I guess I'd better get back to work."

That signaled the end of the party and everyone took a couple of final bites of cake and then returned to their jobs. Later, on her way out to a chamber of commerce committee meeting, Shirley gave Karissa's shoulder a pat and said, "You are a gem."

It was nice being a gem.

Later, Karissa and Edward were about to leave at the same time, both on their way to pick up their daughters from an after-school program. "I appreciate you coming up with something for Shirley's birthday. I never remember that sort of thing, I'm afraid," he said.

"I was happy to," Karissa told him.

"You must have found it somewhere in Lystra's date book."

"Actually, I haven't consulted that in a while," Karissa confessed. "I found out when Gerald stopped by with the candy earlier."

"That was impressively fast."

Karissa was pleased by the admiration in his voice. "You can't waste time when there's a party to plan."

"And you are good at it," he said.

She was basking in his admiration when the office door opened.

"Looks like I got here just in time," said Emerald.

Just in time to ruin a sweet moment. Didn't the woman believe in phoning?

The answer to that was simple. Of course not. That would remove the element of surprise.

"We're closing up for the day, Emerald," said Edward.

"That's why I came. You know the last time you were supposed to take me to dinner we wound up stuck with the happy hour menu, Edward. It was very disappointing. But I'm willing to forgive and forget. In fact, I'm so willing that I'm going to pick up the tab tonight."

He shook his head. "I'm sorry. My daughter's waiting to be picked up and I'm going to be late if I don't get going."

"Oh, not this again. Let Melissa pick her up," Emerald said. "Aren't your girls friends? They can play together," she said to Karissa.

Edward answered before Karissa could. "They are. But I'm not going to impose on Karissa. And tonight won't work. I'm sorry," he said stiffly.

Emerald's smile flattened. "You know this is my last book under contract. I think we should talk."

Was that some kind of threat? And why didn't Emerald have an agent? Most writers had agents.

Edward's jaws clenched. "We can talk about that tomorrow," he said firmly. "Karissa can make an appointment for you."

"I don't have time tomorrow," Emerald said irritably. "Honestly, Edward, why are you turning down a free dinner?"

"Because I need to spend time with my daughter," he replied.

Emerald's cheeks reddened. Then she lifted her chin. "Very well. If you can't be bothered."

"We'll have more time to talk if we do lunch," he said. "Maybe day after tomorrow? Karissa can set up the appointment first thing in the morning." He opened the door and stood, waiting for the women to walk through.

"I'll have to check my schedule," Emerald said haughtily. "Really, Edward, I thought we'd reached a point where we didn't have to stand on such formality." With that parting remark she sailed out the door.

"Would you have preferred me to pick up Lilith?" Karissa asked. Maybe she should have offered.

He shook his head.

Here was where he'd say something like, "Emerald monopolizes my time too much and I need to break her of that habit." Karissa was ready to wholeheartedly agree.

Instead, he said, "I promised Lilith we'd go out for hamburgers tonight and I make it a habit not to break my promises to her."

A man of his word. "She's a lucky little girl."

He didn't say anything in response to that, simply nodded. "Shall we go?"

"Of course," she murmured.

If not for the promise of hamburgers, would Edward have gone off with Emerald?

Karissa picked up Macy and went home to make taco pie, all the while wondering where Edward had taken his daughter for hamburgers.

Later that night, after dinner and going over spelling words with Macy and bath time and prayers before bedtime, she went in search of her notebook.

Margot and Josie had both written scenes for her to peruse, but she had a scene of her own to write.

There she is, her head on her laptop as if she's taking a nap. I will never get this image out of mind. It will be my favorite memory to return to again and again. I only wish I could publicly take credit for it. The number of people who would come up and thank me is huge—the husband Mary had cheated on and then cleaned out, the cheater she consequently married and was in the process of stealing blind, the mother she'd declared mentally incompetent and stuck in a nursing home, the younger sister she'd then booted out of their family home. The list could stretch clear across her living room floor. I want to laugh hysterically, but instead I have to gear up to cry uncontrollably. I take a deep breath, practice a sob. Where are the tears? I must have tears. I'll think of losing my grandma, my grandma who always thought I had so much talent, who believed in me, who said I'd go places. Yes, that will do it. I can already feel the tears coming.

I take out my phone and dial 911. Take some fast breaths. The minute the operator answers, I cry, "I need help. Someone is dead."

And the world is a better place because of it.

Karissa read her last sentence. Oh, she was good.

And a little scared. It had been so easy to put herself in the mind of that killer. To think she was justified in killing poor horrible Mary. Maybe it wasn't so healthy for her to keep writing these scenes.

She called Margot. "You'd better finish this book."

"Why?" Margot asked.

"Because I'm getting way too into it. I think I might have the heart of a killer."

Margot laughed. "Or how about a really good imagination."

"No, really. I'm too comfortable in this killer's head."

"Don't you have to get into a character's head to write a convincing scene?" Margot argued.

"Yes, but I think I'm getting too far into her head. I think

I about convinced myself that murder is a wonderful way to solve your problems. I feel…creepy."

"Okay," Margot said slowly.

"It's hard to explain."

It did sound silly. Mystery and thriller writers weren't murderers. It was only fiction. But this work of fiction had sprung from a poisoned well of envy, and Karissa realized she was tired of drinking from it.

"The book is mostly done. How about you guys write the rest of the gory scenes and then I'll organize them and finish it off."

"Okay, we can do that." There was a pause. "You are going to let her get away with murder, aren't you?"

"I don't know," said Karissa.

She did though. In the end the murderer would have to either be caught or do herself in. People shouldn't be allowed to get away with murder, even in their fantasies.

She ended her call with Margot and went to get ready for bed. By the time she was under the covers she was satisfied with the ending she'd come up with. The murderer would die. Some sort of accidental poisoning, which would be poetic justice. And Karissa knew the last thing she'd see, and her last words on the page. *Mary, no!*

That was good. And right. She felt relief as she snuggled into her pillow. She hadn't been able to save the woman who murdered the evil fictional Mary, but she felt as if, in a way, she'd saved herself.

"He's free at noon," she said the next morning when Emerald called to make an appointment with Edward. "May I make a reservation somewhere for you?" She even managed to say it with a smile.

September was just beginning when Andrew texted Margot.

It's in the App Store!

After countless hours of brainstorming and hard work, My Dressing Room was finally finished and ready for women to enter. And sooner than Andrew had originally thought. He was a tech magician, and he'd pulled a golden rabbit out of his hat.

A thrill ran through Margot as she read his words. Something she'd envisioned was now a reality. It felt surreal.

I'm going to download it right now, she texted back.

Wait! Do it with me. We need to make a reel.

Of course. This was a big moment for both of them. Everything from here on would be about promoting the thing they'd created. She had her press release ready to go and had budgeted for ads. But reels were free and they could go viral, and that would be the best kind of advertising.

Come over, he texted.

Be right there, she texted back. As soon as she'd changed into her cutest jeans and top and put on her makeup to make sure she was camera ready. And refreshed her perfume. Because, of course, you needed perfume if you were trying out your app for the first time.

He was waiting for her when she walked into the office and had a bottle of champagne in an ice bucket.

"Have you downloaded it?" she asked.

He nodded. "I wanted to make sure everything was working. It is."

She pulled out her phone. "I've got butterflies."

"I had pterodactyls. But it's good. Here, sit down," he said, motioning to a chair. Then he got his phone ready and aimed. "Okay, go to the App Store. Let's see what happens."

The butterflies were going berserk. She took a deep breath, went to the App Store, and hit "download" on her future.

23

"One moment, teetering on the precipice of time,
was all it took to change her life."
—from *A Moment in Time* by Amara Williams

MARGOT DOWNLOADED THE APP. THE DRESSING ROOM
icon looked great on her phone. She chose the online store
where she wanted to shop and selected a dress, put in her measurements and chose from the body shape and height options,
input her hair color and skin tone, and clicked "try it on." There
it was, the image of what the dress would look like on the ava-
tar of her that the app had created.

It looked snug in the bust. She chose the try another size option, picked the next size up and re-hit "try it on." And there
it was, adjusted to show her how the dress would look with
the new size. Great!

"Oh, my gosh! It works!" She looked up at him and beamed.
"I love this!" If he hadn't been filming her reaction for a reel
she'd have jumped up and thrown her arms around him.

"So, we did it?"

"We did!"

He stopped filming. "Great reel. This will make an awesome ad. I'm sure my sister will be all over being in one, too."

"Of course, the true test will be when I order that dress and see if it really looks good once I try it on," said Margot.

"What are you waiting for? Order it. It's deductible."

She grinned and ordered the dress. "I hadn't even thought of that. Online shopping is now a business expense. This is amazing."

He thumbed in a text. "I'm letting my sister know she can download it now."

"You shouldn't have made her wait. Other women have already downloaded it."

"I know, but it didn't seem right letting her do it before you. After all, you're the creator."

"Co-creator, and that was really sweet of you," she said.

He rolled his eyes. "That's me, Mr. Sweet."

"I think you are," said Margot.

He cocked his head. "Yeah?"

"Yeah."

"I don't know if I want to be sweet. That's kind of... innocuous."

"You're not innocuous, trust me," she said.

"Yeah?" His voice had changed from lightly teasing to something more sensual. So had his expression.

She knew they had turned a corner and were seeing a new vista open up for them, and her heart began to beat faster.

He set down his phone. "We've kept it professional these past months."

"Yes, we have."

"You happy with keeping things that way?"

She set down her phone and stood up. "No."

"Good," he said, and closed the distance between them. "Because there's something I've been wanting to do for a long time."

"Me, too," she said as his arms slid around her waist and she wrapped hers around his neck. "Isn't it interesting how we seem to be on the same page a lot?"

It was true. They'd worked well together. They'd had a couple of disagreements but those had never gotten heated, partly because she appreciated his expertise, and he appreciated her creativity.

Here was one idea she really appreciated. She closed her eyes and savored the delicious feel of his lips touching hers. She was sure that no writer could have imagined nor actors portrayed a better kiss. Lips to lips, body to body, heart to heart. She could have stood there kissing him forever.

"Where did you learn to kiss like that?" she said when they finally pulled apart.

"Licking the beaters when my mom baked a cake," he joked, and tucked a lock of hair behind her ears.

She laughed. "I'll have to be sure to thank your mom next time I see her."

"I hope you'll be seeing a lot of her in the future. And all my family."

"I think that could be arranged."

"I want to meet yours, too."

"I think that could be arranged as well."

She was looking forward to showing off her successful app to her mother. She was equally enamored of the idea of showing off Andrew. *Don't get ahead of yourself*, her cautious side advised. It was good advice. She decided to take it.

"Let's break out the champagne and take some pictures," she said.

He got the message, stepped back and got busy opening the bottle.

"Dom Perignon," she observed. "Wow."

"I thought we should celebrate in style. Anyway, it's deductible."

"I'm liking these deductions," she said with a grin, "but remember, deductible doesn't mean free, and we're not making any revenue yet."

"All in good time, boss," he replied, pouring the champagne. His phone pinged with a text. He picked it up, read, and chuckled. "Angie just used the app," he reported. "She says it's a super bargain and worth twice what we're charging."

Margot had put in plenty of research and thought into what they'd charge and she was sticking with her plan, but it was great to hear that someone appreciated the value of the service so much. "Tell her a big thanks from me."

His phone dinged with a fresh text. "My sister says you're a genius," he reported.

"One of the geniuses," she replied, which made him grin.

They set up both cameras and took pictures of themselves toasting. Then they took a shot with one of their phones with the app displayed sitting alongside their champagne.

"Thank you for making this happen," she said when they'd finished.

"Thanks for letting me be part of it," he said. "How about dinner to celebrate?"

"Absolutely," she said. "Stanley and Seafort?"

"Always wanted to go there. What time works for you?"

"Seven?" she suggested.

"Seven it is. That will give us more time to celebrate here."

And celebrate they did, but not with champagne.

Going slowly, she reminded herself. But with the way he kissed, that was going to be a challenge.

Karissa finished the book club read the night before their September meeting. She shut the novel with a satisfied sigh. The story of two star-crossed lovers torn apart by a quirk of fate and yet determined to find each other in a search that spanned both time and continents was the stuff of dreams.

Maybe someday, somehow, some way, she would share that kind of love with someone. It wouldn't be Edward, and that was okay. Better to keep him as a friend. She wouldn't want to compromise the first job she'd ever really enjoyed, anyway. Love was a river that flowed where it would and wishing it would flow your direction wasn't enough to change its course. But she also believed the message of the book, that a deep and committed love could change the course of a person's life. Her story wasn't over yet. She could still hope for such a love.

"I think stories like this are inspiring," she said when the group gathered to discuss the book.

"I hope the author writes a sequel," Margot said, "I'd like to see how their lives played out after they found each other."

"No, you wouldn't," said Josie. "It would be dull, with unimportant conflicts and everyday drudgery of work and chores and kids."

Margot frowned at her. "There's a shining testimonial."

Josie shrugged. "That's reality."

"Is that your reality with Gerald?" Margot challenged.

Josie blushed. "That's different. We haven't hit the boring phase yet."

"Does there have to be a boring phase?" Margot argued.

"No," Alice said firmly. "You have times of quiet waters, though, and there's nothing wrong with that. You can't shoot the rapids all the time. It would be too stressful." Her smile faded a little. "I miss those quiet times."

Karissa was sitting next to her on the couch, and she reached over and laid a comforting hand on Alice's. It was fun to see Josie getting another chance at love. If only they could find someone for Alice.

Alice gave hers a pat. "It's all right. I didn't have my man for as long as I'd hoped, but the time I did have with him was wonderful. And I loved this story. It was beautiful. It's a good reminder that love is worth fighting for."

"The kind of life you want is worth fighting for," Josie added. "Don't you young 'uns lose track of that."

"Mine is falling into place so well it scares me," said Margot. "I'm working with the author Karissa sent me, plus I've picked up another client—a small business owner who needs help organizing her files and inventory. And the app is selling like crazy."

"And what about the app guy?" Josie wanted to know.

"He's a keeper," Margot said.

"I'm glad," said Alice. "It's past time you found someone." She turned her smile on Karissa. "You're next, Karissa."

"Oh, I don't know about that," Karissa said.

"That hunky boss of yours needs to open his eyes and see what's right under his nose," said Josie.

"He sees me," Karissa said. "And I've decided I'm okay that he only sees me as his editorial assistant and Macy's mom. And a friend of sorts, maybe."

"I suppose that awful Emerald is still around," said Josie.

"Yes, she is, but I'm done letting her get to me."

Emerald had been in that very morning. Now that she'd signed a new three-book contract she was pressing Edward to push her books more, and insisted they needed to go out for coffee to discuss.

"Hold down the fort, Melissa," she'd said airily as she hauled him out the door. He'd been frowning.

Karissa had shrugged off Emerald's rudeness. She was fine with her place in the world of Edward Elliot and Heron Publishing. She was pretty sure that Edward wasn't interested in anyone romantically, not even Emerald who, for all her beauty and manipulation, didn't seem to be capturing his heart. So, what was the point of envying the woman? Jealousy was a waste of emotion.

"I'm going to quit wishing I was someone else and focus on what's positive in my life," Karissa said. "And the more time

I spend with all of you, the better I feel about myself. You've all helped me grow so much. I feel so much better about myself. Seeing my daughter happy and finding true friendship has made me happy."

"It should," said Josie. "That's the stuff that matters."

"You've helped us, too," Alice said. "I've really been enjoying our book club. And helping with your book."

"Speaking of the book, where are you on that?" Josie wanted to know.

"I'm glad you asked." Karissa hurried to the spare bedroom that she'd turned into a combination office and reading room for herself and Macy and came back with three copies of the finished manuscript. "I want you to read it and then call me or text me what you think. If we're all happy with it, I'm going to send it to Shirley."

"Why not Edward?" Alice asked.

"I think that could be awkward," said Karissa.

"Think he might recognize Emerald?" Josie guessed.

"You never know, although I doubt it. Mary may have started out as Emerald, but she's a witch all her own now. Anyway, I think Shirley is our best bet. But don't get your hopes up."

"If they don't want it, we can publish it ourselves," Josie said. "People do that all the time, right?"

"True," Karissa allowed.

"I'm just happy we did it," Margot said. "Well, you did it mostly, Karissa."

"I had fun just getting to help," said Josie. "I always wanted to write a book."

"I wish I'd contributed more," Alice said.

"You contributed plenty," Karissa assured her.

"What if we don't like the ending?" Margot asked. She was the only one who knew Karissa wasn't letting their killer get away with murder.

"The ending has to stay," Karissa said firmly.

Josie nodded. "Okay. We all helped but this is your baby, so you get the final say. Meanwhile, we have something to toast besides the book getting done, right, Alice?"

"We do," said Alice. She reached into the canvas book bag she'd brought and pulled out a box of candles. "To go with the cupcakes I brought," she said. "I know you're going to be celebrating your birthday with your family, but we wanted to celebrate it with you, too." She pulled out a book-shaped wrapped package and a card.

"Oh, you guys," said Karissa, touched. "You didn't have to."

"Sure we did," said Margot.

"And never mind the card. Open the present," urged Josie. She did. Her friends had given her a turquoise leather-bound journal.

"It's beautiful," she said, running a hand over it.

"So you can record all your profound thoughts," Margot said.

Karissa could feel herself tearing up. "This is…" Too choked up to go further, she could only shake her head over her friends' kindness.

"Never mind the profound thoughts. Write all your racy fantasies in there," said Josie. Then to Alice, she said, "Let's get on with the cupcakes and pick our next read. I'm itching to go home and start on this manuscript."

"Does anyone have a suggestion for next month?" Karissa asked.

"I do," said Margot. She brought it up on her phone and handed it to Josie to pass around. "I started this last week and it's really good and creepy, kind of a thriller like what we just wrote. We can compare her writing to ours."

"*The Widower*, huh?" said Josie.

"I think it would be a good read for our October meeting," said Margot. "I've read another of Terrance Tolliver's books. It was a page-turner. This one is, too. It's about a man who kills his wife for her money and then she haunts him and his lover."

"A nice, cheery read," said Alice. She frowned at the image on the phone and passed it on to Karissa.

"We need a change from sappy advice books," said Josie.

"This from the woman who only last meeting told us what a game changer Muriel Sterling's book was?" Alice shot back.

Josie was never one to back down. "It was. Now I've had enough game changing. Anyway, we need variety. And since we all just committed murder on paper it will be fun to watch someone else do it."

"It really is a good book," said Margot.

"Let's read it," Josie said.

Alice sighed. "All right."

Karissa had been mind-deep in murder and anger working on their book. The idea of plunging deeper still was hardly appealing.

"Karissa?" Margot prodded.

"I guess, if you all want to read it."

"Why don't you want to?" Josie asked.

"I don't know. I think I'm sick of awfulness."

"You don't have to finish it if you don't like it," Josie said. "Life's too short."

Karissa nodded. "Good point."

After her friends' kind gesture, she would have felt snotty not going along. Anyway, she'd picked the last book. Book clubs were democratic gatherings. Everyone got a turn to choose. She would try to keep an open mind, although the premise of a man getting rid of his unwanted wife crept a little too close to home for comfort.

It's only fiction, she told herself, although it seemed inconsistent to read the same type of thing she hadn't wanted to continue writing. At least she wasn't having to pull any of the darkness out of her own mind. Also, she suspected she would feel a measure of satisfaction with this particular novel if the husband got what was coming to him in the end. Someone getting what he deserved would be a nice change from reality.

"Thanks for watching Lucky, Mom," Callum said, as Lucky happily bounded into Alice's living room. "I feel kind of bad leaving him with you since you're not feeling well."

Alice waved away her son's concern. "It's only a cold. And I know you two have been looking forward to this trip to Leavenworth. It's such a great time of year to go—all those lovely fall colors."

"And Oktoberfest and beer and brats," he added.

And romance. He didn't need to say that. It was a given. Kara had been tracking her ovulation and the odds were in their favor for the weekend. It was going to be their last try before consulting a fertility doctor.

"I'll bring you back a book from A Book For All Seasons," he promised. "Anything in particular you want? Lucky, down!"

Lucky sat down with a doggy whine, and Alice patted his head. "Vanessa Valentine is doing a signing at the store this weekend for her new book, and I'd love a signed copy. I hear this is going to be her last. She's retiring."

"Then I'll make sure we get a copy for you." He gave her a hug, gave his dog a quick ear rub, and then went off down the walk.

"Let's keep our fingers and toes crossed, Lucky," Alice said as she waved goodbye. "How about a doggy treat for my grand-dog? Treat? Want a treat?"

Lucky was back on his feet at the mention of a treat. He barked an affirmative and wagged his tail.

"Let's go get you one. Then we're going to relax and watch a movie. Grandma is pooped so it's going to be a quiet evening."

It was a semi-quiet evening. Alice made the mistake of streaming a movie with a dog in it, which got Lucky all stirred up and barking. She tried two more, but each one had a pet that had him nearly jumping into the screen.

She'd barely settled in with her third try when Lucky was scratching at the door, wanting to go out. It was cold and drizzly out and Alice felt crummy, but out they went. Dogs' needs couldn't be neglected.

She'd taken a pill, but cold medicine, while it treated symptoms, didn't give a woman energy. By the time they'd returned and finished the movie she was ready for bed.

"Maybe I'll feel better in the morning," she said to her four-legged charge. "Then we can take a nice walk."

If Karissa and Macy were in town Macy would have been happy to come over and entertain Lucky. Sadly, Macy was with her father and Karissa was with her family, celebrating her birthday.

Lucky was content to accompany her to her bedroom. He settled down in the doggy bed she kept next to the bed and Alice got out her copy of their book club read. It would be interesting to compare to their book club project, which Karissa had turned into a brilliant novel. Alice had gobbled it up in one day.

This novel was, indeed, creepy. The wife was now dead, but not finished with her wicked husband, and the scene where he woke up in the middle of the night, turned over and saw her face staring at him made Alice shudder. This was probably not good bedtime reading.

Sure enough, it wasn't. She dreamed she was with Charlie, back by his side again as he lay dying, and when she reached out to touch his face, it crumbled to dust before her, and she awoke on a sob. It was hard to sleep after that and come morning she felt worse than she had the day before.

She managed to take Lucky out for a quick potty walk, then came back inside and filled his dog dish. While he ate, she had some toast and tea and sneezed and blew her nose and sniffed and sneezed and blew again. And sniffed.

She hated taking medication, but this was ridiculous. She was going to have to take something.

There were only a few pills in foil in the box of cold meds in her medicine cabinet. Hopefully, she wouldn't need to take too many more. Lucky watched with interest as she wrestled to pop out the little red pill.

She finally succeeded, but it not only popped out of the foil, it also popped out of her hand and onto the floor.

Lucky saw it and went for it, and before Alice could say, "bad dog," had it in his mouth.

"Lucky, no!" Horrified, she bent and tried to pry his mouth open. "Give me that right now!" He pulled his head back and clamped his teeth together. "Spit that out!"

Lucky had no intention of spitting it out. He jerked his head away and started backing up.

"Open up, baby," she cried frantically.

Lucky growled and wagged his tail and panic flooded Alice.

She tried every trick she knew to get his mouth open, but nothing worked. What was she going to do? Adult medications could be harmful to dogs, even life-threatening. She couldn't ignore this.

Margot was off somewhere with her new boyfriend. Josie wasn't around, either. She was hiking with Gerald. Karissa was all the way up north in Anacortes.

Alice looked down at Lucky, who was now looking up at her, wagging his tail. She grabbed her phone to hail an Uber or a taxi, but in her cold medicine fog, she'd forgotten to charge it, and the thing was completely dead.

Her heart was pounding like mad. She knew what she had to do.

24

"He'd had enough of her. It was time to move on."
—from *The Widower* by Terrance Tolliver

HEART STILL RACING, ALICE PICKED UP HER CAR KEYS with a sweaty palm. She couldn't do this. She was going to have a heart attack. But she couldn't be responsible for something bad happening to her son's dog, either. There had to be another way to fix her terrible problem, yet in her panicked state she couldn't think of one.

"Okay, we're going for a drive. Come on, boy."

Lucky was delighted to follow her to the car and happy to hop onto the back passenger seat. Her son had a dog seat belt in his car but Alice, who'd never intended to drive, had none. She tried to fit Lucky into the seat belt but between his squirming and her shaking hands it was impossible, and she gave up. She'd barely got behind the wheel when he jumped over the seat and joined her. Okay, he'd have to stay there. She tried not to think about getting in an accident and having him go flying through the windshield.

She realized she had no idea where she was going. More panic! She had to try and stay calm. She closed her eyes and tried to remember where the animal hospital was—she knew she'd seen one not too far down the road. The last road she'd driven, right before...

Her mind veered away from the memory of what had happened the last time she drove, but not soon enough. Her heart rate sped up even more and she began to cry.

Lucky wanted to lick away her tears and she gave him a gentle push out of her face as she pressed the button on the remote and let up the garage door. Her hand was shaking so much she could hardly turn the key in the ignition. She wished she had one of those new cars where all she'd have to do was push a button. She wished she had a self-driving kind of car. She wished she'd never decided to take that pill.

She was breathing hard when she backed out of the driveway, gripping the steering wheel with white knuckles. Oh, how was she going to manage this? Was she hyperventilating? Was she going to pass out?

The street was deserted and the only living being was a cat, sitting on the hood of a car. Lucky got excited and barked a greeting, rattling her nerves further.

"At the next signal, I'll make a left," she said out loud, hoping the sound of her own voice would calm her.

The speed limit said thirty-five. She looked at her speedometer. She was going ten miles over. If only a policeman would show up. Maybe that way she'd get a police escort to the animal hospital. More turns, more stops. She ran through a yellow light just as it turned red and rolled through a stop sign, which earned her an angry honk from another driver. She should have plugged her phone in and called a taxi. What had she been thinking!

Lucky didn't care what she was thinking. He was enjoying

the ride, barking at dogs in passing cars and making her jump with each bark.

At last, they reached the animal hospital, which was when she realized she hadn't brought Lucky's leash. This shot her heart rate up even higher.

"Okay, Lucky, you're going to have to be a good boy and stick right next to me," she said. "No running off."

She came around the car and opened the door and Lucky bounded out before she could get ahold of his collar, nearly knocking her over, and started to race off. "Lucky!" she screamed. "Treat, treat. I have a treat."

He knew the word *treat*, and, amazingly, bounded back to her.

She grabbed his collar. "Come on, now. We have to go see the doctor."

"Who have we here?" the receptionist greeted them.

"This is Lucky. I poisoned him," Alice said. "Accidentally," she added. "He swallowed one of my cold pills. It's my son's dog and he's out of town." She wiped at the tears racing down her cheeks. "And I forgot his leash."

"Don't worry, we keep spares on hand," the woman said. She went to a cupboard and pulled out a cheap leash and handed it over and Alice thanked her gratefully and clamped it onto Lucky's collar.

"Let's get some information," the woman said with a smile.

Alice supposed the smile was meant to reassure her. It didn't.

The vet was kind and understanding. "These things happen," he said. "But you were right to bring him in right away. We'll get him good as new, I promise."

The vet's receptionist was the picture of kindness, settling Alice in a chair in the waiting room, fetching her water, patting her on the arm and assuring her that Doctor Durham was the best.

Alice managed a nod and tried to stop the tears.

"This happens more often than you'd think," the woman said. "Your dog will be fine. Try not to worry."

Alice tried and failed. Time crawled by, and when Lucky was finally brought back to her alive and well, with the nasty pill removed, she cried and hugged the vet's assistant. Then she hugged Lucky, who showed his love by squirming and licking her.

She paid the bill gratefully even though Lucky's adventure had proved to be an expensive one, then they went back to the car.

Which she'd have to drive again. She took a deep breath and opened the door and the dog got back in, not quite as energetically as he had earlier. Poor little guy. His ordeal had really taken it out of him.

It had taken it out of her, too. She felt shaky and slightly ill as she got back behind the wheel, but she made it out into traffic, made it down the street, made it home, and pulled back safely into the garage.

"We did it, Lucky!"

She'd done it. She'd driven. And now she needed a cup of tea and a cookie. And she needed to lie down. One thing she didn't need was another cold pill.

Josie and Gerald stood by the Sol Duc River, catching glimpses of silver from the occasional trout. "Good fishing in this river all year long," he said.

"You mean the kind where you have to wade out into the water in those clunky hip waders?" Josie asked.

"I guess you've never fished."

"No, I haven't. I draw the line at having to put worms on a hook."

He laughed. "You don't use worms. You use flies. You know, the fancy things you buy at sporting goods stores."

"I know what they are," Josie said. She wasn't that ignorant.

"It's a good sport," Gerald insisted. "You'd probably like it if you tried it."

"When you say sport you don't mean that catch and release stuff, do you?"

He looked appalled. "No. If I'm fishing, I'm camping, and I have to eat."

She smiled. "I'm with you on the eating thing. If you're going to go after some poor animal it had better be for food."

"Fishing's as far as I go," he said.

"I hope you also go as far as cleaning the fish," she said, and he chuckled.

He leaned back on his elbows and gazed up at the sky. "Look at that sky. You know, there's nothing like being outdoors to help a person find peace."

It was peaceful, and the further they got from civilization the more relaxed Gerald became. "You know, you're a different man out here in nature."

He frowned. "What's that supposed to mean?"

"Don't go getting prickly on me, mister. I mean that you seem happier."

He shrugged. "I guess I am. Nature makes sense. It has its rules, and it sticks to them."

"Unlike people," she guessed.

He nodded. "Present company excepted. You're a rare breed. You say what you think. You're honest. You don't play games."

"Other than cards," she joked.

"Trying to be serious here," he said with a scowl.

"Okay, seriously, you're right." She cocked her head and studied him. "You wouldn't, by any chance, happen to be comparing me with your ex-wife, now, would you?"

"I guess, a little."

She nodded. "I'm no gem. You saw that early on." Sometimes she was still a little embarrassed that she'd leaked so much about her strained relationship with her daughter, that he'd seen her imperfections so early in their friendship.

He smiled. "Yeah, you are. And you've got heart. You care." He paused a moment. "I like being with you."

The words gave her heart a pleasant zap, and she leaned against him. "I like being with you, too. You're pretty cool for an old coot."

"I'm not that old."

"You're not that young, either."

"You have got such a mouth on you."

"And you love it," she said.

It was perverse of her, but she enjoyed their occasional bouts of verbal sparring. Joe had always been so easygoing—something that had attracted her to him in the first place. But as he'd gotten older easygoing had changed into apathetic and, worse, passive-aggressive. She'd rather they'd have fought. It would have felt more honest.

They sat in silence for a moment, listening to the rushing water, then Gerald spoke again. "When am I going to meet your long-suffering daughter?"

"Why do you ask?"

"Because I'm thinking we're probably going to spend a lot of time together in the future and I should meet her. Or am I wrong?"

She cocked her head and studied him. Spending more time together in the future, having adventures—yes, she was ready for that.

"What?" he demanded.

"I was just thinking how different you are from Joe."

"Good or bad different?"

"Good," she said. "And I think you're right. We are going to spend a lot of time together in the future."

It was nice to be with a man again, and this man suited Josie very well. She knew Alice would never remarry. Charlie had been the great love of her life. She, on the other hand, didn't want to stay married to a memory. She was ready to move on. Moving on with Gerald sounded fine to her.

"How about I take you all out to dinner tomorrow?" he suggested.

"How about you invite your son to join us and I cook?" she countered.

"How about we cook up something together?"

"I think we already are," she cracked, which made him chuckle.

Lucky was a happy, healthy dog when Callum came to pick him up, and Alice was a very happy woman. The dog was okay and so was she. "I am so sorry, though," she apologized after telling her son what had happened. "He was faster than lightning."

"I can't believe you drove, Mom. That's huge."

"I couldn't let something happen to Lucky," she said. "I'd never have forgiven myself."

"I'd have never forgiven myself if something had happened to you," he said, and hugged her. "But I'm proud of you for being so brave."

It had been brave, hadn't it? "I'm proud of me, too," she said.

"So, maybe you'll try and get behind the wheel again," he suggested.

"Oh, I don't know. That was an emergency."

"I get it, and I won't push you. But you did prove to yourself that you could do it."

Yes, she had. She chewed on that for a while after he'd left, sitting at the kitchen table with a cup of tea. Could she get behind the wheel again?

She looked to the junk drawer where she'd kept the keys. Simply looking made her heart bounce. No, she couldn't.

What about just down the street and back? Could she manage that?

She bit down on her lip, walked to the drawer and took out the keys. "I don't need to do this," she told herself.

But what if another emergency of some sort came up? She stood for a moment, gathering her courage. Then she went to the garage.

Her hands were damp when she opened the car door, they were damp when she got in and let up the garage door. Her heart rate wasn't exactly resting. She took a deep breath and backed the car out slowly. Backed onto the street after checking every two inches to make sure no one was coming. Then she drove. All the way to the end and back. By the time she returned her hair was damp and she was exhausted. Okay, that was enough for one day.

On Monday she called Josie. "Come over. I want to show you something."

"Did Callum bring you back a great gift from Leavenworth?"

"Yes, he did."

But the small helping of courage she'd gotten was the best gift of all. If she could manage to drive a little further this time, she'd feel like she was making real progress. If she had her sister with her, she could possibly manage it.

Josie arrived fifteen minutes later. "Let's see what you got."

Alice already had her purse and the keys in her hand. "I'll show you."

"It's in the garage?"

"You could say that." When they got in the garage Alice walked to the driver's side of the car. "Get in, Jos, we're going for a ride."

"What?" Josie stared at her. "Okay, what planet are you from and what have you done with my sister?"

Alice giggled. "I've been out twice, but once was an emergency and last night was only down the street. I want to see if I can get to the grocery store, but I don't want to go by myself in case I have a panic attack."

"Emergency?"

"Get in. I'll tell you once we get to the store."

It was a drive that should have taken less than fifteen minutes. It took almost twenty-five, with Josie saying things like, "Green light. You can go," and "Nobody's behind you, you're good," but they made it.

Once in the parking lot Alice let her heart rate settle down and told her sister what had happened. Josie smiled at her and hugged her. "I knew you could do it, sis."

"Life goes on, right? I have to keep moving forward."

"You did, and you will," Josie assured her. "I'm so proud of you, and I know Charlie would have been, too."

Yes, he would have.

"I want to send you something that might be a fit for Heron Publishing," Karissa said to Shirley, as she settled in the chair on the other side of Shirley's desk.

"Oh? One of the unsolicited ones?" Shirley asked, and Karissa nodded.

It certainly was. Karissa hoped the Northwest setting on nearby Raft Island with its amenities and exclusive setting would help tip the scales in favor of the book she and her friends had labored over. But she also felt the story itself was good, so who knew? She cautioned herself as she had the others. First books rarely sold.

Still, she felt proud of their accomplishment. She was feeling pretty proud of her own accomplishment as well. She'd come a long way since leaving behind her collapsed life. She'd risked friendship again and it had paid off in a big way. She was happy in her job and, while she supposed she'd never feel completely confident in her looks, she was realizing how little thought she gave them when she was with her friends. Her glass was almost to the top.

"Is there a reason you're not talking about this with Edward?"

Other than feeling ridiculously awkward? "I thought you might like this one."

"You hit it out of the park on the last manuscript you found. Tell me about this one," said Shirley. "What do you think makes it a fit for us?"

"It's got a Northwest setting," Karissa offered.

Shirley was not impressed. "We've had lots of Northwest settings."

Karissa thought a moment. "I guess it's about people getting what they deserve."

Now Shirley was interested. She leaned back against her chair and settled in for a summary.

"It's about murder. A woman kills off her egotistical, mean boss, who's a writer."

"Oh, picking on writers, that's cruel," Shirley joked.

Karissa thought about a certain selfish writer she'd been happy to pick on. "Yes, it is. The murder victim has it coming. But, in the end, so does the woman who kills her, and even though she doesn't get caught, she, too gets what she deserves in the end."

Shirley nodded thoughtfully. "Interesting. Why did this appeal to you?"

Karissa tried to look nonchalant. "I guess because it speaks to what women who see themselves as underdogs sometimes feel. It's easy to have vengeful thoughts toward people who take advantage of others and don't deserve the good things in their lives."

Shirley nodded thoughtfully. "Although you said this murderer doesn't get away with murder."

"She doesn't get caught but she pays. In the end, we all pay for the choices we make," Karissa said.

Even the small crimes of jealousy and anger and resentment extracted their price. None of them paid off in dividends of happiness.

"Okay, I'm intrigued," Shirley said. "Shoot it to me."

Shirley being intrigued enough to take a look was the next

best thing to making an offer. Karissa wanted to text everyone immediately, but she decided against it. Better to wait and see what she said. Meanwhile, though, Karissa could enjoy this fun secret.

It made her morning, and she was still smiling when Mark's text came through right before lunch. Wanted to let you know before we tell Macy. We're pregnant. We're getting married New Year's Eve.

She stared at the words, her smile now a distant memory. It felt as if she were trying to decipher a foreign language, and she couldn't wrap her mind around what she was seeing. Pregnant. Mark and Allegra were pregnant. Mark was going to have a baby. Karissa had wanted to have a second child and he'd always balked at the idea. "One and done, babe." But he wasn't done with kids, just done with her. The opportunity he'd denied his wife he'd given to his girlfriend.

For a moment, Karissa couldn't catch her breath. When she did, it came back out the keening of a wounded animal.

Shirley was on the phone, but she opened her door. "Karissa, what's wrong?"

Edward wasn't on the phone, and he, too, opened his door. He held up a hand to Shirley. "I've got this. Karissa, why don't you come on into my office."

Karissa wasn't sure she could see to find her way. Her tears were blinding. She couldn't seem to get her sobs under control. So much for all the emotional progress she'd made. This wasn't a case of one step forward and two steps back. It was more like standing in place and getting pushed back fifty feet by some evil wind.

Once she was in his office he pulled out a chair for her. "What's happened? Is it Macy?"

She shook her head. That would have justified the way she was feeling. This...how on earth did she explain to him what was roaring through her when she could hardly explain it to herself?

"My ex and his girlfriend are pregnant." She sounded petty. "It's, it...it feels like the final betrayal." That needed explaining. "They had an affair. She was my best friend."

She'd thought the wound had healed. It hadn't. Maybe it never would. The tears fell faster.

"I'm sorry," he said softly.

He left the room, probably because her reality star moment was embarrassing him. As it turned out, he'd gone to fetch the box of tissue from the bathroom.

He handed it to her, and she sobbed a thank-you and pulled one out. Blew her nose and dried her eyes, both of which immediately needed another tissue. "I thought I was over all this, but now...it's all so final. He doesn't want me, and he's moved on with someone be...be...beautiful."

Suddenly she wanted to write another book and bump off a fresh character, one who looked exactly like Allegra. She wanted to go someplace dark and camp there.

"Oh, Karissa," he said softly.

She could hear the pity in his voice and that made her cry all the harder.

He knelt in front of her, and she threw herself on his shoulder and began soaking his shirt.

"Everything will be all right," he murmured, stroking her hair.

"I've tried. I've tried to appreciate my new life, and...and I do. I just...this is... I always wanted another child and now..." She gave up on finishing the sentence and went back to crying.

"I know," he said. "I get it."

"I should go home." Crawl away like a wounded animal and wait to die.

"By all means, take the rest of the day off. Let's just give you a minute here."

She pulled away and looked at his tearstained shirt. "Your shirt."

"You certainly matter more than my shirt. You matter a lot."

His door suddenly opened and a female voice crashed in on the moment. "Your guard dog's not at her..." Emerald stopped in her tracks and gaped.

Karissa's mortification was complete. Her nemesis had seen her weak and miserable. It was bad enough Shirley had heard, and that Karissa had imposed on poor Edward, but now this. She should have hidden in the bathroom or gone out to her car.

"What on earth?" said Emerald.

"A bit of a crisis," Edward said, and escorted her out. "I think Shirley's got some time to talk."

"Of course," Emerald murmured. "Whatever it is, I'm sorry, Melissa."

Edward shut the door and returned to kneel in front of Karissa, who was in the process of soaking a fresh tissue. He studied her face. The concern on his had her reaching for yet another tissue. She was building a small mountain of them in her lap.

"I never saw this coming," she said, and took a ragged breath.

Edward took her hand in his. It was warm and solid, and gratitude rose like a small island in the middle of her misery. "I'm so sorry, Karissa."

If only sympathy was enough. "He's got everything he wants now. A new life with a beautiful woman."

Edward's brows drew together. "You don't think you're beautiful?"

All her insecurities rushed at her. "I'm not, I know it," she said miserably. "I'm not the kind of woman you see on social media showing off her hair and clothes. I'm not—"

"Stop right there," he said firmly. "I know you're upset but you can't be thinking like that. You're a lovely woman, and I'm not talking about surface beauty. Yours comes from your heart. It lights up your eyes and makes your smile memorable. I think our authors who come in would rather spend time talking with you than with us. Good Lord, you've turned Gerald into a house pet."

"You don't have to tell me things like this to make me feel better," she said miserably.

"I'm not. Why would you want to be a clone of every other woman out there? Think of all the classic heroines of literature—think of Elizabeth Bennet."

"Not nearly handsome enough to tempt me," she quoted from *Pride and Prejudice* and the words tasted bitter.

"But she did tempt him. That is my mom's favorite book, by the way, and I swear she's seen every movie version of it that ever came out."

"If only I were a fictional character."

"Then I wouldn't get to spend time with you," he said, and smiled.

It was such a sweet thing to say. She smiled back at him through her tears.

"Edward Elliot, you are the kindest man I've ever met," she said gratefully.

He dropped her hand. "No, I'm not. Karissa, I wish…" He pressed his lips together, stood up and moved away.

"Edward?" she prompted.

He looked like a mourner at a funeral. "I wish…"

"What? What do you wish?" She sounded desperate, she knew it, but she was desperate. What had he been about to say?

He shut his eyes and shook his head. "I wish we'd met years ago."

"Are you saying you care about me?"

Even if he did, just a little… She had told herself a thousand times not to even hope for anything more than friendship with this man. She was sure any feelings were all on her side, but the thought that he might have feelings for her in return unleashed repressed hope. A kaleidoscope of visions raced through her mind—the two of them on Heron Publishing's deck, relaxing with glasses of wine and watching the sunset, a family dinner with the girls and Honor, walking hand in hand on a beach, cuddling on his couch on a wintry day, each of them with a book in their hands. But then they'd forget the books and…

"I'm saying I can't." His words came out sharp as shards of glass.

Karissa stared at him in shock. "I don't understand."

"I'm married."

25

MARRIED! NO, IT WASN'T POSSIBLE. THIS WASN'T HAP-pening.

"It tore me up seeing you so broken, but I should have kept my mouth shut. I'm sorry," Edward said.

"I don't understand," said Karissa. She could feel the tears rising yet again and tried to blink them back. "Lilith said she didn't have a mother. I thought you were…widowed."

He moved further away, rubbed the back of his neck. "She has a mother, she just hasn't seen her since she was a baby."

"Her mother left?" Karissa asked, shocked.

Edward kept his back to her. "After Lilith was born, my wife changed. Baby blues, my mother called it. 'Postpartum depression. Don't worry, it will pass,' said the doctor. She cried and I couldn't console her. She didn't want to see family. Sure didn't want to see the doctor again. She didn't want to hold the baby. I tried everything I could think to do, was sure we could turn things around in time, but then she told me she didn't want to be a mother. She left before Lilith's first birthday. I thought she'd come back. Or at least stay in touch. Instead, she disappeared."

Karissa couldn't begin to comprehend what Edward had gone through, was still suffering. Now she knew why his smiles had been so rare.

"Do you know where she is now?" she asked.

"No. I tried to find her and couldn't. Even hired someone. Her parents tried, too. My old friends said I should divorce her, but I couldn't. I kept hoping. Shortly before you came here I'd contacted someone again to try and find her. Lilith is growing up so fast. We've kept things vague so far, telling her that her mommy had some troubles and had to leave. But she's going to start asking questions soon, going to start wanting her mother. I thought…" His words trailed off.

"You could fix things," Karissa supplied. She understood wanting to give a child what wasn't in your power to give.

He heaved a great sigh. "I'm still married and hanging in limbo. I can't offer you anything but sympathy. And friendship."

"I'm so sorry," Karissa said. "All these years you've been alone."

Running a business, raising a daughter, mourning the loss of a wife who couldn't bring herself to come back to him. The magnitude of his troubles made her own shrink.

"I've given up hoping that Amanda will come back, but I still feel like I owe it to Lilith to keep the door open."

"Amanda, that's her name?"

He nodded.

"It's a beautiful name."

"She was a beautiful soul. I feel like I broke her."

"Something broke her, but it wasn't you," Karissa said. They were both broken, and Karissa ached for them.

She ached for herself as well and she, too, wished that she

and Edward had met years earlier. They could have had a good life together. Unlike the lovers in the book she'd read for book club, they'd never even been able to start at the same marker in time. They'd been in a fourth-dimension fun house, with sliding invisible floors keeping their lives from touching until it was too late. Her head felt like someone had buried an axe in it.

"I don't feel well. I really do need to go home," she said weakly.

He nodded and she stumbled out of his office. She grabbed her purse, fled to her car and, once in it, laid her head on the steering wheel and wept.

Finally, she made it home. Before crawling into bed, she called Margot and asked if she could pick up Macy at school.

"Are you okay?" Margot asked.

"No, and please don't ask me to tell you right now."

"I'll pick her up, no problem. She can hang out with me and stay for pizza."

"Thank you," Karissa whimpered. She took an aspirin and crawled into bed, half wishing she could stay there forever.

She couldn't and she wouldn't. Later, when Macy came home, she'd help her with her spelling words, get her ready for bed, and hear her bedtime prayers. Then she'd go to her own bed and wish she'd moved somewhere, anywhere but Gig Harbor.

She'd just gotten Macy in bed when she got another text from Mark wanting to know if she'd gotten his earlier one.

Yes, she texted back. It was the only response he was going to get from her.

She barely slept that night. She called Shirley in the morning and told her she was sick. She drove Macy to school, then she came home, made herself coffee, and sat on her living room couch, staring out the window. Everything looked the same as it had the day before. One of life's ironies—the world around you always looked so normal when yours was crumbling.

"It's not crumbling," she told herself. "Just changing."

Okay, Mark and Allegra were pregnant. People got together and had children. Macy would probably love having a half sister or brother. Karissa would get used to the idea.

As for Edward, nothing had really changed in their relationship status. Except now she knew he wished something could have. And she wished something could have. But nothing would. *You'd known nothing would ever happen between you anyway, so what is your problem?*

The answer to that was easy. Her problem was that she now knew how he felt about her and the fact that nothing could come of it hurt. Even worse, she hurt for him.

And for his poor, wounded wife. Was she safe? Was she trying to build a new life somewhere? Was regret and shame blocking her from contacting her family?

Karissa downed more coffee and turned on the news. It helped put her own life in perspective. She wasn't living in poverty or a war-torn country. She had her family, her great new friends, her health. And her mental health. And she had her daughter, and they were happy together.

"I need to be grateful for what I have," she told Margot when Margot called to see how she was doing.

"But still, yikes," said Margot. "I don't even know what to say."

"Say, 'You'll be fine.'"

"You will. But darn. Poor all of you." She paused. "Do you want Alice and Josie to know? I'll tell them if you want me to."

"Yes, and thanks."

"We're here for you," Margot said.

Karissa's mother told her the same thing. "And you will be fine, darling."

Being fine was a better choice than being miserable. But how to get there?

Karissa went in search of Muriel Sterling's book. The woman

had endured her share of heartache. Karissa knew she'd find something helpful in there.

When I'm struggling, Muriel wrote, *I remember the Bible passage that tells me there is a season for everything. If you live long enough you will experience all seasons—times of joy and times of sorrow, times of success and times of failure. Joy eventually follows sorrow as sure as day follows night. If you're going through a dark time hold onto the people who care about you and keep walking. Daybreak will come eventually.*

She shut the book with a sigh. She sure hoped Muriel knew what she was talking about.

Meanwhile, her friends were quick to offer comfort. Alice delivered home-baked shortbread. Margot sent her texts with encouraging sayings throughout the day and Josie showed up bringing a pillow with a needlepoint single red rose on it.

"When you want to have a good cry or scream or swear but you don't want the kid to hear do it into this. I used it after Joe died and it helped me get through those days when I was supposed to be strong and look like I had it together."

"Oh, Josie, you're the best," Karissa said, and hugged her.

Josie hugged her back. "You'll be okay. Hang in there."

Karissa used the pillow that night, escaping after Macy's bedtime prayers which ended with "And God bless Lilith and Grandma Elliot and Mr. Elliot."

It was a rough night, but by morning Karissa was ready to return to work. Nothing had changed. Emails needed to be dealt with, meetings scheduled, submissions searched.

Except everything had changed, she thought when Edward came in and gave her a subdued, "Good morning," and she murmured it back to him.

His office door closed, and she sighed. There had been a wall between them from the beginning. The only problem was that it had once been invisible. Now it was brick upon brick of disappointment staring her in the face, and it stretched on forever.

She turned her attention back to her computer screen, wishing she'd brought Josie's pillow to work with her.

A few minutes later he called her into his office. The first thing she noted was his sorrowful expression. The second was the ring on his finger. If she'd seen that ring months ago she'd have doused her attraction the moment it started to sizzle.

"Are you okay?" he asked after she'd shut the door.

She leaned against it and managed a nod.

"Are we okay? I mean..." He shook his head, frowned. "I was way out of line. I hope we can get past that."

"I wish we didn't have to," she said, then regretted the words the minute they were out of her mouth. That was a selfish thing to say. "Now look who's out of line. We'll put this behind us and I'll join you in hoping that, at some point, Amanda will return and want to be part of your lives again."

He sighed. "Thank you, Karissa."

She gave him a quick nod, then went back to her desk. Try and pretend nothing happened, she counselled herself.

Easier said than done. The day went smoothly but was the hardest day at work that she'd ever had.

"Maybe it's time to look for a new job," her mother suggested when they chatted.

"Maybe," she said, but she stayed put. And continued to water the rose on Josie's pillow.

It took several days for the flood of tears to subside, but they did, leaving Karissa with a melancholy emptiness. She quoted Muriel Sterling's words to herself and kept working on moving forward and finally ditched the pillow.

The day after she did so, like some cosmic reward, Shirley called Karissa into her office.

"I finally had a chance to read that manuscript by MK Wood that you sent me and I love it, but I'm not finding the author's contact information anywhere."

That was because Karissa and team were MK Wood, a pen

name she'd created from the initials of Margot's and her first names and Josie and Alice's maiden name, and it was all Karissa had provided. If Shirley decided to make an offer, she'd planned a happy reveal moment. *It's my friends and me. Ta-da!*

"About MK Wood," she said. "She's not one person, she's a team."

"A team? Did the person say that in her original query?"

"There was no query."

"All right, I'm confused."

"I'm MK Wood, along with the three other members of my book club."

Shirley whipped off her glasses and stared at Karissa. "You're kidding."

"No, I'm not. We did it for the fun of it," Karissa said, opting not to mention that the project had started out as therapy.

"You did it beautifully. We're going to want to make an offer, but it won't be much split four ways."

"We already figured that," said Karissa. "My friends will be thrilled no matter what."

"So, how was the labor divided up? In light of what you just told me the voice is amazingly consistent."

"Everyone contributed but I pulled it together."

"So, it's your voice."

"It's all of us, really."

"Whose idea was the ending?" Shirley wanted to know.

"That was mine."

"You have a lot of talent. Are you going to let me offer you a two-book contract?"

A two-book contract with Heron Publishing. Under other circumstances it would have been a dream come true.

"I'll have to see what the others think," Karissa said. "But I don't want to write that genre anymore." She needed to be done with that type of therapy. She was probably done with writing, period.

"Ask them and get back to me. You know that even though we're small, we prefer to invest in authors who can give us more than one book."

"I know. I'll talk to them."

"Either way, Edward and I have talked about it, and we're going to make an offer on this one."

Karissa was glad they'd discussed it before she'd told Shirley. Once Edward knew who MK Wood was, she was afraid he would have offered a contract out of guilt. She half wished she had never written a word.

But her friends were thrilled when she called them all over to her house to make the big announcement.

"Oh, my gosh, I can't believe it. This is the most exciting thing that's happened to me in years," Alice said.

"We're going to be famous," crowed Josie.

"More like semi-famous," Karissa cautioned. "Heron Publishing is only a regional publisher."

"I'll settle for semi," Josie said. "Wait till I tell Gerald he's got competition," she added with a smirk.

"Thank you, Karissa. We owe this to you," said Margot. "I'm only sorry about the timing."

That introduced a somber note to the celebration.

"I'll let you be the contact person. You'll most likely be working with Shirley and she's great," Karissa said. "There is one more thing. Shirley would really like to offer a two-book contract, but I don't want to write this type of thing anymore. I don't know about the rest of you."

"I don't know if I could come up with another idea all by myself," Josie said.

"I'm happy with a one-book deal," said Margot. "I'm busy with the app, and my other business."

"I certainly can't write a book all on my own," said Alice.

"So you're all good with a one-book contract? You won't make much."

"We were good with that from the beginning," said Josie. "Let's make a deal and become famous in our own backyard."

"Agreed," said Margot.

"Yes!" said Alice.

Karissa smiled as she opened the champagne she'd bought for the occasion. It was the first genuine smile she'd managed since receiving Mark's text, and the perfect moment for one. Something good had come out of her time at Heron Publishing.

Seeing her friends so happy and knowing she'd brought about that happiness was the broom she needed to begin sweeping away some of the garbage that had spilled into her life. Cleanup had to start somewhere, and this was a great place to begin. Once more, she had liftoff.

Macy's delight the next day on hearing that her mommy was going to be a published author took her higher. This time she was determined to stay airborne, no matter what.

26

"He could easily forget.
He could easily get on with his life."
—from *The Widower* by Terrance Tolliver

"THE APP IS DOING GREAT, AND ANDREW AND I ARE already brainstorming ideas for one to help people organize their lives," Margot told Karissa as they did their Saturday morning jog around the neighborhood.

"This is turning out to be a great partnership," Karissa observed.

"On so many levels," Margot said with a smile. "He is such a great guy."

"How did dinner out with your mom go?" Karissa asked.

"Success. He's the first man since Jackson she's approved of. But then how could she not approve when he kept thanking her for raising such an incredible daughter?"

"Smart man."

"Yes, he is. And you know what's crazy? If I hadn't gotten laid off, I'd have never decided to create the app and I'd have never met him. Life has a way of working out."

Karissa suspected those words were meant for her, so she agreed. Who knew what the future held? She had to hope there would be no more garbage to sweep up for a while. No more horrible surprises.

They jogged on past several houses with pumpkins on their porches and Halloween inflatables and fake headstones on their lawns. "Looks like everyone's getting ready to celebrate Halloween," Margot observed. "Have you and Macy gotten your pumpkin yet?"

"I promised her we'd go tomorrow afternoon when she gets back from Mark's. Macy and Lilith are going to carve pumpkins together."

Honor would be picking up Lilith afterward and it would be Karissa's first time seeing Edward's mother since he'd shared his feelings and his troubles with her. Karissa hoped he hadn't said anything to her. It would only make for awkwardness.

"If you need help, I'm available," Margot offered.

"Thanks. That would be great. I'm in charge of pumpkin carving. Honor and Edward will take the girls trick-or-treating on Halloween."

"It sounds like you're working things out."

"We are," Karissa said. "Macy already had one friendship altered thanks to what was going on with the grown-ups. She didn't need that happening with a second one. It still hurts though."

"You don't heal from this kind of sadness overnight," Margot reminded her.

"I know," she said. "I wish I could though."

"Maybe you need more writing therapy."

Karissa frowned. "Who would you have me kill?"

"No one. Write something that makes you smile. Remember, in fiction you can make things turn out exactly the way you want them to."

"Too bad you can't live in a book," Karissa muttered.

But you could when you were writing one. Maybe she did need to think about writing herself a happy ending.

Life wasn't all bad. In between moments of longing and sadness Karissa found pockets of happiness, like when it came time for Macy and Lilith to carve their pumpkins. Memories of her own delight doing the same thing as a child warmed her heart as she and Margot helped the girls turn their pumpkins into fairy houses. As soon as it got dark they set the finished products on the front porch steps to see how their creations looked. With the flicker candles turned on the figures carved in the pumpkins looked like miniature fairies were dancing inside them.

"They're so pretty!" cried Macy. "Thank you, Margot!"

"They did turn out great," Margot said.

They were finishing up taking pictures to post online and send to grandparents when Honor pulled up to take Lilith home.

"I'll see you later," Margot said, and gave Karissa's hand a squeeze, then she crossed the lawn back to her own house.

"Aren't these pretty!" Honor exclaimed as she came up the walk.

"Mrs. N's friend Margot helped us," said Lilith. "We had sloppy joes for dinner."

"Who doesn't love sloppy joes?" Honor said and smiled at Karissa. It was the same kind smile she'd always worn, so hopefully Edward hadn't shared what had happened between them. "Think you can manage to carry your fairy pumpkin to the car?" she asked Lilith.

Lilith nodded and picked it up. "Bye, Macy. See you tomorrow."

"See you tomorrow," Macy replied and hung on the porch post.

"Karissa, I wonder if we could talk a moment," Honor said.

Dread settled in Karissa's stomach. Edward had said something to his mother after all.

"Honey bunny, how about you go in and brush your teeth?" Karissa said to Macy.

"But my fairy pumpkin," Macy protested.

"You can come and shut off the candle after your teeth are brushed," Karissa said, and Macy heaved a sigh and went inside. As soon as she was out of earshot, Karissa made the first move to get them past the awkwardness. "I guess Edward told you about our conversation." Conversation, what a mild description of emotional upheaval.

"Edward told me. I just wanted to tell you that I'm sorry for all of this. Sorry for all of you. I loved Amanda, and would have welcomed her back with open arms, but she's not coming back. When you came on the scene, I'd hoped Edward would realize that, would give up and let go of his hyper-inflated sense of obligation."

"I'd thought he was widowed," Karissa said.

Honor sighed. "As good as."

"He didn't wear a ring."

"That's my fault. I urged him to take it off. I'd hoped the next step would be to start divorce proceedings. He's put it back on again. I hope, somehow, you both will be able to get past this, and I appreciate you not letting what happened between you affect the girls' friendship."

"Never," Karissa vowed. She managed a smile. "Thanks for coming to get her."

Honor nodded, smiled herself and gave Karissa's arm a squeeze. Then she turned and walked back to her car where her granddaughter was waiting. Karissa sat on the porch, wrapped her arms around herself to ward off the cold, and watched as they drove off while at her feet the fairies danced.

That night she dreamed she'd walked through a gate in a street in some Mediterranean town into a lush walled garden with a fountain. A setting sun made the sculpted woman at its center glow and the water spilling from her pitcher sparkle with golden flecks. She was beautiful, with long stone curls and delicate features. The woman seemed to be calling Karissa over. She moved closer.

The woman's stone mouth didn't move but she spoke anyway. "Tell my story."

"I don't know your story," said Karissa.

"You will. Tell it and we can both be happy."

Karissa awoke and looked at her bedside clock. It was 5:00 a.m. What was she doing awake at five in the morning?

Thinking of the woman at the center of the fountain. What was her story? What did that dream mean?

She got up and made herself some coffee. Then she went in search of the last legal pad she'd purchased to finish *Murder She Wrote No More*. She climbed into bed and tore off the used pages and looked at the new blank page. She was going to write again. Not something grisly, but something encouraging, something beautiful and romantic. Something involving a woman about to meet love, and a special place where she would find blessing and hope. She took a sip of her coffee, then she took a deep breath and began to jot down ideas. All while a voice echoed at the back of her mind. *Tell my story.*

The statue in her dream had promised they'd both be happy. In a small way, Karissa felt that was already coming true because here she was, smiling. And yes, happy.

She was especially happy after she read an excerpt to her friends when they met to discuss their Halloween read by Terrance Tolliver.

She didn't know whose face she'd just seen in the faint image shimmering in the water of the fountain, but she somehow knew it was a face she needed to remember. She knew that, somehow, the legend of the fountain was reaching out to her, wanting to gently touch her heart and her life.

She looked up at the stone figure. The woman's smile was a sad one. I lost my heart's desire, but I can help you find yours.

"Oh, my gosh, that gave me chills," Margot said when Karissa had finished reading.

"This is going to be amazing," Alice predicted.

Determined to have the last word, Josie said, "You're on a roll."

Yes, she was. "I want this to be something women will read and come away from encouraged."

"They will," Alice assured her.

"You've got talent, kiddo," said Josie.

"I don't know how much talent I have, but I'm sure enjoying this," said Karissa. "That's enough about me now. What did you all think of *The Widower*?"

"It was creepy," Alice said with a shudder.

"Creeptastical," said Margot. "I loved the way he kept the suspense going with the dead wife's different manifestations. Everything kept building and building. That's what had me turning the pages."

"Those two cheaters both got what they deserved in the end," said Josie.

"Poetic justice, Karissa would say," Margot said, shooting an encouraging smile at Karissa. "If you're not seeing it in life there's something comforting about finding it in fiction."

"Amen to that," said Josie.

"I don't want to read any more scary books for a while," Alice said.

"I have the perfect next pick," Josie announced. "I found it when Alice drove me to the bookstore," she added, and Margot gave Alice a thumbs-up to acknowledge this latest evidence of her conquering her fears. Josie held up the book. It featured a woman in a long gown and sunbonnet standing in front of a sod house. The title read, *The Friendship Pact*.

"Historical. What's it about?" asked Margot.

"It's about two women in some frontier town who become friends. One's trying to start a school and the other runs the local cathouse."

"Now there's an unlikely friendship," Margot said. "I definitely want to see how that plays out."

"As long as it has a happy ending," said Alice.

Karissa concurred. She was determined to flood her life with as much happiness as she could.

"We are certainly reading a variety of books," Alice observed as they all dug into the pumpkin roll she'd brought.

"Variety is the spice of life," said Josie.

"Speaking of, it looks like Gerald is spicing yours up pretty good," Margot said to her.

Josie's cheeks turned pink, but she refused to confirm or deny. "I want to spice all our lives up with a Halloween party at my place. The Saturday before Halloween. Feel free to bring a guest. Margot," she added pointedly.

"I will," Margot said with a grin. "Is this going to be a costume party?"

"Yes. I want you to all come dressed as a character in a book."

"I have no idea who to come as," said Alice.

"You have time to think of something," Josie assured her.

"I really can't think of anyone," Alice confided the next day to Karissa when they sat enjoying an evening visit.

"Let's look online and see if we can get some ideas," Karissa said. She brought up a website that listed famous female characters. "How about Alice in Wonderland? You already have the name."

"I'm a little too old to dress like a child."

"Then what about the Queen of Hearts?"

"That could be a possibility. Oh, no, that's it," Alice said, pointing to an image of Agatha Christie's Miss Marple.

"You're too young," Karissa protested.

"I won't have a hard time looking older, believe me. Now, what about you? Oh, wait. Here you are."

Karissa looked to where she was pointing and smiled. Yes, Elizabeth Bennet was, indeed, perfect. She was strong and stuck to her beliefs. That was the kind of woman Karissa wanted to come as and the kind of woman she wanted to be.

She enjoyed putting together her Regency-era costume. She liked how she looked in the empire-waisted blue gown and long white gloves. In that time of simple beauty enhancement like pinching cheeks for color and styling hair with ringlets and ribbons she could have been considered attractive. Alice had told her she was a lovely woman. Edward had thought she was beautiful. Like Jane Eyre, she didn't need to be considered beautiful by one and all, only by the ones who counted.

Edward. She had to stop letting her thoughts wander back to him. Hard not to when they were still working together.

"You look like a princess, Mommy," Macy approved when Karissa modeled it for her.

The pretty outfit did lift her spirits, and she was glad she had something fun to do while her daughter was off visiting her father and future stepmother.

Never mind their life, she told herself as she slipped on her gloves the night of the party. *Live your own.* Look forward and move forward was her new motto. Find joy in every possible corner. It sounded like something Muriel Sterling would say. Muriel would be proud. So would Annie Wills.

Josie had gone all out for the party. She'd strung garlands of discs of book pages all around the house—"Got 'em on Etsy"— and had helped Alice create a cake shaped like an open book. They'd taken two pages from their *Murder She Wrote No More* manuscript and printed them on the pages in icing. Everyone was to bring a wrapped paperback so they could play a readers' version of her favorite Christmas game and steal books back and forth from each other, and the literary treasures were piled on the coffee table.

Margot had showed up dressed like Katniss Everdeen from *The Hunger Games*, rocking her dark camo outfit and bow and arrow. With her was the new love of her life, Andrew Logan, who had come as the Mad Hatter in an outrageously large stovepipe hat and a vintage purple smoking jacket worn over jeans and Converse tennis shoes.

Alice had donned a gray wig and paired it with a vintage dress and hat and made a convincing-looking Miss Marple, while Josie was in a gown with a hoop skirt. She wore a cape over her shoulders made from a curtain rod and some dark green curtains.

"What the heck?" demanded Margot.

"I'm Scarlett O'Hara. This is from the scene where she needed a dress to impress Rhett Butler and made it out of the curtains."

Margot nodded slowly.

"You never read the book," Josie guessed.

"No, and I don't particularly want to," said Margot. "That is one that's probably going to vanish from the shelves."

"Probably," Josie agreed. "But I still like my costume."

"Yes," said Gerald, who had come as Beowulf. "Everyone should walk around with curtains on her shoulders."

"And horns on his head," Josie shot back, pointing to his Viking helmet. "You'd better watch it or I'll whack you with your broadsword."

Andrew chuckled. "Interesting friends you have," he said to Margot.

"They're the best," she replied.

Yes, they were, and Karissa was thankful that even though she'd lost out on love with Edward she still had her friends. It was easy to smile when Margot insisted on taking a picture for Instagram.

Josie had their evening's activities all planned. In addition to stealing books back and forth she insisted everyone play charades. "Only book titles," she instructed once she had them all loosened up with her witches' brew, which she'd served in a cauldron set over dry ice to create a spooky mist.

They teamed up with "oldies" versus "young'uns," and there was much bragging when the oldies won.

"We let you," Margot teased.

The book stealing was highly competitive, especially over a Nancy Naigle book and the latest John Grisham. The big fight between the men was over a vintage Donald E. Westlake novel that Josie had found at Earthlight Books in Walla Walla, Washington, on a wine trip with Gerald.

"Oh, man, I love this guy," said Andrew. "He was writing way back in the seventies and eighties," he explained to Margot, "but his stuff is still funny."

The two men made a nice addition to their group. Maybe they'd want to expand their book club at some point.

The best moment came when Gerald and Josie produced a blank journal. "Final game. This was a gift to me. Guess what it symbolizes."

"You're writing a book?" guessed Andrew.

Josie grinned and looked at Gerald, whose face was edging toward pink. "Not a book, but a story."

Alice was the first to catch on. "Oh, my gosh, are you two getting married?"

Gerald's face went from pink to sunburned. "Somebody's got to keep her in line."

"Good luck with that," joked Margot. She hugged Josie. "I'm happy for you."

"I'm happy for me, too," said Josie, and accepted hugs from her sister and Karissa as well.

"You might have told me," Alice chided.

"We opted for the element of surprise," Josie said.

"As if any of us are surprised," said Margot. "So, spill, how did you propose, Gerald?"

"Brilliantly," he answered.

"He gave me this journal and asked me to help him write the next chapters of his life's story," Josie said, and the women gave a collective sigh.

"Rad," said Andrew.

"We're going ring shopping on Monday," said Josie.

Gerald grinned and Karissa could have sworn he even puffed out his chest a little. It was great to see someone getting her happy ending.

There are all kinds of happy endings, she reminded herself. She was working on hers. She'd be fine.

Later, as she drove home, she couldn't help reflecting how far she'd come from when she first moved to Gig Harbor. Yes, she'd experienced more heartache, but she still had her friends and she'd found her self-esteem. Those two things surely qualified as a happy ending.

27

"As they sat together, sharing a rare moment away
from their problems, Mercy realized that friends,
like wildflowers, sprang up in the most unusual places."
—from *The Friendship Pact* by Allison Knowles

"SO HOW MAD ARE YOU THAT I DIDN'T TELL YOU BEfore everyone else?" Josie asked when Alice picked her up to go thrifting.

Alice wasn't mad. She was hurt, and she said so. "We're sisters, Jos. We've always shared everything. I felt cut out."

Was this how it was going to be now that Josie was getting married? Probably. She'd been spending increasingly more time with Gerald and less with Alice. It was to be expected, but reducing Alice to one of the gang, not letting her in on the secret first, it hadn't set well.

"I'm sorry. You're right, I should have told you. I guess I was a coward. That's why I waited until we were all together."

"A coward?"

"I was afraid you'd be mad about Gerald."

"Why on earth would I be mad about seeing you find someone to spend the rest of your life with?" Alice demanded.

"Because you were the one who was first interested in him. I came in and took over."

"We settled all that," Alice reminded her. "Gerald is perfect for you, but he wouldn't be for me. No one could ever measure up to Charlie, and I know, in the long run, I wouldn't be happy with anyone else."

"You're right. You and Gerald wouldn't be a fit. You're simply too sweet and tender. He'd always be saying something to hurt your feelings. He likes to dish it out and he needs someone who can dish it right back."

Alice nodded.

"You are happy for me, aren't you?" There was a touching bit of a need to be reassured.

"Yes, of course I am," said Alice. "I know you and Joe had grown apart those last few years. I'm glad you found someone active that you enjoy being with."

"Almost as much as I enjoy being with you," Josie quipped, which made Alice smile.

Catching the glint of the diamond on her sister's finger out of the corner of her eye shrank the smile a little. "I won't be seeing as much of you now that you're engaged."

They'd always been close, had done things together their whole lives, first as sisters and then with their husbands added in, but never more than after they were both widowed and had become each other's main companion. This marked a fork in the road.

"We'll still do things together," Josie assured her as if reading her mind. "Gerald and I aren't going to be glued at the hip 24/7, you know. And you have to help me plan the wedding. You're going to be my matron of honor, right?"

"Of course," Alice said. "Want me to make your cake?"

"Absolutely," Josie replied with a smile. "It will be the weekend before Valentine's Day, at his house, since he has a view. Only immediate family and a few friends."

"It will be lovely," Alice said.

She was, indeed, happy for Josie. She couldn't help feeling a little wistful though, like another piece of her life was getting chipped off. First her husband, now her sister. No matter what Josie said, things would be different. She wished she could add in someone special to fill that empty spot.

At least she had book club. She went in search of her book.

Karissa found herself counting her blessings as she read the novel Josie had suggested. Like the pioneer teacher and the madam, who had found friendship in an unexpected place, she, too, had found friends when she hadn't been looking for them. One woman had betrayed her, but three others had stepped in to fill the gap.

"Did you all buy the story, though?" Margot asked when they met to discuss it.

"I wouldn't have bought it a few months ago," Josie said. "I was always convinced that people who were so different couldn't be friends. I think I was wrong about that."

"Wait, let me get my phone and record that," Margot teased. Then she sobered. "Seriously, I think maybe we can be too quick to judge people. I know I can be."

"But then you get surprised," put in Alice. "I love how the author kept putting these women in each other's paths."

"I thought the scene at the mercantile was cute," said Karissa. "It was really clever how the author brought them together over bolts of cloth."

"Well, who doesn't love shopping?" said Margot.

"I think women can always find something in common. Like baking," said Alice.

"Or eating," cracked Margot.

"Books," said Karissa. "Even though we all have different tastes."

"Differences aren't always bad," Josie said. "Unless you don't agree with me," she added, which made the others laugh. She sobered. "Thank you all for letting me join you. You know, if it hadn't been for book club, I'd have never met Gerald."

"Or written a book," said Alice. "I'm glad we get to keep the title, and I can hardly wait to see what they come up with for the cover."

"I shared your idea about the scattered pages on the floor and the pen leaking red like blood over them and Shirley liked it," Margot told her, and Alice beamed.

"I'm so glad I got to be part of this," she said.

The talking continued. Everyone had something to be grateful for—their friendship, the success of their collective creative project, the new people in their lives.

"It made me happy to see how many good things have come out of this," Karissa said to her mother the next evening when Mom called. to see how things were going with the book club.

"I'm glad you're doing okay," Mom said. "And I'm excited about your new book idea."

"I don't know if anything will come of it, but I'm enjoying writing it."

Pouring herself into her new story and stepping into another world was proving therapeutic, much more so than committing fictional murder. She loved her main characters, loved growing their relationship and rooting for them even as she put obstacles in their paths. Fiction beat real life, hands down. She was the god of that world, and she would make sure her lovers got the happy life they longed for.

Meanwhile, the holidays were coming, and she was reading the book club's next pick, Muriel Sterling's *A Guide to Happy Holidays,* with the determination of a marathon runner focused on making it to the finish line. It had been her pick, and everyone, including Josie, had been enthusiastic.

Really, the only one who hadn't been excited had been her, which she found depressingly ironic. Still, she was reading it, not because she wanted to but because she needed to. It was going to be her holiday castor oil. She intended to ingest it and flush out any bitterness, resentment or depression that might try to take her down.

Holidays can be difficult, Muriel had written in her introduction.

There was an understatement. They were especially difficult when you knew your ex was getting remarried.

But bad situations can be redeemed, and we can always find something to be thankful for. I hope if you are going through a dark time this holiday season that you will look for the candle in the darkness. There is always one somewhere.

Karissa hoped she would find it.

The families gathered at Callum and Kara's house for Thanksgiving dinner. Gerald and Josie had arrived with his mayonnaise roasted turkey, Gerald carrying it out of reach of Lucky, who was sure what was in that aluminum pan had to be for him. Alice showed up bringing the pumpkin and pecan pies. Coral and Errol arrived with Blossom. Their contribution was sparkling cider, milk, and biscuits that Coral bragged Errol had made. He still wasn't Josie's favorite person, probably never would be, but she'd stopped calling him a loser. Progress came in small steps. Gerald's son, who had also been invited, was as soft and easygoing as Gerald was tough, and Josie knew he'd be good for a funny story or two about his adventures as a camp director. His contribution was pickles and olives and wine. He and Josie had hit it off the moment they met. He'd been properly dazzled that Josie had contributed to writing a book, which would forever qualify him as her favorite stepson. Even if he'd had siblings, she'd assured him.

It would be a feast, with all the usual trimmings and a ham. But the turkey was going to be the star of the show. Sadly, after being parked in the oven to stay warm, the star of the show had a mishap going from the oven to the serving platter when the foil pan folded and Mr. Bird did a dive onto the kitchen floor. A waterfall of drippings followed him.

Lucky, who had been hovering in the kitchen doorway, dashed for the bird, and chomped onto it just as Gerald was bending to pick it up.

"Let go of that," growled Gerald, and tried to pull it away.

Mine, growled Lucky and tugged on the delicious bounty he'd found.

The bird split in two and Lucky dashed off with Kara in hot pursuit, crying, "Lucky, no. Drop it!"

Like misbehaving children the world over, Lucky developed a hearing problem and kept on moving, and commotion could be heard from the living room as everyone made a team effort to part him from the turkey.

Meanwhile, in the kitchen, Gerald was muttering some choice words, along with what he'd like to do to that dog.

"I think we can save some of this," said Alice as Josie fetched paper towels to begin cleanup.

"I'm not sure anybody's going to want to eat that knowing Lucky had his mouth on it," said Josie.

"If we wash off this one end?" Alice suggested.

"Let's roast the dog and eat him," Gerald said, and Josie scolded him for saying such a thing even in jest.

"Who's jesting?" he retorted.

"At least we still have the ham," said Alice.

"Great," said Gerald sourly.

"I'm so sorry about your turkey," Kara apologized to him after she'd recovered the remains of the bird and Lucky had been banished to their bedroom.

"I guess now you've got dog food for the next couple of days," Gerald said, resigned to his loss, and Josie wanted to hug him then and there. She would reward him properly later.

Dinner, minus the turkey, eventually made it safely onto the table and Callum said grace, thanking God for the bounty on their table and that Gerald was letting his dog live to see another day. Then the food was passed around.

Soon plates were mounded with stuffing, potatoes, green bean casserole and cranberry sauce, as well as ham. With ham gravy instead of turkey. And Errol's golden-brown biscuits.

"These look awesome," said Callum as he smeared butter on his.

"Errol's getting into cooking," said Coral, obviously happy to find something about her husband to brag on.

"Got it right on the first try," said Errol.

Big whoop, thought Josie, but she kept her mouth shut.

Smiling, Callum took a big bite. Then he blinked and his eyes rolled upward, and his mouth went three different directions at once. He swallowed but he looked like a drug mule trying to get down his packet of cocaine.

"What's wrong with the biscuits?" Coral demanded.

"They're a little, uh, salty," said Callum, reaching for his sparkling cider.

"Huh?" Errol took a bite of his and instantly coughed it onto his plate.

"You bunch of wimps," said Gerald. "I eat all kinds of stuff when I'm out in the wild." He picked up his biscuit, stuffed half of it in his mouth and his eyes bulged out in a good imitation of a frog, which made Josie laugh.

Meanwhile, Errol's face was as red as the cranberry sauce.

"How much salt did you put in these?" Coral asked him.

"A tablespoon?"

"That's how much baking powder the recipe called for," she informed him, and he frowned at the biscuit crumbs on his plate.

"Well, I'm eating mine," said Gerald. "Pass the gravy."

Josie watched in amazement as he drowned the rest of his biscuit in ham gravy, forked it up and shoved it in his mouth.

He swallowed with great effort and barely controlled facial contortions, and then nodded.

"Not bad," he said. "You can come camping with me any time, Errol."

The cranberry stain faded from Errol's face, and he smiled at Gerald. So did Josie.

It was time for dessert when Callum made his announcement. "We're pregnant."

Alice gave a delighted gasp.

"All right," said Josie. "More future poker players."

"And hikers," put in Gerald.

"And family," Alice said, beaming, and Josie knew she wouldn't have to worry about her sister not having anyone in her life.

It was the perfect Thanksgiving.

Margot and Andrew had gone to his parents' house for Thanksgiving and her mother had been invited as well. The app was the talk of the table and Margot was pleased to see her mother smiling as if she, herself, had created it.

"Margot also has her own company," Mom had shared with one of the aunts.

She'd looked across the table and smiled at Margot, and Margot had smiled back. Mom still liked to nag—now it was about Andrew. Were they getting serious? How serious? But that was Mom. That would always be Mom, and as Josie once said, mothers loved their daughters and wanted what was best for them.

And the daughters didn't always have to answer when their moms called. Spacing out those mother-daughter conversations was the secret to a good relationship.

With dinner over, she'd gone to Andrew's house to enjoy a fire in the fireplace, do some gaming and then find a movie to stream. *Planes, Trains and Automobiles*, he'd insisted. "It was a holiday tradition when I was growing up."

So as Steve Martin and John Candy endured their holiday adventure together, she sat cuddled up next to Andrew, playing with the app, looking for the perfect outfit for the book club's Christmas party.

"Try on the red one," he said, pointing to a dressy red jumpsuit. "I bet you'll look hot in that."

"All right," she said, dropping it into her virtual dressing room, "let's see." Sure enough. It did look good.

"What about looking at bathing suits," he said as the ending credits rolled.

"Bathing suits?"

"I think we should go to Hawaii for New Year's," he said. He ran a hand up her neck and into her hair. "And what do you think about checking out wedding venues while we're there?"

She set down her phone and stared at him. "What?"

"You know, being business partners has been great, but I'd like to enter into a different kind of partnership with better benefits."

She half smiled. "Now, there's a romantic proposal."

His expression turned serious. "Margot, I loved developing the app together, but now I want to build a life. For me it's all about being with you. I can't get enough, and I don't want this to ever end. What do you say?"

"I'd say creating a great life trumps creating a great app," she said.

"So, will you marry me?"

"Gladly," she said, and rubbed her hands along his stubbly cheeks. "I don't want this to end, either."

No one loses all the time, Annie Wills had said in her book. *Forget your losses and move forward and you'll become a winner.* Annie was right. Margot had won the life lottery. Checking out bathing suits and then wedding gowns sounded like an excellent idea.

But first things first. She kissed him.

★ ★ ★

Family holiday gatherings were food for Karissa's soul, although this Thanksgiving celebration she wasn't taking in as much nourishment as she could have. It was hard not having Macy with her. Mark had claimed her for a trip to Disneyland.

"But there's more to life than Disneyland," she said to her mother that morning as they worked together in the kitchen.

"I'm proud of you for not letting this get to you," Mom said.

Karissa shrugged and went on peeling potatoes. "It did at first, and I still hate having Thanksgiving without her."

"But you'll have her for Christmas. You got the better end of that bargain."

"I did, and I still have plenty of blessings to count."

Still, counting wasn't always easy. Her brother and Jill, the woman he'd started pursuing over the Fourth of July weekend, had become an item, which, of course, made her happy, but she also couldn't help feeling a little sorry for herself. Everyone sitting around the table—aunts and uncles, mom and dad, and now Ethan were all paired up. She was the only one who had come alone.

Still, she did the traditional wishbone pull with her brother. He won the wishbone competition and held his piece up for Jill to see, and the small gesture gave her a shot of happiness. It was about time her brother found someone.

The next day she went home via the mall, where she purchased a Christmas candle, a light garland for the mantel and a snow globe to surprise Macy with when she returned on Sunday. They always put up their tree and decorations on Thanksgiving weekend. She'd save the tree for when Macy got home, but decided she'd set out a few things to try and keep up her positive attitude. Eggnog was also a must and she bought some of that as well.

But once she was home, she lost all desire to decorate. It was no fun making her new house pretty when she was the only one in it. She should have stayed longer at her parents'.

She binge-watched *Mrs. Davis*, drank a giant glass of eggnog, and then went to bed. Where she found Muriel Sterling's book sitting on the nightstand. She really wasn't in the mood for Muriel Sterling. But that probably meant she should do some reading.

This is the time of year to give thanks for all the wonderful people in our lives, Muriel wrote. *Counting your blessings may sound old-fashioned and what my daughters would call cheesy, but it is still one of the best remedies for unhappiness that I know. Why not try this? Starting with Thanksgiving and every day up through Christmas morning, list one thing you can be thankful for. If you run out of things, it's okay to repeat. There's nothing wrong with positive repetition.*

It was good advice coming from a good book written by a good woman. "You're right, Muriel, I'll try it, starting with you. I'm thankful you wrote this book," Karissa said.

It almost helped. She passed Macy's empty room and wiped away a tear.

The next day, she arranged her new purchase on the mantel. It looked so pretty, and admiring her handiwork lifted her spirits. Time for an eggnog latte. *There* was something to be thankful for. A text came in from Macy telling Karissa that she met Ariel and Jasmine, her two favorite Disney princesses. I love you Mommy, she ended the text. Her daughter was having fun. She could be thankful for that.

The sun was out. She should work in a jog. Even though Margot was gone for the weekend, Karissa put on her running shoes and jacket and got in two miles.

As she jogged, ideas for her book popped into her mind, so after coming home and showering, she made herself a cup of tea, got comfortable on the couch and got to work. Once she'd entered her fictional world the real one faded away and time became irrelevant. By the time she stopped it was four o'clock and she'd had a very good day.

She checked in with her mother and reported her day's events.

"I'm glad you had a great day," said Mom. "What are you going to do tonight?"

"I have a date with Muriel Sterling and the leftovers you sent home with me."

"Sounds like a perfect evening," Mom approved.

There was perfect and then there was not so perfect. This would fall in the latter category, but that was okay.

She enjoyed her leftover turkey and dressing and cranberry sauce and decided to save the pie for later. Then she turned on the gas fireplace, took a picture of how pretty it looked to text her mom, and curled up with Muriel Sterling's book.

What you focus on will affect how you feel, Muriel wrote.

She was right. For a while, Karissa had lost hope, but hope was a renewable resource. She was already renewing it. And she was feeling better about herself.

Like a ghost's whisper, Edward came to mind.

How she wished things had worked out for them, but even with everything that had happened she would still be okay.

She hugged the book to her. Of all their book club reads, so far, this one was the best.

She was roused from her reverie by the doorbell. All her friends were busy. Who would be ringing her doorbell at eight at night?

She pulled the curtain and looked out the window and was sure she was hallucinating.

28

"The holidays can be difficult,
but we can always find ways to make them better."
—from *A Guide to Happy Holidays* by Muriel Sterling

KARISSA OPENED THE DOOR AND THERE HE STOOD.
She blinked in surprise. "Edward?"

He'd taken the week off and left town. But even if he'd been around, the last place she expected to see him was her doorstep.

He looked past her. "Do you have company? Am I interrupting anything?"

She stepped aside. "No, come in."

He nodded and came inside.

"Sit down," she said. Nerves and a thrill she was trying to tamp down had her feeling as if she had a string of holiday lights blinking on and off inside her.

He sat on one end of her couch, and she sat on the opposite end, facing him, unsure of what to say other than, "Why are you here?"

"I should have called, but I didn't know what to say on the phone. I hardly know how to start now that I'm with you."

"What's going on?"

"We found Amanda."

The news crashed down on Karissa like a landslide. She sat, staring, unable to form a coherent sentence.

"Her parents and I flew to San Diego and saw her," he continued.

"Did it go well?" she managed. She hoped so, for his and Lilith's sake.

He nodded.

"Where was she? What had she been doing?"

"That's a long story. Basically, rebuilding herself and her life. We were able to work through some things."

"Good," said Karissa, and meant it.

"But we won't be getting back together. I've known it all along. I just couldn't accept it, felt too guilty to accept it."

The whirlwind of emotions circling inside her almost made Karissa dizzy. Poor Edward. Poor Lilith. She felt badly for him and guilty for the hope at the center of that whirlwind.

"I'm sorry you weren't able to work things out," she said. "I'm sorry for Lilith." There was the true sadness in his situation.

"It's not all bad. The good news is that Amanda would like to try to establish a relationship with her," he said. "Not a custody sort of thing, but visits."

"That is good news," said Karissa.

"We're starting the divorce process," he said. "It's past time, and I want to move on with my life. I want to move on with you, Karissa. If you'll let me."

The tears rose quickly and spilled over. All she could do was nod.

He closed the distance between them and took her hand. "You have no idea how I've wanted to just be able to sit with you and hold your hand like this. I felt like a traitor for the way I felt about you. I didn't want to quit on Amanda. It didn't seem right or fair to Lilith. But now…do you think there's a chance we could build something together?"

"Oh, yes," she said, and wiped away the tears that had spilled.

He cradled her face in his hands. "This is the sweetest face I've ever seen. I could stare at you forever."

"I'd rather you kiss me," she said.

"An excellent idea," he murmured. He removed her glasses and set them on the coffee table. "I don't think you're going to need these for a while."

She saw her dreams coming true as he kissed her. It was a gentle touching of the lips at first, the kind of touch that made her heart flutter and her eyelids drop closed. Then it was a gentle teasing to spark her happiness. Finally, it was a demand for all of her—for her passion, her heart, her life, all of which she'd happily give. It tasted of wishes granted and new beginnings. There were no words, only feelings of joy, excitement, and, best of all, assurance that the rejection and unhappiness of the past was banished. The future was waiting, and her glass was full to overflowing.

29

*"What necessity is there to dwell in the past,
when the Present is so much surer,
the Future so much brighter?"*
—Mr. Rochester, from *Jane Eyre* by Charlotte Brontë

MURIEL STERLING WAS RIGHT. THE DARK TIMES DID eventually end. Once more, Karissa's life had turned, but this time it had landed right side up. Emerald had stopped popping in unannounced and was dropping strong hints that she would be giving back her advance and looking for another publisher, after Edward had made it clear their relationship was strictly professional. Which was fine with all concerned as they now had MK Wood under contract.

"Do you think Edward will want to publish your new book?" Alice asked as they baked Andes Mint cookies for the book club's Christmas party.

"I don't know, but even if he did, I think I'd want to try and sell it somewhere else. I don't think I'm ready to work quite that closely with him." Although she suspected it wouldn't be so hard to change his attitude on romance novels now that they were looking at a happy future together.

"I think it's wonderful for both of you how things have worked out," Alice said. She took out a sheet of cookies and Karissa started balancing the thin chocolate candies on top of them to melt into frosting.

"I have to keep pinching myself," said Karissa. "Being together still feels like a dream."

"It's one you deserved to have come true. And I'm glad things are working out with Lilith's mother."

"She's going to come up for New Year's. Edward's taking Lilith over to Amanda's mom's house on New Year's Day to meet her. Familiar for Lilith and kind of neutral ground. I'm hoping it all goes well, for both Lilith's sake and hers."

"It's a first step," Alice said. She took a spoon and began spreading the melted chocolate over the cookies and they worked in companionable silence for a moment.

Until Karissa worked up the nerve to say something that had been on her mind for the last few days.

"Alice, sometimes I feel a little badly that we're all finding someone but you're still on your own."

"No need to feel bad for me," Alice said. "I had my Charlie, and we had enough love to last me for a lifetime. And now I have someone new coming into my life in just a few months. I'm going to be very busy helping with my grandbaby. And traveling."

"Traveling?"

Alice beamed. "This summer I'm taking a road trip with an old friend."

"That's awesome! It looks like we'll have a lot to celebrate as we go into the new year," Karissa said.

"You know what Muriel Sterling says. 'There's always something to celebrate,'" Alice quoted.

"Yes, there is," Karissa agreed.

Like Andes Mint cookies, which were a big hit when the book club gathered for their Christmas party at Karissa's house.

Her table was loaded with everything from salmon dip and crackers to bruschetta to bacon-wrapped dates—a hit with the three men who were present. In addition to Edward and Gerald, André had come, bringing his famous oatmeal cookies. Edward and Karissa had made stuffed mushrooms together, and he stood proudly, with his arm around her shoulder, accepting compliments from one and all, including Shirley, the book club's newest member.

Macy and Lilith wore matching green velveteen dresses and curled ribbons in their hair and were excited to get to be with the grown-ups. They had been given free rein with the eggnog punch, which Karissa had made sure would be kid friendly, and were soon having their own book club meeting in Macy's room.

"It's been quite a year," said Alice as everyone settled in with champagne.

"That it has," Josie agreed, winking at Gerald, who was sitting next to her and looking smug.

"I'd like to make a toast," Alice said. "To Karissa, for bringing us all together. You've been the catalyst for a lot of good things."

Everyone smiling at her had Karissa's cheeks feeling suddenly warm. Almost as warm as what she was feeling in her heart.

"Thank you," she said. "That means so much, and I'm so grateful for all of you." But one more toast was in order. "I'd like to make a toast of my own." She raised her glass. "Here's to our book club. And to books, and the lives they change."

"To books," everyone echoed.

There were no more toasts after that. After all, what more was there to say?

* * * * *

Acknowledgments

I'D LIKE THANK SOME WONDERFUL PEOPLE WHO helped me reach the finish line on this book. A big thank you to Ruth Ross for being my first reader and offering her wise insights. Also, to my friend Paula Eykelhof, who helped me very much. I am hugely grateful to have such a brilliant editor in April Osborn. Thank you, April, for all your advice and much needed suggestions that so hugely improved this story. Thank you, also, to my agent, Paige Wheeler. You are the best! A heartfelt thank you to Patti Callahan Henry, author extraordinaire, for so kindly giving this story her stamp of approval. I am truly honored. And a big shout out to the Mira team for helping me bring this story to life and for the great, fun cover. Finally, let me take a moment to acknowledge you, the reader. I understand that your time is valuable, and I appreciate you spending some of it with me.

THE
BEST LIFE
BOOK CLUB

SHEILA ROBERTS

Reader's Guide

1. When Karissa Newcomb arrives in her new neighborhood after hitting restart on her life she's timid about forming new friendships. What have been your experiences when moving to a new location?

2. Could you identify with Karissa's fear of risking a new friendship? Have you ever been betrayed by a friend?

3. If you were Margot, how would you handle her mother?

4. Alice must overcome a case of PTSD. Have you ever been involved in a car accident or experienced another kind of traumatic situation? How were you able to cope?

5. Josie has some rough edges. Do you know anyone like her?

6. Have you ever invited someone into a group or club and then regretted it?

7. Does your book club have certain expectations regarding potential new members?

8. Alice insists that not only can the young learn from the old, but the old can also learn from the young. Do you agree with Alice?

9. Do you think office romances are a good idea?

10. Should Edward have shared more of his situation with Karissa earlier?

11. With the exception of *Jane Eyre*, none of the books the book club reads exist in the real world. Which of the made-up books would you choose to read if it did exist?

12. What book has your group read that sparked the most heated discussion?

13. Do you agree with Alice that there is a perfect book match for everyone?

14. What would you say are the benefits of being in a book club?